I CHOOSE
PAIN

A NOVEL BY

EROS DA ARTISTE

The eclectic Eros Da Artiste is a unique Renaissance Man. He is a singer, songwriter, musician, digital painter, and visual artist. He currently resides in Baltimore, MD.

I Choose Pain is his very first literary work. He started the book twelve years ago, while going to Morgan State University. Due to his church upbringing, he hesitated to complete this book, due to fear of criticism and passionate rebuke from the church. But when circumstances were altered, he decided to finish and publish the book and let the chips fall where they may.

This is a huge jump from the church to the literary chair, but he believes that sometimes you have to be brave and stand up for those who cannot fight for themselves. He believes that there are people (gay or straight) who deal with depression, sexual abuse, child abuse, guilt issues, and suicidal thoughts. He hopes that this book, if people can look past the sensuality included, will help someone to understand that they are not alone, and that it really does get better.

DISCLAIMER

I Choose Pain: A Novel
By Eros Da Artiste

The Library of Congress has established a record for this title.

Paperback ISBN: 978-0-578-46516-6

Printed in the U.S.A.
0   1   2   3

ACKNOWLEDGEMENTS

Special Thanks go to:

GOD for the gift he bestowed to use a different medium to bring about healing to our wounded rainbow family.

The Adodi Brotherhood
Big Boy Pride Family
SGL Cruise Family
Rainbow Soul of Morgan State University
Marla McKinney (Auntie Marla)
Chandler Moore
Kevin Carter
Elonda Russ and the Russ Family
And Everyone who Purchased this book!

This book is dedicated in memory of my dearest friend, A.D. Richardson.

Special Shout-out to my three best friends, Daniel, Grayling, and Joseph, for your encouragement while completing this book.

FOREWORD

This story is inspired by those who hear music. Those who speak in verse. Those who dance in the rain. Those who paint visions of love in their hearts and in their minds, using their souls as the paintbrushes. Those who love creation and the Creator and can flow in both… spiritually and truthfully free. Those who can roll upon the earth and enjoy the crackling of the leaves and the rustling of the reeds as our bodies crush them only for them to spring up again. Those who enjoy being a little crazy.

It is for anyone who has ever felt depressed. Hurt. Lonely. Angry. Discontent. Those who must take medication to get through the next minute. The next second. Those who must take medication daily just keep the Virus down. Those who must continue to talk themselves up to avoid shooting themselves down. Those who chuckle to avoid a whimper. Those who roar to keep from wailing.

It is for the little kid who had his innocence taken from him from a grown man who couldn't keep his hands to himself. The little child who was raped at an early age. The little child who sits in church every Sunday and Listens in desperation as the preachers damn them to hell. The little child standing in the corner by himself wondering why no one will play with him. We carry these children with us when we think about our childhood. We ARE these children. Some of us have been molested. Some of us have been raped. Some of us have been publicly vilified by those who claim to speak for God. Sadly, all of us have been ostracized just for being who we are.

It is for any preacher who preached death to "sissies" from the pulpit while hiding their own secret desires.

It is for any Super Saint who reads it. I hope that they can imagine the pains we suffer that we DON'T choose.

It is for the choir member who sings loud in church but is afraid to sing in life.

It is for the musician who is chained to the organ or the piano and told that secular music is of the devil. Who are prostituted by the religious leaders and thrown out because of who they choose to love.

It is for anyone who has ever loved.
Anyone who has ever dreamed.
Anyone who has ever hoped to find a love of their own.
Those who can lie naked and feel no shame.
Those who can bear their soul without restraint.
Those who can live free
…. and even those who are caged that they may live free.

This story is for the "fairies", the "bulldaggers", the "punks", the "faggots", the "queers", the "funny" ones, the "queens", the "bourgie", the "butches", the "weird" ones, and the "dykes". In short this is for the hated who have it in them to love those that hate them and could never refer to them as who they are, A PERSON.

It is to encourage all to find the truth within themselves, to believe in themselves, to love what they see in the mirror.

The story is for us, by us, about us, in us. I pray to God, in thanks to Him and all who supported this effort, that we all continue to tell our stories and live them better than we can tell them.

The common denominator of all forms of love is hurt. You cannot have one and discard the other. Show me someone who has chosen pain to uphold the lives of others, and I will show you someone who has learned how to love.

Eros Da Artiste

TABLE OF CONTENTS

PROLOGUE

PART ONE: TO THINE OWN SELF

PART TWO: HELP

EPILOGUE
DISCUSSION QUESTIONS

PROLOGUE

"The Mask"

Lionel Davis

A Mask hides
A Mask covers up
A mask smiles
A mask laughs
A mask gives off an aura of sarcasm
A mask sneers
A mask scorns
A mask befriends
A mask ignores

Who Am I Behind this Mask??

I write these words for my journal entry as I sit at my drafting table. I sit back and gaze at my man as he reads. Questions bombard me. *How did we end up here? How did I get on this rainbow rollercoaster?* The question I ask above all is this:

How did all the drama begin...?

PART I:

TO THINE OWN SELF

CHAPTER ONE:

"LION"

Lionel,

So, the truth comes out. You are a purse toting, finger snapping, man stealing fag! Have you stopped to think of what this is doing to our family? Before you answer that, I already know you haven't.

When you told me that you were a homo, I wished you were in the same room, so I could beat the tar out of you. Thirty-six years of my life wasted on you. I am shocked. I am completely disgusted. This lifestyle is a sin. You know it is. I raised you better than this. I am ashamed of you and what you have become. A weak shell of a man with no values, no morals, and no spine, just like your shit-heel brother. But at least with him, he's not trying to screw every man he sees. You are a total embarrassment to me, and a dishonor to the life I raised you to live.

This letter is to tell you to lose my number. Lose every contact you could possibly have to me. A faggot for a son? If I had known you were going to turn out this way, I would have killed you in my womb.

No signature. Just the smell of the same perfume that she used to wear. I got this letter four months ago. The tears begin to run down my cheeks.

Tear number one.

This was not my best month. I had a huge credit card debt I Just found out about. My ex-boyfriend, Nathan Pierce (Nate for short), went to Vegas after we split and maxed out his credit card, and since I co-signed for him to get it in the first place, the bill was my responsibility. So, I had to call and give him hell until he paid back what he owed. My house was broken into. The burglar took my watch, my amethyst and diamond ring, and three hundred bucks in cash that I had in my nightstand. To top all this off, I called my mother five days ago on Mother's Day, thinking she had cooled down and she went bat-shit the minute she heard my voice. How well I remember the conversation...

"Hello Ma."
"Who is this?"
"This is Lionel."
(Pause. Dead flat voice.)
"What in the hell are you calling here for?"
"I'm just wishing you a Happy Mother's Day."
"I made myself absolutely clear in the letter I sent. Don't call my house no more."
"Ma..."
"Don't call me Ma."
"Where is all this anger coming from?"
"It's how I feel. People like you make me sick. Dressing like girls. Putting on makeup and shit. Afraid to be a man who knows how to fight. Afraid to be a man who knows how to take care of business. Afraid to just be a goddamned man!"
"Enough, OK. Let's not do this..."
"What? Am I saying something you don't want to hear? You know, I think that bitch ass Joseph Thompson is to blame for this. He told you it was ok to be a homo and you fell for that shit."
"Let's not bring my best friend into this. Alright? He has nothing to do with me being gay."
"Then what made you choose this mess?"
"What makes you think I would choose anything like this?"
"Everything in life is a choice. You chose sin and like it or not, this is a sin. You got a special place to rot in hell for it. As for this family, you made your choice. You wanna be a faggot? Then, stay your ass away from us and don't you ever come back. Not while living and not even after I'm dead."

(Pause)

"If that's the way you want it, fine. I don't have a mother who loves me, but the other side of that is you just lost a son who loved you and tried all his life to make you happy. So, have a Happy Whatever Day. I hope you and your children will be happy." Click

Family is not always much when you know you have one, but it's like a hole in your heart when you lose them. After that conversation, I sank into sorrow. I called my boss and took a week off, and now I am sitting here in the same clothes I wore two days ago and armed with a bottle of Doxepin. I got the prescription when Nate and I busted up, and I took them almost every day to lull my depression. I put them off when I was going to that support group. But then I got the letter, and I started them again and, this week, I have been totally doped up and numb. Sleeping and crying…

The phone rang on numerous occasions, mostly calls from my three best friends. My answering machine message light shows number twenty-five. I know they must be going frantic by now. I hear their voice messages, but I'm so depressed that I cannot listen to them. Armed with those pills, I am deaf and dumb to everything around me but sleep; the one thing I run toward to embrace the oblivion that it offers. Today, I didn't take any pills. Maybe that's why I feel so depressed. No sleep to lull the pain.

Tear number two.

This shows me what being honest with my mother can do to me. Why did I tell her? Why?

Tear number three.

It was that damned LGBTQ support group that said coming out of the closet to the people we love would be the best thing to do. How did I get here? When did this start? My mind travels back to the tender age of thirteen. My fourteen-year-old cousin Jamaal and I were wrestling playfully at his house. Then he landed on top of me and our faces were inches apart. Trying to break the uncomfortable tension, he playfully bit me on the nose. But when he drew back, he just looked at me. His eyes held mine captive as he moved in slowly to kiss me. Why I let him, I don't know. It just felt good. He put his hand in my shorts, wrapped it around my jimmie, and started jerking me off. Now, before this, I didn't know anything about masturbation. Lost in the feeling of it all, I laid back as he pulled both of our shorts down and got on top of me. My jimmie pressed against his as he continued to kiss me passionately. Suddenly, I sensed a strong pleasant shudder that went through me as I felt abundant, sticky liquid on our crotches. It was after the last spasm that I heard the pastor's voice in my head. "Abomination". "Sin". "Hellfire". The guilt that rained on me was horrible. I pushed Jamaal off me, pulled up my pants, and ran twenty blocks back to my house. Once inside, I went to my room and locked myself in. Then, I looked in my shorts to see this dried white stuff was caked on my dick... and it was still coming out! I called Jamaal and asked him what the fuck he did to me. "It won't stop coming out. Now I gotta go to the hospital because of you," I said. Jamaal let out a huge flood of laughter. He told me to calm down. "Just go to the bathroom, take a piss and a shower, and you'll be fine!" Well, that night in bed, all I could think of was him and our encounter. The images were too hard to ignore. Instinctively, my right hand found my jimmie and before I knew it, I was doing the same thing alone that he did to me that afternoon. While I climaxed, A loud howl escaped my lips! My father yelled up the stairs saying, "What's going on up there?" I lied and said I stumped my toe on the bedpost.

The sex we had after that was crazy! He attacked my shaft with such ferocity that he had my toes curling. He was the first one that opened my eyes to the joys and pains of getting penetrated, starting with eating my ass to get me ready. I sometimes wonder how he learned how to eat it like he did. Who taught him? It had to have been some older guy who introduced him. Maybe he learned it by watching those fuck films. Who knows? Anyway, I was sleeping over at his house one night while my aunt was working a graveyard shift cleaning the office buildings downtown. He ate my ass like a three-course meal, twisting his tongue into my asshole, drool pouring from his salivary glands. He drove me wild! I wanted him in me so bad, my ass was wet and throbbing. But he kept saying, "Not yet. You ain't loose yet." After an eternity of him pulling my jimmie and nuts and alternating between eating and sucking, He then laid on his back and told me to squat on his thick pole, which was nine inches long. I was shocked at his size. He had a lot of dick for a teenager. When it wound into my constricted hole, he kept saying, "Go slow. Relax." The sensation reminded me of a balloon that was being blown up inside me. It almost felt like I was shitting backwards. I had a little discomfort, but after the initial pain, the pleasure of his shaft opening my walls caused my breathing to become labored. I gasped for air as the temperature in the room rose, causing the sweat to emerge from our bodies. I found myself swearing, something I was scared to do. All kinds of "motherfuckers", "shits", "damns", and "fuck me's" were issuing forth from my core and out of my mouth into the sex-scented air! I was screaming Daddy, Papi, Baby, and everything else in between because his head hitting my prostate was insanely stupendous! He turned me out! We fucked several times that night and he came in me every time. Of course, HIV and AIDS were on the scene for more than a decade. But being young and dumb, we were fucking like rabbits and there was no shame in our game.

We fucked around until right before my senior year. He had graduated, went to college, and came back with a girlfriend and an engagement ring. He tried to pretend like nothing ever happened between us. How vividly I remember when we were at his welcome home party and he made it a point to find something else to do so he wouldn't have to face me. Towards the end of the party, I pulled him onto my Auntie's back porch and asked him what his problem was. He told me that while he was in college, a preacher called him out about his messing with men, and as a result he had gotten saved and that he had to marry to curb those feelings. He and the girl got married two months after that and had a baby girl. Five years later, they got divorced because she found out he was driving to Birmingham at least five times a month: sucking, slinging, and taking dick in the adult bookstores. His life didn't go so well after that. I was the only one he could come to for comfort because his mother and the rest of the family cut him off. We had the time to reconnect, but it was a very short time. He contracted HIV at age twenty-nine. Shortly afterwards, he committed suicide by hanging himself from the balcony of his apartment.

Tear number four

I rise to put the letter in my bookcase. Slowly crossing the living room floor, I catch sight of an empty space on my wall. A space emphasizing a lifetime of past occasional happiness and of future sadness and loneliness. There used to be a portrait of me and my family hanging there. *Used to be.* The moment I got off the phone with her, a surge of anger went through me. I charged through my lavish townhouse like a man possessed, ripping the family pictures out of the frames. I grabbed every family keepsake I could find, from the family albums to the eight solid gold paperweights my dad had appraised and gave me. Family treasures that Dad told me to keep. I dumped them and the family pictures in the garbage. Later that night, I retrieved the paperweights. They are still on my bookshelf. I couldn't allow them to be thrown away. They cost two grand apiece!

Tear number five.

I stand in front of the bookcase. I look at the letter in my hand. Wow. She just cuts me off without a thought that I may need her at this stage in my life. Never mind that I am a pillar of success in the marketing and advertising field. Forget that I am the first of my siblings who scraped, saved, scrimped, and clawed to rise to the top. I worked for ten years at Robertson & Moore Marketing Firm, climbing the ladder from intern to marketing executive without breaking others' backs. Let's disregard the fact that I have tried to be there for my family, just like my father would have done. She easily forgot that I took care of the second mortgage on her house when she was trying to bail my oldest "brother", Andre, out of jail for drug possession… and his ass still went to prison for ten years. I, being the second oldest along with my twin brother, Dean, had a hand in raising my younger brother and sister. I was there for her when Dad was shot and killed. She was distraught and wouldn't do for herself. Roland and Brenda were too busy being kids. Andre was in prison. Rhonda was too busy running the streets to do shit. Dean was away at college. He came for two weeks and did what he could until Mama became irritable, then he went back to school just to get away from her. But I took a semester from school. I stayed with, prayed for, and cooked dinner for her when she didn't feel like cooking. I also made sure my two younger siblings got fed. I had to coax her to eat when she was wasting away to nothing. I helped her get back to her old mean and nasty self. How could she write me off as bullshit this easily?

Tear number six

I put the letter in the bookcase and walk like a ghost to my sofa. I think this is that dumb-ass support group's fault. Then again, I joined them. I started going three months after the four-year relationship with my lover ended. I found him in bed with one of my co-workers and frenemies, Shawn. It was no secret that Shawn wanted Nate from the time he saw him. Nate just lies in bed looking like a deer in headlights.

"What the fuck?" I remember screaming.

"Lionel, please listen to me."

"You cheated on me… with Shawn?"

I turn my eyes on Shawn. He has this smug, self-satisfied look on his face that clearly said, "I got your man and you can't do shit about it." Before I knew it, I blacked out. My hands went around Shawn's neck, and his face was turning blue. I kept hearing, "Let him go! You're gonna kill him!" After a few seconds, Nate succeeded in yanking me away from him. I watched as he crumpled on the floor, choking and coughing, and I told Nate five words. "Pack up and get out!" *Sigh.* Now, all I have for company is an empty house, and old songs that make me break down and cry when I listen to them, like "Through the Fire" by Chaka, or "I Miss You Like Crazy" by Natalie, and that whole "Waiting to Exhale" album. Shit. One of the songs that we christened our special song was "Count on Me". I can't count on him now, can I?

Tear number seven.

I am thirty-six years old, recently single, and alone. What kind of disaster will life throw me now?

I lay down on the sofa and push the power button on my remote control. Some old show comes on... but I can't concentrate on it. I turn my TV off and lay back. As I stare at the ceiling, pictures of Nathan and I are vividly depicted. The first picture was of the day we first met, at the City Café on Cathedral Street. We bumped into each other as he was coming from the bathroom and I was carrying my food to my table. Obviously, neither one of us were paying attention because... WHAM! We collided, my Pepsi splattered all over his pink shirt and gray slacks. I apologized and good sport that he was, he said it was ok. Then he gave me a cock-eyed, humorous grin that melted my heart. Oh, how I loved that grin! I forget how the conversation started but after that day we were inseparable... until recently.

The second picture flashed: the day he moved into my place. It was a year and a half ago. We fought over whose stuff we were going to keep and whose we were going to give away. Then we decided on a game of chess, after which the loser was to get rid of his stuff. I'm pretty good at chess, but Nate did not mention that he was captain of his chess team in high school. So, he won... But I'll be damned if I was carting off *my* shit. All my stuff is in a storage unit, unbeknownst to him. A storage unit I've been paying on since the fated game.

The third picture flashes: the day Nate lost his management job at the grocery store and I had to work overtime to pay the mortgage, both of our car notes, and the utility bills. Through it all, he was complaining about me spending too much time working and not tending to him, calling me while I'm at work, and irritating me so much I had to tell my secretary to block all calls coming from him just so I could get some peace and quiet.

Picture Four: The night Nate left. But I don't want to dwell on that picture. Besides I'm hungry. I reach for my phone to order Chinese, when it rings. I don't want to answer the phone. Let it ring.

Ring… Ring… Ring…Ring…Ring…Ring…

The answering machine: "Hi, this is you know who. I'm either busy, out, or I saw your number and opted not to answer. Just kidding. But leave your name and business after the beep." *Beep.*

My friend Jojo's smooth voice caresses the walls. "Lion, I know you are there because you don't go anywhere. I haven't heard from you in four days. Now if you don't pick up this phone, I am coming over there, and bringing Peep and Corey with me. Don't forget we all got keys to your place." Do I want them coming over here feeling sorry for me? They wouldn't. But I really don't want my best friends to see me like this. I pick up the phone.

"Hey, Jojo."
"Boy, you had me and the guys worried sick about you!"
"I'm ok."
"Quit lying. I know that voice. I've heard it too long not to. Now, what is wrong?"
"I really don't want to talk about it."
"Fine, I'll come over there, and we'll talk about it then. Your voice might be able to lie, but your face can't."
"Jojo, Please…I'm ok."
"No, you are not. Like I said, I know that voice. You couldn't tell a straight lie to me when we were kids and you can't tell one with us being grown. Now, are you going to voluntarily tell me what's wrong over the phone, or do I have to come over there and get it out of you?"
I let out a long sigh. "My mother."
"Oh, that… I already know. She blew up."
"How did you know?"

"Hello?! It was Mother's Day and I figured you would call to check on her. Besides, My Aunt Lois told me that she ran into her at Big Star and said she went on a rampage when your name came up. Listen, I know you are hurting, but remember this is new for her."

"I know. I just thought that..."

"You just thought that since you have been standing by her from Day one, that she would be more understanding, am I right?"

"I guess."

(Pause)

"What am I supposed to do?"

"Give it time. It'll work itself out."

"Yeah, right. She started in on *you*, you know? Talking about you lured me into this."

"Why am I not surprised? We have been close since boot roller skates came out, and everybody in the neighborhood knew I was different. Anyway, another reason I'm calling is because Peep is concerned. You had a standing gym appointment with him on yesterday and he said you never showed up. He called but received no answer."

"I know. I just don't feel like discussing this with anybody right now and if I go with him to the gym, he's going to want to talk about what's going on and I just don't have the energy to discuss it."

"That's ok, although you know he would never force you to speak about it. But you need to get out of that house. Being cooped up is not the best way to be when you are depressed. Especially with you taking those sleeping pills. I keep telling you, those pills are dangerous."

"I know... I will... eventually. Uh look, I gotta get off the phone. I have something cooking on the stove," I lie.

"Yeah, OK." An uncomfortable pause elapses. Then, a voice filled with caring beckons. "Lion..."

"Yeah?"

"You know I love you. Right?"

"I know. I love you back."

"If you ever need to talk, I'm here."

"Thanks, Jojo. I'm fine though... Really." I must tell him something to make him stop worrying and get off the phone. I need to take these pills because another wave of depression is threatening to drown me. "Look, why don't we get together next Monday? Tell Peep I'll be available next week for gym and salads."

"Yes, for getting together. No, for telling Peep. You'll have to tell him yourself. He would feel better if it were coming from you."

Damn... "Ok."

"Be easy. I'll catch you on Monday...and I'm holding you to that. Otherwise, I'm using my key to drag your ass out."

"Fine."

"Good night."

"Good night." I hang up.

I pause a minute, then I start to dial Fung Chao's. Suddenly I don't feel all that hungry, especially for anything from that MSG Tabernacle. I lumber up the stairs to my bathroom. I open my medicine cabinet and pull out the prescription bottle of Doxepin. Only, surprise! There is no medicine left. Dammit!

I amble into my bedroom... A hard room to go into since every night I walk into this room and climb into a lonely bed. I glance and then do a double take at my reflection in the mirror. My usually close cropped wavy hair has grown to an unkempt state. My lips are chapped and cracking. My eyes are terribly bloodshot, and my skin is looking a bit grayish. Oh God! What am I doing to myself? I wallow in the deceiving sanctity of my own self-pity as the tears begin to flow, again. Tears that sting my eyes as they stream freely down my face. I can't help but think back at the times I used to have with my family; the happy Christmas Days, the family vacations, and the day I left for college as I drove from Yeti and the sight of my mother's constant disapproval. So many memories flooding back... and visions of my ex barrel into my brain...

No! I don't want to think about him. But the memories come without restraint. I want to go downstairs and pour a shot of vodka, but I am too mentally drained to make the trip. Still in the unrelenting throes of my despair, I strip, climb into bed, pull the covers over my head, and let the tears drench my pillow as I cry myself to uneasy sleep.

"Rrrrrrrrrrrrrrrrring!!!!"

I jerk awake. Damn. What time is it? I look at the clock. Oh, it's 9:26. Who would be calling me now? I answer the phone.

"Hello?"

"Boy, I oughta kick your ass for not responding to my calls! What da hell is the matter with you?" The crazed, nasal, high-pitched voice yells. It's my best buddy, Corey.

"Wassup, Corey. I'm sorry. I just didn't want to talk to anybody. I've been dealing with a lot of crap lately."

"Baby, when you are dealing with crap, you need friends to pull you out of it. Listening to your voice right now, my mission has just become bell-clear! Darling, put on your sexy clothes. We are going to the Link tonight."

"Aw man," I sigh, exasperated.

"And don't give me that "Aw man" crap! It is time you got out of that fuckin' house and had some fun. We ain't gettin no younger, especially you. You and Jojo turn thirty-seven in October. Three years from forty, old man!"

"Bitch, hush," I countered.

"Get wit' it, Lion. It's been seven months since you and Nathan split. It's over, and I know you are depressed about your Ma being her bitchy self."

"Oh, so we're calling mamas bitches now?" I defended, smiling.

"Baby, you know me. I 'ma call a spade a spade. It's the country boy in me. Like I said, 'I know you are depressed about your Ma being her bitchy self', but let it go and keep it movin'. You did the right thing by being honest with her. If she cannot love you, then that's her problem. Now come on out and let's get busy!"

"I don't feel like going out."

"Bitch, you better change out of that pajama shit that I know you are wearing at 9:29 at night. I am coming over to pick you up in thirty minutes, and I ain't taking no for an answer! Believe that!"

I started to tell him that if I wanted to go out, I would jump in my car and go, but I heard the dial tone instead. That's how Corey is, and always was. He has a strong personality and often uses it to encourage people to say yes to life when circumstances tell them no. Besides, I know Corey. When he takes that tone, there's just no talking to him. Shit, maybe it's not such a bad idea. I need to get out of this house and find some new scenery.

I cross the bedroom and open my closet door. Cardigans, Polo shirts, sweaters, and slacks as far as the eye can see. How boring! Nate picked out these clothes for me and because I didn't want to hurt his feelings, I kept and wore them. Yet, one time when I went shopping, I felt kind of frisky and I put together this hot little number. It was a white tank top, a transparent white silk shirt, tight black pants, and a black wool scarf. Nate drooled to see me wear this outfit; only in his view of course. With good reason, I say. Since I am kinda buff, that outfit showed off my muscle. I spy that outfit at the very back of my closet. Hmmm… I wonder if I should wear it tonight. Of course, those pants would show off a muscle I didn't have to work out. That is, until I found someone to work it out with. (Chuckle). Anyway, I am not trying to attract men. I'm only doing this to get my friends off my back.

*****

It is ten-fifteen. I am sitting here, listening to the voice messages… and waiting. It would be just like Corey to be fashionably late. I hate the outfit that I chose. A baby pink shirt, black loose slacks, and brown penny loafers. Damn. Where am I going, to a country club? But it's too late to change, and Corey will be here any minute. Sometimes I hate going to clubs, especially the Link. It's just a place where a bunch of men size each other up for sex. The clientele at the Link can range from stick-in-ass folks to drug dealers and coke addicts. A person can't even leave without checking their pockets to make sure they have everything they came with. After a while, I stopped bringing my wallet to keep it from being stolen. I would just bring the money. The person at the door knows me, so I don't need an ID.

Another reason that I hate the Link is because it set the stage for yet another fucked-up decision I made when I was twenty-seven: bare-fucking guys I hardly knew. This one guy I met was a self-proclaimed ho, and a bitter one at that. But he had the type of dick that reminded me of Jamaal's. Life changing! Unfortunately, it didn't just change my life sexually. It also challenged my health and left me with HIV. I kept it quiet from my family and blocked it out for four and a half years. I wouldn't take meds or see doctors because that would mean admitting that I have it. If it wasn't for my friend Corey, who's also positive, I would be in the same screwed up condition. Worse than that, I would have killed myself just as Jamaal had.

Even with meds and counseling, it still did not curb my penchant for bringing home male strangers, from avid drug users to affluent businessmen. Very unwise. I remember one occasion I came home with a young buck I met at the Link. He had this air about him that radiated eighty feet of arrogance and self-importance, and its very potency attracted me to him. He was six-foot eight, a giant compared to my six-one frame. His arms, shoulders, and chest were doubled over with caramel muscle. He was wearing a black tank top and black spandex shorts, which showed the extreme definition of his powerful, bodybuilder's legs. His hair was cut short to fit his virile yet boyishly smooth face. This man was fine! Anyway, we made small talk, and I learned that he was a Kinesiotherapy Major at Johns Hopkins University and would soon be graduating. That sealed the deal. There is nothing I like more than a brother with brains, as well as brawn. This lifestyle is so full of folks with shit between their ears. To find someone with a purpose and a future would be nothing short of a miracle only God could perform.

After forty-five minutes of idle chit-chat, the conversation takes a provocative turn. He asked me what I liked sexually. I told him I was easily pleased and open minded (Big Mistake). He reached out and touched my face with his smooth, soft palm. It was a soft touch, yet firm and fervent, demanding more. His eyes burned into mine, and we agreed silently to ditch the Link and prepare for an evening of physical pleasure. We came back to my place and as soon as we walked in the door, his arms enveloped me in tight and hot embrace! His lips crushed down on mine with complete authority and control. A few minutes later, our clothes were on the living room floor. Brutally, we groped each other, and my body seemed to levitate in his strength as he lifted me off the ground and carried me into my bedroom. He laid me on my bed and tongued me down firmly and slowly. But when he got to my jimmie....

"Time to flip the switch!"

He grabbed my legs with a dangerous glint of thuggish cruelty in his eyes. An alarm bell went off in my head! But I didn't trip, because I can deal with a little hard-core every now and then.

"Come on, bitch!"

I was so lost in what was going on that I didn't realize his proceeding in an attempt to rape me; I mistook the savagery on his face for passion. But when he tried to enter me missionary style, dry and without protection, I knew that he was going to rape me, and if I didn't fight back, I would be sitting in the county hospital where they aren't always helpful to gay black men. Ten whole inches of thick punishment and the shit hurt like hell!!

"I am gonna take that boy pussy!"

I told him to get off me, but he told me to shut the fuck up. It was then that I remembered my loaded gun in my nightstand. In struggling to get away from him, I was somehow able to land a hard punch to his jaw, dazing him to where he reeled back. Without hesitation, I planted my feet directly on his chest and pushed with all my might. He landed with a crash on the opposite wall. Damn! Leg Presses really DO work! His dazed confusion gave me enough time to grab my gun, point it directly at his chest, and order him out of my house before I put a hole in him, and would you believe it? He *still* came for me! Talking about "You're too chickenshit to pull the trigger." Ha! I fired one off that barely missed his nuts. "You got a choice. Get out of my house voluntarily in one piece or be thrown out... dickless." He hastily grabbed his clothes and darted out of the house, still dressing and yelling, "Crazy bitch!" I just sat there in shocked silence, and then a tsunami of hilarity flowed out of my mouth and bounced off the walls of the room.

Men... They can really take you there. He wanted to flip the switch, but I beat him to it and made him run out like the bitch he wanted to make me. I guess he thought that I was something of an easy target just because he's half a foot taller. Now when he sees me at the Link, he turns and walks faster in the opposite direction. Ha!

As humorous as that was, it also put a permanent halt to my trolling for dick and looking for love in fucked up places. This was where Nate came in. Nate. I could think of his sleek chocolate slim body, his perfect snow-white smile, and his intense dark eyes that could look right through you, and I would squirm. His ethnic masculinity exuded a radiant energy and strong presence. He knew of my status but said that it didn't matter. He loved me anyway. Speaking of love; boy, did he know how to make it! Many guys just fuck for its own sake. He started off slow and it mounted with a shocking intensity that almost frightened me when we first did it. But when he kissed, Oh my GOD! He kissed as if he truly meant it and his kisses were electric! Soft, but electric! When his head inclined to mine, and his eyes would hypnotize me in their dreaminess, I would find myself smoking cigarettes later, even without us doing the full deed. I am thinking about this even while I am waiting for the doorbell to ring... Where is that boy? Corey is always annoyingly late.

Ding-dong! About time! I open the door. "Hey bitch!" There stands Corey in his clubbing outfit: a tight red muscle shirt and his black leather pants and black leather boots. I can see the defined contours of his body under the clothes. He gives me a wide, vivacious grin, which I reciprocate.

Let me tell you. In life nowadays, if you're lucky, you only have one ride or die best friend. I lucked out three times! Corey, Peep, and Joseph. Now Joseph, affectionately called Jojo, I have known since birth. We both went to Morgan State University and met Peep and Corey. We all wound up being best friends for the last seventeen years to date. Jojo and I met Cordell Rodgerick Kennedy at a concert in the chapel. He was the featured pianist of that concert and he was magnificent! We were astounded at how his fingers flew over the keys and played the notes with a mixture of beauty, precision, sadness, and foreboding.

Jojo and I introduced ourselves afterwards and we became fast friends. Peep met him later and he disliked him on the spot at first. They had personalities that were exactly alike, as well as opinions as different as east and west. But, after a few weeks, Peep grew to love him with a fierceness. Peep, Jojo, and I had varied ways of relating with Corey. Peep and Corey's relationship was a bit like that of those fairies in Sleeping Beauty. Peep said pink and Corey said blue. There was a mutual sweetness between Corey and Jojo. The hugs and brotherly ass pats were most abundant between the two of them. Yet, while he was very close with Peep and Jojo, I always felt like he had a deeper connection to me than anyone else. I think it was because we gave each other a measured balance between Peep's outspoken nature and Jojo's sweetness.

He is a music professor at Towson University and Minister of Music at Unity and Love Community Church, the most affluent and LGBTQ affirming church in Baltimore. He is also one hell of a concert pianist and the sickest Hammond organist I have ever heard! He can play Robert Schumann's Piano Concerto in A Minor with vigor and feeling, then turn around and blend his soaring counter-tenor voice to the keys while sharing a soul stirring Gospel selection. He teaches piano to snot-nose bastards who don't practice. His words, not mine. I was initially attracted to him, but nothing ever came of it. With his six-foot frame, his tight dancer's build, and his clear, flawless butterscotch skin, he would always end up going home with one, sometimes two or three men. Yep, he is just that freaky!

"Wassup Corey."
"Oh no. What in the hell are you wearing? Don't tell me you are going in that!"
"What? It's comfortable," I defended.
"Lion," he snaps, exasperated. "This is a club, not an interview for a job. Loosen up for once in your life."
"I don't have time to change."
"Shit, we'll make time. You are *not* going in that!"

Corey charges up to my bedroom and into my closet. His face is alight with mischief and impish charm. He has always been like this. Wild and free, not apologizing for the life he lives and the decisions he makes. He is the rougher, bolder half of me, always the life of the party, the quick-wit, the jokester. Hell, he is my best friend, and to tell you the truth, I wouldn't have him any other way.

But now, he is tossing my clothes out of the closet, making a total mess out of my bedroom, trying to find an ensemble I can wear; his body a defined and muscled, red and black blur.

"Corey, Need I remind you that I have to clean and sleep in this room?" I admonished.

"Babe, you get the right outfit, you may not be coming back to this room tonight! But, if I have to, I'll come by and help Mr. Corporate America fix his precious closet," he quips, grabbing my chin. I jerk away. Then, he looks back in the closet, and sees the hot number I bought. He snatches it up. "Dayum!" he squeals. "How long have you been keeping this outrageous outfit in your closet?"

"Oh, that old thing."

"Yeah, this old thing!"

"I bought that a year ago," I stammer, embarrassed.

"You tramp. They say the quietest ones are the biggest freaks. Now I believe it. Good to see that Nate hasn't taken all of your fashion sense. Change into this," he muttered, nonchalantly throwing it at me.

"I don't know…"

"Wake up and smell the K-Y," he says. "You are going on forty years old. You don't get that many chances to have fun."

"I am thirty-six and almost three quarters. There is a difference!"

"Whatever! The way you're dressed right now, people would think you are forty. Read my lips. *Put on this outfit!* You got the perfect body for it. Oh, and another thing, while you are out, don't be looking depressed. Men sense that shit and they stay away from you. You have to be bold enough to stand up to your depression and say, 'This is where it stops!' Now put this on and let's go. Peep and Jojo are probably already at the club."

"Alright, alright, you twisted my arm! I will be out in fifteen minutes."

I went into the bathroom to take another shower. But as I look down, I see an empty bottle of my favorite smell-good. Damn!

CHAPTER TWO:

"JOJO"

Some say that life happens to us and we are not prepared for the occurrences. I certainly was not prepared for the words, gay, faggot, fairy, or queen to be used as a description of me. My lifelong friend, whom I just hung up with, wasn't prepared to be disowned by his mother and family either. But hey, these are the cards we were dealt.

I, Joseph Stanley Thompson the III, financial secretary for Oakley Law Firm, hail from the small town of Yeti, Alabama. The IQ of people down there can be compared to that of a slug. When I grew up, the last thing anyone would ask to be is a homosexual, especially in our bigoted little town. If the gangs weren't beating up on you every day, the church was telling you how you'd be on a first-class train to the lowest level of Hell. I experienced both, and like my true blues that I hang out with regularly, being gay was not what I desired. But hey, that's what I am, and it took forever for me to be comfortable with that. Now, having the same comfort level with my exterior features, that's completely another set of sessions with my shrink.

I was raised by my mother, my aunts, and my mother's friend, Rodney. I called him Uncle Rodney. My dad was an absentee father. He split from Mama when I was a one-year-old and moved to Seattle. Rumor had it that he was always hopping on a boat heading to parts unknown due to his job as a captain of Funtown Cruise Ships, never a thought for the woman and child he left behind. So naturally, it was just Mama and me.

My childhood was filled with myriad memories, both good and bad. I was teased daily about my mannerisms and the way I was built. I was a thick (not fat) chocolate boy with a high ass and had hair as coarse as a Brillo pad. It took forever for my mother to comb through it. Mama dressed me in Bugle Boys, Lord and Taylor, and Gap. She always said that she wasn't raising a hoodlum, and looking at myself in the mirror, I see that she didn't.

A dark chocolate, 5'11, full faced, thick guy with even teeth stares back at me. Lord, my teeth ache when I think of all those many years of braces. An inch-long scar is visible on the right side of my forehead. I got that scar through one of my mother's boyfriends, Mike. He came around when I was eight years old and stayed around for two years. His favorite pastimes were drinking, cussing, and beating up on Mama and me almost on a regular basis. Of course, she covered this up. Estee Lauder could have cleaned up by how much money Mama spent on foundations, concealers, and other makeup. But one day, at age ten, I came into the kitchen and saw my mother pinned down on the kitchen table, while Mike was brutally hitting her. The back of his hand slammed on her face repeatedly. Call it instinct, anger, or just plain fed up, but I ran over, grabbed a heavy cast iron skillet, and slammed it down on his back. He whirled around, punched me on my right jaw, and sent me spinning. My forehead hit a corner of a sharp counter edge and I blacked out. It was the first time he ever hit me in front of her, and that was what it took for Mama to send him packing. Mama had many boyfriends before him, but she was through with men after he split.

As far as my sexuality is concerned, I came out to my mother when I was eighteen and it was not because I wanted to. I tried my damnedest to hide this from her. But eventually, I was forced to come clean. While clearing the clutter from under my bed, Mama found several magazines of big dicked, big assed guys performing sex moves that defied the laws of gravity. When I got home from shopping for college, my mother was sitting at the kitchen table with the magazines spread out and she was looking at one of them! Can you imagine? My heart was racing quicker than a race car! My fingers felt like slippery worms from the sweat that formed on my hands. When she saw me, she said, "Hmmm! So, this is how men have sex with each other. Freaky! Maybe I need to have a threesome with two of them so's I can watch." Just then, an avalanche of laughter flowed out of me and she laughed right along with me!

After we settled down, she told me to sit down and we had a long talk. I asked her if she had any problems with my being gay. She told me no and that she always knew. Shocked to my bone, I asked her how and she told me that she would watch my eyes when we were out shopping and my interaction with Lionel, my best friend. She also told me that if this is the path I was set to follow, I should just find love and be careful how I go about it. Then she gave me the best present a mother could give. She came around that table, hugged me, and told me that she loved me and that she was proud of me. That was just what I needed. After that, she became my closest confidante besides Lionel, and my shoulder to cry on. Of course, she also became my kick in the pants if I made a bonehead move. I felt comfortable talking to her about almost everything, including my boyfriends.

I know you're going to say, "I can't believe your mother was ok with your being gay." But Mama was a rarity. In the seventies, she protested for peace and she made friends with almost everyone that crossed her path. She was especially close to Uncle Rodney, the gayest, handsomest fish in the sea. He was her friend from college. She used to let me stay over his house all the time while she went to work. Maybe that had something to do with how my boat swung, huh? Not really… and if so, it was only to a small degree, and through no fault of his own. I had two experiences with older men before I was eighteen. Yes, I was exposed to gay sex early on, but the second time I loved it! My "uncle's" nine-inch chocolate pole was like a tower begging to be sucked! Trust me, he didn't seduce me. I seduced him! I was sixteen at the time and boy did he resist. I wore cutoffs. I wore tank tops. I even wore booty shorts. Oh yes, his mind resisted, but his pole cried for more.

One day while he was asleep, I went down on him and tasted his beautiful joystick. It got bigger and bigger! Then he woke up and saw me, he tried to push me off, but I begged him to let me do it just one time. He consented at length, and it was like paradise for me. But when he went down on me, my GOD! Ecstasy pills ain't got shit on my uncle! He took me to heaven and back! Uncle Rodney stayed on my pole for at least seven minutes straight. He also had the type of ass that would not quit! I fucked him all night that night and when it was all over, I rested in his big beautiful muscular arms and we fell asleep. We had plenty of sessions after that "one time", and he was so patient with me when I let him open me up. Unfortunately, six years ago, he died of cancer and our secret was buried in his grave with him. Tears still come when I think about that man. Our escapades were something that I kept from everybody, even my mother!

The first time was not an experience I would wish on anybody. It happened with Mike, the abusive one. I will not go into too many details about this because it's painful to relive. All I can tell you is that it involved a repeated fist coming towards my face…
a butcher knife to my throat…
vegetable oil in my crack…
a painfully thick eight-and-a-half-inch violation in my ass…
a hard, badly-worn kitchen table with splinters lancing through the skin on my back….
and a look of the deranged pouring out of a lunatic's eyes as he fucked me over and over…

Ok, I'm going into details. I kept that a secret too. My mother was already stressed, and I didn't want to stress her more. She did see the splinters on my back and asked the reason. I told her a bullshit story and she rushed me to the hospital where they dug them out, stitched me up, and nothing was mentioned of it again. I didn't even tell Lionel because I thought he would turn against me. In some ways, I thought it was my fault for pissing Mike off so much. I especially did not want to lose Lionel's friendship. I did not know his orientation then, so I kept quiet.

Lionel. How I love him. We were friends since we were born. We share the same birthday. He is so smart, self-assured, calm as a puddle on a summer day, sweet, and as gorgeous as he can be. At 6'1, his caramel skin layered with hard muscle, kept with a velvety sheen. I've had so many occasions of a hard masculinity, and a moist hole while watching him sweat in tank tops when working out! His face contains the biggest, most luminous light brown eyes that are perfectly spaced, a straight finely shaped nose that flares when he is angry or aroused, and puckered red lips surrounded by a sparse goatee with a sinister line connecting his bottom lip with his chin. He is dreadfully insecure about his face though, because it features a strong sharp irregular jawline and a devil's cleft on his chin. Even when he was a teen, he was packed with muscle. My mother called us The Odd Duo. For instance, take complexion. Now, he's a peanut butter color and I am very dark. I'm talking Hershey's Special Dark

Chocolate. He was into athletics. Wrestling. No one could match his hammerlock that clamped like an iron vise. I was more into band and chorus. Before Nate came along, He dressed in more flair and style and I dressed in preppy nerd attire. There were many other differences between us. But when it counted, we always were there for each other. Of course, it took him forever to come out of the closet. He did it finally when he and Nate busted up. I was glad they split up because it depressed me when they became an item. We were so close that I always thought we would end up together. No surprise that his mother freaked. Lynetta Davis was always someone you'd feed with a long-handled spoon. She would always be talking about "faggot" this and "sissy" that. She always felt that I was a bad influence on Lionel. Hell! Maybe she's right.

I survey my reflection in the mirror. My ass is way too big. I got huge thunder thighs. My skin is way too dark. I know I should be happy with the body I have, especially after being dragged kicking and screaming to the gym by my friend Peep.

Fat faggot!

I hear the words echo in my head and I wince. Tears begin to flow as an unpleasant memory forms in my brain. I see a flashback of myself taking the shortcut from band practice. I see Lionel's brother and sister, as well as five hyper-masculine street punks, looking for someone to bully. I could hear the snickers and the jeers as I walked by them. *"Fat Faggot!"* The words were like a razor slicing my back. I just kept walking as they kept the insults coming. I got pissed when I heard the words, "Hey, Tutti-Frutti, does faggotry run in the family?" but I kept walking. "Hey, muh sista's talkin' to yuh, pansy motherfuckuh!" A rough hand clamps down on my shoulder and turns me around forcibly. My eyes scan over the contemptible forms of my best friend's brother, sister, and his cronies. They all stand one to four inches taller than me, the shortest being Andre. Tank tops and jeans with Air Jordans and Caps cover the muscular bodies of drugged out Neanderthals with hollowed out eyes, sunken jaws, and a combined IQ of forty-seven. Rhonda is wearing a tight pink shirt and black shorts, stockings, and stiletto boots. They all surround me. Rhonda gets up in my face and screams, "I said, 'Hey Tutti-Frutti, does faggotry run in the family?' Can't you hear?" I state, "My name isn't Tutti-Frutti it is Joseph." Andre mimics my statement in a stereotypical lisp to the jeering benefit of his stooges, and then he gets in my face saying, "Yuh name is Tutti-

Frutti. That's whatcha bull-dagguh mama shoulda named yuh." I dropped my books and my trumpet case. I then deliver a hard punch to Andre's smirking face, causing him to reel backwards. A belting whack hammered into the back of my head and everything went black. When I came to, I was in the alley and those same Jordans and stilettos were kicking me in my ribs. Then, Andre gets on top of my chest and starts beating me. Five excruciating punches slam into my face as the gravel tears patches of my hair off. Then, Andre gets off. "Faggit motherfuckuh!" Andre breathes out. Then he… Well…

Riiiiiiiiiiiiiiiiiiiiiiiiing goes my phone. I rush to get it and, blinded by my tears, I crash my toe into the corner of my couch. Shit, that hurt like hell.

"Hello?"
"Jojo, what's wrong?" Peep's voice rings out.
"Nothing."
"You sure?"
"Yeah," I wipe away my tears with the back of my hand. "What's going on?"
"Well, Corey went to drag Lion's hermit ass outta that house. We're having a fellas' night out. Get your tail down to the Link."
"Why is it that every time we have a fellas' night out, we always have to go to the Link? Why not anywhere else but there?"
"Honey, where else can we go on a Friday night? Baltimore is a cool city and all, but it bores the shit outta me. And for the record, we don't do the Link for every fellas' night out. Sometimes we go to the movies, and let's not forget that gay ballet you dragged us to three weeks ago."
"You didn't like it?"
"Well now, I wouldn't say I didn't. I mean, watching those bare-chested men in those white tights bumping and grinding on each other had me gushing in my draws. I think I dated one of them."
"What?"
"Yeah, chile'. But, about the Link, and you know I'm telling the gospel truth. You are not going to meet your Prince Charming sitting on your ass watching porn."
"And what in the hell makes you think I'm going to find him there?"
"Baby, please. If guys see that you can live a little, maybe you have a good shot. Besides, we have been working that body out for some time now. Don't you want to show off the results?"
"Well, you got a point there."

"I know I do. Now... Let's get a move on. I'm leaving the house in thirty minutes and I want you to wear that outfit I made you buy last week. It accentuates your ass and that chest of yours."

"I don't know."

"Oh, come on! You and Lion both with the corporate dress bullshit. When are you going to live a little? Life is short, and you better enjoy it while you can."

"OK, fine. I will wear the stupid outfit."

"Now if you would just agree with me in the first place, we could avoid all this back and forth. See you in a bit, my love." *Click.*

I amble upstairs and into my closet to pull out the outfit. I am still tempted to wear the "corporate dress bullshit". Peep did not know this, but the reason I dressed the way I did was because I didn't want those sex-crazed pervs at the Link eyeing me like I'm a piece of meat. I have had my share of guys to cross my threshold and they ranged from good-looking to drop dead gorgeous. Alas, very few of them wanted a solid relationship. I had a short stint with a good-looking guy that came in the office one day. He was a cute caramel guy with dimples, large ocean blue eyes, and long curling lashes. He had a large, hairy, stocky body and a pole that was thick and juicy! I was attracted to his smile that lit those beautiful blue eyes. At the beginning of the relationship, he wined and dined me, called constantly to check on me, and surprised me with little trinkets that he knew I liked.

Unfortunately, he only lasted a year. I began to notice changes in him seven months into the relationship. He became emotionally and mentally abusive. He would call me Tar-baby, Coal-Black, or Black Seal out of spite and he added terms like "bitch", "fat bastard", and "dumb punk" to the list. He was insanely jealous of my friendship with Lionel and Peep. He hated Corey with a passion because Corey would tell him that his draws stunk in a second. He complained every time I wanted to hang out with them instead of listening to him bitch on the phone about everything. My friends kept warning me to get out of that toxic association, but like a fool, I overlooked all of this, thinking it would pass. It came to a head one day when we got into a scorching argument. The motherfucker lied about his HIV status, and I ended up getting it! When I confronted him, he called me a bitch and hit me across the face. In that instant, I thought of Mike's abuse and kicked him in the balls, watching him sink and writhe on the floor. I then thought of Andre, Rhonda, and those thugs, and I did the same thing to him that they did to me: I kicked him in the ribs. Then I straddled him and slammed my fist into his face repeatedly until I got tired. I then removed myself from him and told him to get the fuck out of my house. Shit, I may be a bitch, but my sweet Uncle Rodney didn't just teach me how to fuck. He also taught a bitch how to fight!

The others I met weren't any better: users, freeloaders, deadbeats, and liars. The halfway decent ones I met were just interested in sex. We would fuck a few times and when I started wanting to get serious with them, the fucking would stop for months. Then I'd get a late-night call asking if I want company, to which I say, "Hell No!" One thing guys can say about me is this: once you leave my bed, you don't come back. I then made up my mind that I was going to make the next guy wait before I give him any. Maybe I'd have a better chance at love if I ditched the revolving door to my bedroom.

I take my outfit to the bathroom with me. I lay out my orange scented facial scrub, my loofah sponge, my body wash, and the rest of my grooming products. Lathering my face and neck, my thoughts steal back to Lionel. *Hmm. I wonder if he sees me in this outfit and starts thinking "thoughts"*. On times when he doesn't think I'm looking, I do catch him sneaking peeks at my ass and thighs. Many times, I have seen him adjusting his jock due to some "discomfort". I chuckle inwardly. Of course, I don't mention it. I know he doesn't like screwing friends because it always tends to complicate things and he doesn't want to ruin what we have already built. I have fantasized what it would be like to be with him exclusively. I relish the idea of being in a committed relationship with him. It would be a dream come true for me, but I would always perish the thought due to how he feels. However, there is nothing wrong with a little harmless flirting. I just have to make sure I don't go too far.

After my facial, I strip out of my clothes and step into my shower stall. On my way in, I catch a glimpse of my ass and hamstrings while walking in. Hmm! If I were him, I would think thoughts too.

Wink, Wink.

CHAPTER THREE:

"PEEP"

"Jimmy, will you please slow down? Those patients are not going anywhere!" I exclaim, rushing down the stairs after my man. He is moving at breakneck speed.

"Feli baby, I gotta get to the hospital. I want to get as much time in as possible," Jimmy replies, going into the kitchen and packing his snack. "Besides, I'm dealing with Ms. Harrison and she is the hardest patient to please. You know she's been giving the other registered nurses a hard way to go."

"Yeah, I know. I have a few friends who work at the hospital that have to deal with that old witch, drop the 'w' and add the 'b'."

"Feli, be nice!" Jimmy says. "That could be one of the women in your family you're calling that, ya know."

"They would have had better sense than to be weeding the yard at one hundred and two-degree weather. That old grouch had a stroke and now she's making y'all pay for it."

"It'll be fine, baby. Come here," Jimmy invites, stopping his snack packing and holding out his massive arms. I fold my body into his. God, how I love this man! Sometimes in bed at night, I look over at him just to smile. When he smiles back, my heart melts. I rest my chin on his rock-hard, hairy shoulder and he squeezes me tight. Jeez, I hope my bones don't crack. This boy doesn't know his own strength!

"Ow!" I exclaim.

"You ok, baby?" He pulls back, concerned.

"That hug was so tight; I thought I might break."

"I'm sorry, baby. Sometimes I don't know my own strength."

Mind-reader! "I didn't say I didn't like it," I tell him teasingly.

He laughs and hugs me again. Gently this time. "Baby, you've been a trooper. These two months have been hard with both of us working extra time to pay off this tax bill."

"Well, it had to be paid, papi."

"I know. I still think you should've let me earn the money by myself. I mean, this back-tax bill isn't your responsibility. It happened before we got hitched."

"Jimmy," I say, pulling back and looking into his eyes. "How many times do I have to tell you that we are in this together? I wanted to help pay it off. Besides, we cut the odds in half by both of us taking on the extra time at work. This way..." I say, grabbing his crotch, "we can get back to our regular schedule of loving a lot sooner."

"And not a minute too soon, baby," Jimmy muses devilishly, his hands on my ass and his eyes looking straight at me. Those eyes! How I love them. I can always look in them and see love only for me. As my eyes connect with his, our breathing becomes labored. The only sound heard is the clock ticking the seconds away. His huge hand caresses my face as he goes in for the dive. Our faces grow closer, and then...

Rrrrrrrrring!

Dammit!!!

"Saved by the bell, baby," He breathes out and grabs his snack. "I gotta go. Have a good time with the fellas. I'll see you tomorrow morning." He kisses me quickly and heads out the back door.

Damn! Here I am with my lips still puckered looking like Booboo the fool and this phone is ringing off the hook, irritating the hell out of me! I snatch it up and answer in a sour voice, "Hello?"

"What's with the shit-tone? Did I interrupt something?"

Hell to the yeah! It's my sweet and darling mother-in-law, Irene. I love her dearly, but she has the worst possible timing!

"Hello, Mamacita. No, everything is fine."

"Good, where's Jimmy?"

"He just left for work."

"Ok, I am on my way over there."

"Over here?"

"Yeah, I ain't got no place else to hang and I am bored as hell."

"You don't have any friends to hang around?"

"There's Cristal and Gladys. But all them old biddies wanna do is play cards and gossip about everybody on our block. It is always the same 'who's sleeping with who' bullshit. I'd have more fun hanging out with my favorite son-in-law."

"I'm your only son-in-law."

"I ain't gonna have another, am I?"

"Of course not, and your favorite son-in-law is heading out to hang with the Three Musketeers at the Link."

"That sounds good. I know I would enjoy myself with y'all."

"Uh, Mamacita, it's more of a fellas' night out. Besides, with everything that's been going on with Lionel, he just needs quality time with his boys."

"Oh, that's right. I forgot you told me about that shit with his mother. So, she's still tripping, huh?"

"Yep, she is. He just needs his buddies to hang with him and get him out of the house. I tell you what, though. Let's plan something for Sunday evening. Since Jimmy is off, we can go to your house and cook dinner. I'll ask the fellas to come."

"OK, baby. Now if you do that, you tell that Jojo to bring that sweet ambrosia salad. He knows how much I love it. Y'all go'n and have a good time. I'ma call Sandra Jean over and see if she wants to swing by and cool out, but I'm gonna be looking to see y'all rusty butts on Sunday!"

"Alright, Mamacita. Love you."

"Love you too, baby."

I hang up the phone, suddenly deep in thought. I feel a twinge of sorrow for her. Twice widowed to men who she said loved her beyond reason. Shortly after her second husband died, she threw herself into her work; Meals on Wheels, President of the Association of Equal Treatment for Women, Volunteer work at the hospital; and Liaison for the Baltimore LGBTQ Coalition. Jesus, she really *does* need a personal life. The thoughts of sorrow begin to morph into a familiar feeling of guilt. Maybe I should have let her come. No, we'll see her on Sunday. I go upstairs to get myself ready for the club. Yes, I do go to the club. I might be married but I am certainly not dead. I can look and not touch. Why do that when my Jimmy takes care of home?

After a long and soothing shower, I step out, dry myself off, put on my smell-goods and pit fresheners (deodorant), and stroll into our bedroom. I peer into our closet at the sea of sparkling and stylish garments. My eyes peruse over them to decide what I want to wear tonight.

Let's see. My satin, diagonal striped, green and white shirt. *Yes! This is good!* I take it off the hanger.
The pants? Hmm… Ah! White linen capris. *Perfect!*
Shoes? White loafers with green laces! *Love it!*
What kind of chain should I wear? Herringbone? *Nah, too thick.* My silver Omega chain? *Just right!*
Socks? *Ditch 'em!*

My name? It's Felipe Alexander Walker-Hartfield. My man calls me Feli for short. My friends call me Peep. I'll let Lion tell you where *that* one came from. I am a financial advisor at SunTrust Bank and a certified personal trainer. I was born in San Antonio, Texas to mi Madre and Padre, Carmen and Juanito Perez. I am of a mixed heritage. Latino and Black to be exact. Black on my mama's side and Hispanic on my papi's. The last memory I have of my parents is when I was seven. They stood over my bed and kissed me goodnight, left me with a sitter, and went out to some party. They were killed that night. A drunk driver was barreling down FM 1604 and my dad swerved the wheel to avoid him. Unfortunately for them, the tires were worn. The car skidded out of control, went careening off the bridge, and exploded. My paternal family was in no position to care for me because they could barely support themselves, so I was sent to Los Angeles to live with my grandparents on my mama's side: Robert and Margaret Walker.

I loved my grandparents just as much as I loved my parents. My Granddad was the gruffest, feistiest, and most big-hearted man I have ever encountered, besides my Jimmy. 5'11 with milk chocolate complexion, he was the most attractive, most athletic, most active granddad I'd ever seen. He was about the only man I knew who could wake up at 4:30 in the morning and go for a two-mile jog, teach school, make out lesson plans, and *still* have time to run around and play with the neighborhood kids and me. Granddad was fanatical about exercise and proper health, and he passed that trait down to me. I wanted to emulate him because he was everything I believed a man should be. He served in the Air Force during World War II, but he couldn't continue in service due to a broken leg in a plane bailout. After an honorable discharge, he went to college and graduated with his bachelor's and master's degrees. Thereafter, he became a Social Studies teacher. Robert Leon Walker was one of those men who believed that the man was solely responsible for the financial matters of the home. He would work odd jobs on the weekends to get things paid off quicker. In fact, that's how he paid for the house we lived in.

The thing I most remember about him was that Granddad had pizazz! He just had a style that could not be duplicated, and he always spent *mucho dinero* on his clothes, whether they were for church, for work, or for leisure. He spent an equal amount of money on Granny's and mine. I remember asking him why he spent so much on our clothes, and he told me this: "Philly, when people look at how you and your granny are dressed, that reflects on me. When people look at how I'm dressed, that reflects on my father. We don't come from slovenly people, so we have no option to look slovenly."

Granny was a buxom, five-eight, brown skinned woman with a melodious voice and a graceful stroll, and what a fireball she was! She was just as feisty and fun loving as her husband. I still remember her hands. They were wrinkled and worn, and her nails were chipped. But they felt so soft and I smelled Vanderbilt when she touched my face. Her eyes were huge and brown with curling lashes and she had the thickest and most gorgeous hair you ever saw. It was salt and pepper in color and hung down her back in a cascade of curls. I finally found out the secret behind how her hair got that long. She didn't believe in perms and a straightening comb went nowhere near her hair. She massaged, combed, brushed, parted, and braided it every night before she went to bed.

I tell ya right now. My grandparents weren't people anybody wanted to mess with. He kept a Colt .45 in his desk and she kept a pearl handled Smith and Wesson in her closet behind her fluffy pink slippers. Frankie, she called it. That gun was willed to her by her father who taught her how to shoot. Whenever some shit popped off or there was a relative cutting the fool and trying to break bad, she would grab Frankie, make sure he was loaded, and fire off some warning shots. If the fool kept it up, she would strategically shoot him in his ass. It didn't happen all that often though. But as hard as nails as they could be, they had just as much love for me and everybody who crossed their paths. The smells in that house are still lodged in my nostrils. Granddad's Cuban cigars, the constant smell of food cooking in the kitchen, the lemon scented ammonia, and Granny's Vanderbilt perfume and bleached sheets represented the happiest years of my life.

My sexuality... Hmm... I started screwing the girls at fifteen (a girl in my Biology class) and the boys at seventeen (Our neighbor's son). To top that off, I was confused about who I was since I was eight years old. I accidentally walked in on my Granddad when he was getting out of the shower. I said he was athletic, but NAKED? Lord! He had a banging body for someone over sixty. Thick, football player build with love handles, huge calves and a big sex toy that hung at least eight inches *soft*. It had to have been well used, because almost every night, I would hear Granny hollering, moaning, panting, and swearing, while he grunted like a stuck pig. I had to turn away, but when I was old enough to understand about sex, the image of my naked grandfather conflicted me for years. I know... Crazy, right? A grandson thinking of his grandfather in the sexual sense. But it was what it was. Thank God nobody ever knew, or they would have nailed me straight to the cross.

Now mind you, with my family being heavy in the church, premarital and same gender sex was something the pastor said we would go straight to hell for. Sunday after Sunday, that's all we ever heard. Hellfire and brimstone. "There is a sweltering place in Hell for whores and sissies," the pastor would say. It didn't matter about the rumors that our married pastor was putting the missionary sisters in "missionary" positions. It apparently also didn't matter that he was making the organist sing high notes while bending him over his desk in his study and giving him a beef injection. I know this because I witnessed it once when I was a teenager. *Yes, baby!* I went to the church thirty minutes early for youth choir rehearsal. I stopped by his office to drop off Granny's tithes money and I was about to knock when I heard moaning and panting voices. I carefully eased the door open and there stood the pastor and organist in naked glory. The pastor's big hairy ass was turned to the door and he was fucking the hell out of that rail-thin organist, who had his legs flailing in the air. I thought he would split his ass in two. It took everything in me to hold my laughter in, but when the pastor peaked and let out this loud phrase, "Huh! I'm cumming! Huh! I'm cumming! Huh! I'm cumming! Huuuuuuh!" I lost it! I covered my mouth with my hands and darted out of the church, forgetting to close the pastor's door. When I got back home and went up to my room, I opened my mouth, threw my head back, and laughed my little ass off! Every time I tried to quit laughing, I would think of that crazy moan and I would start all over again! After that, I couldn't look at him, let alone greet him, without having this shit-eating grin on my face and a huge hawking laugh that threatened to emerge from my core!

As hilarious as that was, it was also very disheartening. Apparently, homosexuality was a sin for everyone but him. My grandparents heard the rumors but never discussed them. I asked about the rumors once, but Granny simply said, "Stay out of grown-folks business. Go somewhere and play." This would be the one sore spot I had with my grandparents. In that church, everything the pastor said was sacred law, while everything he *did* was swept under the rug. A sad commentary on how the "body of Christ" operates to this very day.

Despite my conflicting sexuality, I was a contented, precocious kid who grew into a happy, rambunctious teenager. Unfortunately, when I was fourteen, Granddad passed away from a heart attack when I was a freshman in high school. It was a tough time for both Granny and me. It was just the two of us. Granny went to work as a clerk in the post office, as well as a housekeeper for the Westin Hotel near LAX. I promised at once that I would do my best to fill Granddad's shoes, but he believed in the highest education… and my grades, while a C-average, were not the highest. I buckled down and graduated in the top half of my class. Then, armed with partial scholarships, Pell Grants, and loans (so I assumed), I was packed up to attend Morgan State University in a car she paid cash for through Granddad's pension. Another death happened a week before graduating with my three best friends, Lionel (my roommate), Jojo, and Corey. I remember being out with them laughing, drinking, and having a good time celebrating all of us graduating with honors. We bombard into the dorm, tipsy and holding on to each other, and the Resident Director drops the worst news I could have ever received. He said that my great aunt Myrtle went over to check things out, because the hotel and post office managers said that Granny had not been to work in four days. She knocked, let herself in with her key, and there, sitting motionless and slumped over while decomposing and bloated, was Granny. She died in her sleep. A written letter was lying under a pen-clutching hand plagued with arthritis. That letter is still in my shoebox.

My dearest and only grandson,

If you are reading this, that means that I have gone to glory. But before I go, I am writing this to tell you that I love you. You've heard me say it many times before. I am so proud of the man you have become. Even while I'm writing this, I look over at a picture of you in your ROTC uniform. Memories are flooding my mind as I remember what a wonderful child you were. You have always been my sweet baby.

Your Granny is old and tired, and I have a strange feeling, one that I've never had, that the Good Lord is getting ready to send his angels to escort me up to His bosom. But I want to leave you with something as you cross the stage to get your degree and I cross the river to meet my Lord. I want you to live your life the best way you can live it. You go on to graduate school with no fears, no regrets, and no guilt. I say that because I know that even as you read this letter, you are feeling some kind of way, just like you always felt when we spent money on you and gave you everything we could. The giving was not just on our side. The greatest gift you have given us is the love and respect you have given all your life.

So, promise me in your heart that you won't blame yourself for my dying. The hotel rooms I cleaned and the packages I mailed for your education and support were my pleasure. Your Granny and Granddad lived a long and happy life and because my grandson is graduating from college with honors, I am dying happy. I know that you are going to be something very special… and I will be watching you from Heaven.

All my love to you,

Granny

Well, of course, I did feel guilty. I was floored. I never knew how the school bills were paid, nor did I know how I got the books. All I knew was that when I walked into the registrar's office or the book store, they told me it was taken care of. I found out later from her boss that almost everything she earned at the post office, she sent to the school every month to pay for anything the partial scholarships and Pell Grants didn't cover on that first year. Even after I started getting full scholarships, she *still* worked, squirrelling away money to give me once I graduated. It totaled to over one hundred grand which was enough to pay for graduate school, room and board, and other expenses. She literally worked herself to death, or so I told myself. Later, Aunt Myrtle told me that she enjoyed every bit of the work because it gave her a sense of accomplishment. She left me over five hundred thousand additional dollars, the remaining benefits of Granddad's pension, and the house. I tearfully sold it to my cousin after graduate school because I couldn't handle the upkeep. I used some of the money to make a down payment on this five-bedroom house I am living in and put the rest in the bank.

It was on the Metro subway in Baltimore that I met the love of my life, James Hartfield. Six feet and two inches of pure love. Moroccan, baby! He has these light grey eyes that always gave him an adorable, "lost-little-boy" innocence. His body is huge with a solid football player build. You know the type; Half thick and half muscle. Skin of a deep olive color and covered with a carpet of black, bushy hair. You know, in many ways, he reminds me of my granddad; the way he lifts me off the ground when he is happy, the way he holds me with care, and the way he looks at me with pride in his eyes. I'll never forget the civil ceremony we had. It was a beautiful intimate gathering with friends and members of his family. *My* family vocally disapproved of my marriage and did everything they could to break us apart, including telling the pastor that I was "lost" and needed to be led back to Christ. The pastor, being the hypocrite that he was, called me to the altar in a church service while I was visiting L.A. With the anointing oil in his hand, he proselytized that my upcoming marriage was against God's law and that I needed to marry a woman to suppress my sinful urges. I don't know if it was the condescending, self-righteous look on his face or the hateful one on the faces of the church members, but I knew then that I'd had enough. I cracked his face when I said in an oily voice dripping with sarcasm, "Yeah, that is the way to go. I mean, A lot of good that must have done you, acting all holy while you screw every man and woman you see." Lord, the ruckus that erupted when I said that! The mothers got up and cussed me out with words I thought they were too saved and sanctified to utter. A couple of tenors and sopranos in the choir were looking at each other with smirks and titters, obvious tell-tale signs on their faces. The deacons started rebuking me. One of the ushers nudged another and said, "I told you! Didn't I tell you?" The minister of music and the organist just started laughing their asses off. The pastor told them to shut up, but they just laughed even harder. The pastor ordered me out the church and told me hysterically that I was no longer welcome. I left, with hard ass pocketbooks and Bibles being swung at me and amid the sounds of cussing, screaming, laughter, and discordant organ pedals. The organist fell out on top of them, still laughing his ass off. I walked up to the corner, but then I heard somebody calling my name. I turned and looked into the laughing eyes of the minister of music. Well, that one look sent us in! We fell to the pavement lost in our own laughter, cars slowing down to stare at two crazy guys rolling around. When we had calmed down, he said, "I wish you the best happiness you could ever have." He then proceeded to write me a check for two grand and gave me a piece of advice that I hold in my heart to this day. "One thing you ought to never apologize for is love." That advice was the burr I needed in my saddle to marry James. I love him dearly. I love him so much that I can even put up with him forgetting to wipe down the sink after he finishes shaving, neglecting to put his funky ass draws in the hamper, and his loud and long snoring at night. I also have a close and binding love to my three friends, Corey, Lion, and Jojo. We have laughed together, cried together, talked about sex, and dished dirt on the men we met and displeased us. In all my years of living, no past friendship could equal the friendship we have. Even now as I grab my keys and head out the door, my eyes glance at a framed college picture of us. I smile, thinking of days gone by.

In life, you only have a small circle of best friends… and, if you are lucky, you get a man who adores and worships the ground you walk on.

Thank God I got both!

CHAPTER FOUR:

"*COREY*"

"So, what is really the problem, Lion?" I say as I steer my car down North Avenue.

"What do you mean?"

"I mean, there has to be more to it than your mama's rejection."

"Not really. What else could it be?"

"I'll tell you what it is. This life scares you."

"What?"

"You heard me. In all the years I have known you, the word 'gay' has never come out in self-description. Even now, although you came out to her, you are still afraid to live and really be who you are. You would say 'my gayness' or 'my struggle', but never the words, 'I'm gay'. You had this same issue in college."

"What do you mean? It's nothing that I'm ashamed of."

"Then why did you wait so long to tell her?"

No answer.

"Look, I'm not trying to get on your case. I feel where you are coming from. Accepting who you are is scary, whether you are gay or straight. But once you make that leap, I think you will be much happier in life."

"Maybe I am scared. I've been attracted to guys ever since I was thirteen, but it seems like every day brings something new and frightening about this lifestyle."

"Let me stop you right there. I am going to need you to quit calling this a lifestyle. A lifestyle deals with material things. Something that is appealing to the natural eye. Life is something we can't see, but we know we have it and that it appeals to the soul. It's kinda like faith. You do know about faith, don't you?"

"Who doesn't?"

"Many people, but that ain't the point. Doesn't the Bible say, 'Faith is the substance of things hoped for, the evidence of things not seen'?"

"Yeah."

"Well, have you ever seen life?"

"What are you talking about? I see life whenever I look at people walking and talking. Flowers and birds and shit."

"Those are only signs of life. I am talking about real life."

Another pause.

"You can't see life, just like you can't see the air you breathe. But you need air to live, right?"

"Of course, you do." I detect exasperation in his voice.

"Do you know that it is possible to have breath in your body and still not have life?"

"You are not making any sense."

"Just hear me out. How many rich people have you seen on 'Lifestyles of the Rich and Famous'?"

"A whole lot. What's the point?"

"How many have you seen on the fashion magazines?"

"Again, I say, 'A whole lot. What's your point?'"

"What was the expression on a lot of their faces?"

Pause number three. I'm getting through!

"I mean, you look at their wealth, which means they have a lifestyle, but you look in their eyes and see a dead look. No life. You know, it's been proven that the eyes are a mirror to the soul. Lifestyle is different from life. Lifestyles are easy to fake. But you can't fake life. You have to live it."

"Corey, you've been reading too many of those self-help books."

"Hey, they work. Maybe you ought to try reading some of them. Perhaps then, you'll stop caring about what your mama, Nate, or any of those homophobes got to say. Look, someday you will get what I'm trying to tell you and I promise you this; once you do, everyone else's estimation of you will shrink in comparison to the estimation you have of yourself."

Pause. I sense that he is really considering what I am saying.

"Your time is up, love. My fee, if you please."

Lion reaches in his pocket and retrieves his wallet. He pulls out and presents a dollar, saying, "Here, take your stinking buck!"

I pluck it from his fingers and say, "Thank you, dear."

This is our standing joke. If one of us needs a read, the other would give it in exchange for a dollar, which the reader would put in his jar at home. I don't know about his jar, but mine is overflowing with one-dollar bills. I love Lion, but sometimes he and Jojo can be dense as shit when it comes to "This Life We Call Gay". I swear I could write a book about this and call it 'Gay 101'". I listen to my best friend rattle on and on about his family and his past. While I'm listening to him and giving advice, my mind travels back to where I came from.

My name is Cordell Rodgerick James Kennedy. My birth name was issued by the state, Simon Lee Bradley. I was born and raised in Miami, FL. The only thing my birth parents contributed to my life was the motivated swimmer that fucked the egg in my mama's twat. My formative years left much to be desired. Both of my parents, John and Carolyn, were involved in drugs. One was the supplier and the other was hooked on cocaine and heroin. I found this out through a personal investigator. The rest of their story I got from my mother's sister, Freida, whom I recently connected with. The sperm-donor was graduating from college and on his way to law school. I say here and now, I will never call that asshole my father or my dad. I call him Spermie. My mother had one more year to go before she graduated. She was as sharp as a tack. In the college debate team, she was very persuasive in winning people over to her side, and she was shrewd in her knowledge of the law when they had mock trials. They became a hot item, destined to be together forever. They were going to be America's top lawyers, Spermie kept saying. Then they went to this pre-graduation party given by this friend of his. At this party, they were passing cocaine around like it was water. Unbeknownst to my mother, Spermie sold cocaine from his dorm room and his car. I guess to sail through school with no worries. Anyway, it was at this party that his friend and he got my mother to try cocaine. She wasn't buying it at first, but she gave in after he lied and acted like it was his first time too, He said that one time didn't make you an addict. Then he pulled the "If you love me, you'll do it," routine. It was then that she snorted line after line of coke. After that, it was partying and cocaine for her. The freebie she enjoyed that night became a hundred-dollar-a-day habit. She started not to give a shit about school, her life, or her career. For a year, she went on like this, her addiction getting worse toward the end where she started doing heroin to kill the cocaine tolerance. My grandmother and Aunt Freida started noticing changes in her that affected her thinking as well as her drive to succeed. They did their damnedest to talk sense into her, but she would not listen. All she cared about was Spermie, the next party, and the next fix. By now, Spermie became nothing more than her supplier. He dumped her and went on to the next gullible woman. Her chances at law school were shot to hell. The worst thing is that Spermie got accepted to law school while she started hooking to support her habit. It is a very hard pill to swallow that I was conceived through a bad drug deal between my mother and Spermie the day before he left for law school. A shortage of money from her… and a violent beating and rape from him in a dark and dirty alley.

When she found out about the pregnancy, she was floored. That sorry motherfucker split, but not before spitting out the old line, "That baby ain't mine." To add salt in the wound, my own grandmother who wanted her to get off the stuff told her that keeping me was not an option. She almost persuaded her to abort me, but Aunt Freida told her that abortion was murder and she needed to get her ass in rehab to clean up and have a healthy baby. With Mom aspiring to be a lawyer, Aunt Freida also told her that if man's law lined up with God's universal law on what murder is, she would be just as guilty as those gun-toters she would have helped put away. Mom still wanted the abortion, but it was when she stepped inside the abortion clinic that my aunt's words hit home. She did not want to live with the idea that she was responsible for killing someone. She turned back around and walked thirty blocks to a rehabilitation center, where she checked herself in for treatment. She got clean and nine months later, I came into this world. Unfortunately, she didn't want me. My grandmother was not going to take responsibility for me, and Aunt Freida couldn't do it because she was running after her own kids. The rest of my family were either dead or in jail. She gave me over to child welfare that very night.

In my life, I have had two sets of adoptive parents, and sandwiched between them was the Yancey Home for Boys. The first parent was a sweet, yet strict fiftyish German-American spinster named Miss Ingrid Schumacher, a violinist and pianist in one of the city's premier orchestras. She was the one who first started my long career in music. At the age of three, she started teaching me piano and how to read music. Five days a week for three years, I was taught the piano as well as appreciation of the tones that flowed from it. I still remember the sharp slaps she gave me on the hand when I didn't arch my fingers or play with precision or with feeling. She would always say, "Simon, you are expected to give your best. Less will not do." In addition to the hour lesson I had with her, I had to practice an additional thirty minutes. She would drive me to school and would quiz me on note values, key signatures, and solfege during the ride. She would give me a fact about a composer which she would quiz me on after school. When she would pick me up, she would ask me about my day and then start the quiz. If I got the answer wrong, she would lecture me on the fact, as well as the composer and his accomplishments. On the dashboard, she had a long sticker of piano keys on the passenger side. She would tell me to demonstrate the fingering of this key and lecture me on the values of perseverance and hard work.

For every hand slap and every quiz she threw at me, she gave me just as many hugs and kisses. She had a beautiful smile and an infectious laugh. Her face would light up when I read and played a song to perfection. She then told me afterward that, as talented as I was, I would probably write my own symphony one day. She would then give me a huge hug that ached my bones and I would smell the scent of her favorite perfume, White Diamonds. My eyelids puddle up when I think about Ms. Schumacher. I was *Ihre Nachkomme* and she was *Mein Mutter*. I loved her so much and I mistakenly thought I be with her forever. I was wrong. It ended just after I turned six.

One day, I was waiting on the curb, and our neighbor's car pulled up. I got into the car and immediately noticed that he had this lost look on his face. I asked him where *Mein mutter* was. He hesitated with tears in his eyes. He told me that I had to spend the night with his family that night. I asked him why, but he wouldn't tell me. All he would say was that I would know the reason soon. That night, my sleep was fitful and disturbed. I kept waking up wondering what the problem was, and when I finally stayed asleep, I dreamt of *Mein Mutter*. In my dream, she held me close to her and said these words, "*Ihre Nachkomme*, I'm always with you". Then she disappeared, and my arms were empty, I frantically ran to find her and alone in the darkness, I heard her echo, "*Ihre Nachkomme*, I'm always with you. *Egal was komme, Inganghalten!*" Those were the words she told me even as she slapped my hand at mistakes. "*No matter what, Keep Going!*" Then the voice faded, and I was alone.

I woke from that dream to see a mannish lady perched on my bed, our neighbor, and another syrupy sweet-faced lady with dead eyes in a white uniform. The first lady gave her name as Ms. Howell and told me she was a representative from the Yancey Home for Boys. What I heard next gave me nightmares for years. I hear her words tell me that *Mein Mutter* had a heart attack and died. An avalanche of screams erupted from me. I screamed over and over again until my voice went, and I fought her and our neighbor like someone demon-possessed. Unexpectedly, I felt a sharp pain enter my arm, which the women forced to keep still. I watched wearily as my neighbor turned away helplessly, I felt weightless as arms lifted me and I saw blurry motion as my vision blackened. The last words I heard were my neighbor and the sing-song voice of the nurse.

"Was it really necessary to stick him with that needle? He has been through enough!"

"Believe me, sir. It is in his best interest, so he doesn't harm himself."

When I awoke, I was in a large room with wood paneled walls, a multitude of whitewashed cast iron beds, and some boys staring at me. As I attempted to sit up, the social worker, the nurse, and a middle-aged white man in gray slacks and a white shirt entered the room. He told the other boys to go downstairs and play. They are talking to me but I, through my grief, am deaf and dumb to most of their words. I do hear the man say that he is the person who runs the boys' home. His name was Mr. Elbert Krone.

From day one, life got hard for me. I was teased and picked on every day by the bigger white boys. They would call me a nigger faggot and a sissy because I liked music. I wasn't interested in sporting events or schoolboy pranks, so I became an easy target for ridicule. Not a week went by that one of them did not start a fight with me. They would trip me often, knock my books out of my hands, and sometimes they would punch me for no reason. I only had two friends: Lawrence Tatum and Zachary Middleton.

We had two dorm counselors: Mr. Haines and Mr. Baker. We also had an in-house mental therapist named Rev. Harold Kennedy. The first two were problems to deal with, because they were bigoted, white pieces of shit. Every time I said something about how I was being treated, the reaction from them would always be the same. Mr. Haines would look at me and say, "Are you sure you aren't doing something to anger the other boys? Maybe you are just imagining things." Mr. Baker would simply tell me, "Quit being a goddamned pussy. They ain't doing shit to you!"

Those two gave me so many problems that I didn't even bother to talk with Rev. Kennedy, who was black. He was the bright spot of being there. He would always smile at me with a face that lit up like a Christmas tree. I thought that he was a little weird though. He would spend hours in the chapel, just meditating and talking to himself... or so I thought. But the one thing that drew me to him was his voice and the way he played the keys! He had a spellbinding way of singing that captivated you into believing that there was a God. His playing was gospel-tinged and inspirational, something *Mein Mutter* would have frowned on. She didn't believe in anything that wasn't classical, and she intimated this every chance she got. Through watching Rev. Kennedy, I found another side of music that I did not know about before. I learned that music wasn't meant to be restricted to meter and black markings, but to make the artist free to embrace creativity and imagination.

Unfortunately, the white people in Yancey felt that a black boy playing keys was unheard of. In fact, they didn't believe blacks could do much of anything. I remember an occasion that proved that fact to me. One day, I snuck into the chapel to practice on the piano. I pulled out a piano score and began to play it. After playing it as written at first, I played it again, this time improvising notes like I saw Rev. Kennedy do... and it sounded so good! I even felt the music flowing through me. Mr. Baker viciously bounded into the chapel and suddenly slammed the piano lid down on my hands...hard. I started to scream with pain, but Mr. Baker came behind me and clamped his hand over my mouth, telling me to shut up and get my ass to my room. "If I catch you in here again, I am going to break more than your fingers, boy." I ran from that chapel. The tears that flowed from my eyes were tears of anger and hurt. When I got back to my room, I checked my fingers and hands. They hurt. They bruised. But miraculously, they didn't break. That was the first time I experienced what real hate felt like and I hated him, Mr. Haines, and all those white bullies from the marrow of my bone. I hated Mr. Chrone for allowing this abuse to happen in an orphanage he called a safe haven. Worst of all, I hated myself. Still, what I dealt with then was nothing compared to what I dealt with five years after going into that place.

I remember I had grown into one very high strung ten-year-old who was perpetually withdrawn and ashamed to be black and different. Ultimately, a night passed that changed my outlook on life forever. I was sleeping in my bunk and hands nudged me awake, I awoke to the youthful face of Mr. Haines. He motioned me to come follow him because he needed some help with something, so I got up and followed him. Down the long halls, we trekked, and I'm thinking the whole time- *What does he want with me?* Finally, he opened the door to his apartment, which was dim and dark. He sat down and told me to sit on his lap.

I remember thinking at the time, *I don't like where this is going. I am too old to be sitting on some grown man's lap.* Reluctantly, I obliged. He said, "I have been watching you ever since you came to this place and I believe that you really have been going through a hard time."

"You do?"

"Dealing with those bigger boys can be hard, I know." He put his hand on my shoulder. With his other hand, he touched my face softly. I flinched and jerked back. He gave me a contemptuous smile as he continued, "But boys will be boys, you know? Their hormones are going out of control. You see, it is scientific. When a boy's hormones are out of control, he acts out of control. He needs release. Something to calm him down."

"Calm him down?"

"Yes," he said. He stood me up and lifted his hand to caress my neck and travel down my chest. "Now, I want to show you something. And if you do exactly as I say, the boys won't pick on you as much, and they may even become your buddies. Would you like that?"

I nodded yes. Then he got up and told me to sit in the chair. He stood up in front of me, unzipped, dropped his pants, and pulled out his dick.

"Now, I want you to kiss this."

"Mr. Haines, it smells like piss. I don't want to ..."

"You want the boys to like you, don't you?"

"But..."

"You want them to stop teasing you, right?"

"Yeah, but ..."

"Then do what I said."

I slowly and reluctantly inclined my head closer to it. My stomach turned at the stench of urine mixed with funk. But I managed to put my lips on it and kiss it.

"Good boy. Do it again. This time I want you to hold the kiss longer and lick the tip."

"Mr. Haines, I really don't want to do this."

"Come on, it's not going to hurt you. Kiss it."

Again, I moved closer and put my lips on the tip of his hardening, veiny, ghostly white manhood, tears rolling down my face.

"Good boy! Lick it."

My tongue licked his tip. The taste was revolting. What he was making me do was sinking my self-esteem lower than it ever went. I pulled back.

"Open your mouth for me."

"No, I don't..."

"Open your fucking mouth and stop crying, or I'll give you something to cry about."

I opened my mouth and suddenly, he rammed his dick in it, letting out a sick, twisted moan. I tried to pull away, but he caught my head and held it so I couldn't move or do anything except what I was forced to do.

"SUCK IT."

His hand felt like a vise, yet I took the violation into my mouth. I felt it expand. I gagged.

"IT'S OK."

I felt a constant stream of tears coursing down my face.

"SUCK DADDY'S COCK."

I tried to wriggle away but his hand was too strong.

"SUCK DADDY'S COCK."

I wanted to go back to my room. I would rather have been bullied than to do what he made me do, seeing his torso advancing and retreating, and hearing his sickeningly sweet voice crooning.

"COME ON. SUCK IT, NIGGER."

I had no choice. If I was going to get any sleep that night, I had to get him off. My ears heard the sounds of my own slurps and whimpers, and his disgusting voice as he said, "DADDY'S GOT A PRESENT! DADDY'S GOT A PRESENT FOR HIS LITTLE DARKIE! HERE'S YOUR PRESENT! DADDY'S CUMMING!

AAAAAAARRRRRRRRRRRGH!"

Hot and bitter juices squirted in my mouth. Sickened to my stomach, I tried to pull away, but he kept me there.

"Swallow it… Yeah… Yeah!! Good boy!"

Shame held my head in downward position, as I felt him release my head, heard him pull up and zip his pants, and heard him saying, "Don't tell anyone what we did. The boys would pick on you worse than before."

I don't remember how I left his apartment.

I don't remember how I got back in bed.

But, I do remember pulling my covers over my head and crying myself to a frightful sleep.

Instead of things getting better for me, they ended up getting worse. I ended up having to give Mr. Haines head four nights a week. Part of me died every single time he made me do it. This went on for a year and a half. The boys picked on me even worse than before, especially after some of them saw me leaving with Mr. Haines. Some of the older boys even started to force me to give them regular blowjobs in every single nook and cranny of that orphanage. After making me give him head, Mr. Haines started shoving his fingers in my ass while making me suck it and, as I winced, that sickening voice kept saying, "Just relax." After a few times of him doing this shit, I became sick and tired of it. I started getting more aggressive with the boys who tried to make me blow them. By now, Zachary taught me how to box and Lawrence taught me how to hit and kick in the nuts. Afterwards, the boys started backing off because they wanted to keep their dicks intact, especially since I developed a habit of biting them when they tried to force me to give them a blow. I was careful not to bite all the way, so I wouldn't be criminally punished for dismemberment! I just bit them enough to get the message across that I wasn't a punk or scared to fight back. After biting two of them, they all left me alone.

The bright spot about all of this is that Zachary and I became close and we began to get sexually involved. We had a place we would go in our free time where no one could see us: in the attic. Nobody ever went up there because it was full of junk that they didn't want to be bothered with. This dusty place gave us freedom to be intimate. Painfully armed with the knowledge of what could please a man erotically, I pleased him repeatedly. But imagine my shock, when I discovered that he could do the same thing. When he went down on me, I felt a sense of euphoria while thinking, *So, this is what it's all about. Damn.* Who knew that something which served as the catalyst for my pain could also be an act of beauty and love? We became inseparable! He protected me, and I did the same for him. He was the first male I knew that found me romantically desirable, knew and kept all my secrets, and loved me just as I was. I longed for him to say the words, while knowing he wouldn't. It didn't matter because I knew he loved me. He proved it through everything he did for me.

With some fighting skills, I began to feel strong and more confident. I snatched back a piece of my soul every time I fought back. Try as I might though, I couldn't fight Mr. Haines because he was surprisingly stronger. I tried kicking him in the nuts one time. He doubled over but, he rebounded and punched the daylights out of me. The only redeeming quality is that he left me alone for several months. During that time, I started relishing and strutting in my bravado. Yes, I was locked in closets for fighting, assigned extra duty for talking back, and beaten by both dorm counselors for even looking at them cross-eyed. But, I wasn't being molested. I figured if I fought back more, nobody would think of hassling or touching me. Again, I was wrong.

On the night of my twelfth birthday, Mr. Haines called me to his office to talk about the stance I was taking. He was frighteningly calm and collected. He offered me some apple juice from a carton. I was suspicious. I knew I should have followed my first mind.

I sniffed the juice. It smelled ok.
I sipped it. It tasted like regular juice.
Thinking it was safe enough, I drank it all.

In the space of two minutes, I started feeling so woozy that I could hardly stand. I heard Mr. Haines voice, but I couldn't decipher what he was saying. I felt a liquid darkness wash over me as my vision blackened and I fell to the floor. There was a brief moment that the blackness cleared. Through my stoned haze, all I could see was the picture of Jesus blessing the little children advancing and retreating jerkily over a headboard, and sharp pain tearing my asshole. Stabbing again... and again... and again. I heard a breathy androgynous voice saying,
"Relax, don't fight it."
I passed out in my exhaustion and drug-induced trauma.

When I awoke from the sedation the next morning, I was back in my bed. All the other boys were outside playing. I tried to sit up, but my ass felt like it was on fire. I reached my hand down and the first thing I felt was blood. I saw that blood and screamed like I was going insane. Over and over, I howled like someone gone crazy. Suddenly I felt arms grab me and say, "I got you! Calm down, son. Calm down!" But I kept screaming. I felt my body being turned around and my eyes locked with the eyes of the mental health therapist, Reverend Kennedy. My screams choked off and I just started crying. I showed him my fingers coated with blood. In disbelief, he asked me where that blood came from. All I could say was, "I hurt back there." Abruptly, I feel his arms holding me tight and saying, "It's going to be ok." Unlike the sick grips from Mr. Haines, Rev. Kennedy's grip felt like that of a father comforting his son, something I never experienced before.

He took me to the hospital and Zachary snuck out of the home to visit me every chance he got, sneaking huge candy bars and cans of my favorite orange soda. When I felt a little better, Rev. Kennedy came in the room while Zachary was there. Zach offered to leave but Rev. Kennedy told him he could stay. He asked me many embarrassing questions. One of the questions he asked me was, "Who did this to you?" I told them that I couldn't tell him because I would get worse than I already got. He told me that I had to tell so that he could keep the person from doing it again. He then said these words, "I will not let them hurt you. I promise you that. You can trust me." In that instant, something broke as an abundant overflow of tears gushed from my eyes and I told him everything. Suddenly, Zach told Rev. Kennedy that he could back up my facts because Mr. Haines did some of the same things to him. The next thing I knew, he was on the phone with a detective, telling him to get the files on Mr. Farley Haines, as well as Mr. Lester Baker. When I came back to the home, Zachary told me that they were arrested. It seems that I wasn't the only boy that was being beaten, molested and raped. They did the same thing to five other boys. But what put the nail in Mr. Haines' coffin was that empty juice carton he gave me. They found it in his trashcan. At the top of the carton was a small hole. They had the inside of the carton tested and discovered traces of a sedative. In his desk were hypodermic needles and an array of sleeping pills. Under his desk was a small bottle containing a clear liquid that he used for sedation. At the request of the board of Trustees, Mr. Chrone lost his position for allowing this to happen. Those that replaced them were light years better. Not long after that, Pop Kennedy, as I began to call him, became my foster parent. Then he adopted me.

The night before I left to live with Pop Kennedy, Zachary and I spent our last night in our special place. We talked long into the night and held each other so tightly, we almost merged into one being. No sex, just two boys in love with each other, embracing and talking. He told me he would miss me. I told him the same. Then, in a voice that sounded like a frightened little boy mustering his courage, he said these words, "I... I love you." I was shocked to hear it because I always thought he would never say it. He asked me, "Do you love me?" I was breathless and joyous as I said, "Yes." Upon hearing that, he kissed me deeply and passionately. Then he held me tighter than before. He had boyish arms, but I felt safe and found wonderful peace when I was in them. He then told me that a very loving family adopted him, but he was leaving Miami. I then cried harder than I ever had. I thought we would still be in the same city, but now that I find someone who really loves me, he leaves me. I turned on my side away from him, but he scooted behind me, hugged me, and put his school picture in my hand saying, "If we love each other, we'll find each other again."

Even though I was moving to a better home, I was depressed. I miss Zachary just as much as I missed *Mein Mutter*. However, life with Pop Kennedy was as good as it was with her. At my request, he legally rechristened me with the name I now answer to, Cordell Rodgerick James Kennedy. With exception to my time and relationship with Zachary, I wanted to erase those years from my memory. I still have that dog-eared picture of Zachary in my wallet.

Pop Kennedy was wonderful to me! It was under him that I learned how to play by ear and to feel the music. He also gave me voice lessons and showed me the correct ways to breathe and phrase the words. He had me listen to the gospel greats as well as old school R&B and gave me assignments to play what I heard as accurately as possible. He didn't allow rap or new school R&B because ninety percent of the lyrics called women bitches and hoes, pushed Black on Black violence, and instructed impressionable minds on how to get girls in bed. He told me that he expected more from me because he believed I was capable. When I was fourteen, he thought I was ready to do more than just practice music on his piano. Under his guidance, I started singing solos and playing the piano in the church he pastored, Champion Baptist Church. Later that year, he gave me the directorship of the music ministry. Eventually the church grew in number. He also talked to Miss Edwina Morrison, a sweet chorus teacher at my high school and told her my gift for music. Since I read music like a pro, I became the accompanist for the choir and Miss Morrison pulled some strings and convinced the school to pay me one-fifty per gig. He told me to bring the checks home from the school and He kept the ones from the church. Out of every check I brought home, He paid me thirty-five, tithed fifteen, and kept the rest. He told me if I wanted more, I had to get a part time job, which I did. Many an argument we had about that, but the statement he would always make was, "Trust me. After a while, you will see why I'm doing this."

Pop Kennedy was strict and was very heavy on education. If my grades dropped below a "B", all my privileges were taken away and I had to surrender both checks without allowance. Plus, I couldn't work my part time job. But those periods never lasted too long, and I didn't mind it much. The rules were strict but fair and the discipline I received was only a small part of six wonderful years with him, filled with big bear hugs and man-to-man talks about life. I loved seeing his bright smile and dreamy fatherly expression as he propped his head on his fist and listened to me rattle on and on about my pleasant experiences with the choirs I served, interrupting only with advice on how to handle certain types of people and situations.

When I graduated from High School with Honors, Pop Kennedy sat me down and asked me what my plans were. I told him that I wanted to find my parents. I thought he would be upset, but all he said was, "I figured the day would come when you would ask. It's natural for you to want to know who your family is." He hired a private investigator and they both combed the city looking for them. A month later, we found out that Spermie was disbarred due to information about the drugs he sold in college and went to prison on federal charges. While in the joint, he was stabbed to death. My mother fared worse. She died of a heroin overdose shortly after she gave me up. That night, I cried for hours for parents I felt cheated from knowing. Pop Kennedy sat up with me all night and prayed. As he talked to God, I noticed that this man was crying too. When he finished, I asked him why he was crying. It was then that he told me that he had a son and a wife, but they died shortly before he went to work for Yancey. It joyfully dawned on both of us that we not only became father and son; we also became kindred spirits to fill the familial voids in our lives. He brewed lots of coffee and we talked for hours that night about music, the church, God, and our lives. We did talk about my sexuality. He didn't make a big deal about it. When I told him how my boat swung, he said, "I'm not surprised. You were painfully introduced to this and the wounds you suffered are things you must contend with. Now I don't particularly care for it because I've seen it hurt many people and turn them bitter against God and others. But, I am not here to condemn you because the nature of the heart is a constant conversation between you and the Lord. As for me, the only thing I got to say is that I love you and I always will." Wonderful words from a wonderful man. I told him about Miss Schumacher and the love she gave me. He told me about his family. Their anger issues and hatred made them terribly dysfunctional. The bright spot is that their issues strengthened his resolve to help other people through social work and mental therapy.

The next morning, he repeated the question about my plans. I told him that I wanted to attend his alma mater, Morgan State University. Tears rolled down his face as he embraced me. He told me that this news made him happier than he had felt in years. I told him that with everything going on, I didn't have time to look for scholarships and I didn't know how we were going to pay for it. He then said, "*We* are not paying for anything. *You* are paying for it." At first, I was upset because I thought he was bailing on me. He got up and went to his office, came back with a bank book, and told me to open it. When I did, my mouth dropped open. I saw that all the funds I turned over to him had been deposited into a bank account. One number I saw repeatedly was five hundred dollars, beginning the day I started playing for the church. The total was one hundred and eight thousand, one hundred sixty dollars.

He then told me, "Remember how I always said, after a while you'll see why I'm doing it. Well, through all those checks I made you sign over to me, you were investing in your own future. I did this for two reasons. One, to look out for your schooling and two, to eventually teach you that to be successful, you must invest in yourself. I believe that anything you invest in, you will take it seriously because you paid for the right. Now, all of this is not for your tuition. I think you will only need a portion to cover expenses for your freshman year. I'm sure you will get many scholarships to cover your remaining years and you can keep the rest of your earnings in the bank for a rainy day." At that moment, I rushed at him and gave him the biggest hug I could, and felt his arms circle me as he laughed heartily.

I went to Morgan on a full ride, built on my own labor and the investments of someone who cared. I got scholarship after scholarship during my first year and I worked hard to keep them. Unfortunately, while finishing my junior year in college, this man I came to love died from a brain aneurysm. Tears fall as I think about that dark day. His family showed their colors at his funeral. I wanted to kick their asses right there in the church. Except for his big brother, the only decent one in the lot, none of them came around at all when he was alive. Jealousy, I suppose. The house we lived in was their mother's. She gave it to him when she died, and they resented him for it ever since. Amazing, how the dead brings the love of family when it wasn't there before.

They came and stripped the house of all it was worth. Thank God, they couldn't touch the bank accounts which amounted to over eight hundred thousand dollars. Twenty percent of it went to the church, and the rest went to me, along with the house. When the lawyer read the will to all of us, the daggers coming from their eyes pierced me to the bone. I could see that every day I possessed that house would be a day where the family would give me hell. His older brother tried to reason with them, but they kept saying, "He's not even part of this family." So, to keep peace, I told the lawyer to let the family have the house. Of course, I knew they were going to fight among themselves about ownership, but that was not my problem. I kept the money though. I wasn't stupid!

The pain of being molested, raped, and beaten never left because I never addressed it. I never talked about it. Pop wanted me to, but I blocked it out. Lion, Jojo, and Peep still don't know. That says a lot, because we talk about *everything*. I stuck college out for the remaining year and graduated with honors. But a year into graduate school, I began to slide back. My grades dipped. I slept with different men almost every night of the week. I gorged myself in alcohol and even tried cocaine. But I remembered the report from the private investigator on how my parents died. I took that into consideration and after talking with my Philosophy professor and my three true blue friends, I kicked cocaine because I didn't want to be anything like my parents. I gritted my teeth, stood flat-footed, buckled down, and breezed through graduate school with numerous accolades. I still can't talk about what happened. I thought about seeing a therapist, but I feel self-conscious about telling a stranger all my problems. I am doing ok now, I guess. I have had this strong goal of writing one of the greatest symphonies ever penned by a Black composer. I started it at fourteen by composing my piano solo movement "Anger". Since then, two additional movements have been written, and those took me twelve years to compose because I was always adding and subtracting passages and ideas. Moreover, there are three things obstructing the composition's completion; my tortured silence concerning what happened, my inability to confront the demons of my past, and my being a ho. A fine ass ho. But a ho, nonetheless. But that's not my fault, is it?

"Corey!" Lion's worried voice cuts through me.
"Huh? What?"
"You are in a daze and you just sped through a stop sign. Can you slow down and pay attention, please?"
Red and Blue lights.
A Short Siren.
A "Pull over please".
And the two words we utter as many others have said whenever trouble comes knocking. *"Aw shit!"*
The officer steps out of the squad car. Thank God he's black... and what a thick muscular black gumdrop he is, too! OK, Corey, turn on the charm.
"Sir, do you know you ran that stop sign?" He asks in a sexy baritone voice.
"I'm so sorry, officer. I was in a daze thinking and I wasn't watching."
"License and registration, please."
I reach into my glove compartment and retrieve my registration and license. I hand them to the officer, brushing his muscular hand. I look up at him. 6'7!

Oh my GOD, I would *love* to climb that tree. I look at his bread basket. Wow, the print entices me, and it looks like it's growing! Hmmm! Uh oh, he caught me looking. I look away. But when I look back at him, I see a smirk on his face and a seductive glint in his eye.

"Where are you guys headed anyway?"

"Oh, we are going to the club to enjoy a single guys' night out. My friend here needed to get out the house and meet some nice men... OW, bitch!" Lion digs his elbow in my ribs.

"Running stop signs is very dangerous, ya know."

"I'm sorry, officer, but I must say it's nice to find somebody as fine and big as you upholding the rules of the road. I know it must be exhausting! You know what? You are one tall drink of water." I look out the side of my eye, and I can see Lion's mouth dropped open in disbelief. "Close your mouth, Lion. You'll let the flies in."

"Alright, alright, cut the flattery, sir," the officer says sarcastically as he leans on my door, "Don't leave this car." He turns and walks back to the squad car. In my rear-view mirror, I catch a glimpse of an ass built like two large honeydews, held up by thick muscular thighs stretching the hell out of those pants.

"I cannot believe you said all that shit...and did you have to drag me into it?"

"What?"

"You trying to pick up that cop? Lord, he is probably going to arrest the both of us."

"Aw, quit your panicking! It ain't go'n go there."

"Oh, it ain't, huh? This is not the club, Corey, and the cop is not one of your conquests. He is an officer of the law."

"And underneath that uniform repping the law is a MAN! You must have missed the way that boy was staring me down. Watch what I say. There will be no ticket and no arrest."

The officer walks back to my car and gives me a piece a paper, then tips his hat. "Have a nice day, boys and watch yourself on the road. Safety first." He goes back to the squad car and drives away.

"You see, Corey?" Lion fusses. "I knew he wasn't going to fall for your coy flirting bullshit."

"Oh yeah? Well, read it and weep," I retort as I hand the paper to him.

Lion looks, then his eyes widen in disbelief. "A warning? No way!"

"Way, baby! Way! Check out the back." I say as I start the car and pull out into the street.

Lion reads, "Officer Kenneth Sellers, 443-999-1902. Call me tonight, no matter how late." He looks at me and shakes his head.

"Slut!"

"Proud to be one!"

CHAPTER FIVE:

"STEPPIN' OUT"

Corey and I, after getting stopped by the police for running a stop sign, made it to the Link. Unbelievably, Corey made a date with the police officer!

"You are the biggest ho' I've ever seen," I wisecrack at Corey as we walk into the Link.

"What? He needed some flirtin'. You know how these police officers are; upholding the law one minute and fucking the offender in the alley the next. You better be glad I wasn't as horny as I *could* have been. I would have made the officer bend me over without delay and you would have gotten one hell of a show," he retorts. "Besides, I don't have one-fifty for a ticket."

"You oughta stop," I laugh out.

The person working the door spots us, "Wassup, bitches!"

"Wassup, Darrell. Where's yuh man? Usually he works the door with you," Corey asks.

"Don't ask. Right now, he is in the dog house. I caught him making eyes at my married twenty-five-year-old cousin," Darrell says before looking at me. Then his eyes pop open and he starts yelling, "Dayum, what possessed you to wear that out the house? You are trying to nail every guy up in here?"

"Naw, naw. It's just a little something I had in my closet," I blushed.

"Aw shit! Look at him blushing. If you ask me, I say it's about time. Many a night, I have seen you stroll in here, and I'm thinking, 'What is his problem, dressing like he just came from the office.' I mean, geez!"

"That's because many times, I *am* coming from the office," I half-joked.

"With that outfit, you go'n make me come out from behind this counter and test out that salami you got blowing in your pants. What is it, nine, ten inches?"

"Darrell, cease and desist. You are embarrassing the boy," chided Corey.

"His fault for coming out de house half nekkid! Even the corporate shit can't hide the rump roast and kielbasa sausage you got. It's about time you showed it off. Five each." We pull out our cash and pay Darrell the five. He gives us a ticket and rings the buzzer to let us in the door.

Walking into the Link is like walking into another world: a world where being gay is not only welcome but fervently displayed. In every corner, you saw two guys making out: and since there were four large rooms in the Link, make that sixteen corners occupied on a good night.

There, beyond that huge red iron door, awaits the blaring sound of electrifying house music and a huge array of Black men. Old, young, short, tall, big, small, muscular, average... well, you get the point. Some are at the bar, drinking and cursing like sailors on a four-day pass. Many are on the dance floor, moving with such a fluidity that would baffle the most experienced choreographer. Alvin Ailey would be proud to sit there and watch the flexibility of the dancers.

From the moment I walk in, I am conscious that guys are staring at me. Some with admiration, some with envy, many with hunger. I hear them saying:

"Work it, boy!"
"Where the hell have you been?"
"Who's tapping that ass?"
"Can I take you home with me?"
And the usual, "Where yuh man at?"

Being a frequent and oftentimes reluctant clubber in the Link, I'm very familiar with the mindset of the guys spitting these lines. They love you until the time they nut; then if you are lucky, you get a booty call in a month. Ever so often, you meet a man of substance, but they end up being married, involved, fathers, or screwed up assholes. No secret why sometimes I hate the Link; I feel like a minnow among killer sharks.

I hear a loud, boisterous voice calling out, "Hey Lion! Corey! Come over here!" I turn to see Felipe, whom we call Peep, sitting on the bar stool. His full name is Felipe Alexander Walker-Hartfield. I met him in college. At first, he did not like me because he thought I was conceited, and he told me this on several occasions during our friendship. Then we went on a freshman skating trip. I was a pretty good skater, but Peep wasn't. As soon as he got on the rink, he fell flat on his ass. I rushed over to help him up and when I gave him my hand, he pulled me down with him and I landed right on top of him. He said, "Damn, boy! You're supposed to be helping me up, not pinning me down." We took one look at each other's faces and started laughing our asses off! Somehow, we got off the rink and into the snack area. Over cherry soda and cheese puffs, we really hit it off. Armed with this rapid and pleasant camaraderie, we decided to become roommates. I call him Peep because one night while I was sleeping, he came over to my side of the room and peeped under my covers to see my jimmie. Being that I was horny, I cop a few good feels. Before I knew what was happening, he straddled my torso and plopped his ass down on my dick. We were drenched in nut four times that night. We had a serious "friends with benefits" thing going. But once we graduated, it stopped. We decided to just be the best of friends, but I called him Peep ever since that night and, as I called him Peep, Corey and Jojo began calling him Peep too, without even knowing why. He saw himself as the papa bear of the bunch. An even six-footer with an ample and sexy physique that boasted huge thighs and legs and clear golden-toned skin, he certainly was the pride and joy of the Latino descent. As usual, he sits in the middle bar stool with four or five guys competing for his attention while he simply captures theirs.

"Wassup Peep," I say, sauntering over to him with Corey in tow. All of a sudden, he punches me on the shoulder... *three times!*

"*Ow!*" I cry out. "What was that for?"

"For having me and Jimmy worrying sick, for skipping your gym appointment, and for failing to call! You know, an old bird like me can't take too many surprises."

"I'm sorry, O Mighty King Felipe! I humbly beg thy forgiveness," I say as I bow in mock humility.

Peep playfully touches me on the forehead and says, "I dub thee forgiven, peasant." He hops off the bar stool and gives me a hug, lifting me off the ground. When he sets me down, he says, "The dead man has come alive. Damn, I know Corey had to drag yo' ass out the house."

"Damn straight," Corey agrees.

"Corey ain't had to drag me anywhere!"

"Lion, come on! We all know very well that if he had not come with that "Don't fuck with me" mood, you know your lying ass would still be sitting in front of the TV or listening to Phyllis Hyman," He counters.

"What can I get you?" The shirtless bartender asks with a seductive smile and swagger, his lean sweaty body glistening under the lights.

"Uh, let me have a blue Motorcycle. Heavy on the tequila."

"You got it."

After paying for and getting my drink, Peep gestures for me to come with him to a quieter part of the club. "Seriously, Lion," Peep asks with concern. "How are you doing? Jojo told me about your mama."

"I figured he would."

"Well, it's good to see you out of the house. We have really been worried about you."

"I'm ok. Just processing things."

"Process away, my love."

Corey comes with drinks in his hand. "You know, you gotta be careful when going to the club. You left your drink on the bar. I saw someone eyeing it like they were planning to slip something in. Here," he says, handing Peep a drink. "I bought you a fresh one. Courvoisier, right?"

"Wow! Good lookin' out! I was so busy trying to talk to Lion that I didn't even notice. How much do I owe you?"

"I got this one."

"Thanks again, love. Oh, don't jump, but I saw Nate walking in here about an hour before you did," Peep says, turning to me.

"Did he have Shawn with him?"

"Yeah. But Nate went back home to grab something, and while he's doing that, Shawn is back there bumping, grinding, and making out with some other dude. They went back there the minute Nate left."

"Hmm, I guess the cheater is being cheated on."

"Yep! But you know how bitchy and stupid Shawn is. He doesn't want somebody until he knows he is not supposed to have 'em. I got sources that gave me the tee about him fucking around with every man he sees, and he started doing that shortly after he snatched Nate away from you."

"Does Nate know?" I ask.

"If he has eyes, he should."

"Hm. Well, his problem. Not mine," I say.

"I know that's right, baby. Let him sniff the shit *and* clean it up," Corey says.

It was at that moment that I catch sight of six feet and four inches of pure heaven. A tried and true chocolate Hershey's Kiss! I have always been attracted to darker men. I told you how dark Nate was. Well, this dude was blue-black. He had neat medium length dreds styled to flatter his full, defined face. Full lips that rivaled Naomi Campbell. He was tastefully dressed in White Linen Pants, white loafers, a red polo shirt, and a white jacket, but even those clothes could not hide the beauty of his toned body. Wow, he must've ran track in college because he has it goin' on! His head turns toward our direction. Oh my God! He smiles. What a beautiful smile! It is a smile of absolute approval and pleasure. His eyes dance with amusement and laughter. I start to approach him…

"Come here, I wanna talk to you."

I snap out of the fog and whirl around to confront my ex-boyfriend, Nate. "What the hell do you want?"

"I want to talk to you."

"I don't want to talk to you."

"Look, it ain't gonna take but a minute and then you can go back to cruising this fool."

"Fool? That is *your* territory, remember?"

"I need to talk to you!"

I look around for the guy. He stands there with a baffled look on his face. I turn back to Nate. "Outside. Two minutes," I say between clenched teeth.

We start to walk outdoors; I catch Corey and Peep's eyes as I go. As soon as we get outside, he starts ranting and raving.

"What in the fuck are you doing here… and wearing that?"

"It's a free country, I can go wherever the fuck I want to. We are over. Let's not forget, you quit me by cheating on me with Shawn."

"Don't start that shit, alright? You are just as much to blame. We wouldn't be here now if you tended to our relationship like you were supposed to, instead of being at work all the time and hanging out with your bitch ass friends."

"OK, A few corrections seem to be in order. First of all, we wouldn't be here right now if you weren't trying to control the relationship and everything pertaining to it, let alone cheating on me! Second, you know as well as I do that I was working because you lost your job. With you maxing out that credit card, I'm beginning to wonder if you didn't get yourself fired on purpose after you saw how I was living. Finally, you ought to look in the mirror when you say *bitch*. It suits you a hell of a lot more than my friends and me put together."

"Watch your mouth with me!"

"Look, we are done. Your bullshit ended when I caught you fucking Shawn. Jesus, to think I introduced you to him. Now you're trying to be in my mix, telling me where I can go and what I can wear? Not cute at all!"

"I just think that you shouldn't be here and wearing that."

"I don't give a damn what you think! I'll go wherever and wear whatever I'm good and goddamned ready to... and you can go to hell for all I care."

I hear the big iron door open and as I turn, I see Corey walking out here. He comes up to me and grabs my arm. "Lionel, let me tear you away from Nate for a minute." He looks at Nate with contempt. "Excuse us."

"What, Corey?"

He turns his back toward Nate and whispers to me, "Lionel, we came to have a good time, not to get caught up in his foolishness. Let's go back in the club."

"I'll be in there in a minute."

"Let's go now, Lionel! Nate isn't worth a drop of spit it takes to cuss him." Uh oh, He's raising his voice. I know where this is going.

"What did you say?" Nate shouts.

Corey turns slowly around. His voice is tight and cold as he spews outs, "For the hearing impaired, I said, 'Let's go now, Lionel. Nate isn't worth a drop of spit it takes to cuss him.' Are you deaf?"

"Look, you flaming motherfucker," Nate fumes. "This ain't got shit to do with you so you need to move your ass back in there before I do it for you."

"Come wit' it! Land one punch so I can mop the fucking floor with your ass." Corey lunges at him, ready to fight! He would have gotten to him too, if I hadn't stepped in front of him.

"Alright now, Corey! Calm that shit down! I am not trying to spend the night in jail. Go on back inside."

"I ain't going nowhere unless you come in with me."

"Corey," I repeat calmly, "Go back inside. I will be in there shortly."

"I said no! Look Nate, do us all a favor and go find that bitch ass Shawn... and let me give you some advice. Instead of your eyes being on Lionel, you need to be keeping an eye on the nympho you left him for! Looks like he still can't keep his pants on!"

Oh no, why did Corey have to tell him that? Nate's eyes widen as he begins hyperventilating. Watching him run back in the club, I start to pity him and wish that things turned out differently with us.

"Forget what you are thinking, love."

"What are you talking about?"

"You are thinking about giving that asshole another go-round, Especially after the *look*."

Sometimes I think he is psychic! "I am not!"

"Yes, you are! Look, the man is scum. He cheated on you! Remember that."

"Yeah, I know. You don't have to remind me."

"Yeah, my ass! Look, you are thirty-six years old. Supposedly wiser and more experienced. Too experienced to be makin' the same dumb-assed mistakes twice."

Just then, Jojo walks up. Joseph Stanley Thompson the III is my childhood friend. We were born on the same day, four minutes apart, in the same hospital. Rumor had it that our mamas screamed so loud having us that the nurses were betting on who was the loudest. Our parents became close, probably due to what they heard about the betting, and as we grew up, we became the best of friends, although our mothers fell out with each other for religious reasons. Jojo is a sweet and quiet type of guy, a little slow on some things but extremely intelligent on others. He was very stocky as a teenager and young adult, but his overall body had a makeover in the last five years since Peep started dragging his ass to the gym every other day. I look him over. Now his body has a solid, muscular build, a perfect complement to his smooth clear ebony tone. He has a face with full pink lips, curly brown hair, and soulful brown eyes. His barrel chest has hard nipples that poke the fabric of the cut off shirt exposing his navel, and a clean line of noticeable hair trailing down to his big thick... *Whew... Back to Earth Lionel!*

"What was that all about?" he asked

"Oh, nothing. Just the same bullshit between Lion and his ex-asswipe. Damn, Jojo, it took you long enough to get here."

"I don't know why I came. You know I hate the Link."

"Oh please, You and Lion both need to lighten up. You are not going to meet anybody sitting on your asses watching TV. Life is a sausage, take a bite," Corey exclaims.

"I will, after you finish sucking it dry," Jojo joked.

We kee-kee and haw-haw and then we walk back in the club. But as Jojo walks in, I catch a glimpse of his back. His solid back muscles strain the shirt he is wearing. A high, firm, and round ass stretching his jeans, held up by legs that could choke a tiger... And that outfit... I have never seen him show this much of himself! *Lionel!* I say to myself. *What is wrong with you? Best friends shouldn't be checking each other out like that. You are on the rebound. Get it together!*

Corey and Jojo go to the bar to get drinks. As soon as I reclaim my former seat next to Peep, I look for the guy I was cruising earlier, but he is nowhere to be found. *Damn! I didn't even get a chance to talk to him. There goes my chance of meeting someone cool tonight.*

"Looking for someone?"

I turn to see Peep with a sly look on his face. "What makes you think I am looking for someone?"

"The way your eyes are darting around, trying to find the guy you were staring at earlier."

"I was not staring at him."

"You lie through your ten thousand-dollar capped teeth."

"I wasn't!"

He smirks, "So, you are saying that you don't have the slightest interest in him at all."

"Not even in a little bit of the slightest," I lied.

"Ok. Then you won't be needing this," he says, furtively holding a slip of paper.

"What is it?" I ask, excitedly grabbing at the paper before he snatches it back.

"Ah, But I thought you weren't interested," Peep says slyly.

I grab at it a couple of times as he holds it away playfully. Then he surrenders it to me. I read it:

Garrett Peterson
410-687-2991

I am shocked! "How did you get it from him?" I asked him.

"Simple. He saw me talking to you and assumed that we were cool, so he gave me the number to give to you."

"Did you give him my number?"

"Lion!" Peep exclaims. "I am shocked that you would think I would give your number to someone you don't even know."

"Did you?"

"Yes."

"Damn, Peep!"

"How else was he going to contact you? By séance? Besides I gave him your home phone number, knowing that you rarely answer that phone."

"OK, OK. But he probably won't call."

"How do you know that? He may surprise you. Besides, if you don't jump to him, Corey will! You can believe that shit!"

"I can't take you anywhere without you making a goddamned fool out of me!" A deep familiar voice yells out. I turn around and see Nate and Shawn arguing.

"Get outta my face, Nate!"

"I ain't in your face yet! Get your ass outside. We're going home right now."

"I ain't going anywhere. I'm staying my ass right here."

"Baby, you ain't gotta go nowhere! I'll handle this motherfucker," A deep voice says. I look and almost wet myself laughing. The voice came from a little gnome that stood in front of Shawn.

"You cheated on me with a goddamned midget!"

Well, after that, everybody in the club fell out, laughing. Except the security officer. He came and stood in the middle of the ruckus folding his arms. He said, "I don't know what's going on. But you three got to roll!"

"I didn't do shit! It was this whore of a boyfriend messing with this sawed-off Munchkin!"

"Oooooh! Did you hear that shit?" Someone from the crowd yells out. All I hear is this abundant chorus of raucous laughter.

"I ain't no fucking Munchkin!"

Now, there are sounds of wheezing and back slapping!

"Get da fuck outta here, you Pygmy!" the security guard says.

The three of them head for the door. Nate is the last to leave. As he walks by, he stops at looks at me.

I can't resist! I have to get one jab in. "You, uh, have yourself a lovely evening."

He leaves in a huff. I take one look at my friends and we start rolling! Maybe it was a good idea to go to the Link tonight. God knows, I needed a laugh!

*****

An hour later, Corey, Jojo, and I are toasted. Tossing back vodka like it's water, we laugh our heads off over the men we meet. Peep drunk a little bit, but him being the designated driver, he's playing it cool. Damn, this outfit really did the trick! I caught the attention of a lot of guys, and I have nine phone numbers to prove it.

"Chile', that boy got ass," Peep exclaims.

"Nah, baby. It's too loose," Jojo says. "I tell you, when the mood is right, I love fucking a nice tight ass that jumps only a little bit."

"Yeah, like yours," Corey snickers.

"Shut up, Corey."

"Anyways, back to the slut of the hour, how many guys did you pick up?"

"Why I gotta be the slut of the hour?"

"Excuse me!!! Ain't you the one who came out the house with that outfit."

"Ain't you the one who made me put it on?"

"Ain't you the one who got a mind of his own? You ain't had to listen to me!"

"So, you're saying that I shouldn't have listened?"

All of us exclaim, "*Hell naw!*"

Jojo says, "Though I heard he almost got you in trouble with Nate."

"Oh, Jeez," I exhaust. "I could have gone the whole night without hearing that name."

"Yeah, I saw the friction between you two before that other shit went down. What's going on?" Peep asked.

"Would you believe that he was pissed that I came out tonight *and* wore this outfit?"

"What I wanna know is why. You aren't together anymore," Jojo said.

"Repeat that again, for his benefit!" Corey quips, pointing at me.

"I think once is enough. But really, you are free agent now so if you want to wear that outfit, wear it with your booty out!" He jokes, poking his ass out on the last two words.

"You are sick," I laugh out. I start counting my numbers.

"Obviously, the outfit worked in your favor," Corey jokes. Then he snatches the numbers out of my hand. I tried to get them back, but he holds them where I can't reach them. Then he started reading off the names one by one. "Mark, Daryl, James, Garrett..."

"Come on, Corey. Cut it out!"

"Lane, Harry, Steve... Oh no, not Steve," He looks at me sarcastically.

I grab the numbers back. "Thank you," I say, "And what's wrong with Steve?"

"Nothing, except I like polish sausages. *Not* cocktail weenies!"

We all are doubled over, laughing our heads off.

"Imagine if I was a woman with no man, trying to get an orgasm from sticking a Vienna Sausage in my twat," Peep retorts, between guffaws.

By now, we all are literally on the floor, rolling around so much that the people at the bar are staring at us. My stomach is hurting so much from laughter that when I finally can talk, I utter only one word, "Ouch!"

*****

What a night! In addition to those nine numbers, I got about seven more. All of them prime meat… Well, except Steve. We left the club at 2:43 a.m. and went to IHOP to grab some grub. After eating and innocently flirting with the male waiters, we head home. As I put the key in the door, My mind wanders. Hmmm... The times I went to the club before, nobody ever gave me that much play. Of course, the way I dressed played a part in that. Damn. It's no wonder why Nate didn't want me to wear that outfit in public. He was afraid I'd get too much attention. I chuckle to myself. Tomorrow, I'm going to the same place I got that outfit from and buy up some more. No more of those tired old outfits for me!

I walk into my darkened house and switch on the lights. I survey the space about me. The realtor was right when she said that there was plenty of space… but look at the space I own! Mahogany, burgundy leather sofa set, black curtains, and black lacquered table set. Two words begin to form in my brain, "cold appearance". Now, I believe in coordinating and matching colors to balance out the room, but this setup is too drab. Not just this room, but this whole damn house. What was I thinking? I wasn't. It was Nate. I remember wanting more color, but Nate wanted less. He kept saying less is more. So, I decided to live with the furniture. Now that he's gone, fuck the furniture. I'll sell it, as well as what I got in storage and buy new. This time I'm decorating the house how I want.

I catch sight of the blinking light on my answering machine. Yes, I still have an answering machine. My cell number is for my friends, my family, and my job. Nate had it, but I've since gotten a new number. I go over to look at the screen. Two messages. I press Play while putting my keys on the rack.

The first is from Corey. *"Hey chile'. You were so busy being the slut of the bunch that you forgot your scarf on the bar"*. Oh shit! I knew I was forgetting something. *"Lucky for you, Darrell picked it up and called me on my cell. Said he'd hold it for you 'til next Friday. Of course, I could go back and get it tomorrow. Which would you prefer? Call me back around ten a.m.. Kiss-Kiss. Later!"*

Thank God. That scarf cost seventy-eight bucks. I push the button to hear the next message. Pleasantly, my large living room was filled with the sounds of a deep full bass voice.

"Hi, this is Garrett Peterson from the Link. I got your number from your friend. I hope you don't mind." Hell no, I don't mind! *"I wrote down my number and asked him to give it to you. I guess I just couldn't wait to call. I assume that you are still out, so I will call you Sunday around 3pm and maybe we can schedule a game of tennis."* My favorite sport? Hell Yeah! *"Talk to you Sunday. One."*

The smile I had almost hurt my face. This well-built chocolate man calls me before I can call him! Hmmm... There *is* hope! I turn off the lights and proceed to go upstairs to my bathroom to take off my "outrageous outfit" and to take a shower. The cold water feels so good and refreshing on my naked skin; it was over ninety degrees outside on this summer night. After fifteen minutes, I step out and dry off. Going into my bedroom, I remember that I have to straighten out my closet after Corey wrecked it. Hmm... Most of that stuff will have to go anyway. I'll go to the mission tomorrow and give it to good will. I sank onto my bed, relishing the feel of my satin sheets against my naked skin. Slowly and peacefully, my eyes close. My nose breathes in the sweet aroma of repose as I fall deeper, and deeper into the release of blissful sleep, unaided by the assistance of Doxepin.

CHAPTER SIX:

"SWITCHIN' UP"

"Get your asses outta bed! Get up, get up, get up! This is yuh boy, Laughing Larry Caldwell, on yuh radio at 9:40 in the am. Today's weather is *hotter* than a nekkid girl on Playboy! Highs are in the lower one hundreds, lows in the upper eighties. So, if you're goin' out, rock yuh tank tops and yuh capris. It's Jamaican weather out there."

I awaken with a start. My sheets are thrown to the other side of the bed. My nude body drenched in sweat. Damn, Larry wasn't lying. It *is* hot. *Hmm... I need to get to the mall. I wonder if Corey's going.* I roll out of bed and head to the bathroom to wipe the sweat off, brush my teeth, and wash my face.

Rrrrrrrrrrrrrring.
"Hello?"
"Hey babe, did yuh get my message last night?"
"Yeah. I slept kinda heavy."
"I'm not surprised, with all the liquor you drunk last night."
"Please, boy. You drank just as much as I did, if not more!"

"I guess I did, huh? Earlier, Jojo and I had to get Ubers to get our cars. What you got goin' on today?"

"Don't know yet."

"I got your scarf. I can bring it over. You wanna go to the mall?"

"I was going to call to ask if *you* wanted to go!"

"Ok! Well, we are about ten minutes from your house."

"We?"

"Yeah, Peep and Jojo are with me. We're riding in my car."

"Oh Lord. There goes the neighborhood."

"I heard that!" I hear Peep chime in.

"Whatever. I'll see you in a minute."

"See ya then, Kiss."

"Kiss-Kiss."

I go to the bathroom to shower and slip into khaki capris, a lime green tank, and some casual white sneakers. I go downstairs to my kitchen to retrieve three huge trash bags, then rush back up to my bedroom to fill the bags with all the clothes Nate bought me. In less than five minutes, I had the bags stuffed to capacity. I look at the barren coat hangers swinging back and forth on the rack. The only thing left in the closet are the seven standard suits I wear to work and a few dress shirts. A sigh of relief as well as a sweat of trepidation escapes me. It's really over... Really over... Over... Over... *Snap out of it, Lionel!*

I go back to my bathroom to rinse and dry my sweating face again. I need to get something to eat. I always wake up with a ravenous appetite. It would be nothing for me to clear out half a carton of eggs, half a saucepan of grits, four pancakes, and three sausages in one serving. I grab the bags and trip down the stairs to my living room where I drop them on the floor. Knowing Corey, he stopped off somewhere to pick up a bite to eat... and it would take him twenty minutes instead of five to drive down ten blocks. In this case, it's good, because that gives me seven minutes grace to eat something light.

Ding-dong! He always picks the wrong times to be punctual! I go to the door and open it.

"Alright, where he at?" Corey says as he barges in.

"Was it good?" Peep follows.

"Is he still undressed, hmm?" Jojo teases.

"Nice to see you too. Won't you *please* come on in?" I mutter sarcastically as I close the door.

"I don't hear anybody movin' around upstairs. You didn't call him, did you?" Corey finishes unbelievably.

"Geez, Corey! Let me at least give it a few days before I jump his bones!"

"You keep waitin' if you want to. Pretty soon, there will be no bones to even rattle," Corey retorts.

"Come on now, Corey. He doesn't want to look desperate. Calling him the night of receiving his number would do just that," Peep reasons.

"Finally, someone with some sense!"

"All I'm saying is that you are letting this dude pass you by," Corey defends.

"And all *I'm* saying is that I'm not ready for this yet. It's, uh, too soon," I counter.

"Right. What's the harm in waiting," Jojo says.

"That's what your mama should have said to your daddy," Corey quips.

"That's what you oughta say to over half the men you fuck," Jojo snaps back.

"Aight now. Calm that down. Now, I know I laughed and teased Lion 'bout this but I think he's got a point. To jump on that fine, delicious, black, succulent slab of beef..."

"Peep!" Jojo, Corey, and I exclaim.

"What?! Ok, ok! But to call him now *would* be one step away from being desperate. I think you are doing the right thing by waiting. Just don't wait *too* long."

"Don't worry, I won't. Besides... it's not like he didn't already call," I say coyly.

"What?" they chorus.

"Yeah, he left me a message last night."

"What does he sound like?" Corey pounces.

"Uh, like a man. Duh!" Peep snaps.

"I want to hear it!"

"I already heard it when I gave him your number."

Corey presses me until I can't hold out. I go to my machine, locate his message, and play it on speakerphone. As his bass-booming, masculine voice fills the room. I look at my friends. Corey is melting in his clothes, Peep is heaving huge breaths of air, and Jojo looks like he is about to cream his draws. As the message closes, Peep shouts, "Call his ass today!"

"Dammit, Peep. Would you pick a side and stay there? One minute you tell me that waiting is cool, then as soon as you hear his voice, you flip and rush me into calling him."

"Think about this now. He gives you his number and gets yours from Peep. Then he calls you less than three hours later. Few guys do that," Corey says, matter-of-factly.

"Didn't we just have this conversation about being desperate?"

"Yeah," Peep says. "We were talking about *you* not being desperate."

"Then what do you say about him calling me the same night he gets *my* number."

"Smart," Corey banters.

"I should have my head examined for telling you."

"Whatever," Corey follows. "Call his ass! The way I see it, you are free to test the waters since you got rid of Nate."

"Speaking of getting rid of stuff," Peep interjects mercifully. "When are you getting rid of this boring ass shit you call furniture?"

"I know you ain't coming up in my house talking about my decor."

"Looks like I just did. Anyway, I remember the day Nate bought this shit and you came for lunch looking like your brother just died."

"Whatever. Anyways, it's funny you should mention that. I was thinking about the furniture last night."

"So, what are you gonna do?" Jojo asks.

"What I should have done when his ass left. Get rid of the shit. I'm gonna put an ad in Craigslist and see who bites."

"Are you sure you wanna do that? A bunch of crazies hang out on that site," Corey says.

"Can't be any crazier than half the dudes you sleep with," Peep jokes.

"Jealous, are we?" Corey quips. "I am not that much of a slut."

"Uh Lion, I think we need to move a few spaces away from Corey. We don't want to be in lightning striking distance," Peep says, laughing.

"After all the action you pull every time we go out, I know your old ass ain't talkin' about me!"

"I may pull, but I don't touch. I am married, remember? Jimmy handles home…and very well, I might add."

"Oh Corey, what happened with that cop?" I quiz.

"I called him when I got back home, and he came over. It was good. But I'll say this. As fine as he is with all that dick, he needs some lessons on how to keep someone in the mood."

"What!"

"Yeah. I tell yuh, somewhere during his conquests, somebody ought to teach him how to properly lube the hole, tease it, and then go for what he knows. He made me so mad, I could've screamed, 'Do what you gonna do and get the fuck out. I need my itch scratched and you ain't doing jack shit.'"

"Corey, you are crazy."

"Fortunately, he did know how to eat ass and after he did that, it was gravy! I might call him in a few days, so he can get lessons on Sex 101."

"Um hmm. Like we said. *Slut!*" I tease. Then I point to the bags. "Y'all help me get these bags out to the car."

"What is all this stuff," Peep quizzes.

"All the clothes thrown outta my closet when Hurricane Corey hit it last night!"

"Good gracious, there is a God! Are you finally gonna switch up your wardrobe?" exclaims Peep.

"I am considering it. My play clothes, at least."

"Oh, babe! I got so many stores I need to take you to. You definitely need spandex. Body hugging spandex."

"Ever heard of baby steps?"

"Ever heard of boring? Baby, you got a banging body. You need to wear stuff to highlight it."

"Alright, now. Break it up, y'all," Jojo says, grabbing one of the bags and gesturing to the door. "Let's get these bags out to the car."

"Where is this stuff going anyways?" Peep asks, grabbing the other two bags and heading out the door.

"Good will, right?" Jojo quizzes.

"I don't think even anybody from good will would wanna wear this boring office garb," Corey retorts, as they both follow Peep out.

I say to myself, "Amen to that."

My phone rings. I move to pick it up and shout to the fellas outside. "Be out there in a minute. Hello?"

"Lionel, this is Rhonda."

(Pause)

"Rhonda, what's going on?"

"Nothing good. I talked to Mama, and she ain't doing too well."

"I'm sorry to hear that."

"Is that all you gotta say, 'I'm sorry to hear that'. This is our mother we are talking about. You are acting like I'm talking about a stranger on the street." *Jesus, I know that tone. She's trying to start some dirt.*

"Well, what's wrong with her?"

"She got Cancer."

Oh no. When I went to see her before "the news", she looked fine. I had to catch my breath, but the resentment of her dismissal overtook me as I said, "I'm sorry she is sick. Look, I really gotta go."

"What is with you? Obviously, you don't give a shit about the woman who gave you life."

"The same woman that read me for filth, then renounced me when I told her I was gay."

"Just because she didn't agree with you being a fag doesn't mean you can't be here for your own mother."

"Goodbye, Rhonda."

"Lionel, wait." Five seconds. *Dead silence. I know exactly what's coming...*

"What?"

"We need your help. She's gotta have an operation that costs five grand. We thought maybe you could pay for it, and we pay you back."

"No."

"Lionel, we..."

"I said no."

"So, this is how you do family?"

"Look at what family did to me! Every time family needs something, I always have to be the cavalry. But when I'm in need of love and support, nothing happens. This time, I'm not doing it."

"Lionel, quit being a bitch. This ain't about you, it's about Mama. She is still your mother regardless of whatever little lifestyle you choose to live. If you want to be a fag, that's your business. But who said you had to broadcast that shit? That was on you, not Mama."

"You know, it seems to me that you will accept my money, but you won't accept me."

"Lionel... get off your high horse, for Chrissakes."

I pause, weighing the pros and cons of this. I think to myself: *When will I ever be free of the guilt hold this family has over me? I know that this will bite me in the end. But still, she is my mother and even though she denied me, deep in my heart I know I could never deny her. There has to be a way that I can help and buy back a piece of my soul.*

The horn honks. "Get your ass in gear! Let's go!" Corey hollers.

"Are you still there?" Rhonda asks.

I half hear these voices, one in the car and the other on the phone. But I'm still thinking.

There has to be a way…

There just HAS to be a way…

I know there has to be a-

I got it!

"Lionel!" Rhonda nearly shouts impatiently.

"I'm here. When is her operation?"

"Three months from now."

"OK. I will pay for part of it."

"*Part* of it?! We need it all paid!"

"You just said the magic word… *We*! There are six of us! It's not going to be another Lionel-pays-all situation. Everyone with a well-paying job ought to pay an equal share towards her operation. That makes *four* of us. We can let Roland and Brenda off the hook because they are in graduate school and they need to focus. But you, me, Andre, and Dean are different stories altogether. Twelve fifty from each of us, and I'm not contributing one red cent of my part until I get documentation from the surgeon's business office that everyone else has paid theirs!"

"Always the suspicious one."

"Call it what you want, but you seem to forget that she gave birth to six children whenever family bills need to be paid. If I can get the money, surely you three can too."

"You know I don't have that kind of money."

"Well, the surgery is in three months. You can surely save that kind of money as part of the cost for *our* mother's surgery, because that is the only way you will get the 'fag's' part of the cost. Now, I really have to go. Goodbye, Rhonda."

"Don't you hang up on me…" *Click!*

I love my family, but some of them suffocate me with their bullshit and every time I talk to them, especially Rhonda, I feel two familiar emotions: guilt through all their talk about "Family's gotta stick together" and anger at myself for agreeing to be the sugar titty all the time.

Corey walks in. "Lion, what's going on? You know that heat and I don't mix well." Noticing my facial expression, he says, "Are you alright?"

"Just got some rough news."

"What?"

Snapping out of it, I say, "No need to go into it right now. I want to enjoy today. Let's get going."

*****

"So, Peep, what is up with your husband?" Corey says, as we are tooling up York Road in his 2015 Mustang convertible. Jojo and I are in the back seat since Peep called shotgun.

"Baby, Jimmy has been working double shifts down at the hospital. To be honest, it has him a bit on edge. Sometimes, he's grouchy when he comes home and all he seems to want to do is sit and look at TV or play video games."

"How long has he been working these double shifts?" Jojo asks.

"For two months."

"Is there a problem with money?"

"Yeah, do you need anything?" Corey follows.

"Just a tiny one. But, no... and thank you. We have a huge thirty-two hundred-dollar Maryland tax bill that Jimmy owed before we got married. Our accountant confirmed it in late March, but it's nothing we can't fix. We figured... Well, I insisted that between me working overtime at the bank and him at the hospital, we'd have it paid in three months."

"Looks like you got a month to go," I say.

"Right on schedule, and I can't wait. Two months of going without is too much for me."

"Wait a minute," Corey says. "You haven't done it in two months?"

"It would be the end-all slut to point that out. No, we have not made love in two months. I mean, he is gracious enough to deep throat me at least five times, but that's it. I guess the only good thing is that both of our asses are tighter than a nun's legs and our balls are nearly blue. So, when we finally do it, we go'n have one hell of a freak session."

"Uh, TMI," Corey quips, gagging.

"Bite me, asshole."

"Where?"

"You wish. Anyways, that's not my biggest concern."

"Well, what is?" I ask.

"His mother. I mean, I really love Irene. She is a joy and she's OK with the fact that Jimmy is gay and we both are married. But ever since her second husband died, she's been working herself to death and when the work is done, she gets incredibly bored. That is when she wants to hang around us. I feel sorry for her though, especially with all her health issues."

"Health issues? Is it her Diabetes again?" I quiz.

"Yeah, and Jimmy is really starting to worry. She's smoking like a chimney and eating the very things she's not supposed to. She's overworking herself with all these organizations and out in the yard." Peep sighs. Boy, he really sounds just as worried as Jimmy. There is something deeper going on. "I suppose she is trying to keep active. But we think, and her doctor agrees, that she is taking on too much."

"You know what I think?" I observe.

"What's that?"

"I know you are worried about her. But, I'm hearing guilt in your voice."

"What are you talking about? I don't feel any guilt."

"Come on, Peep," Jojo says. "It's your friends you're talking to. You went through this when your grandma died."

"Yeah, remember? You said she worked herself to death putting you through school. You felt guilty about that, and you've been dealing with that same guilt ever since," I remind him.

Peep gets quiet for a few seconds. Then he agrees, "Well, maybe that is the case. I look at Irene and I see Margaret Walker all over again. She doing the same overkill shit Granny did. I am really worried. Jimmy and I both think she needs more of a social life. Just not the one she is hinting at."

"Uh, ya lost me. What do you mean?" Corey asks.

"Well, would you believe she wanted to go to the Link with us last night?"

"Shit, hon, you should've let her."

"What?"

"Yeah. Let me tell you. The older fag hags are, the more fun they can be, especially when they are pissy drunk!"

"Uh, Corey," Jojo says. "I've met her, and she doesn't seem like the type of gal to even be in the area of fag-hagging, even if she is open-minded about most things."

"Of course, she's open minded. She's a pussy-bumper too," Peep says.

"*What!*" Corey, Jojo, and I exclaim.

"Do I stutter? You heard me right. Some time ago, we were at the grocery store on 33rd, and there was this pretty little lady checking our groceries. My gaydar went crazy and I looked at Irene and she was checking sister out."

"*Stop!*"

"I ain't lying, baby! If that grocery store was a hospital examining room, homegirl would have been a seventy-one-year-old x-ray machine! She was looking at this girl's rack and started drooling so much they almost needed to put out a wet floor sign."

"So, Mama's crossing over," Corey observes.

"I'm might need for her to cross back. She is already something to deal with being closeted. Imagine what a boil on everybody's ass she would be if she was out."

"Does Jimmy know about her?" Jojo asks.

"He does. Although he hasn't told her yet."

"How did he find out?" Corey queries.

"Let's just say he found some stuff in her room while looking for a safety pin two Thanksgivings ago."

"What stuff?"

"Ah, the usual… dildos, vibrators, all female porn…"

"*Ew!*" We all say collectively.

"How does Jimmy feel about it," I ask.

"He says that it's weird. I mean, he would live with it if that's what she wanted to do. But you don't hear every day that a gay son later down the line has a gay mother, or at least bisexual."

"Imagine how funny it would be if you told her that you know about her 'lick-her' license."

"Please, I'm asking God to kill the visual!"

We all laugh.

"By the way, we're all invited over to her house tomorrow after church."

"What time?"

"Three o'clock. Will that work for everybody?"

"Cool with me," Corey says.

"Me too."

"And me."

"Anyway, getting back to you," Peep says, glancing at me. "What's going on?"

"Yeah, you said you had rough news," Corey says.

Long pause. After which I say, "I had a conversation with Rhonda. She was trying to get me to pay the cost of Mama's operation."

"What's wrong with Lynetta?" Jojo asks.

"Cancer."

"Oh…"

"I don't know how bad it is, but the way Rhonda's carrying on, it may be life threatening. Of course, in true Rhonda fashion, she had a lot to say about me and how I live my life."

"You told me about Rhonda. She's the sister that makes Lizzie Borden look like Little Lulu," Peep recalls.

"Yeah, that's her. I think she gets that mean streak from Mama. Maybe that's why she's Mama's favorite. When we were little, she used to do some stupid shit just to get Dean, Andre, and me into trouble."

"Wait a minute- Andre? Is that the sick homophobe you told me about?" Corey muses, looking at Jojo through the rear-view mirror.

"Sick homophobe?" I join the look. "Jojo? What gives? Why are you discussing my family with Corey?"

Long pause.

"I had to tell somebody. Corey happened to be there when I was in one of my low moods. Your brother and Rhonda did some foul shit to me when we were growing up."

(Pause.)

"What do you mean? What did they do?"

"For one, Rhonda, Andre, and their moronic friends bullied me at school almost every day when they weren't being suspended or expelled. I used to have to take the long way home just to avoid them. But one day, I decided to take the short way home, and…" He pauses for several seconds.

"Well, what?"

"Look, can we just drop this? I really don't want to go into it."

"What did they do to you?"

(Pause)

"Joe, tell him," Corey asserts authoritatively.

"They kicked my ass, that's what they did… They kicked this 'Fat faggot's' ass'. Then after they were through… they pissed on me, one by one. Then Rhonda kicked me in the side with her high heel and they walked off laughing."

The car is quiet. All we can hear are the street sounds of Baltimore City, but our minds are thinking about our friend's traumatic childhood memory. Even Corey was at a complete loss for words. I look over at Jojo and an unbound tear hesitates around his eye then drops down his face. "Wow," I say, shocked. "I didn't know." The next seconds seem like hours, then I break the silence.

"Why didn't you tell me?"

"I didn't tell anybody then, and I had to be drunk to tell Corey. It was humiliating to relive it just by telling it. Besides, I didn't want any trouble between you and your family… or you and me."

I reach for him and hug him tightly, his tears wetting my bare shoulders. We hold on to each other and, when we drew apart, our eyes locked. A sense of déjà vu engulfs me. A feeling tells me that, long ago, we were in this same romantic space before. There is unnatural tension. Luckily Peep and Corey are in the front seat, sharing their own thoughts. They resume conversation. I can hear snatches of words like, "I'm glad you finally told Lion" and "It's sad how sick people can be". But at that moment, all I can see are those big brown eyes staring back at me. We sit breathlessly close, our faces almost an inch from each other. Wow. There is a heat in my groin that makes my jimmie press against the zipper of my capris. A tent! He looks down at it. *Uh-Oh*. But we can't move. He lifts his eyes and smiles into mine. I feel myself smiling into his. *Wait a minute! What in the hell are we doing?*

"What's going on back there?" Peep demands.
We draw apart quickly. "Nothing," I stammer.
"It doesn't look like that to me," Peep quips.
"Nothing is going on," I defend, more emphatically than I felt.
Peep doesn't say a word more, but out of the corner of my eye, I see a pained look on Jojo's face. A wave of awareness sweeps over me. I can't ignore what had just transpired. I looked into his eyes and I saw love. That's ridiculous though. Why wouldn't I see it? After all, we've been friends all our lives. Yet... *this* look of love? I have never seen before. A torrent of questions begins to bombard my brain.

Was it always there?
Is it just because he knew me all his life and I'm a safe option?
What did he see in my eyes?
Did he see love? Or only lust?

I look at him. He glances back at me, then turns his head to stare at the passing mundaneness of Baltimore. Then, in a gesture which surprised me, my hand finds his hand. He squeezes my hand tighter. Then he looks at me and smiles sweetly. *Oh God! He has beautiful eyes. I wonder why I've never noticed them before.* But, you can mess up a good thing when friends become lovers... so the line must be drawn somewhere. Having a romantic thing with my best friend would *not* be an option.

*****

"So, what's up with you and Jojo?" Peep asks as we were perusing the aisles of Rodchester's Menswear. Corey and Jojo went to McNasty's to grab some grub, which puts me in an uncomfortable position. Not even a second after they leave, Peep gives me the third degree. So, what do I do? I play dumb.

"The same thing that has been up with us for thirty-six years. Friendship." With that casual declaration, I cross the aisle to awkwardly focus my attention on a pair of neon pink and black biking shorts, and to avoid a conversation that was surely on Peep's mind. But Peep wasn't letting me off easily. He follows me.

"Oh, come on, Lion. I saw *the look* between you two."

"The look? Uh...What is the look?"

"Don't play dumb with me, Lion. You know exactly what I am talking about."

"No, I don't."

"Ok, you don't have to tell me if you don't want to. But, Felipe Alexander Hartfield was not born yesterday. I know the look when I see it, and there was some chemistry between the two of you in that backseat. Now tell me I'm wrong." Long pause.

"Thought so."

"Ok, so what if there was chemistry. We've always been close."

"Close, my ass. I've been watching you two in the gym. In the last year, even when you and that ass-wipe were together, you have been drooling over Jojo's ass and crotch, although you won't admit it. And the conversations that you two have while working out? Lord. You two are in a whole different world than Corey and me."

"Ok?"

"So, maybe you are starting to see him as more than just friends."

"Naw."

"Yeah, Mr. In Denial and Can't Admit It. Ooooh, look at this little number!" Peep pushes past me and picks up an orange and black sheer shirt. "Yaaaas, darling… and here are the pants to go with it."

"That might look good on you."

"And ya know that, but this ain't for me, hon. This is for you."

"I don't know," I mutter skeptically.

"Don't tell me you want to go back to the good will and pick those old fogey clothes up to wear again. Boy, put this mess on and stop it."

"Like I said, Peep, I'm trying to do this in baby steps. I'm not trying to *plunge* all the way in!"

"Ok, Ok, I get it. But I hope you don't think you are only going to wear those suits in your closet."

"No."

"Alright then. We are going to another men's store to pick you out a whole new wardrobe of clothes and they are going to be clothes that look nice, presentable, and will *fit* you like a skin-tight condom, OK?"

"You aren't going to have me looking crazy?" I ask cautiously.

"Chile', you're acting like you just met me today. Take a good long look at me. Am I wearing anything crazy?"

He got me there. In all the years I've known him, his clothes were always on point. Even when he went to the Link, He dressed in a notch of class, sexiness, and daring. Even now, His beige linen shorts and white shirt with rolled up sleeves and sockless feet shod in matching loafers fitted him perfectly, complete with a gold herringbone chain which lay against his defined neck of golden brown skin.

"No," I say quietly.

"Baby, I am not going to steer you wrong. I just want to accentuate your best features. You have so many. Look, I know you want to be conservative and proper, but ask yourself this question: Why have a banging body and nobody can see it because you are doing the layered look?"

"Fine," I vouchsafe, after a pause.

"Good! Now put this on and hurry up. I have more stores to take you to."

I head towards the fitting rooms, but I stop in my tracks and turn around to face him. "Peep... assuming that what you are saying about us is true, how do you feel about it? Should I even attempt to pursue that? I mean, this is my best friend for Chrissakes."

"Well," Peep says very matter-of-factly. "It's not important how I feel about it. I'm not the one with the attraction. That's for you to answer. But, off the record, I would say that it would be kinda cool to have a romantic relationship with someone you've known all your life. It saves time trying to get to know them."

"Yeah, that is true."

"I will say this though," Peep says in a very serious tone while placing his hand on my shoulder. "Be careful about that. Both of you have had bad relationships... and you *are* on the rebound, so to enter a relationship right now might not be the best thing, because you could end up hurting people that don't deserve to be hurt, including yourself. Take this time to get back to what makes Lionel happy. Don't rush into anything. That goes for that tennis player you are so hot for."

"You said at the house..."

"I know what I said, but I was teasing. Now I'm being dead serious, baby. Don't be afraid to wait for the right one. Time has a way of revealing things, and trust me, if either Mr. Tennis or Ms. Jojo is the one, you'll know it."

"And what if neither one of them are?"

"You'll still have Jojo as your best friend, right?"

"You're right."

"And if Garrett is friend material, you'll gain a new best friend to add to the ranks and we all will drag your ass to the club, to the mall, to a bar mitzvah, or even to church until you do find the right one!"

"Peep, you are crazy," I let out, feeling myself grin.

"Crazy, but right," Peep retorts, following with a chuckle.

"What are you two talking about?" Corey says as he and Jojo bounce their way towards us.

"Mind your business, nosey. It's a little boy talk," Peep says as he looks at his watch. "Lord, it's 12:38. Lion, get yo' ass in that dressing room. We got way too much shopping to do!"

CHAPTER SEVEN:

"DELAYED BUT WORTHWHILE"

Here I am with a full closet of new clothes and shoes. Some of them conservative, some casual, and some that are flattering yet scandalous at the same time. But all of them fit me to a tee, and DAMN! Do I look good in them, or what?

There were many selections he chose that had my left eyebrow shooting up, but the gesture was met by a pointed finger at the dressing room and a quick read from him to get in there. I must admit though, Peep knew exactly how to style and fit me, because all this week, I got compliments, some of them obvious flirtations. The most outrageous flirtation came from my boss, Mr. Floyd Alexander: a tall, stocky, blue-black man who reminds you of a young Ernie Hudson. He has always been extremely professional, but he came to my office on Wednesday and said, "Looking good, Davis." He came around my desk to "look at some marketing numbers from the last ad campaign" and as we were perusing, he brushed his body against mine and I felt an erection that had to have been at least eight inches. I had to restrain myself from moaning, because many of the times that Nate and I had sex in the difficult part of our relationship, I imagined it was him! I heard him say, "Why don't you come to my office and we can, uh, put our heads together about these numbers... In private," and he was licking his lips the whole time. Of course, I don't shit where I eat, so I told him, "Uh, why don't we meet for lunch at Sorbét's and talk about the numbers you have in mind". In the restaurant, he repeatedly made seductive remarks at me, and I told him that employees don't screw employers and I considered him not only as my boss, but as a friend. Thankfully he understood. I will have to tell Peep that his plan worked a little too well.

Even though Corey said I was crazy, I put an ad on Craigslist asking twenty-five hundred for the living room set in the storage unit, and two grand for the one in the house. Within the space of three days, I received heavy breathers, people trying to beat down my price, and crank calls. Fortunately, right before I decided to change my number, an offer came from a delightful elderly black couple, Mr. and Mrs. Washington, who bought a house in Timonium to be near their children. When they came by to see the furniture, the vitality they shared took me by surprise. I staggered when they volunteered their age. In their late seventies, they looked like they were in their late forties. I had to sit down when they said they wanted to buy *both* sets for five grand. The lady then looked at the bookcases and asked me was I interested in selling them for five hundred additional dollars. Talk about blessings! They came in and bought almost everything they saw in the storage unit and in my living room, including the curtains.

There were two things I would not sell, no matter what price. The first was my brown leather Queen Anne chair. Call me superstitious, but sometimes when I sit in that chair, the most amazing advertising ideas come rushing to my head and I run to my drafting table to sketch what I envision before I forget. The second were the paperweights my father left me. Lord, did they make a hefty offer for them! But, some things you keep because you have a strong attachment. Anyways, they paid me in cash and called their two sons to get a moving van and help move the furniture out. One of them was very friendly and talkative, but his brother was the very same guy that tried to force himself on me. I smirked like the Grinch that stole Christmas and he started breaking out in a sweat. He practically moved the stuff out to the van with very little help from anybody else. Mr. Washington said, "Damn, what the hell is wrong with him? It usually takes an act of Congress to get that boy to move a finger to do anything." No answer from me, although any reason *I* would have given would have made his hair fall out. The second the van left the curb, I called Corey to pick me up and we went to Conn's. I bought a nice and eclectically stylish sectional chaise and loveseat as well as side tables and curtains. I also bought modern art to lend creative balance to the room. NOW it looks like the living room of an advertising executive!

As far as Garrett is concerned, the question remained all last weekend, "Am I going to call him?" He called me on that Sunday like he said he would, but I was at Irene's house with the fellas. I don't understand what Peep is talking about; she seems the same to me. Then again, with Diabetes you can never tell. She is a lively woman with eyes that always seem to dance every time I see them. She is the same feisty hot tamale she always was. I asked her how she was doing, and she said, "Oh baby, I'm doing fine. Busy as a bee."
"Maybe you are too busy," Jimmy says.
"Who pressed your button? I'm about my business. Now, mind yours!"

I waited to call Garrett and there were two reasons why. One reason was because work kept me hopping so much that I haven't had the time to call anybody, even Corey, Jojo, or Peep. I did manage to get to the gym to workout with Peep and Jojo. Speaking of the latter, I was doing my barbell curls and Jojo was doing his squats. But mid-squat, I caught a look at his waist which is really slimming down. Then I noticed his dark chocolate skin stretched across his defining hamstrings, large calves, and the spectacular mold of his ass. I really had to get a grip and remind myself that this is my friend, not my lover. I felt a little bit guilty, but then an onrush of sensual breathlessness overtook that guilt when I caught him staring at my biceps, my forearms, my shoulder blades, my quads, and my "lead pipe". Peep caught the both of us staring each other down and he just chuckled and went on explaining the latest exercises with a knowing grin.

The second reason was because, as I said, I did not want to appear desperate and over-eager. I gotta tell you, I fought the urge to call him back, especially since he left me two more messages on my machine, both eager and wondering if it is the right number. He has the cutest little stutter at times when he is at a loss for words.

It has been a week, and I am sitting in my favorite chair and sipping Sangria on this lovely Friday evening. What time is it? I look at my wall clock. Six thirty-four. OK, let me call him. Hopefully, he's home from work by now.
I dial the number and after two ringback tones, a sweet sounding *female* voice answers, "Hello?"

What the hell? Either I dialed the wrong number or he's one of those confused boys that have trouble deciding what team he's catching for.

"Hello?" The voice says, with slight impatience in her voice.

Though my palms and armpits are sweating, and my face grows hot with disappointment, I stammer, "I'm sorry I must have the wrong number" then start to lower the cordless onto the receiver when I hear, "Wait! Who are you looking for?"

"Uh, Garrett Peterson."

"Oh, he's my younger brother. Let me get him. GARRETT, PHONE!"

My ears pop. A sweet voice that can scream loud!! But, my body relaxes with utmost relief. I hear a few voices saying, "Ok, I'll be over there."

"You'd better! Or Mama will have both our heads on a pole. Junior, hug your uncle goodbye. We gotta go. Sam is waiting."

Hmm... a family-oriented person. Point one for Garrett.

After a few seconds, a low bass booming voice taunts, "Speak."

My knees buckle as I melt while saying, "Hello, Garrett?"

"Yes."

"This is Lionel, Returning your call."

A strange hush comes. After a pause, he says, "Hey Lionel. How are you?"

"I'm doing alright. I'm sorry I'm just returning your message. Work has been crazy. I took time off last week and now I'm paying through my ass for it."

"No apology necessary. I'm just glad that we can talk. I wasn't sure if I had the right number because your answering service didn't have your name. You are Corey's friend, right?"

"Yes. You know him?"

"I introduced myself to him a couple of months back. He was a friendly face in the crowd and looking at you, good taste in friends. You see, I really don't go out that much. I hate the Link."

"Wow, I thought I was the only one. The only reason I went the last time was because my friends dragged me."

"Well, my best friends came from outta town. They didn't drag me, but I sure got a tongue lashing from them. They say I don't get out too often and I'm always holed up in the house."

"I hear you."

"So, we are both homebodies."

"It appears that way, doesn't it?"

"What do you like to do when you are at home?"

"I like reading, watching TV, sitting out on my backyard deck relaxing, writing poetry in my journal."

"Poetry?" He says with an interested tone.

"Yeah. The type that sometimes rhymes, sometimes flows, and sometimes just talks."

"Alright, Mr. Smart Guy. Talks of what?"

"Life. You know. The dilemmas we face in life. Why we are what and where we are and how we got there."

"Hmmmm…Well, currently, I would assume that you have a lot to write about as it relates to dilemmas… and it's good to follow trails of self-reflection, so I applaud you on that, as long as the trail leads to a productive end."

A smart man. Point two.

"True. Of course, there are degrees of productivity. It could range from productivity attributed to one's own life to the same attributed to those around him."

"Yes, but eventually, one person's productivity has the probability to have a snowball effect, that as it rolls it assists others in their own productivity. Just an observation."

Mmmm… I think I like him. He's a forward thinker. It sounds like he has a bit of the poet in him. Points three, four and five!

"Clever observation, my dear sir," I tease.

We talk for over an hour. In that talk, I learned that he came up here from Austin, TX. No wonder he's so big and tall! He lived with his sister and cousins for a while, then got a good job. After years of saving, he bought a condo for him and a house for his mother after he moved her up here. His father died, and he didn't want his mother living in Austin by herself. He played both high school and college football and he graduated with a Bachelors' and Masters' in Accounting. There goes the myth about all brawn and no brain! He is an avid tennis pro, and he plays the saxophone. He said that his mother made him take lessons at age fourteen and he hated every single minute of it, but he developed a passion for it as he grew up (Now *this* is someone Corey would think is fabulous). He loves painting abstract art and the color azure blue.

Of course, there were other things we talked about. but I was taken by how self-assured and confident, yet sensitive and vulnerable he seemed. The combination was extremely appealing. There were quite a few times when he would stutter, and my heart melted every time he did.

"So, what are your plans for the rest of the night," he asks.

"Probably catch a good movie and relax, and you."

"I'm going to my Mama's house to help with some stuff."

"That's decent of you," I say, feeling slightly envious.

"Yeah, got to be there for Mama," he proudly declares.

"Uh, Garrett, can I ask you a personal question?"

"Uh-oh!"

"It's not that bad, trust me."

"Ok, hit me with the boom."

"Well, does your mother know about you?"

"No. It's not because I don't want to tell her. But, my oldest sister knows. That was her that answered the phone."

"Yeah, I remember she told me. What's her name?"

"Rachel."

"She seems cool."

"She really is. She's been telling me that I need to tell Mama, but every time I attempt it, I... I…"

"You chicken out?"

"Yeah, you could say that. Does your mom know?"

My lips fly open to tell him yes and fill him in on what happened. But the memory of her reaction stayed my tongue. I did not want to scare him off coming out by telling him my sordid story. Besides, all mothers aren't the same about these things. So, I endeavor to falter the word "No" and swallow to keep the lie down. It doesn't work. My mouth is dry. "Can you hold on for a minute?" I barely croak.

"Ok…" He hesitates with puzzlement.

I go to the kitchen and grab a glass of water to clear my throat. As I drink it down, I decide to myself that honesty is best. After all, my relationship with Nate was built on lies. Why not start with the truth but keep it short?

"I'm back."

"Did I say something wrong?"

"No, you didn't. Yes, my mother does know, and she's not happy about it."

"That is scaring me."

"Why?"

"I mean, after hearing about your mother's reaction, I'm a little bit apprehensive about telling mine."

"Listen, don't let my story with my mother color your perception as to how yours will take it. No two situations are alike. Remember that."

"I know, but you hear all the horror stories about the people who come out, and the news can sometimes wreck families, and my family is one of the many things I hold dear. We are all very close."

"Well, maybe I'd better tell you a tidbit about a friend of mine. His mother found out by accident when she was cleaning under his bed and found boy magazines."

"What? You got to be kidding!" he exclaims, laughing.

"If I'm lying, I'm flying. And you'll never guess what *she* did."

"No, but I'm certain you will tell me."

"She sat down and flipped through them, even reading the articles and learning the names of the porno stars!"

"Ok, now I'm *positive* you are lying!" By now, he is laughing his fool head off... and his laughter is so contagious that I have to join him.

"What are you laughing for? My friend actually walked in and caught her reading them."

"What in the world?"

"And my friend's face fell with she looked up and said, very matter-of-factly, 'I might need to have a threesome with two guys, so I can watch!'"

Suddenly, I hear a thud and for fifteen seconds I hear a distant constant stream of loud hearty laughter and wheezing, and before I know it, I'm laughing right along with him.

After the hilarity subsides, he gets back on the phone.

"I'm sorry, my phone dropped! That was hilarious, but I can't believe how cool she took it."

"Well, she was pretty liberal even when we were kids."

"She actually sounds like my mother. Like I said, Rachel's been telling me that Mama would understand. I mean, I got a cousin my mother's age whose door swings to the pole instead of the hole."

Now, that sent *me* in! My turn to drop the phone and hoot. I hear him chuckle.

"Well, let me ask you this," I ask, calm resumed. "Does your mother talk bad about your cousin?"

"No. They are like two fingers, man. In fact, she would kick anybody's ass for approaching him the wrong way and quote a Scripture to refute the holier than thou church folk sending us to hell."

"Seems like your Mama and mine oughta trade places."

"Oh no, I am going to keep mine, thank you very much," he teases.

"But, you got two things working to your advantage. You got a mother who has a gay cousin she's crazy about."

"True."

"Additionally, you just said that your sister was older, right."

"Yeah."

"So, I guess she would know more about your mother's temperament and her level of acceptance better than you would, right?"

"I guess so. I never thought about it that way."

"I'm just saying that no situation is the same."

"Yeah, you are right, my dear sir. Well, listen, I better get over to Eunetta Peterson's house before she chops my head off."

"Ok," I relent, saddened by his need to hang up.

"But, I'd like to talk some more, later."

"So would I," I perk up.

"Can I call you tonight?"

"Yes."

"Ok then. Maybe we oughta schedule a game on the tennis court for next week when we talk tonight. I can pick you up and we can go in my car."

"Ok, but I warn you. You might not want to play anymore after I beat you."

"Is that a challenge?"

"It isn't a valentine."

"Well, we'll have to see about that then, won't we?"

"I suppose we will."

He chuckled. *Oh my God, his laugh!* "OK then. We'll talk tonight. Stay up until then."

"You too, man."

"And I'll keep you in my prayers about your mother. Things will work out." *Wow, how considerate and decent.*

"Thank you. I appreciate that. Talk to you later."

"Later." *Dial tone.*

*****

We are now sitting outside on a Wednesday evening in a nearby restaurant, recounting the game over Mochaccinos. My ego is bruised because Garrett beat me in that tennis match. It was a five-set match where I won the first and fourth. He won the second and third, but we were neck and neck on the fifth. Then he called time and said he was hot. He took his enormous water bottle and drunk some, then he poured the remaining contents on his head and the water trickled down his strong shoulders, drenching his white tennis shirt where it clung to his chest and stomach. Oh, what a remarkable sight! I squirmed to view his fully erect nipples on top of that lean, sculpted chest. I was already turned on by those blue-black dancer's legs under those white tennis shorts. Anyway, he served and, due to my distraction, I failed to return it. He whooped and hollered with joy.

"You do know you cheated!" I said in mock rebuke.

"I don't know what you are talking about," he rebuffs, opening his wide, beautiful eyes and grinning like a Cheshire cat.

"You know exactly what I'm talking about. Drenching yourself in water, indeed!"

"Well, you know, I'm not the only guilty party here. How many people would call a time out, then go to the bathroom to remove his underwear."

"What?! Oh Nooo!"

"Oh Yeees! Kind of weird that a pole was swinging after you got back where I could see the print!"

I start to counter defensively, but then I feel a smile stretch across my face.

"Something to say?" Garrett queries mischievously.

"Yes," I assent. "Touché!"

Garrett nods smugly, raising his mug and taking a drink. Then he tells me, "But all jokes, and cheats aside, you are one hell of a tennis player. You give me competition, and you certainly didn't make it easy for me to win."

"Well, that's me. An all-around challenge."

"All-around, huh? Suppose you tell me what other challenges you offer. The good ones. We all have challenges that are not so good."

"Why don't we find out each other's challenges as we go along? If we share too much now, we won't have enough to talk about or share later."

"Fair enough, but there is one challenge I have to ask you about."

"You may ask, but whether I endeavor to answer is another matter altogether," I say as I sip my Mochaccino.

"What was the challenge you had that night at the club? I saw you with this brotha' and it seemed pretty intense."

Uh, can we say awkward? I slowly remove the cup from my lips and set it back on its saucer. I'm not sure how my face looks, but I notice Garrett's face as his eyes clearly spell out, *"Uh-oh. I crossed the line. Way to go, stupid."*

After an unbearable few seconds, I hear him say, "I'm sorry. I didn't mean to pry."

"No, it's OK."

"You don't have to talk about it if you don't want to. I mean, you don't even know me, so I really have no right to ask."

"Well, it almost became a spectacle for you to see, so the question is well founded. That man was my ex-boyfriend."

"I figured that."

"How?"

"Well, I sensed the 'romance lost' tension between the two of you."

"I guess I'm not the only one that is psychic. Let's just say that we never resolved the issues surrounding our breakup. We had a lot of them, but the clencher involved a once mutual friend he couldn't keep out of our bed."

"Gotcha. I have been through that. It's not cool at all."

"No, it's not. Would you believe that he got upset at me for wearing the outfit I wore?"

"And why was that?"

"Beats me. I guess he likes to think he still holds the reins."

"Heeey, baby brother," A loud sweet voice calls out. I whirl to encounter a beautiful young lady with an inquisitive, wide-eyed boy at her side. Her skin was a honey brown color and she had a valentine shaped face with full lips as well as a slender and shapely figure. On her body hung a very pretty pink sundress. At first glance, I can't see any resemblance between Garrett and this lady. But as I look up into her luminous and bright eyes, their family tie is unmistakable.

"Rachel! What's going on," Garrett beams as he gets up to embrace her. She returns the embrace. "What are you doing here?"

"Oh, just active. Spending time with my baby and walking the Towson streets."

"Well, this is a nice enough day for it. Uh... Where's Sam?"

"He is in the clothing store. You know that man is a suit junkie."

"He would save a lot of money if he wasn't trying to move up by impressing those corporate clowns at work, then getting pissed when they are not moved by his toadying." The vibe changes as I read disapproval in his face.

"Garrett, don't start."

"Well, you married him, so what can I say? Sup, Mike Junior," he addresses the boy as he slaps him five and hugs him.

"Hey, Uncle Garrett. See my baseball?"

"Yeah, where did you get it?"

"Mama took me to an Orioles game and one of the players gave me this," He talks in rapid fire style with an angelic grin on his face. As he talks, I study him. He has a remarkable face alight with innocence and wonder that only an unfettered child can possess. Dressed in yellow, his skin tone glowed. On his head was a full head of curly hair fluffed out in brownish red glory. I look at him and his mother who is now palming his head with a loving smile, and a feeling of sadness overtakes me. Why couldn't my mother and I have that type of relationship? My thoughts are interrupted by his clear tone.

"Hi, I'm Michael Lewis-Kincaid Jr. and I'm six years old. What's your name?"

"I am Lionel Davis."

"Hi Lionel."

His mother cuts in, "That's Mr. Lionel to you."

"Oh, I'm sorry, Mr. Lionel. Do you live in Baltimore?"

"Yes, I do."

"Did you ever want to live somewhere else?"

Now that's a question. "Sometimes."

"Me too. Sometimes, Baltimore is so boring. I was telling my friends in school that I would love to live in Disneyland."

"Why is that?"

"Because I can ride the rides all day and get a whole lot of funnel cakes! I am *mad* about funnel cakes!"

There is something very different and endearing about this kid. He has his uncle's personality and His mother's sweetness mixed with his own virtues. *Lord, please,* I pray to myself, *Give me some of my own innocence back.*

"Alright now, don't talk the man's head off," Rachel chides. She then looks at me with approval and says, "You must be good people because he doesn't rattle on like this very often."

"He doesn't?"

"Not to adults he doesn't know."

"That makes me feel special," I say as I look at him, smiling.

"My baby has that effect. Oh, I'm so sorry, where are my manners? I am Rachel Kincaid, Garrett's sister. We spoke on the phone." She smiles warmly and extends her hands. I accept them in mine.

"It's nice to see the beautiful face that matches the voice."

"Oh, you are a flatterer! Garrett has been talking about you so much that your ears should have fell off by now."

"Is that so?" I ask, beaming and glancing at him.

"Yeppir!"

"Are you and Uncle Garrett on a date," Michael asks.

"Mike Junior! What kind of question is that?" she asks, trying to hold in her laughter. Garrett and I share an amused yet astonished look between us. *Kids really do say the damndest things.*

"I wasn't sure. I mean, they could've been talking about stuff we ain't supposed to know."

"*Aren't* supposed to know," Rachel corrects, tousling his hair. Then she turns back to me. "I'm sorry for interrupting y'all. I just came over to speak to my precious Blueberry."

She then jabs him with her finger and a short laugh escapes his lips. *Ah, he's ticklish!*

"Rachel, you promised me you would not call me that," he says, embarrassed.

"Uh, Blueberry?" I question.

"Yeah, I call him that because of somethin' that happened when he was little."

"What happened?"

"I, uh, think I need to let him tell you that. We done embarrassed him enough. Look at him blush." I look. Well, I'll be damned. Under his rich blue-black skin, there is a hint of reddish tint.

"Rachel!" I hear a harsh voice and turn as a tall, muscular light skinned man is standing on the opposite side of the street. Suddenly, a coldness sweeps over me, chilling me to the bone. There is something about this guy that rubs me the wrong way. It's not his tall frame, his sinewy arms, or that grating voice, because Peep is tall and sinewy, and Corey has the most irritating voice when he is really pissed. It was those hateful eyes that jolted my mind and choked my voice. I look down at Mike Junior. He was talkative with me, but now he retreats to silence. His brown eyes that held such childhood wonder and naivete changed into an unspoken adult barrage of fear. I look at Rachel, and she seems to wilt in that pink dress as she winces and fidgets with her purse.

He moves with purpose, looking like he wants to drag her across the street. Then he spots Garrett, and suddenly a megawatt smile spreads across his thin lips. He reaches us and chides to Rachel, "You must have been in a hurry. I looked around from trying on clothes, and Poof! You disappeared." An uneasy quietness hovers over the table, as the sounds of conversations and engines along York Road are intensified. He reaches his hand out. "Hi, my name is Sam Kincaid."

"Lionel Davis," I mumble as I take it gingerly.

"Nice to meet you."

"Pleasure."

"Garrett, what's going on?"

"I'm making it. How about you, Sam?"

"Oh, you know, it's just work, work, and more work down at the office. The shit you have to do to make partner. Trying to appease the boss and being overworked. I don't get nearly as much loving as I used to," Sam said as he moves behind Rachel and humps her, making her flinch.

Smiling, Garrett stands up and stealthily positions himself between Sam and Rachel. He clamps his hand on Sam's collarbone while standing beside him. He narrows his eyes. "Well, maybe you ought to take some time to yourself. If they are stressing you out that much, why deal with them, especially when they drive you to drinking and showing your ass at the wrong people?"

"Just a lot of stress, man. Just a lot of stress. Don't worry. It won't be long before I have the word partner behind my name." The hand clamp seems like it's morphing into an iron grip. I can't tell whether it's a massage or a subtle "don't fuck with me" move.

"Well, let's hope it is soon," Garrett's voice comes out in a low, airy, and threatening hiss as he removes his hand and watches Sam massage his collarbone.

"Damn, you got some heavy hands!" Sam says, smiling nervously.

"Sorry, dude. Every now and then, I forget my own strength," He says in a deep intimidating voice. He holds Sam hostage in a deadly stare.

"You know what I'm saying?"

Sam starts to stammer.

"To be sure. Well, I hate to rush along but we have a lot to do today. Say goodbye, Mike Junior."

"Goodbye," Mike Junior says inaudibly. How can a boy who talks with such confidence retreat to such reservation where he does not sound like himself?

"Goodbye, Garrett," Rachel stammers. "I'll call you later. Lionel, it was wonderful meeting you."

"It was wonderful meeting you too. I hope we'll meet again soon. Bye, Mike Junior."

He looked at me and gave me a smile that broke apart the gray clouds and the radiance came back to his face.

"Goodbye, Mr. Lionel."

We watch as they walk away. Man, wife, and child, walking stiffly on the sidewalk. Chilled, I turn my eyes towards Garrett and wonder if pursuing him as a love interest is such a good idea. The last thing I want to hear about is family drama. I got enough of my own.

CHAPTER EIGHT:

"WHY DO THEY HATE US"

"What was *that* all about?" I asked, turning to Garrett

"What do you mean?"

"I felt that something wasn't right with that guy."

"Funny, I felt that way when she brought him home a year ago."

"So, that's not Mike Junior's father."

"No, Sam is his stepdad."

"That explains a lot."

"His father, Mike Senior died from Heart disease three years ago. Now when Rachel brought him home, we eventually became cool. You know, brothers won't like anybody their sisters bring home. He proved to be ok after a while. But when it came to Sam, every time I looked at that stupid motherfucker, I got a horrible feeling in the pit of my stomach. I could tell when I first met him that he had a mean streak and a way of hurting folks where it leaves no physical marks."

"I got that vibe. How did she meet this guy?"

"At a singles event."

"Well, at least she didn't meet him online."

"Yeah. With all the sexual assaults and fatalities we hear about nowadays, we can at least be thankful for that. But I think he is really breaking her down. What you saw today was just half of what she used to be. She was so lively and fun to be around. But as you saw, she tenses and gets very quiet when Sam comes in the picture."

"You don't think he is physically abusing her, do you?"

"I hope to God that he is not. Because I would have to hunt him down and kick his ass until he can barely breathe."

"I felt that you would."

"What?"

"You gave him quite a scare with your body language. It clearly said, 'I'll kill you if you mess with my sister.'"

"You caught that, huh? Well, if you think *that* was a threat, you should meet other members of my family, and may God help him if my two cousins from Cherry Hill find out. If Craig and Melba get wind of it, his body would be tied up in plastic and thrown into the Inner Harbor."

"You got roughnecks in the family too, huh?"

"Every family has black sheep that they love as people but hate to claim as relatives. Whenever Craig and Melba go somewhere, there is always some fight popping off."

"Well, let's hope that he is *not* abusing her," I say as I drink my now cold coffee.

"Yeah."

"So, tell me. Why are you called Blueberry?"

"Dammit, I was hoping you wouldn't ask."

"Well, she said she would let you tell me why. Something tells me if I hadn't asked for the info, you would not have volunteered it."

"I guess I'm cornered. Ok well, when I was a junior in High School and on the football team, I ate almost everything in the house. My mother made a pie and I thought it was my favorite, blueberry pie. And it was, but what my sister failed to tell me was that it was a laxative blueberry pie that Mama made to get back at our neighbor for dumping sloppy joe sauce down her dress."

"You are lying!"

"The hell I am! That pie had me shitting the whole damn night. My ass felt like it was deflating. My sister and mother laughed at me for years after that."

I laugh out loud. "That is terrible!"

"Yeah, they gave me the nickname 'Blueberry'. The worst thing about it is that blueberry pie makes me sick just looking at it now."

"Well, I know not to serve you any at all, especially at my house. I don't need you blowing up my bathroom to where I have to wash the curtains to get the smell out."

"Alright, Smart Ass."

I smirk at him and take another sip. Then I resume the convo. "So, what is your idea of a solid relationship?"

He sits back, folds his brawny arms, and focuses on the centerpiece meditatively. He then says, "That's kind of a broad question… and to be honest, I don't know. I don't think anybody knows anything concerning what builds a solid relationship, except for the stock answers like communication, commitment, and teamwork."

"I suppose you're right," I assent. "Well, let me ask a different question."

"Ask away."

"What are your best qualities?"

"Hmmmm. Well, I think I care about people to where it is considered a fault. I am very affectionate. I love giving big bear hugs. I think I'm intelligent but still able to learn more. I can beat people at tennis!" He beams a teasing smile at the last question.

"Uh, actually, you did not win."

"Have you checked the score?"

"I checked the score. Remember drenching yourself in water?"

"Yes."

"That's intent to distract, so it doesn't count."

"So, you are saying that you won?"

"Exactly."

"Due to 'Intent to Distract'. Right?"

"Yeah."

"Need I remind you, No underwear?"

"It was pulling my skin," I stammered weakly. "I had to take it off to get comfortable."

"Did you have to shake your hips so that a certain something swung in seduction?"

"OK, OK, no I did not have to do that."

"Um, hmm!"

"Call it a tie?"

"Fair enough."

*****

At the end of our coffee, he takes me to the Harbor where we just walk and have friendly conversation. He tells me about his career and how he always had a head for figures as a kid. He went into Accounting after seeing his mother pay through her nose for accounting advice and tax preparation. I tell him about my career and how I was always good at drawing and art, as well as finding out what draws people to different products. Before I know it, three hours have passed. The sun paints the sky a rosy red, saffron, and burgundy. We watch as the sun sets, leaving darkness. I feel something. I feel the same way I felt when I told Jojo that I was gay and afraid of what Mama would say. He grabbed my hand in both of his to show he understood. The same way I felt when Corey wrapped his arms around me and held me when I told him my father died. The same way I felt when Peep and I talked at that skating rink and he told me that we'd have a close and wonderful friendship to last for years to come. I feel... Trust. An affection for a man wise beyond his years. A perfect gentleman. A humorous man. Hmm... Yes, I have my reservations, but is this the start of romance or the start of another close friendship? I don't know. All I know is that this feeling is a beautiful feeling and I want to keep it close to me... for always.

*****

Sitting in his car in front of my townhome, he says, "I had a really good time hanging with you."

"I did too."

"What is your schedule like next week?"

"Kinda slammed, with all the campaigns we got coming in."

"I understand."

"But that doesn't mean we can't chat over the phone."

"Really?"

"Of course! That *is* one of the ways we get to know one another, ya know."

"You're a smart ass, you know that?"

"I would hope so. Otherwise, college would have been a waste!" We both laugh.

"So, call you tomorrow?"

"Sure, but make sure you text me on my cell tonight to let me know you got in safe."

"Ok, same number?"

"Oh, that's right. I'm sorry, that's my landline and I recently got it changed. Here's my cell. 443-992-7129.

"Got it." He locks me in his phone. He then glances at me radiantly, his smile lighting up his face. "Well, let me get on home before it gets too late."

"OK, we'll talk tomorrow. Maybe schedule another tennis match. One where we don't cheat!"

He laughs heartily. "Fair enough."

"Take care, Garrett. Drive safe," I say as I step out of the car.

"G'night, Lionel."

I can feel his concerned eyes follow me as I move up the stoop and put my key in the lock. Opening the door, I turn to see him still watching to make sure I got in safely. I wave and smile at him and he reciprocates. How I savor the pleasant feeling of the night as I watch his car drive away.

Suddenly I feel a vibration in my pocket and as I pull my phone out, I see Peep's name flashing across the screen.

"Hello?"

"Lion?" Peep's voice floats out bringing a feeling of urgency and dangerous alarm.

"Peep. What's wrong?"

"Baby, you need to come down to the hospital. It's Corey."

"What? What happened to Corey?!" The pleasant feeling is now replaced with dread. *Oh God. What happened?!*

"He was beaten and stabbed. His neighbor called me from the ambulance and he's here beside me now."

"Where?"

"St Agnes Hospital."

"Is Jojo there?"

"No, not yet. But he said he's on his way. How long before you can get here?"

"I'll be there in fifteen minutes. What are they doing to help him?" I ask hurriedly.

"They cleaned the wound, but they are afraid he may have internal damage."

"Ok, sit tight. I'm on my way."

*****

Corey is all I can think of as I speed up Charles Street. The age old, one-word question resounds in my head, *Why? Why did this happen? Not my Corey. My bold voice. What am I going to do if I lose him? What are we all going to do?* Out of the four of us, Corey is always the one who speaks his mind without fear or favor. Even Peep, as opinionated as he is, has considerable restraint when it deals with expressing how he feels. But Corey can do it freely without apology.

It's hard to focus my eyes on the road with stinging tears blinding my view, and imagining life without Corey, or any of the fellas, is even harder. *Ok. You gotta think positive. He's gonna be fine. He's got to be fine. He still has that dream of composing the great Black American symphony to rival William Grant Still's. God, I know you aren't going to take him without giving him the chance to complete it. Please say you won't. We need him here. A dead man can't inspire the world and he has so much to give.* I run a red light. *Oh shit!* I look around for the next ten seconds. Whew! Thank God the police aren't around to ticket me. *Please Lord, let him be OK.*

When I walk into the waiting area of the emergency room, I see Peep and Jimmy huddled together and a pale and wiry white man next to them, nervously flipping through magazines. Upon seeing me enter, Peep rises to embrace me. My plentiful tears fall on his white T-shirt, soaking through to his skin. My arms cannot let him go. Neither can he release me from his iron grip. I feel Jimmy's hand rubbing my back fervently as if transferring good energy and reassurance to my desolate spirit. I then feel him hugging the both of us as we stand in a triangle, heads pressed together with our tears falling to wet the hospital floor.

We pull back from the hug to see Jojo walk through the door. His expression frantic with bloodshot eyes, a sweaty brow, and chapped lips, he begins to ask question after question.

"What happened? Where is he? Is he OK? I want to see him."

"Calm down, baby. They have him in ICU and they are keeping him under observation," Peep soothes.

"Observation?! Why aren't they doing more than that?"

"Well, they said it's standard procedure. They don't want to go through the trouble of a surgery before they are sure that it's needed."

"Are you kidding me? They are just going to let him sit there in pain while they are watching and not doing shit?"

"Jojo, you have *got* to calm down," I reproach carefully.

"Calm down, hell! That's my friend in there!"

"And he's our friend too. Believe me, we are just as shaken up about this as you are."

Jojo sits down, and his left leg starts shaking. Oh Lord, I know that sign. He is about to go into meltdown.

"Look, can somebody just tell me what happened?"

"A street gang jumped him. They beat him up, broke his wrist, and stabbed him in the side," Jimmy informs.

"Why?"

"Only Corey can answer that."

"Was there anybody that saw it?"

"No, but his neighbor rode with him in the ambulance."

"Where is he?"

"Over there," Peep says, pointing at the pale, trembling man flipping through the magazines. "Alex? Come here. These are my friends Lion and Joseph. Tell them what you told me."

The young man shuffles over, His rusty blond hair was disheveled, and his blue work shirt was drenched in Corey's blood. His thin voice cracked as he related what he saw.

"Well, I was coming home from work and I saw Cordell staggering weakly up his stoop, trailing blood behind him. There was a bigger pool of blood at the foot of the steps. I ran to help him and saw the stab wound. That was when I called the paramedics."

"Tell them what you saw spray-painted on his door."

"It said, *'Death to all faggots.'*"

A jolt goes through me. I look at Peep's face, melancholy cloaking it in it's dark shadows. Jimmy looks like he wants to grab the guy that did it and drop him in a river somewhere. But Jojo… his expression is the bleakest of all. His eyes look like they had been searching for answers and coming up short every time. I see my friend's face and spirit crumble as he begins to cry. The walls of the sterile room reverberate the angry, helpless sobs of one without hope. Suddenly, he bounds up from his seat and runs out of the waiting room. I run to catch up with him, calling his name. He runs outside to the circular driveway and pauses at the curb. I stop dead in my tracks at seeing him with his head held down. Catching my breath, I walk up to his side and put my hand on his shoulder. He glances at me then resumes his downward gaze.

After an eternity of silence, he chokes out, "Why do they hate us so much? We are no different than they are. We shit and piss like they do."

"I don't know. I have struggled with that same question and I'm not gonna try to give you the easy cliché answers, because I'm sure you've heard them all."

"Yeah."

A long silence closes in. I can see, even in profile, the hurt and depression on Jojo's face. Finally, Jojo breaks the silence.

"You know, sometimes I really wish I wasn't gay."

"What?"

"Yeah. I mean… most times, I'm ok with it but at times like this, I ask myself, 'What am I getting out of it?' You always have folk judging you. You get your heart broken by trifling ass men who can't decide whether they want a man or a woman. Worse, look at Corey. You get a beatdown just for having the balls to be yourself. And we have these fools who say that this is a choice. Who would choose anything like this?"

"Yeah. I had to correct a co-worker of mine the other day when *she* was ranting about this being a choice. If people only knew what we knew, they would realize how ridiculous that statement really is."

We sit down on the curb and I put my arm around him. My fingers massage his temples and my free hand caresses his cheek. His head rests on my shoulder as the sobs subside. Peep comes out and sits next to us. We join hands as we pray for the life of our friend.

For three hours, we sit on the curb not saying much. The spring breezes of May whistle softly in our ears and play with the hairs on our skin. The wait is unbearable. Peep and I try to make small talk to ease the pain of the circumstances. Jojo just sits there, blankly staring at the buildings on the other side of the street. His eyes are tearless, but anger colors his face a deep and dark plum color. *What can I say to make it better for my friend… and what is taking so long?!*

Finally, when we are almost to the breaking point, we hear Jimmy's voice beckon, "Guys, come back in. The doctor's got news."

We rush back into the hospital, circling the snow-white corridors and praying that the news given to us is good news. When we walk into the waiting room, we see a short white woman wearing a lab coat. She has short red hair and friendly green eyes. Her smiling expression is reassuring and positive. *This is a good sign,* I think to myself.

"Well? What's going on?" Jojo questions.

"Mr. Kennedy is fine. He lost a lot of blood, but the stab wound is nowhere near his vital organs."

Collectively, we all breathe in grateful release. "Thank God," Jojo gushes out.

"We had to reset his wrist, however, so he will have to wear a cast for four weeks."

"Uh, doctor…" I cut in.

"Camden. I'm Dr. Camden."

"Dr. Camden, how bad is the injury to his wrist?"

"Not too bad. I've seen much worse. A few weeks in the cast and he'll be just fine."

"Can we see him?" Peep says.

"Well, he is still very groggy from the sedation. He also needs his rest after going through that attack. I would try him on Friday."

"Can we just sit overnight with him until he comes around and feels like talking?" I inquire.

"Are you all family?"

"He has no blood family that we know to contact. We are his closest friends," Jojo says.

"The privilege for overnight guests is reserved for the natural family."

"We understand that, Frances. But, is there any exception to that rule? His friends are like his brothers. Plus, he has no blood family, like Joseph stated," James cajoles.

The doctor thinks it over. "Ok. I know I am not supposed to do this, but I'll take you to his room."

"Uh… can we hold that thought a minute?" Peep pulls us to the side and says, "Guys, I think we should do this in shifts."

"You're right, baby. People might see four black guys in the room and start tripping," Jojo says.

"Right, I'll cover tonight," I say. "This way, y'all can get home and get some sleep."

"I'll come tomorrow," Peep volunteers. "And we can all come on Friday. He'll be out of the woods by then."

The guys nod in the affirmative.

"Alright, I'll call if anything else happens."

We embrace each other. Then the three of them exit the waiting room.

"Ok, Dr. Camden. We're going to do it in shifts."

"Certainly. Come with me. I'll get you a blanket for the recliner."

As we walk, I ask, "Uh… Dr. Camden, did he happen to say who did this?"

"No. In fact, when he came around from the sedative, he closed up about everything pertaining to the attack… and frankly, that worries me. Hopefully, he will share more with you all, because holding on to it is going to do him more harm than good. Outside wounds heal, but inside wounds can linger forever if he doesn't get help."

*****

"Oh, come on now. Don't be looking at me like that. Old Corey is gonna be fine," Corey banters lightheartedly through his hoarseness. It is Friday and Peep, Jojo, and I are visiting Corey.

I go over to hug him, and as soon as my arms encircle him, he starts yelping. "Ow! Ow!! Watch my side!"

I jump back exclaiming. "Oh, I'm sorry, Corey. I didn't mean..."

"Made you jump!"

Despite myself, I had to laugh. Only Corey could turn something this serious into a joke that loosens everyone up. The only one that is not laughing is Jojo.

"Corey. This ain't no time for joking. This scared the livin' shit out of us!" Jojo reproaches.

"Before or after Lion tried to squeeze the rest of my life out of me with them big ass arms of his?"

"Corey, I'm serious."

"I know you are... and I know how concerned you are. But baby listen," He responds with difficulty, tears in his voice. "You gotta treat it a little lightly... to keep from crying over how bad and sick the situation really is."

"Well, since you brought it up, what exactly is the situation?" Peep asks.

"Two black eyes, a broken wrist they had to reset, and stab wounds. But hey, I've been through worse."

"*What in the hell could be worse than this?*" Jojo suddenly explodes. His rich dark skin tinted a shade of violet as tears flow profusely down his face. "You almost died. That knife could have killed you. At this very moment, we could've been planning your memorial service. And you say you've been through worse?"

Corey looks stunned. "Jo, calm down." He repositions himself to where he is sitting up. A spasm hits his side, making him wince. When the pain passes, he says, "I can't front. What those idiots did was stupid and horrible. But I have to look at it like this. They are not doing it out of personal hatred of us. They are doing it based on the same shit their parents heard from friends, family, and surprisingly the church. They are just reacting on what they were taught. To hate us and everybody that is either like us or understands what we go through."

Jojo turns towards the window. His back is in the same slump it was whenever he was belittled as a teen. Then his voice, deeper and more bitter than I've ever heard it, breathes out, "I just can't see what it is about us that those dumb motherfuckers hate so much. I have been wracking my brain, but that is the one question that does not have an answer."

"You want an answer?" Peep's strong voice booms, his face flaming with fury. He bolts up from his chair and forcefully turns Jojo to face him. "Now, you listen to me! Corey just gave you the answer. Stupid people breed stupid people. And just as sure as we are all standing here in this hospital, it will never get easy for us. That stupidity is never going to go away. You can live in your Candy Land fantasy all you want to, but you would just be doing more damage to yourself than anybody else. Accept that, stick your chest out, and grow the fuck up!" Speechless, Jojo looks around the room, as if he lost something and was wearily trying to find it. Peep becomes conscious of his force. He relaxes and massages the back of Jojo's neck. "I'm sorry for shouting. I know this is eating you up, but questioning other people's fucked up issues is not going to help, baby. Never has and never will."

Jojo looks at him and me, with sadness. Then his eyes rest on Corey, who has his arms up and open. "Come here, Jojo."

Jojo goes to him and takes his hands.

"To hell with that hand shit, baby. You can hug me, yuh know. I still got one working side. You can lean on that."

Jojo bends down and hugs him. Corey's arms hold Jojo tighter. As I watch him hold my childhood friend, love for him fills my heart. In all the facets I've seen Corey in, this is the side of him lesser shown. He shows it in abundance to Jojo. Many a day I wished he would show it more to Peep and me. Not brash. Not loud. Not defensive. But, comforting, loving, and nurturing. Then I thought, *Wait a minute! We are the ones that ought to be comforting him, not the other way around!*

As I hear Jojo weeping, Corey says to him, "Alright now. You only get to cry but so long in here. Listen, baby, this is life… and in life, shit is gonna happen. I can't ultimately answer the question as to why they hate us. That chaos started long before we were born. But I will ask *you* this. Get up, wipe those tears, and look at me."

Jojo pulls back and looks at him.

"Am I dead?"

"No."

"Am I still moving?"

"Yeah."

"Can bones, black eyes, and stab wounds heal?"

"Yeah."

"Well, there you go. I ain't dead, baby. I went through a lot worse. I went through stuff that if I told you, it would turn you straight… and with your ass being more fish than me, that's sayin' a lot!"

Jojo laughs tearfully, wiping his tears with the back of his hand. Corey joins him laughing softly. Then he goes on. "Yes, they hate us. We can't change that, but we can't let them make us hate ourselves. Do you hate yourself?"

"No!"

"Well, alright then! That's what I'm talking about. We're going to get our gorgeous asses in gear and we're go'n keep it moving. You with me?"

After a gulf of silence, Jojo smiles and says, "All the way, baby," Jojo embraces him again. Peep and I join in the hug.

After a few moments, Corey clears his throat and bellows, "Alright now. Gimme some room! I'm glad y'all quit crying like some wet-diapered babies. Now, y'all get the fuck out before Nurse Hatchet-face comes back in and scares everybody to death."

"Are you going to be alright?" I ask.

"Please… This is Corey you're talking to. Of course, I am!"

"You want me to bring you anything tomorrow," Peep volunteers.

"Well, can you sneak me up some Jack?"

"Jack?"

"Uh, yeah! As in Jack Daniels. You know, they call it whiskey."

"Uh, you will *not* be getting that," Peep says.

"Party pooper! Then get me my phone and charger from Alex. And go to my house and get my tablet so I can watch some movies. Can't do anything with my left hand. But I sho' as hell can do something with my right!"

"Ew!" Jojo lets out laughing. "You are one nasty old bitch!"

"And I'll be one until I'm a dead old bitch!"

"Whatever! Bye," Jojo answers as he and Peep exits out of the room.

"You are a crazy ass! Do you know that?" I tell him.

"And you are a naïve ass! Do you know *that*?"

"Who are you calling naïve?"

"You. I swear you and Jojo got that same rosy look about the world. I'm surprised y'all don't have fairy dust to make yuh happy asses fly!"

"Still the trash talker huh."

"You know it! In all seriousness though, as evolved as this world is, there are still a lot of people that are not going to be receptive to us. Like Peep said, it ain't gonna get any easier. We will still have gay bashers, physically like the ones who kicked Jojo's and my ass and mentally, like the mind ass kicking your family is giving you. You and Jojo gotta toughen up." Corey's voice breaks as he continues, "Because if y'all keep traveling down this primrose path where everything seems flowery, you gonna get some thorns in your asses."

"Whatever."

"I'm serious. This is our reality. We gotta accept it and be strong in ourselves. But old Corey can't be strong for all of y'all, because old Corey got weaknesses and issues too. Do you hear what I'm telling yuh?"

"Yeah."

"Good. Now, get on outta here. Talk to that fine ass Garrett. I wish I had tried to talk to him first, but I got a good feeling about him. You are coming back tomorrow, right?"

"Of course!"

"Good, then you can give me the 411 on your little date!"

"Nosy ass!"

"Kiss-Kiss, bitch!"

"Kiss, ho'!"

I start for the door and open it. I pass through it. But before it closes, I glimpse Corey's profile as he stares at the ceiling. The tears waiting to fall from his moistened eyes, the crumpled look on his face, the pulse of his jawline jumping. When the door finally closes, I hear beeping machines, nurses chattering and having lively, humorous conversations, doctors ordering tests in their medical jargon. But none of these are as loud as the sound of a gay battered man sobbing at the hatred of society and the horrors of a trampled life. A broken and dejected man crying himself to fitful and anguished sleep.

I walk by the desk and watch as the hospital receptionist brings in a huge bouquet of red roses. She sets it on the counter and says, "Clarice, can you give these to Mr. Kennedy?"

"Sure, girl. Who are they from?"

"Hell, if I know! Some tall, wiry, coal-complected fella about 6'4 came by my lobby with these roses and asked me to bring them up. I asked him why he couldn't take them himself. He said he wanted it to remain anonymous."

Anonymous? The features are familiar. Could she be talking about Garrett?

CHAPTER NINE:

"NECESSARY CONVERSATIONS"

Well, I can't say my three weeks after Corey's attack were the best I have ever had. For starters, a week before the bashing, I got stuck with the Nightmare Client from Hell. He is twenty-one years old and still has nut on the brain. He kept changing his mind about *everything*! He is the creator of "Jump!" Cologne and boy, that cologne is awful as fuck. It matches his arrogant and condescending personality. He wanted me to try it out to prove how good it was. Now this is where I tell myself that I really value my job, because on Wednesday I substituted my regular smell good for that manure in a bottle. The attention I had received due to my new wardrobe was halted, because the second people smelled that scent coming from me, they made a point of walking the other way. Well, I switched back to what I knew, and my pulling power returned. Ha!

The campaign? Well, he wanted a forest scene where a man was swinging on vines like Tarzan, rescuing Jane from some calamity. After he saves her, she melts in his arms and says, 'What a man. Rescues like a man. Looks like a man. And (sniff sniff) smells like a man! Take me!" Then she swoons and "The Man" looks in the camera with a seductive smile and then jumps high with her in his arms as the picture freezes and fades into white with the words, "JUMP! Like a man!" Corny, right? Anyway, the storyboards for the commercial were already designed, and here he comes with another idea for replacement. This one involved a man entering a Wild West saloon and five women falling all over him talking about how manly he smells and they all kiss his face at the same time. Then he runs out of the saloon and down the street towards the sunset where he jumps, shouts, "YAA-HOO!" and kicks his heels together while the picture freezes and the same slogan comes up. The Storyboards are done, but *again* he has another different idea. After a month of this nonsense, I sat down with Mr. Alexander and told him that there is no way I could further work with this client because he was indecisive, impulsive, and implacable. It was on the tip of my tongue to say that his cologne was trash, and he should be the last one talking about manliness when his mannerisms are more fish than Flipper.

Garrett and I haven't seen each other since our tennis match, but we talked by phone almost every day. We talked about life and shared our stories. He told me about how he was picked on in middle school because he was skinny, had glasses with thick goggle lenses, and a terrible stutter. But once he and his family moved from down south and he became a freshman in high school, he developed an interest in lifting weights and playing football. He practically begged his mother to get him contacts and once he got them, he started lifting weights and toning up. At his mother's advice, he began weighing what he said before he said it, which considerably helped with his stuttering. Suddenly both the girls *and* the guys started taking notice of him.

I asked him about his first encounter. His voice had a funny pause to it as he asked to tell me about another experience because he didn't want to relive that one. After I consented, he said that at thirteen, he and his best friend traded oral sex and afterwards it became a regular and enjoyable pastime between the two of them, as well as a door opener to get to know each other better. He had love in his voice when he said that. When he got on the football team, he met a closeted teammate who further taught him the joys of anal sex and foreplay between two men. The affair lasted until their junior year. I in turn shared with him my story of how I was introduced to the life. I could tell he was shocked at how I knew nothing of masturbation until thirteen. Of course, we talked about other things too. We were on the phone for three hours one night, and we had to reluctantly hang up the phone when we became conscious of the time. Honestly though, as far as where we are romantically, it's hard to tell. While I find myself sexually attracted to him, I don't feel as though we would make a good fit as a couple. I notice many different drawbacks, one of them being that he can sometimes be a bit opinionated.

I found this out when we were discussing the hard issues concerning us as a race, starting with the genocide of our Black people. I lamented how disgusted I was to watch the news and see another innocent Black teen gunned down or choked by the police. He said that if the victims would put up zero resistance during the arrest, they would have the opportunity to talk with their lawyers upon their release and learn to fight within the system. Now this is something Corey and I battled about constantly. I pointed out to him that nowadays the percentage of Black men surviving that long is rapidly dropping, to which he replied, "That is very sad, but that shows that we need to come together as a race and when the murder is at the cop's hands, it's up to us to fight to bring the responsible parties to justice." While I agreed on us coming together, I felt the need to remind him about that asshole, Zimmerman, who was acquitted of the murder of Trayvon Martin because of a racist system geared against people of African descent. That was the first of our many debates during that month, but we would always end them by focusing on a general truth that made sense and gave us common ground.

I also noticed that our conversations led back to Corey. I am convinced now that he's more than a bit infatuated and he sent the flowers. Color me jealous. I did not share of my knowledge about the "secret" admirer, but I told him about the attack during one of these conversations and the line went silent for a few seconds. Then he spoke, "I know. Ricardo told me the day after it happened. It sickens me that Corey had to endure that, and that we as gay men have to hear about crap like that. I wish I knew who did it. I'd go fuck him up."

"Forgive me for saying this. But I thought, with your usual rationale, that you would think of something that Corey could've done to prevent it."

"What do you mean?"

"I mean, in the conversations that we have had, you would play Devil's advocate, trying to see things from both sides, and you would state your own opinion."

"And I'm stating it now. Just like those white police officers have no right in taking our innocent black folks' lives, those punks had no right to beat up Corey for being who he is, a proud Black gay man. I think Corey has more balls than any of those sexually insecure cowards put together."

"I agree. But, I'd like to hear your reason as to why."

"Well, it takes *cajones* to be who you are unapologetically. Many of us spend too much time trying to fit into other people's expectations and demands. I like and respect a man who knows who he is and does not dim his candle to match everyone else's darkness."

"With that being stated, why are you so afraid to tell your mother about who you really are?"

"I guess I walked into that one."

"You really did. You seem so poised with every other area in your life. But that is the one thing you take issue with."

"I'm working my way up to it. Giving her clues, but she is not catching the hints."

"Have you ever considered the possibility that she already knows and that she's waiting for you to just come clean and tell her?"

"That thought did cross my mind."

"Mm-hmm. Now, I'm not telling you what you need to do. But I am saying for you to think about it. It may do more help than harm."

"You're probably right."

"I know I'm right."

"Do you think there is a possibility that I can have lunch with you and your friends? I would like to properly meet them, especially Corey."

Um hmm. He likes Corey! I chuckle to myself as I replay my feelings of jealousy and realize how ridiculous they are, especially after pulling back from getting into another relationship. "I don't see why not. We need to give Corey some space, though. He's trying to process what happened and he's not too keen on communication right now, even with his best friends."

*****

I managed between the drama on my job and phone joys of talking to my now friend, Garrett, to workout with Peep and Jojo. That's where we are now, on a hot ass Friday evening. I skipped lunch because of a meeting at the office with a potential client. This workout is kicking my ass and I am starting to feel dizzy, but I press on. I kept mums on Garrett's burgeoning infatuation with Corey. In fact, when they bring Garrett up, I change the subject, which I know is driving Peep crazy. We've been having many conversations while on the ellipticals, and they are all centered around what to do about Corey. I suppose he is recuperating from the accident. But none of us heard anything from him for the past month. The attack really did a number on his mind. All three of us went by to see him but he wouldn't let us in. He just called through the door and said he was fine and to go away. Last week, I used my key to try to open the door, but the door wouldn't budge. I called to Corey, but I heard nothing. This worried me so much that I called Dr. Camden, and she said that this was to be expected considering his trauma, and that it would pass.

Although none of us want to bring it up, we reflect on what would've happened if we were in that situation. Would there have been any escape? Would we retreat behind a wall of fragile protection? How much would we break? We all can see that a part of Corey's spirit broke under the blows. Our Corey, the bold, quick wit, life of the party, was now afraid of his own shadow. But how can we help him? It despairs me to see him like this. Moreover, I am getting these feelings that there are some issues that surfaced before we all met, and he kept them from us. I felt it that night when I left his hospital room; and saw the look of dejection and hopelessness in his silhouette. It was saying, "What else am I going to be faced with?" My friend had built up this imaginary wall of the past to keep even us out. He laid it brick and mortar. But now he is so ensnared that he can't even step outside the literal bricks of his home.

Also, I think about Jojo. I look at him as we step off the ellipticals. I have felt that same feeling for him. It went far past what happened with Andre and his gang. My friends are keeping secrets that are killing them inside. But then, I look at Peep, and he always exudes a happiness that is unexplainable, a contentment with his life, and a man that loves him. What did he do that we are not doing? What phenomenal facet of life has he found that has always alluded us? How did he learn to love himself? He seems so free with his life, while Corey and Jojo are trapped by their secrets

"TAKE IT AWAY FROM HIM, JESUS!"

Suddenly, the words echo through my brain, and at this moment I realize that I have a painful, dirty secret of my own.

"REMOVE HIS SICKNESS! HEAL HIM OF HIS DISEASE!"

I feel the world retreat as I fall to the floor and black out. Bathed in dream-like red hue, I hear my mother's voice.
I see the cross with Jesus nailed on it.
I feel my mother's hand on my neck, forcing me to my knees.
I see the pastor pouring oil over my head. The oil blurs my vision. My mother forces me to say the words.

"I will not be gay!"
"I WILL NOT BE GAY!"
"I WILL NOT BE GAY!"

I see the pastor yelling at me with his hand on the top of my head. "PRAY, LIONEL! GOD IS NOT PLEASED! YOU ARE TURNING INTO A HOMOSEXUAL AND GOD DESPISES HOMOSEXUALITY!"

I hear the words faintly escape from my lips, "Lord, help me not be gay."

"PRAY HARDER TO THE LORD!"

"Lord, help me not be gay!"

"PRAY HARDER TO GOD! PRAY LIKE YOU MEAN IT!

"LORD, HELP ME NOT TO BE GAY!"

"YOU ARE NOT PRAYING HARD ENOUGH! LIONEL! LIONEL! LIONEL! Lionel!"

"Lionel, can you hear me? Wake Up. Lionel!"

My eyes flutter open. I see my friends, Peep at my head and Jojo, bending over my side. Quite a crowd has built up around me, witnessing the commotion.

"Thank God! Are you okay?" Jojo lets out in a panicky voice.
"What happened?"
"You fell and blacked out on us. You've been out for fifteen minutes," Peep breathes out.
"I was?"
"Uh, Yeah?"
Suddenly, I hear Corey's voice. "Where is he! Where's Lion?"
As Jojo and Peep support me to sitting position and leaning me against the massive post, I blearily focus my eyes on my friend, Corey, kneeling in front of me. He looks thinner and has unkempt hair, chapped lips, and bloodshot eyes.
"I'm okay."

"Oh my God, you scared the holy fuck out of me! I worried all the way over here." He grabbed me and hugged me tightly.

"I'm ok."

"Baby, did you eat anything today?" Peep questions

"I had a big salad and some water this morning."

"Lion, you need more sustenance to do these workouts. You been lifting weights, drinking water, and exercising today, but you overexerted yourself."

"I know, I was just in such a rush to leave the house and get to the office, and I had to work through lunch. I thought I would get something after the workout."

"Lion," Corey says, "What the fuck is wrong with you? You, of all people, should know that it is risky to be running on fumes."

Concerned, Jojo says, "Baby, you are done for today. You are going home right now!" He tries to help me up, but I wave him away.

"Come on, y'all. I'm not an invalid! I just need to eat something and get back to the house." We walk out the door, my friends still on either side of me holding me up. I look at Corey. "And speaking of houses, let me ask *you* something."

"What?"

"Why did I have to fall and blackout for you to leave your house?"

"Oh, shut up, bitch! You were in trouble. Be glad I got here!"

"Well, somebody is sounding like himself!" Jojo says. They all support me as they lower me into the backseat of my car.

"Please, Old Corey wasn't go'n stay down for long. You oughta know that. I just needed some time."

"First, we tend to Lion," Peep says. "Then we kick your ass for making us worry!"

"Cool, as long as you kiss it before and after!" Corey says, getting in his car.

"Corey, we love you dearly. But this is one time your joking will not work," Peep interjects indignantly, getting in the driver's seat. "Follow us to Lion's house. You've got some explaining to do. Not leaving your house for a month. Not letting us in to help you. And when you do come out, you look like a wino on Prohibition. Oh, yes, mister! You've got some explaining to do!"

"Just lay back, baby. Don't move," Jojo says, as his lap cradles my head and his hand caresses my forehead. I relax in the coolness of the night air, blowing on my skin. It is as sweet as Jojo's lips kissing my face.

*****

Back at my house, I'm in my living room eating a sandwich slowly with all three of my friends surrounding me. Corey is sitting beside me talking about his ordeal. His voice has a dreamlike quality.

"I felt unsafe. I was holding it in for y'all in the hospital but I guess it was delayed reaction. When Alex brought me back home and I saw that tag, for the first time in years, I felt dreadful... fearful... depressed. I walked in that house and tried to sleep but the tag was in my dreams." He pauses, tears streaming down. Then he went on. "I started sleeping with a bottle of whiskey and a loaded 35. in the side drawer of my bed. I got so paranoid about everything that I put deadbolts on all my doors. I couldn't walk outside at all. The fear was just that strong. So, I put in a request to the university and the church for stress leave. I still gave piano lessons to my out of school students, but in my house. When I needed groceries, I had one of my students bring them. I had an appointment with the psychiatrist Dr. Camden referred me to, but I couldn't go. I kept saying that I would reschedule, but never did. I tried to walk out that door so many times, but every time I did I saw 'Death to all Faggots!' Even when the painter came... stripped and repainted the door, it was like I could still see it. I felt like the walls were closing in on me. I couldn't breathe. I could barely move."

"What made you come out today? How did you hear that Lion blacked out?" Peep inquires.

"Kenneth Sellers, that police officer, saw that you passed out in the gym and called me, I didn't even think about the tag. All I could think was that you were in trouble and I rushed out the door, got in my car, and sped down Northern Parkway." I tried to comfort him by putting my hand on his, but Corey pulls away. The tears began steadily streaming down his dull cheeks.

He gets up and walks to my bookcase. He rests his hand on the shelf. We hear choked sobs. "I don't know if I can deal with this, y'all... Jojo, you asked a question in the hospital. 'Why do they hate us?' That question turned in my mind ever since you brought it up, and it bothers me that even the answer I gave in that room is not the absolute answer, only a portion of it. It scares me shitless."

"Why didn't you come to us? You have friends who care. Why did you shut yourself away from us?" Jojo questions.

"Because there are battles that I have to fight on my own, and those battles have nothing to do with you."

"Yeah," Peep says. "But you can only last but so long when you continue building walls around yourself."

"There are some walls that are necessary."

"That is the most ridiculous thing I have ever heard."

"Yeah, it would be." Corey lashes out, turning sideways to glare at Peep, "Coming from someone who has everything he could possibly want and thinks he can diagnose others' conditions when he has absolutely no clue. Don't tell me I'm being ridiculous. You haven't been where I've been or gone through what I did."

Peep crosses the room and stands next to Corey. "Look here. I am not trying to diagnose you. I am only trying to help you. We all are. But you can't say that we haven't been there, so you *could* share what's bothering you. Let's not forget, you shut *us* out! It wasn't the other way around, and now you have the nerve to tell us that we haven't been where you've been. How would we know that if you don't tell us?"

"Peep, calm down," I say. "This is still fresh for Corey."

Peep relaxes his voice. "All I'm saying is that we are here to help you, but if you don't want to discuss it with us, then maybe you need to discuss it with someone who *is* qualified to figure out what you are dealing with."

"Yeah," I chime in. "Corey, you know we love you and you can tell us anything. But, whether you tell us or not, I think you need to see someone not vested in the situation. Maybe you should call Dr. Lofton and reschedule that appointment like Dr. Camden said."

"I don't want them in my business."

"So, you are gonna let your business drag you down?" Jojo says. "Not cool at all."

"Jojo, you are the last person to talk. With all the fucked-up shit you told me about Lion's brother and that scumbag stepfather of yours." Jojo's face freezes in hurt.

"What?" I am shocked.

"I gotta go." He starts for the door.

"No, no, no. Wait. What happened with Mike?"

"Just forget it. I gotta get out of here," Jojo cries as he tries to open the door to leave. Before it opens an inch, I slam my hand on it to close it.

"Jojo, you are not going anywhere. You can't just run away and hide when you are hurting. You did that shit when we were kids. It hasn't worked then, and it will not work now." I take note of my tone. It is a little too forceful. I calm down, putting my hand on his shoulder.

"Jojo, you don't have to tell us what happened. But please stay," Peep requests tenderly.

Jojo sits with his head hanging down. "Now, back to you," I said to Corey, "What is wrong with you? We are not the ones for you to lash out at. We know you are hurting right now, but that does not give you license to hurt others, especially those in your corner."

"I'm sorry."

"Lionel and I are not the one you need to apologize to. Talk to him," Peep says, pointing at Jojo. "He is the one you hurt."

Corey pauses, looking at Jojo. He goes and sits down beside him. I can feel the hesitation as his hand falters and rests on Jojo's knee. Jojo looks up at him.

"I was wrong."

"You're damn right you were!"

Pause.

"You didn't deserve that."

"Right again."

Pause.

"I didn't mean to hurt you."

Pause. "But you did."

Corey hangs his head in shame. "You got a bad habit of kicking where it hurts sometimes. Not often, but enough to make me question where it is coming from."

"I'm sorry."

Jojo puts his hand on top of Corey's and rubs it. "I understand. You are dealing with a tough time right now. I know this feeling. It sucks. But when you operate out of hurt and go firing darts at people, nothing good can come out of it. You just hurt more folk."

"I know."

"I'm glad you know."

"So, we cool now?" Corey asks hopefully, looking at Jojo.

"Yes, of course," Jojo assents. "But you know you are going to have to make this up to me, don't you?"

"An apology is not enough?"

"Uh, no. A good start. But, no. Your atonement is twofold. The apology was the first half. I need a favor for the other."

"I'm listening."

"Go to that psychiatrist."

"Wrong answer!" Corey says as he jumps up.

"Look Corey," Peep demands. "All this anger is coming from somewhere and you need to examine the root of it."

"Right," I jump in. "I think it really might help. If nothing else, you get to release all this static you held in for so long. It helped me in that support group, sort of."

"And talking with a shrink has done wonders for me," Peep follows.

All three of us stare at Peep. We never even pictured him going to a shrink.

"Uh, you want to run that by us again?" Jojo asks.

"Yeah. I mean, to look at you, you would never know you had problems," Corey observes.

"Guilt issues concerning my Grandmother's death. I started going after Corey's attack. I had that issue, and lest we forget, the hurt surrounding that hypocritical church and the preacher that damned me to hell before I married Jimmy. But I'm dealing with it. And just to let you know, seeing a psychiatrist doesn't mean you are crazy. You just have somebody to talk to, and to avoid a lawsuit for breach of ethics, they are under obligation to keep that shit to themselves."

"Right," I agree. "You've got to talk about this stuff to somebody. Why not a professional? If you don't want to go to Dr. Lofton, we'll help you find a counsellor that you're comfortable with that takes your insurance."

Corey blows out air from his mouth. After a lengthy silence, he says, "I've been putting it off for a while. I guess now is as good a time as any to do it. But, I just want to go on record in saying that I have my reservations about doing this."

"Would it help if I went with you?" I ask.

"How can *you* go with me? You already took a lot of time off work dealing with your own depression. I wouldn't want you to get in trouble with your boss."

"Don't worry about it. We just got a new client. But I'll do a huge chunk of work on the day before and ask Mr. Alexander for half a day so I can go with you to your appointment."

Corey assents, "OK. I'll call Dr. Lofton and make the appointment."

"When?" Peep inquires.

"Tomorrow."

"Why not today?"

"Because it's after five. He wouldn't be in the office now."

"Uh, Corey. Newsflash. These doctors do have answering services to schedule your appointment. Quit stalling and call him."

"OK, OK! I'll call," Corey says, pulling out his phone buts Peep stop him after looking closely at him.

"Uh, before we call anybody. You are taking me back to the gym to get my car and we are going to my house and getting you together, baby. You smell ripe. Your face looks ashy and your breath is humming!" Peep stops then looks him over. "Now, I done told Lion about the layered look, and here you are dressing in it. Oh no, chile'! That ain't go'n do!"

"Shut the hole in your face," Corey exclaims, smirking as he goes to the door. "Lion, I'll call you later tonight to let you know when the appointment is."

"I'm holding you to that."

"He will. Trust me!" Peep says.

They both say their goodbyes and walk out the door. Jojo gets up and prepares to leave, "I'd better go too. I have some work to catch up on."

"Uh, Jojo?"

"Yeah?"

"Are you ever going to tell me about what happened with Mike?" *Silence.*

"I will. I promise. But just not now."

"OK, then. I respect that."

"Thank you." He walks to the door and opens it. Then he turns to look back at me. After a long look, he says, "Maybe I ought to follow my own advice and see a therapist. Some shit is hard to deal with on my own."

"Well, it bears thinking about. Just don't overthink it."

"You're right," Jojo says. "You going to be ok? You know you just scared everybody at the gym, not to mention your best friends."

"Oh, I'm ok. I got some leftovers in the fridge."

"OK. Well, c'mere and gimme love."

I walk over and embrace him. Then as we draw apart, we gaze unwaveringly into each other's eyes. I feel sparks flying between us, barely breathing. The unmistakable sexual tension hangs in the air. But he steps closer to me to kiss me sweetly on the cheek, caress my face, then walk out into the night air. I stand at the door, unable to move as I watch him walk slowly up Bolton Street.

"Hey Jojo!" I call out.

"Yeah?" He replies, turning around.

"Wait up. I'm coming with you. It's too late for you to be walking around."

"I just live a subway ride away from here. It's not that far."

"I know that. I would just feel better. I'll drive you. Let me lock my doors."

*****

We drove to his place. When we got to his townhome, we just sat on the stoop and let our voices weave a strong fabric in the loom of the night. We talked about our insecurities, our never-ending abyss of loneliness, and our endless stream of casual encounters.

"What do you think could be the reason for why we are still single?" Jojo asks.

"Beats me. You know, I think we are too busy trying to get a man that we are not taking time to focus on things that we should. Now I don't think there is anything wrong with us. We are just caught up in the turbulent scenes of dating. Nowadays, everyone is looking for sex. We all forget the time when you actually had to get to know the person before you slept with them."

"What time was that?"

"I don't know but there had to have been one. Remember when we were going to school. We didn't have these apps that we have now like Grindr, Jack'd, and Scruff. The net was just coming out."

"Ah, the good old days of dial up AOL."

"100 hours."

"No, 500 hours," Jojo counters.

"And, it always made that annoying high-pitched noise when connecting."

"Yeah." *Silence.* A thought crossed my mind and I had to ask him what the deal was with Mike.

"Jojo?"

"What?"

"I know you don't want to tell me what happened with Mike."

"You're right. I don't... right now."

"But, I'm curious. Why?"

"Too painful."

"He abused you, didn't he?"

He looks at the ground, melancholy in his eyes. Then he closes them and nods his head.

"I knew that already."

"What?"

"Yeah."

"How?"

"I remember you coming to school with bruises, and all of them didn't come from bullies. I also know that Mike was beating on your mother. I remember the day all of that ended too."

"Again, I am confused as to how?"

"Well, I was playing catch with Andre, and I heard all of this commotion coming from your house. I heard Ms. Thompson crying, and the sound of someone hitting her over and over. The sound stopped. But then I heard a dull thud hit the ground and Ms. Thompson was screaming. I saw Mike rush out through the back door, out of breath and crazed. I smelled fear on him and I had a feeling that something else happened other than a random beating. When he ran away, and I was sure he was at a safe distance, I dropped my ball and went to the screen door on your back porch. Through the screen, I saw you lying on the ground with blood oozing from a bad cut. You were unconscious. Ms. Thompson was trying to revive you and crying the whole time. I called out her name and she turned and saw me. She told me to go into the living room and call the paramedics. Andre flagged them down and led them to the back door. I gotta tell ya. He looked even more distraught than we were. They came, loaded you into the ambulance, and drove away."

Meditating, Jojo touched his scar. "It took me a long time to recover after that."

"I know."

"I had nightmares about him for years after he left. I remember when I was in the hospital for three days, and he came to beg my mother's forgiveness. She told him to look at my forehead. He, coward to the end, couldn't look. She told him that she wanted him out of the house and to take his shit with him. He pushed her so hard that her back hit the wall. He would have beaten her up in the hospital room if my Uncle Rodney hadn't heard the noise and rushed in to see what was going on. He took one look at Mama and me and went crazy. He knocked Mike to the floor and straddled his neck as he smashed his face to a pulp. Doctors, nurses, and security guards came on the run. They pulled Uncle Rodney off of him. He stood and told him this. 'Now, that is what a real ass whoopin' feels like… and you'll get a lot worse if you come near them again.' I guess that worked because when we got back home, all his things were gone."

"No wonder Ms. Thompson never married after that."

"Right. I asked her about that and she said that marriage wasn't in the cards."

A long pause. Suddenly, my cell rings.

"Hello?"

"Hey, this is Corey."

"Hey, you alright?"

"Yeah, at Peep's getting a facial and a cut. The appointment is next Friday."

"Oh, well that's good. I usually only have to work half a day on Fridays."

"I know. That's why I made it then."

"Good thinking."

I hear Peep's voice, "Alright now. You done told him about your appointment, now hang up the phone and come get your facial."

"You heard that, right?" Corey queries.

"I heard. I'll holla at you tomorrow."

"Ok. Kiss-Kiss, baby."

"Kiss."

I hit end on my phone and I catch Jojo in deep thought.

"Care to share what's on your mind?"

"Just puzzled about something. You said Andre flagged the ambulance down and led them to the back and that he looked distraught."

"Yeah."

"I thought Andre hated me."

"He didn't. Unbelievably, he does have a soul when he takes the notion to show it."

"Then why did he and that gang pick on me and beat me up that day?"

"Three words. Young, teenaged, and stupid. I get the feeling that Andre liked you, although he was trying to break bad in front of his friends."

Phone rings. "Hello?"

"Lionel, this is Dean." A raspy voice replies.

"What's going on?"

"Nothing much. Are you busy?"

"I'm hanging with Jojo."

"Oh, ok. Should I call back later?"

I gesture to Jojo that this would be brief. He nods.

"No, what's going on?"

"Well, you know Mama has to have an operation and I was calling to ask you to pay for it, and we pay you back."

"Right, and I'm going to tell you the same thing I told Rhonda. I will pay one fourth of the cost, and not before getting proof that everybody else has paid theirs."

"We don't have the time to wait for everyone to come up with their share. We run the risk of her not having the operation at all, which means more pain she has to deal with."

"I'm sorry, but those are my terms."

"I don't remember Mama having "terms" when she brought you into this world."

"She didn't bring me into this world. I am dead to her, remember? I tried to be a good son to her. Over the years, I ended up paying bills of hers that you, Andre, and Rhonda claimed to be too busy or too broke to help pay. Even after she wrote that letter to renounce me, I called her for Mother's Day and that went down in flames." I look around and see Jojo. He's looking a little on the shocked side.

"I have been nothing but a good son to her. But my personal life is the one thing she cannot control. That is the reason she is ready to spit tacks."

"Look, let's put your personal life aside for a minute. She may have disowned you, that's true. But that doesn't give you the right to disown her. She *is* our mother. Did you hear what I just said? *Our* mother, Lionel."

"Dean, I have to go."

"Ok, I'll let you go, but I want to leave this with you, Lionel. Family oughta come first sometimes."

"Not when family fucked me over constantly. You have been saying that shit for years and I am sick of it."

"Lionel, let's be fair. It is true that you helped pay for a lot of Mama's bills. I'll give you that, but you were not the only one paying them. I paid a lot of them as well, and I got a drawer full of receipts to prove it."

"Three words, Dean: tax write off!"

A hush comes over the line. I can feel that Dean is hurt by my words. Of all my brother and sisters, Dean and I were incredibly close. I feel a pang in my conscience.

In a calmer voice, I say, "I'm sorry, Dean. I didn't mean that. If I feel any different before the operation, and that is a big 'if', you will be among the first to know."

"Ok bro."

"Bye, Dean."

"Bye."

I sit back down beside Jojo. After a pause, Jojo says cautiously, "Uh, Lion. I couldn't help but overhear."

"I'm just tired of having to come to the family's rescue all the time."

"I know."

"They drain the hell outta me."

"I know that too." Silence abounds. I catch his hesitant profile.

"Uh oh... where is this conversation going?"

"What do you mean?"

"What I mean is you are working up the courage to tell me something. I know that look."

"You would be right. I think you ought to help your mother."

I can't believe my ears! "What, why?"

"Lion, you've gotta treat folks right, even when they treat you wrong. I am not just telling you a Christian, Buddhist, or Taoist principle. I am telling you a simple truth. When you treat cold-hearted people right, you teach them how to be with their neighbor, especially those who claim to know what's right but don't endeavor to do it."

"What about the screwed-up shit that these cold-hearted people do?"

"Well, that shit is *their* shit! Fling it off you and watch *them* clean it up."

"Maybe you're right."

"Besides, this will show you if she was for real in what she said. If you pay for this, and she's still the same, then kiss her goodbye and just walk away."

"And if she wasn't?"

"Then, let her know that although you love her, you are living life on your terms. Only God has the final say in your life. Not her, not the preachers who pontificate, and surprisingly, not even Corey, Peep, Garrett, or me."

I chuckle. "I wonder, who are you sometimes?"

"Meaning?"

"Meaning, there's the vulnerable person I saw in the hospital and at my house, and this philosopher you're showing me now."

"What can I say, I'm multi-faceted!"

I playfully shove him on the shoulder as we smile and look at the stars past the Hippodrome Theater.

"You know what?" Jojo says.

"What?"

"I was talking to a friend of mine from Atlanta, and he told me of this cruise that goes out October 20th through the 27th of this year."

"Who cruises in October?"

"Some do. It's called Rainbow Pride Cruise, and it was first started by some friends who went on annual weekend trips and over the years it grew and grew. This year, they say they are occupying the entire ship."

"Not one of those gay cruises, Jojo!"

"Just hear me out, will you please? It's for a whole week. Sunday to Sunday. You have talent shows, parties, motivational speakers, comedians, and the chance to get to know other people like us."

"We meet other guys like us whenever we go to the Link. You know what a meat market that place is. The only difference with this is that the meat market is floating on a boat."

"You can't look at it like that. It's not just an all-male cruise. There are women up there too. Lesbians tend to lighten the air more than bitchy queens with male physiques. Also, from what I heard, there are not just gay or bisexual couples. Surprisingly, there are straight people going who are secure in themselves and loving of everybody."

"So, everybody's gonna be on the ship singing, "Kum-ba-ya?" I say, laughing.

"Listen, Lionel. Have you ever been on a cruise?"

"No."

"And you know I have never been."

"No, you haven't."

"My cousin Vera went on one, and she said it was a lot of fun. It might be nice to look out on a watery horizon and seeing the sea in it's blue-green color. They also have excursions where you can see what happens underwater."

"Well, it sounds tempting."

"Look, I think it could serve as a distraction for all of us. With you still nursing a breakup, Corey being gay-bashed, me with my crazy ass boss, and Peep dealing with Irene and her issues, this distraction could be right on the money."

"That's another thing. Money. Aren't these cruises expensive?"

"Have you ever seen a vacation that *wasn't* expensive?"

"Point taken."

"The way I see it, it's worth the money. Let us not forget, we celebrate our birthdays on that Saturday, October 26th. Besides, I figure we can get two cabins. One for you and me, and one for Corey and Peep."

"And what if Jimmy wants to go?"

"Then Peep and Jimmy can get an extra room."

"Hmmm... Wait a minute. What about Corey?"

"Oh, we'll work something out."

I think it over. The prospect sounds good. After a minute, I say while standing up to go, "OK. Let's meet with the fellas tomorrow. You bring your laptop to pull up the website and we'll go on from there."

"Ok." Jojo stands in front of me.

Silence. We both look at the ground, Then at each other. I can feel my manhood beginning to take weight and stiffen. I clasped my hands in front of me, trying to hide my telltale sign. He looks down at my hands then into my eyes, smiling.

"Well..." Jojo breathes out.

"Well..."

"I guess I'd better go inside."

"Yeah. I gotta get home myself."

"I noticed you didn't have anything other than that sandwich. Stop and get something before you go home."

"I promise I will."

"Good night, Lion." He goes up the steps and into his house. He grants me a beautiful and bright smile, then shuts the door.

The night air caresses my face and makes me drunk with pleasure as I say to the door, "Good night, Jojo... *I love you.*"

CHAPTER TEN:

"MAKING PLANS"

The previously mentioned "tomorrow" turned into almost two weeks. Everyone was just so busy. There didn't seem to be enough time to introduce the cruise idea. Garrett suddenly went silent on me. No calls. No texts. I am starting to worry. The fellas and I are all sitting outside at City Café on Cathedral. It is great to see Corey out of the house, being as gregarious as ever. But Corey is less than enthusiastic about the cruise, and that's putting it mildly. Peep is interested, somewhat.

"Have you lost your mind? There is no way that I'm getting on a boat and making myself sick! Absolutely not!" Corey exclaims, upon hearing Jojo mention it.

"Hmmm… It's been a long while since I've been on a cruise."

I am surprised. "You've been before?"

"Lots of times when I was younger. My grandparents used to take me almost every summer. I had a lot of fun. My only problem is whether my Jimmy would want me on a boat with an array of shirtless black men who can tempt the hell outta me."

"I don't think that would be something you would have to worry about," I observe.

"Especially if he were to go with you," Jojo says.

"Now *I'm* starting to think you have lost your mind!"

"Besides, it is June 27th. The final payment is due on July first," Corey points out.

"It's no problem. I did the math. To go on this cruise, it will be nineteen hundred per cabin for a balcony. I figured that we can do two cabins, or three if Jimmy wants to go."

"What would be the rooming situation?" Corey asks.

"Well, me and Jojo would be in one room, and you and Peep would be in another room. Now if Jimmy wants to go, he and Peep would be in a room together and we will just have to find somebody to room with you."

"Oh, that is making me feel better and better," Corey says sarcastically. "And just who are you thinking about asking to room with me?"

"I was thinking about Alex. Y'all get along well enough."

"Alex? Oh, hell no! I don't want him all up in my business. It's bad enough that he knew about my attack. I mean, we are cool, but he would be the last person that I would ask to even go to the store with me."

"Plus, like he said, we are in late June. According to the website, everything has got to be in by the beginning of July," Peep points out.

"Not a problem. I talked to the cruise planner last night and he told me that there are still rooms available. Plus, he is willing to get the cruise line to extend the deadline for those just registering. Come on, y'all. Let's do this. We all need it with everything that's been going on. Besides, Lionel and my birthdays are on that Saturday. We always celebrate on each other's birthday. What better way than on the boat?"

"I don't know about this. I'm having enough trouble on level ground. What makes you think it's going to be any better on a boat?" Corey says skeptically.

Just then, my phone rings.

"Hello?"

"What's going on? This is Garrett."

"Hey Garrett. What's happening? I haven't heard from you in a minute. Is everything cool?"

"Yeah, I was wondering what you had going on tonight. You know we haven't had any time to just hang out since the tennis match."

"I know. Things have been crazy. Between my job and working out, I don't have much time to hang out."

"I understand that. I'm pretty loaded with work and family issues. Some things went down recently, and I want to fill you in."

"Where are you now?"

"I'm at the M&T Building downtown, getting ready to leave work for the day."

"The fellas and I are at City Café. It's not that far from you. You've been saying you wanted to meet them. Do you want to swing through here?"

"Uh…" *Uh oh, Hesitation? Not good.* "Ok. I'm cool with that."

"Are you sure?"

"Yeah."

"So, five minutes?"

"Five minutes."

"All right. See you then."

"Peace."

As I hang up the phone, I notice that the fellas are staring at me. *Oh Lord! What questions am I gonna have to answer?*

"We had been dealing with Corey's stuff and gabbing so much about the cruise that we forgot to ask what was going on with you and Garrett," Peep says.

"Yeah," Corey chimes in. "What is going on? You have to catch me up."

"Well, He is an exceptional and intelligent guy. But nothing serious."

"You're joking!" Corey says.

"Well, with everything going on at work and with your attack, we haven't really had enough time to spend together other than talking on the phone. Besides, I'm keeping my options open."

"Well, it's good to do that. But what does he think?"

"Oh, he knows. We talked about it and it's cool. I believe he could be another close friend. He's a very nice guy and I enjoy talking to him. But, romance is not in the cards. Besides, he has his eye on someone else, although he would die before admitting it."

"How did you find this out," Peep muses.

"Duh! We had conversations about the dude. He's vague about it. But I can read between the lines."

"Anybody we know?"

"Maybe."

Corey suddenly perks up. "Who? Tell me."

"Excited, aren't we? Do you really want to know?"

"I wouldn't have asked you if I didn't," Corey pouts.

Suddenly I catch sight of Garrett. I wave him over.

"Hey, what's up fellas."

"Hey Garrett." I look down and notice a bandage around his hand. I gesture at it and inquire, "What happened here?"

"I'll tell you later."

"Cool. Well, pull up a chair. I want you to meet my friends, Felipe, Joseph, and Cordell."

"Peep, Jojo, and Corey to our friends," Peep volunteers.

"And Larry, Curly, and Moe to our enemies," Jojo follows.

"Well, nice to meet all nine of you," he says, glancing at Peep and Jojo. All of us share a laugh. Then, his eyes rest on Corey. Suddenly, his heart is in his eyes.

"Is something wrong?" Corey says, stammering. I've never seen him so nervous. Hmm. Maybe this is a match. "Do I have something on my face?"

"I'm sorry. You just remind me of a friend I knew from back in the day."

"Oh. Well, was he drop dead gorgeous?"

"Breathlessly. But you are a shade better."

Ok, Sweet talker! Corey looks at him then me with this wonderfully comical look that said, "Well, Well, Well! I like his style." Lord...did he just giggle? That's new! But while witnessing his hilarity, my eyes rest on Peep. Suddenly, he is looking a bit nervous. Hmmm... Strange. Without warning, he jumps to his feet.

"I'll be right back. I'm going to find out if this might be something Jimmy would like. Uh, Jojo, come with me. You can explain the particulars to him better than I can."

"Ok." Jojo gets up and follows Peep. I hope nobody noticed me staring at Jojo's ass.

"So, Corey, how have you been holding up? I heard about the attack. Lionel filled me in." Corey looks at me, staring daggers into my face. "I'm sorry we have such stupid people who can't see the beauty of a person rather than their sexual preference."

Corey glances at him. His face relaxes. "Thank you. It's sad to acknowledge that there are people walking around with that mindset."

"I hope you don't mind Lionel telling me about the attack."

"I did, as you might have noticed. But, because of that sweet remark, I'm prepared to forgive and forget."

"Are you considering filing a report?"

"I don't know," Corey sighs, retreating. I give Garrett a look that spells *Pump your brakes. He's not ready yet.* He caught the hint and changed the subject.

"Lionel also tells me that you are a music professor… and that you are a virtuoso on the keys."

Corey, wide-eyed and with a chuckle, says, "Guilty as charged. At least on the first half. I wouldn't call myself a virtuoso."

"Lionel did. He said that you could play anything from Handel to Hancock."

"Lion sure does talk about me a lot," Corey says, glancing at me with amused and almost grateful eyes.

"Not just you. He talks about all of you in such glowing terms."

"Too bad I can't say the same. He hasn't been able to fill me in about you. I've just been under the radar for a bit."

"I understand."

"So, since he couldn't, why don't you fill me in, sir? Do you play?"

"I play a little."

"Um Hmm! Those who say that usually play a lot."

"Nah. My instrument is the sax."

"Saxophone?"

"Yes…"

"Ok, now I'm intrigued. I absolutely love the saxophone! It's sound is so sensual."

"Sounds even better when the piano accompanies it," He says with a seductive glint in his eye. *Smooth!*

Starting to feel like a third wheel, I excuse myself to go to the bathroom. Striding through the restaurant door, I smile to myself as I listen to the animated sounds of Corey and the low rumbling tones of Garrett. *They really complement each other.* I run to the bathroom and relieve myself. Then, I wash my hands and exit. Spotting Jojo and Peep, I walk along the mosaic tiles of the Café to meet them. Peep looks out the window at Corey and Garrett. Corey suddenly lets out a high pitched, exuberant laugh and Garrett shares in the laughter.

Peep looks concerned. "Uh, Lion?"

"Yeah?"

"Is Corey the one he likes?

"Yep."

Peep rolls his eyes to the ceiling in dismay. Then he covers his lips with his hands, muffling his words as he emits, "Oh no…"

Jojo looks at him and asks, "'Oh no?' What do you mean?"

"Just a mistake I made."

"What mistake?" I ask.

"I'll tell you about it later."

"Tell me about what?"

"Don't grill me about it right now. I'll tell you later."

I am puzzled. "O...K... Fine. Later then. What did Jimmy say."

"Oh, he's in," he says, looking at Corey and Garrett. "He said with having to pay that tax guy, pulling double shifts at our jobs, and fretting about other bills we needed to pay, we really need a vacation."

"Do you have enough money to cover it?"

"Yes." He informs, finally turning to me. "We saved vacation money, but we didn't know where we wanted to go. Now we do. I'm going to pull from that account and pay the travel agent when I get home."

"Well, I guess we are going."

Jojo exclaims, "Yes! Let's go tell Corey."

We walk back to the table, but I take note of Peep's posture. *He is obviously upset,* I ponder as I approach my seat. Corey and Garrett are engrossed in deep conversation. Corey cuts it off to look up at Peep and ask, "Well, what did Jimmy say?"

"He's on board."

"Ugh!"

"Come on, Corey. It's a chance to get away from it all. Nine days of no students, no lessons, no snot-nose kids that don't practice," I point out, reminding him of his own complaint.

"Uh," Garrett chimes in, completely lost. "Am I missing something?"

"Yes, I'm sorry," I apologize. "We are planning to go on a cruise called the Rainbow Pride Cruise."

"Correction...*They* are planning. I'm just listening," Corey interjects.

"Hmmm... Hey, I've heard of that cruise! I have friends in Aberdeen who went last year. They came back raving about the good time they had. I started to go this year, but my funds were jacked up, so I decided to wait until I had enough money to go next year."

"Why not this year?" Peep asks.

"Because two grand is a lot of money for single occupancy and my friends can't go this year. Otherwise, I would room with one of them. If it weren't so high, I would get a cabin to myself."

"Ever thought about sharing cabins with one of the guys already on board?" I say.

"Yeah, but, I'm real funny when it comes to my space. Highly private person here."

"Yeah, I know what you mean. I'm sort of private myself," Corey agrees. Suddenly he perks up, "What time is it?"

"Five eighteen."

Corey jumps up and grabs his bag, rattling hurriedly, "Oh, shit. I forgot I scheduled one of my students for a make-up lesson today at six. Oh God, I have to get past this five o'clock traffic. Uh, listen, Garrett, it was wonderful to meet you. Hopefully we can talk very soon. Jojo, text me the information on the cruise. I'm not making promises, but I am interested. I will let you know my decision soon. Next Saturday at the latest."

"OK."

I cut in, "Uh, don't forget we have the appointment with Dr. Lofton tomorrow. I'll pick you up."

"Ok, I'll be ready. Kiss-Kiss, y'all," Corey calls back while running across Cathedral.

"I'd better go too. Jimmy and I have to go check on Irene."

"What's going on with her?" Jojo asks.

"Oh, I didn't tell you? She went into diabetic shock earlier this week. They admitted her into the hospital."

"The hospital? Oh no."

"She took her insulin, but she skipped eating to run an errand. Kinda like somebody else I know," Peep says, with a shrewd look in my direction.

"Shut up, Peep. Is she going to be ok?" I ask.

"Yeah, she will be. This has happened before. But she is stubborn. She thinks that you just take your insulin and you'll be fine. She forgets that she has to eat."

"Wow. Well, give her my best."

"Of course."

"Wait up," Jojo says. "I have to go too. Can you give me a ride to the parking garage to get my car?"

"Ok, but let's hustle. I gotta go pick Jimmy up." Peep stands up and comes around to bend down and kiss me on the cheek. Then, he grabs Garrett's hand in a distracted way. It's almost as if he is avoiding his eyes. "It was real nice meeting you, Garrett."

Jojo follows, hugging me then hugging Garrett. "In case Lion hasn't told you. I'm a hugger."

"No problem. I like huggers," Garrett says chuckling.

"I also gotta say this. I don't know what you and Corey were talking about, but thanks for snapping him out of his funk," Jojo says.

"Anytime."

"I'll ring you later, Lion," Jojo assures. They both holler their goodbyes as they cross Eager Street.

"Good friends," Garrett observes.

"The best a man can have. Don't you have any friends like that?"

"Not in the city. I have my friends; Ricardo and Harold. They live in Aberdeen. Most of my acquaintances here are either closeted or straight."

"I'm sure there are some good potential friends here in Baltimore that you have overlooked."

"Yeah, true. But, you can't really trust people here in Baltimore, present company excluded."

"They can probably say the same thing about you."

"What do you mean?" Garrett demands, defensively swiveling his head towards me.

"I'm just saying, whatever you perceive about others, others can just as easily make that presumption about you."

"I don't understand."

"I want you to marinate on this. If I were a stranger passing by, and I looked at you with cold eyes, what would you think?"

"I would wonder what the look was coming from when you don't..." He pauses, understanding filling his eyes.

"Don't... what?"

"When you don't even know me."

"Right. So, armed with that fact, how reasonable is it for you to make the same presumptions about others, when you don't know *them*."

He thinks it over. "Ok, I get it."

I write an invisible mark in the air, "Point one for Lionel."

"Smart ass."

"Worked my whole life to be one."

"It shows," he says, smiling.

I look at him and I am reminded of the conversations we had about Corey. The fact that he likes him is evident. But I must know for sure.

"I got a question for you."

"And I might have an answer."

"Well, you seemed especially set on meeting Corey, as well as the others?"

"Again, what do you mean?"

"It was obvious from our conversations."

"I was just interested in meeting him, because I saw him in the Link several times before I met you. I really loved his style and often wondered if he was good people."

Suddenly, it hit me like a lightning bolt. "Wait a minute... You didn't hit me up just to get close to Corey, did you?"

"No. But I haven't been completely honest with you."

"What are you talking about?"

"The number was meant for him. Peep gave me your number by mistake. He thought you were the one I wanted to talk to, so he gave you my number."

My head is spinning at the revelations being unfolded. I suddenly stand up and say, "I gotta go home."

"Wait," he says, standing up as well.

"Wait for what? All of these conversations were based on a mistake?"

"No! Not at all. Come on. Sit down. Let's talk about this." He puts his hand on my shoulder.

"Not now. I gotta get out of here."

I tear away from him and dash across Eager Street, my name being heard among the sound of honking horns.

*****

Peep is the first call I make when I get in the house. I could've called on the way, but I had to be in the comfort of my home. Of course, Garrett was blowing up my phone, but I didn't answer. I needed time to process it.

"Hello?"

"Peep. This is Lion."

"So, you know."

"I know what?"

"I am so sorry."

"I know *what*?"

"That the number wasn't for you. It was for Corey."

"Why didn't you tell me?"

"Because I didn't know. He just came up to me and gave me his number and was stammering out, 'Have your friend call me'. I thought he was talking about you. It wasn't until I saw them today that I realized it was Corey he wanted."

"Oh…"

"You mad at me?"

"No, because you had no way of knowing. But Garrett is another matter altogether. All this month and a half, he should've told me. I told him so many things about myself. I feel so stupid!"

"Why, there's nothing wrong with conversations between friends, which is what you two are starting to be. Am I right?"

"Yeah, we did, but…."

"Listen, he should've told you. No question about that. But you ought to hear his reasons for not doing so before you cut him off."

"I don't know if I want to talk to him right now."

"Up to you. But just think about it."

"I will."

"Ok, call me later."

"Ok. Bye."

"Bye."

I call Garrett. He answers on the first ring.

"Lionel."

"Garrett."

"I can explain."

"So… Explain."

He breathes. A few seconds go by. Afterwards, he begins to talk. "The phone number was for Corey."

"I know that part. The part that I'm having a problem with is trying to find out why you didn't tell me when I was spilling my guts out to you. You knew who you wanted all along. Why didn't you say it from the jump?"

"I was too embarrassed. I talked with him months ago. After that one conversation, I had been smitten. Only one guy had ever touched me that deeply, and that was when I was a boy. But one day, I came into the Link and saw him hugging this guy. It looked serious, so I looked elsewhere, but I couldn't get him out of my head. I was talking to Ricardo, who knew him as an acquaintance and told him how I felt and that I thought he was attached. Well, Ricardo told me he wasn't. Since then, I had been going to the Link hoping he would come, but no such luck…until the night both of you showed up."

"Go on."

"Well, I thought. 'Hey, this is my chance'. So, when you and your ex, and later Corey, went outside, I went up to Peep and intended to tell him to give it to Corey, but my mind went blank, and I said, 'your friend'."

I feel my resentment for him fade. After a long stillness, I say, "Ok, I understand the position you were in, but the question still remains as to why you didn't just tell me on that first phone call that it was Corey you wanted?"

"Initially, it was because I didn't want to offend you. You see, I have been in situations where the men I liked ended up desiring my friends."

"Understandable."

"Then, as we kept talking and getting to know each other as friends, it became harder and harder as we told more about ourselves."

"Garrett, do you know the word I just said?"

"Understandable?"

"Yeah. Just like I understand now, I would have understood then. Besides, the truth would have surfaced eventually. If you hadn't told, Peep would have because he was shocked."

"I can imagine."

"Garrett, I don't ask much from friends. But I do ask for honesty and keeping certain things from me is just as bad as telling a lie, especially when I am involved."

"I understand."

"Good."

"So, are we ok?"

"Of course. And just so you know, I already suspected that you liked him."

"How?"

"I told you... through the conversations, and judging from your interaction with him earlier, I think that maybe you both should sit down and get to know each other. Hey! I got an idea."

"Which is?"

"Listen, would you ever consider changing your mind about that cruise? With all of us going, that would be a good opportunity for you to connect with him more and see how it goes."

"I don't know," He mutters skeptically.

"Why not? You would have time with him that is uninterrupted, unless you want interruptions."

"Well, you got a point there."

"Were your friends adamant about not going?"

"Well, not both. Ricardo is on the verge of reconsidering."

"Ok. Well, if he does reconsider, you can room with him like you said you would, and the guys and I can keep pestering Corey until he agrees to go."

Garrett goes silent like he is mulling over the idea. "Ok, I'll think about it. But like Corey said, I can't promise anything concrete. Besides, things are a bit problematic with the family right now."

"How so?"

"Well, our worst fears have been confirmed, Sam *has* been beating on Rachel."

"What?!"

"Yeah, she's at Mama's house now. The bandage on my hand is because I punched Bright Boy in the face and commenced to beating the shit out of him. He pressed charges and I ended up in lockup for several hours. They released me when Rachel paid bail."

"Do you have a court date?"

"Yeah. August twentieth."

"How is your sister feeling now?"

"That's what is bugging the fuck outta me. She doesn't want to leave that shitheel. Even worse, Melba found out."

"Melba?"

"You know, the cousin I told you about?"

"Oh, yeah."

"She told Craig, and they went to Rachel's house to raise hell and kick his ass even more. But when they broke the door down, he was gone."

"Wow. Well, where does that leave you?"

"Oh, I'm not worried. If he doesn't show up to court that day, the case will probably get thrown out. If he shows and Rachel tells the truth, the judge will dismiss me, and the charges will be dropped."

"I guess that is good."

"Yeah, I suppose so."

We talk as if the day's events had never happened. As we converse, I think to myself. *He could be just the man for Corey. I caught the look between the two. It was a faraway look of two lost souls who found each other at last.*

CHAPTER ELEVEN:

"DO YOU STILL LOVE ME"

Well, I made the decision to go ahead and pay for Mama's operation. I had already decided to go on the cruise, although I had to put on quite a song and dance for Mr. Alexander to get the time off. It is now a week after calling the surgeon's office and sending the funds to Dean, and I get a knock on the door, and a cornfed FedEx man stands there asking me to sign for a package. After doing so, I open the contents of the envelope, and received a pleasant surprise in the form of four certified checks: two checks of twelve-fifty from Andre and Dean, and two of six twenty-five from Roland and Brenda. *Where is Rhonda in the bunch?* I thought to myself. *It's a shame that Roland and Brenda had to pull together to do what Mama's favorite failed to do. Well! This is a good sign.* I grab my keys and rush to the door to drive to the bank. As I open it, I bump into a hard body. "Nate?"

"Surprise…" He says with a sheepish look on his face.

"What do you want here?"

"I was just in the neighborhood and came to holla at you."

"Listen, Nate. I don't have time for this. I have somewhere I have to get to."

"Can I just have ten minutes? I want to talk."

I look at him. His lean, muscular body is clad in yellow. His upper body muscles strain the cotton t-shirt he wears, his hard nipples piercing the fabric.

The yellow jogging pants do very little to hide the beauty and angular definition of his spectacular legs. His ebony skin contrasts with the brightness of the color he wears. His arms are sleek with sweat… and those helpless eyes… Oh God, how I've missed them. But I shake it off. *Remember, he's the asshole who cheated on you.*

"Please?"

I look at him, surveying his face. *Hell, why not? I need to get some shit off my chest anyway.* "Ten minutes. Come on in." I step aside to allow his entrance. As he walks by, I steal a look at his perfectly molded ass. Damn!

Looking around my living room, he says, "Where's all the furniture we chose?"

"I sold it."

"Don't you think I should have had a say before you did that?"

"Cheaters have no say. I seem to remember that the furniture was bought on *my* credit card."

He raises his hands in concession. "Ok, I stand corrected."

"You have nine minutes left. Make them good."

"May I sit down?"

I gesture to the chaise and he sits. I grab a portable chair and sit opposite him, straddling the chair backwards. After a moment of uncomfortable silence, I urge him to have his say. I must get to the bank before it closes. The lines are going to be long because its Friday.

"Well, I just came over to talk about what happened between us."

"Why? 'Us' died when a third was involved."

"I know."

"Oh, do you?"

"Yeah… I don't know why I did what I did. I felt lost with no job and you were always working."

"I was doing it for the both of us, and during the time I was working, you were sitting on your ass not doing jackshit."

"I had problems finding a job then. All of the employers wanted someone young and idealistic."

"That's no excuse!"

"And I'm not trying to make it one! I'm not even trying to justify what I did. Because, I know it was wrong. I was wrong all the way down the line, and I just wanted to say that I'm sorry."

What? Am I hearing right? Did he just apologize? This is so unlike him. I look at him, his dejected form slumping. His eyes cast to the floor. One question turns over in my mind.

"Of all people, why did it have to be Shawn? You knew that son of a bitch hated me and wanted everything I had, and you gave him our bed, with you in it!" The silence is deafening, broken by my own voice shouting, "Answer me!"

"I didn't mean for that to happen," Nate says, apologetically. "He kept going after *me*."

"But he was not the one in a relationship. *You* were! Why didn't you think enough of that, or me, to stand up to him and say no?"

Being weighted down with that difficult question, his eyes skip guiltily around the room. After a hush in the air, he begins to explain.

"I was angry… Hurting… Selfish. I just lost my job and I really needed someone to be there. I needed someone to talk to me and tell me that it was going to be ok. Then Shawn starts coming over and we started talking. It wasn't sexual at first, but platonic. I just felt comfortable telling him about all the hell that was going on. All the rejections. All the stomping I did on the sidewalk trying to find a job. After a while, it seemed that every time he came over, he was wearing less and less clothes. I looked the other way the first few times. But one day while you were at work and it was raining, he showed up in a long poncho. I thought he was wearing a shirt and shorts underneath. But when he took the poncho off, he was naked. That was when we started the affair,"

I am sitting here, getting angry all over again. There is the possibility that Nate is lying, but the straightforward look he gave me through most of it convinced me. He could never look me in the eye and lie to me, and when he tried, he would blink repeatedly and look away. I want to go over to Shawn's house and kick his ass from here to Cold Spring Lane! I knew he wanted Nate, but he schemed to get him and followed that plan to the letter.

"How many times did you fuck him?"

It was then that he looked away without a word. His body language told me that they both had multiple escapades. Now I want to haul off and smack the fuck out of *him*.

"You see, this is what I am pissed off about. If you had cheated on me one time, that would have been bad enough. But you couldn't *get* enough. You fucked Shawn as often as you got the goddamned chance!" I pause to catch my breath and finding it, I continue, "But what's good for the gander is good for the goose. What would you say if I told you that during all those times you thought I was at work, I was really at that sleazy motel on North Avenue, getting fucked by Mr. Alexander. What if I told you that?"

I see his jaw jumping. His breath getting shallower and quicker. An angry expression cracks his face. I look at him and say, "See the expression on your face right now? I felt worse than that when I walked in on you and Shawn."

Seeing his features relax, I continue. "And, no. I never did that, but I could've if I wanted to. God knows, I had plenty opportunities to let him bend me over and fuck me senseless, and you would've hated me for it, am I right?"

A slow exhalation escapes his lips as he breathes out, "Yes…"

I nod my head in satisfaction. Then I say, "A minute ago, you said that you were angry, hurting, and selfish. The feelings of anger and hurt, I can get behind and understand. The selfishness is what I am having trouble with. In a relationship, it's not just about you. It is two people involved. I would've helped you work through it and held you up no matter how busy I was. But, when you got fired, the only thing you said was, 'I lost my job...' and when I tried to reach out for you, you pulled away from me and said, 'I don't want your pity.' You said that numerous times, so I threw myself in my work, to pay both your bills and mine. And suddenly, you tell me, 'I need you home.' 'You ain't taking care of your man'. 'You're hanging out with those bitch ass friends too much.' And while I am on that subject, that is the most callous thing I have ever heard you say, when you know how much they mean to me."

He hangs his head in disgrace. I can barely hear him mutter these words, "I was wrong."

"No argument from this corner. You were wrong. You're talking about my friends who supported me, and you because I loved you so much. Your remarks about them were cruel. You didn't hear me putting down those drunk ass motherfuckers who bombarded their way into my house while I was at work. Scarfing down the food I paid for with *my* goddamned money. Tracking up my carpet with their dirty ass sneakers. Trashing the place and causing me to have to come home and clean it up. I could have put an end to your company coming over, but I held my tongue because I knew that you were hurting. I tried to be there for you, Nate, and I asked you daily, 'How are you feeling?' 'Are you ok?'. You're the one that shut yourself away from me."

"I know."

"But, isn't it amazing? There is a bright spot in all of this. At least today, I got the chance to rationally tell you how I felt. Nate, these 'should've', 'could've', and would've' statements could have been avoided if you had been as faithful and honest, as I have tried to be with you."

A long, painful stillness covers the room. I sit looking at him as he gazes at the floor. I look at my watch. His ten minutes are up. I touch his knee and say, "There were things that both of us could've done better. But you cheated on me and it hurts." I breathe deep and continue. "I'm going to go forward and try to hold no grudges about what happened. I've got to move on with my life, and to do that, even though it hurts … I have to forgive you."

"If I could remove the hurt, I would, Lionel."

"I don't doubt that…now."

"OK, I hear what you are saying about you forgiving me and trying to move on. I know that it's something I myself need to do."

"I couldn't agree more," I say as I get up and stroll to the front door to escort him out. Then I hear these words…

"But… do you still love me?"

What a question. My words are caught in my throat. I hear him stand. I feel his strong presence directly behind me. I feel his hand caress the back of my head. *Goddammit! Why did he have to do that?* I feel his arms encircle me, drawing me close to him and holding me tight. *Mmmmm… He smells so good.* I feel his warm breath stroke the nape of my neck. I turn around and see his eyes, wet with tears. I feel stinging sensations in my own eyes. He takes his strong, heavily veined hand and wipes the tears before they fall. Then without warning, Nate moves his lips closer to mine and he kisses me. The kiss was as soft as a feather, but as heavenly as a star. Before I can understand what is happening, my arms are stealing around his neck and I am kissing him back. Our hands begin roaming frantically all over each other's bodies. Clothes are flying everywhere! His yellow jogging pants thrown across the back of my chaise, his jock dangling from my front door knob, my tank top and shorts strewn about my coffee table…

Bronze and Ebony, standing naked in my living room… Sinking to the floor… The heat of the moment is saturating the room, extracting an aroma of masculine funk and cologne generated by the sweat of our bodies. As we melt together, he lays me back and leaves a trail of wet kisses from my mouth to my chest…

From my chest to my navel…

From my navel to my pubic hairs…

From my pubic hairs to my jimmie…

As he takes in the hardness of my penis, I feel my head involuntarily moving from side to side in ecstasy. His tongue is writhing around the shaft of my jimmie as he sucks it like a milking machine…. I grab his head and thrust my pelvis forward. My hands trace the contours of his heavily muscled blue-black back as his tongue and mouth massage my sex over and over.

He then hoists my legs up and apart as he licks a trail down my jimmie… down my balls… down my crack… until his tongue finds my abyss of love. The only sounds we hear are our own moans of unbridled pleasure. As I feel his pink tornado swirl around inside of me, my eyes roll back in my head as I think these words, *God, how I've missed this.*

After a period of insatiably licking my sensitive and sensual cavity, he licks the trail back up to my lips as we kiss more fervently than before, our tongues dueling like slippery eels. I feel his body against the back of my thighs, as I feel my ass moisten and become wet and sleek. Suddenly, I am wild for him to make his entrance into my portals. He briefly searches for his jogging pants and locates his wallet. Retrieving the condom, he tears the wrapping and slides it on his schlong. It is then that he entered my chamber, exploring its walls drenched with natural lubrication. Slowly at first, then increasing speed and force, he powerfully thrusts his body forward as his phallus opens me to overflowing. I hear our lustful moans saturating the air. I'm holding onto his back as his torso grinds against my ass.

We press skin to skin as night darkens the sky outside. We moan and shout our obscenities in perfect unison. He kisses me as he fucks me. He pinches my nipple as his glans presses my button again... and again... and again. I breathlessly scream his name. "Ebony! Oh... fuck me, Ebony! I need it. Ebony!... Ebony!!"

"Receive me, Bronze. Let me in. Take me in! Receive me! Open your chambers. Receive me!"

I feel an onrush of sexual relief and bliss as my phallic volcano erupts white and warm lava on to my stomach. I feel his sex expand as he yells louder in response to his own incredible climax. I feel each spurt, even with the condom on, as he experiences each spasm. When he falls onto my chest, his arms encircle my body. My hands trace along his sweat soaked back. I am conscious of my own sweat drenching my hardwood floor. Erotically spent, we drift into a sexually exhausted, yet peaceful sleep.

Well... I guess I will not be going to the bank today.

*****

"So, how's work?" Nate says the next morning, as we are in the dining area, eating eggs and bacon. We are fully dressed, with me in my T-Shirt and cutoff jeans, and him in the clothes he wore yesterday.

"Work's work. We had this client from hell, but I'm glad we don't have to deal with him anymore."

"What was the matter with him?"

"Oh, you know. Macho on outside. Legs to the sky on the inside."

We both laugh.

"What about you?"

"Things are looking good. Got a job managing a gym across town. Perfect opportunity to go back to personal training. Between the job and the clients, I'm makin' bank."

"I'm glad everything worked out."

"So am I, after a year of being jobless."

I sip my coffee. We must talk about yesterday. My body is saying, "Take him back and get that good loving you've been missing." Although I yearn to obey my body, my heart and mind says, "Address what happened and let it go."

"Nate."

"Yeah?"

"You know, we need to talk about yesterday afternoon."

"I was wondering when we were going to bring that up."

"Our time together was beautiful, scary, erotic, tumultuous, and exciting all at the same time."

"Yeah. It was."

"Yesterday reminded me how wonderful our time was. It has been a while since a man excited me the way you did."

"You still excite me too, especially when you are mad. You become passionate. Many times, I would intentionally make you mad just to enjoy everything you serve up sexually."

"I thought as much."

"However, I feel a 'but' coming on."

"You would be right... As passionate as our relationship was, it was also extremely painful for both of us."

"But, isn't that what relationships are? Passion and pain?"

"But ours exceeded the normal amount. We were headed down the aisle before life began to test our metal."

He nods. Then, he looks with interest at a small sculpture of two men kissing on the windowsill. He goes and picks it up. Then he looks at me, with shining tears in his eyes. "You kept this?"

"Of course. You bought it for me."

"Wow..."

"What?"

"I thought you would've sold this too."

"There is no way I could have parted with that. It reminds me of all the happy times between us."

"I'm glad you held on to it. Do you remember when I bought it?"

"Yes, it was when you first moved into this house."

He chuckles. Suddenly, he looks in the living room. "I just noticed something."

"What?"

"This is not the living room set you put in storage."

"How did you know I put my living room set in storage? The fellas and I were the only ones who knew about that."

"And that's the way it would've stayed…if you hadn't left one of the monthly receipts in the nightstand drawer."

"Smug ass! Well, I sold that too. I just felt like I needed a change. So, I bought new furniture."

"I really like it. It suits you and your personality. Eclectic and as exciting as a hot pepper!"

"Thank you, kind sir. Do you ever hear from Shawn?"

"Naw."

"Y'all broke up?"

"I wouldn't call it that."

"Why not?"

"Because to break up, you have to have a relationship and we never had one. It was just sex."

"Well, was that good, at least?"

"I plead the fifth, sir."

We both laugh. I then look at him. I'm seeing him for the first time in years. Not as a lover. Not as a boyfriend. But as a friend.

"You know, Nate," I begin. "I like this side of you. Easy to talk to and to laugh. Reminds me of the man I met four years ago."

"Yeah, and I like this side of you. Relaxed and confident. But, it was your sweetness that drew me to you. You know, I still have that pink shirt you spilled your Pepsi on."

"You do?"

"Yeah. It's my keepsake."

A long pause. I rest my hand on his.

"Sometimes, things work out differently than what we plan. We wanted to be romantically together forever, but that is just not in the cards."

"I can't argue with that… and I did cheat on you."

"Yeah. But it doesn't mean we can't try to be together forever… as friends."

"I would like that."

He extends his hand, which I accept in mine. Then I look at my watch. Eight twenty-six. "Damn, I gotta get going."

"Me too."

He heads to the door, opens it, and turns around. I lounge against the post of the archway connecting the living and dining room. "I'll catch you later, ok?" he says. "I'm really looking forward to renewing and growing our friendship."

"So am I."

He smiles as he turns to leave.

"Nate?"

"Yeah?"

"The answer is yes."

"What was the question?"

"I still love you and I always will."

He crosses the living room and embraces me tightly, whispering, "Thank you. That means a lot."

After our embrace, he kisses me on my forehead and traces his forefinger down my nose. Then, grinning his cock-eyed grin I loved so much, he says in a gruff, gritty voice, "I love you too kiddo."

*****

"My God, Lion! You slept with him?!" Corey barks. The two of us are at his house, having white wine and talking.

"Yeah…" I say slowly.

"Do you know what you just did?"

"Yeah… I slept with him."

"You are opening the floodgate again. I am lost as to why you want to give him another chance to fuck you over. He cheated on you, and he'll do it again."

"Uh… when did you hear me say that I am seeing him again?"

"Well, you said you slept with him."

"If you would please let me finish?" Corey sits back and breathes hard. Then he lifts his hand and gestures as if to say, "Proceed!"

"I slept with him last night, yes. But we talked this morning and we came to an understanding."

"Fuck buddies?"

"No, fool! We decided that we still love each other, but romance is no longer in the cards. We want to explore the possibilities that we have… as friends."

"Friends. Yeah, right! I'll believe that shit when I see it."

"Yeah, and you will. Not that it's your business to be assured!"

"Just looking out for you, that's all. You know I don't like that motherfucker. But if it makes you happy, then fuck it."

"Alright, Mr. Snarky! By the way, did you and Garrett ever talk?"

A slow, but uncharacteristically sweet smile spreads across his face. "Yes, we did... Actually, we have talked eight times since I gave him my number."

"Whaaaaaat?" I draw out playfully.

"Yeeeeees! Eight times. You know, there is a calming sweetness about him that I really like."

"Is that right?"

"Yeah. In fact, I think I'm starting to like him. What sealed it was this. He played his sax over the phone for me. My God!!! He makes that saxophone talk! I found myself jacking off to him playing."

"Uh, Ok! I really did not need to hear that part."

"Whatever. I am just imagining us making music together... What a duo we would be!"

His face takes on a childlike expression. It is glowing with wonder, hope, and desire. He catches me looking at him. "Don't get it twisted now. I'm not trying to rush anything."

"Of course not."

"But, I have the strangest feeling of déjà vu. Like we met somewhere before. And when he looked at me at City Café, he did a double take like he recognized me."

"Probably just one of those things that happen."

"Yeah. I've been racking my brain to figure out where I know him from."

"Don't think too hard. Time will bring it out."

"Yeah. Oh, let me get you another drink."

"No thanks. One is enough. I have to drive to the bank and run some more errands."

"Sparkling Apple Cider? I could crack open a bottle."

"I could go for that."

He grabs my wine glass, rinses it, and goes to the cabinet to grab the bottle of cider. While he is searching the drawers for his corkscrew, I remember the conversation I had with Garrett about the cruise.

"Corey?"

"Yeah?"

"Have you thought anymore about that cruise?"

"Yeah, and I'm not sure if I'm cut out for it," he says, retrieving the corkscrew.

"I could say the same thing. But why not? It's something different."

"Being on a boat in the middle of the Atlantic, with no doctor in case I have to ralph from being seasick? Yeah! That shit is different!"

"Oh Corey, set it to music, why don't yuh."

"What?" He says, as he opens the bottle and pours the cider.

"They do have doctors and nurses on the boat. They kinda have to be there," I say sarcastically.

"I think I'd be better off at home. The only water I like is the water coming from my shower-head. Here." He hands me my glass and sits in the opposite chair at the small table.

"What if I told you that I could try to get Garrett to come?" I say, after a silence.

"Garrett? Didn't he say that his friends weren't coming?"

"Yeah, but I talked to him and he said that one is thinking about changing his mind."

"Hmm… But who would room with me? I could swing for a cabin to myself, but I don't really want to."

"Well, do you have a friend that goes on cruises all the time?"

"Hmmmm… Yes! An old friend of mine from Morgan, Danny Hodges. We get along pretty well."

"Do you think he would go on this one?"

"I don't know. I don't imagine why he wouldn't since he goes on several cruises every year. He keeps bugging me to go."

"Ask him."

"Why would I? For the record, I haven't even said *I* would go."

"Look. Didn't Dr. Lofton say that you needed a distraction to take your mind off the attack?"

"Yeah, yeah."

"What better distraction? You know, there is more to fun than going to the Link every Friday. Besides, your best friends are taking the trip with you, two of them celebrating birthdays. Come on, this could be good for you!"

He gets up and goes to the sink. He looks out the window and breathes a long sigh. "I don't know why I'm letting you talk me into this."

"So…," I say playfully, jumping up and standing beside him with my hand on his shoulder. "Is that a yes?"

He says, rolling his eyes, "Yes!"

"Great, then you call your friend. You want to call Garrett and tell him you're going, or should I?"

"I'll tell him."

"Good, and don't worry. I think we will all have a good time."

"We'll see."

I gulp down the cider, then prepare to go. "I'm splitting. Call me later. Let me know what they say."

"Ok."

"If you don't call me, I'll call you to follow up… tonight!"

"OK! I said I would!"

"Fine, grouchy. Gimme some sugar." I, wrapping my arms around his neck, kiss him loudly on his boyish cheek. He waves me away. "Go on! Quit violating me!" He says lightheartedly.

"You wish. I'll see you later."

*****

I drive to the bank and deposit the checks. Then, after deciding that it was too hot to run errands, I head home. On the way, my mind travels back to the former night's events, as well as the difficult periods of our relationship. I have questions. Nate and I spent years in the same house, thinking we knew each other, yet missing the important parts that made us who we were. I was too busy trying to make the relationship work on my terms; and he was too proud to come to me and confide in me about his feelings. The fault we had in common can be summed up in one word… Pride.

Maybe I should've fought him more when he would pull away from discussing his hurts and failures. Yes, I could have gone to him when he called to me and let me know in his own way that he needed me. Maybe I am just as guilty as he is. The only difference is this: I didn't cheat. I smile, congratulating myself for staying faithful to him. I simultaneously commend Nate. For the first time since I have known him, he was open, honest, and took responsibility for what he did. That alone is reason enough to consider a lasting friendship. Maybe we could be friends with benefits....

Then again, maybe not.

I open my front door and walk into the darkened house. Switching on the lights, I kicked off my shoes and went to my bar. I make myself a cocktail and settle down into my well-used and soft armchair. I breathe a sigh of contentment. My phone rings interrupting my thoughts.

"Hello?"

"Lionel, this is Dean."

"What's going on? I got the checks. Just deposited them."

"Ok, fine, but there's something else I need to talk to you about."

Uh-oh, this sounds serious. "What's going on? Is Mama alright?"

"She's fine, as far as I know. But, um. How much do you know about Dad's death?"

"I know he was shot. But, what happened beyond that, I don't know."

"I came across a letter while looking for Ma's health insurance docs."

"Are you at her house now?"

"No, I'm at home."

"What do I care about some letter? That isn't my concern. Yours neither. If I were you, I'd put that letter back where I found it."

"Well, you aren't me, and this letter concerns *all* of us. It was addressed to Mama from Donaldson."

"The prison?"

"Yeah. Came from some man named Troy."

"Troy? The one who killed Dad?"

"Allegedly."

What? Did he say allegedly? "What do you mean?"

"It's some heavy shit. Some real heavy shit."

"Are you going to tell me or are we going to keep circling the mulberry bush?"

"I need to talk to you in person."

"Well, it's not like you live that close. Lest we forget, you live in Richmond. I'm in Baltimore."

"Can we do cam?"

"Yeah."

I go to my desk and turn on my computer. After a few minutes of trying to get to the website, I see the tired face of my brother, Dean, as he clutches a wrinkled sheet of paper in his hand.

"So? What's going on?"

"Did you ever hear anything about Dad cheating on Mama?"

I laugh. "Nah. Come on, Dean. Dad loved Mama! Granted, they had problems and Mama drove him batshit, but he wouldn't have cheated on her."

"I'm not so sure about that. This letter says different."

"What does it say?"

"Daddy cheated on Mama with Troy!"

PART II:

HELP

CHAPTER TWELVE:

"SHOCKING REVELATIONS"

I can't believe it! My dad was gay, or at least bisexual. I am feeling short of breath. When I catch it, I sputter out the words, "Run that by me again?"

"What are you, deaf? Daddy cheated with Troy."

At that moment, the nadir of my mother's resentment of my sexuality became clear. No wonder she reacted the way she did. I can only imagine how a woman would feel, discovering that the one who has your husband by the balls, literally, is another man. I feel so sorry for her. No matter how mean she was, She did not deserve this.

"Read the letter to me."

He proceeds in reading. The letter states this...

Dear Lynetta,

It seems strange to be writing to you after all that has happened in the past year. I did not want things to end up like this. I loved your husband from the moment I laid eyes on him. Maybe I pursued him more because I knew he was forbidden to me. We were co-workers of the same company. I was fresh out of grad-school and an intern, but lonely and very unstable. Kenneth was there for me. He was so patient and understanding as he explained the job to me. We became close friends, but I hadn't counted on a fateful business trip where things became physical and would change everything. Our love lasted for ten years. Kenneth said he loved me, but he also loved you and he didn't want to hurt you or the kids. Those kids meant the world to him, he said. Well, I became obsessed. Remember those calls where the phone would ring twice then the line would go dead? That was me. I was so obsessed that I started calling him multiple times a day. The more he resisted me, the more I wanted him.

I was not prepared for his visit on the night we lost him. He came over to break it off with me, but I seduced him for one more night of pleasure. While in the bliss of what was happening, I didn't think of anything else but him. But when I turned from hearing my door being kicked open, I saw the look of hatred, hurt, pain, and disgust on your face. But the emotion I saw most of all was rage. I can still hear Kenneth pleading for his life when you fired the first shot. Then I felt a sharp piercing pain in my chest. You shot me, and I blacked out. When I came to, I saw my lover, your husband, lying dead on the floor with blood covering his naked body. But you were gone. I looked, and I saw the cops and the paramedics standing over me. At that moment, I felt red hot hatred towards you for killing him. That was my chance to get you back for killing the man I loved. But, extreme guilt for what I started overtook that feeling as I thought about those kids he talked so much about. The worse thing to happen is for children to lose both of their parents, one dead and the other on lockdown. So, I told the cops that I killed him, then tried to kill myself.

I deserve all of this. I knew he was married but all I could think about was how much I loved him. Look where that love got me, The kids without a father, you without a husband, and me without my freedom. I am so sorry. It's hard to live with the fact that I am responsible for the death of such a beautiful soul.

I hope one day that you will find it in your heart to forgive me. But if not, I understand. I hate myself for what I did, and I am right where I deserve to be. You didn't kill Kenneth. I killed him with my love. But this is a chance to give your children a parent, since they can't have two, they can at least have one, their mother.

Always, Troy.

Numbness cloaks my body. There was nobody closer to my father than I was. To hear that he died at the hands of my own mother made my blood boil. I feel my anger making my face hot, washing over my resolve like a tidal wave. The sorrow I felt for her is replaced now with rage.

"Lionel?"

I am spaced out. I cannot hear my brother as he calls my name.

"Lionel!"

"What?!"

"Did you know that Daddy was bisexual?"

"Really, Dean? Y'all tripping about him being bisexual? Are you going to proselytize next? There is a bigger issue here! She ended the life of someone that we loved and needed! That life was not hers to take. And letting his lover take the rap and hang because of what *she* did? That is just low!"

The revelations turned my brother silent.

"You know she has to pay for this!"

"What are you talking about?"

"I'm talking about taking that letter to the police!"

"No, no, no. I won't have any part in that."

"Then you are giving her a rubber stamp saying it's ok!"

"Wait just one minute! What she did was evil and callous! Knowing that, do you think I'd take sides with her? All I'm trying to do is avoid all the drama that's connected to this. All the jail time in the world is nothing compared to the guilt she will have remembering what she did."

"Are you out of your mind? She needs to **answer** for what she did… and they oughta lock her ass up. Dean, take the fucking letter to the police!"

"I won't do anything of the kind! I only told you because I thought you would be level-headed about this as you are about everything else. I am not releasing this letter to the cops. We all have enough shit to deal with as it is with Mama's operation, her medical bills, Dad's death, and the sudden knowledge about you being gay…"

"So, you're saying I'm burdening the family with my personal life."

"I did not say that."

"You didn't have to!"

"Look, Lionel," Dean says with restraint. "I am not the enemy here. I don't care who you are attracted to. That is your own business and if you're happy, I say to hell with what everybody else got to say… I just don't want any more drama in this family."

"So, to avoid it, you would rather sweep what she did under the rug! Why the fuck am I not surprised?!"

"Look, I think we need to just settle down…"

"Settle down my ass! You are a chickenshit! The same way you were when we were kids. You just took everything she and Rhonda dished out and you didn't say a fucking word! You just stayed quiet to save your own punk ass!" I stop myself and I watch as I see hurt crumpling his expression. Then his facial features harden as he says, "Goodbye, Lionel." *Black Screen.*

*****

Two hours later, with four full shots of vodka in my stomach, hate in my mind, and hurt in my heart, I am sitting in the darkness of my living room. This evening, I was as happy as a kid in a candy store. But now, I just want to plunge into a chasm. The walls are illuminated with the bluish white light of the TV, and as I blearily and stupidly look at the mirror through my inebriated haze, I see two glistening tears catching the illumination. *Fine fucking parents I have. A father who was a proven cheat and coward for not living his truth and a mother who is a proven killer.* The ringing sounds of both my phones are scarcely heard as I wallow in angered grief. My eyes, weary from crying, close in the sweet reverie of heartbreak.

I hear a key turn in the lock.

I feel hands lift me up and guide me to a room I barely recognized as my bedroom.

I feel hands undress me and put me in the bed.

I feel hands wiping my tears of torment from my eyes.

I feel lips ever so softly play over my shoulder blade, my cheek, my eyes, and then my own lips. As I force my eyes to open, I see the face of my childhood confidante.

"Jojo," I say. "What the fuck is happening to my life?"
"Ssssh... It's ok."
"No, It's not..."
"Don't talk, baby. Just lay back and rest. I'm here. I got you."

I turn on my side and I feel arms encircle my body and hold me tight. My head is brought to my friend's chest. His shirt dampened by the waterfall of my tears. I am shocked at the sound of my own voice, as I cry out my father's name in my newly felt grief. Oddly, being in the arms of my old friend, I feel a sweetness that I have never felt before. I hear sobs of sorrow not only coming from me, but from Jojo also. Finally, weary of the turns and twists of life, we both cry ourselves to sleep, our bodies glued together and our hearts beating in unison with one another.

*****

I awaken with the sunlight from my window shining in my eyes, I feel arms still holding me. I tilt my head up and look at Jojo's boyish face as he sleeps, his clothes still on. He looks so peaceful, even has a sweet smile on his face as he dreams. I kiss him on his cheek, then I sit up. Whoa! I feel dizzy. Did I drink that much?

"Are you ok?"
I look back and see Jojo's concerned face. "Yeah, just a bad hangover."
"Stay right there. I'm going to get some coffee from downstairs."

He leaps off the bed and makes his way to the kitchen. As he makes the coffee, I blearily transfer my body to my armchair, trying to collect my thoughts. A few minutes later, Jojo walks back in the bedroom with a large mug of piping hot coffee, the aroma of hazelnut filling the air.
"Here," he says. "I know how you love hazelnut coffee. Careful. It's hot."
I nod to thank him as I take a few sips. The coffee makes me feel a little bit better. "This is good."
"Great." Jojo sits on the bed. After letting the stillness fill the air, he asks cautiously, "You want to talk about it?"
"What?"
"What's going on with you?"
"I can't."
"Why not?"
"I just can't, OK?"
Silence. He rests his hand on my shoulder, "Ok, you don't have to. But I want you to know that I am here for you."
"I already know that." I sit back in the armchair. I study the wood on the floor. I hear myself speak the words, "My mother is the one who shot my father".
"What?!"

"I found out from Dean that my mother killed my father. She shot him dead."

"I don't believe it!"

"It's the truth. Dean read a letter from the man who supposedly killed him."

"Why did she do it?"

"He had an affair with the man."

Jojo lets out a low whistle. "WOW!"

"My sentiments exactly!"

"What's the story with the letter?"

"It was an apology. Apparently, Ma walked in on Dad and Troy fucking, and she shot both of them. Dad died. Troy didn't. He thought about what Dad said about us kids being his life and he felt guilty to the point where he took the blame for her."

"How do *you* feel about this?"

"Confused, hurt, angry. Take your pick. I have to find a way to get that letter from Dean and take it to the police."

"Hold on there now. Before you do that, I think you need to find out if Troy is still on lockdown. If he is, pay him a visit, let him know what you found out, and hear his side."

"Why?"

"Because if this is what he felt he needed to do, you need to know why, and not just from some letter. You need to hear it from his mouth. Plus, the only ones that know anything about it are her and Troy. With her not talking with you, that leaves Troy."

"What if I still feel like she should pay for what she did?"

"You don't get to make that decision. This was between Lynetta, your father, and Troy."

"But it was MY dad!"

"That doesn't make any difference. You can advise your mother to come forward, but if you take that letter to the police without considering all sources, you'll only make matters worse than what they already are."

I cannot answer him. All I could think about is the fact that my own mother shot my father down in cold blood. She cheated me out of what could have been an even closer relationship with him. Jojo sees something broken in my face.

"Remember when we were talking about psychiatrists and how important it is to get things off your chest?"

"Yeah."

"Would you have any problems seeing one?"

I think it over. Encouraged, Jojo continues.

"The only reason I am asking is because I think it might help to talk to a professional about all the things you've been dealing with lately. I just started going to one." I look at him, surprised.

"When did you start going? You never told me you were seeing a shrink."

"I started a week ago. It was one session. I go back next week."

"Hmmm… Well, you may be right, but who should I see?"

"Might I suggest that the next time you take Corey to his appointment, you ask him how he feels when he talks to Dr. Lofton. Does he feel safe? Does he feel like he can share whatever it is that's bothering him? If so, set up an appointment with him. I got to say though, judging from how Corey has been over the past few weeks, Dr. Lofton must be doing something right."

An impish and mischievous feeling overtakes me. Grateful to segue into a lighter subject matter, I say in a knowing way, "Trust me. It is not Dr. Lofton that has Corey smiling and giggling all over the place."

"What are you talking about?"

"Corey has the hots for someone. Or, I should say, someone has the hots for Corey."

"Who? Tell me."

"Garrett."

"I knew it! I saw how they were looking at each other when we were at City Café. There is definitely something there."

"I thought I was the only one that saw it."

"Well, you weren't. So, now that we know what's going on, the challenge would be how to get them on this cruise together."

"I don't think we need worry about that. Garrett said that his friend Ricardo might reconsider going and Corey said he definitely will go."

"Oh my God, this is bananas! I cannot wait until October. We have got to get these two officially boo'ed up."

"Since when do you have matchmaking skills?"

"Please, baby. You don't know all the skills I got. That's just one of them."

"I'm somewhat curious as to the other skills you've been keeping from me all these years."

"Curiosity killed the cat. Watch out now."

Laughing, I get up to leave the room. Suddenly, I feel a pillow hit me in the back. I turn.

"Oh, you are dead meat now!" I say, laughing.

I grab that same pillow and hit him upside the head. He grabs another pillow and swings at my side. Before we know it, we launch into an old-fashioned pillow fight like we did when we were kids. Laughing and yelling, we trade licks. Then, in a move that shocks me, I halt the fight by holding him in my arms tightly. I say now that love is in the eyes because as chance would have it, our eyes connected. Suddenly I felt a warm energy in the air and sparkles surrounding us both. Tenderly, I take him in my arms. His hands steal up to my face and into my hair. Pleasantly, our faces draw closer as if magnetized, and our lips kiss. At that moment, my mind envisioned two puzzle pieces, fitting perfectly together. So why am I stopping? Why am I drawing back?

"What is wrong?"

"We are friends. I don't think that we should be doing this."

"Why not? Friends can kiss."

"Yeah, but not when you don't know what is going on with your life. I'm all mixed up. I'm confused, and that confusion makes me do idiotic things, like sleeping with my ex-boyfriend." Holy Shit! Why in the fuck did I say that?

The quiet that stretched between us was so thick that you could almost slice it with a knife.

"What did you just say?"

Well, shit! Might as well tell the truth since the cat's out of the bag. "I slept with Nate two days ago."

I see his face; the expression is that of a building that crashes down. His eyes are filled with despair. Oh no. I hadn't meant to hurt him.

He turns and goes to the window to look out over the Avenue. He says miserably, "So, you two are back together."

"No, but I would be lying if I said that I hadn't thought about giving him another chance."

Jojo turns from the window. His face is contorted in unusual fury. "Lionel, another chance? He hurt you and he'll do it again!"

"But you didn't see how he looked when we last talked. He looked really sorry for what he did."

"Lionel, don't you know that cheaters will say anything just to get back in? I swear to God; I don't know why you are acting so stupid?"

"Who in the hell are you calling stupid?"

"Where, in any part of your auditory faculties, did you hear me call you stupid? I said you were *acting* stupid! You are letting Nate's nut-stream cloud your fucking brain! All you were to him was a free fuck, A loaded bank account, A charge card, and some nice clothes. You didn't mean shit to him then. What makes you think you mean shit to him now?"

I feel searing heat in my chest. "Jojo...Enough!"

"Your problem is you can't see somebody who loves you if they were staring you in the face! Somebody who cares about you. Somebody who wouldn't have cared if you didn't have a dime but would've been with you because he felt that you were worth more than any price. Somebody who loves you even more when you are yourself and not what family wants you to be, a mama's boy who can't get the titty out of his mouth, put some nerve in his goddamned balls, and live his life the way he wants to live it!"

I scoff, feeling bitter. "And who would that someone be? You? You and I are different. You are completely out of the closet for Chrissakes! The difference between you and me is that you would be comfortable leading the gay parade, riding on the head float, rainbow colors and all. You may not mind people seeing you as a faggot. But that's just not me!"

Ooh…If I could only take back the words I just said. Those words really stung him. But he said some stuff that hurt too. A mama's boy with no balls… I look at him, angry tears falling down his face, His mouth opening in shock. He bolts from my bedroom out into the hallway. I hear his footsteps as they race down the stairs. I hear the front door open and slam shut. Then I say the two words that I should've said before I let him leave, knowing that I am saying them too late. "I'm sorry."

*****

Come on, Jojo! I know you see my name on the screen. Answer the fucking phone. I think to myself.

Ring three.

Ring four.

Ring five.

"Hi, this is Joseph Thompson. You called me. Now please be courteous and leave a message. Thank you." *Beep.*

"This is the sixth call I've made. I need to talk to you, Jojo. I don't want to say all this in a voicemail. I need to hear your voice. Please call me when you can." I hang up the phone.

What the fuck just happened? How could a playful pillow fight turn into a potential loss of a friend I have known my whole life. I shouldn't have kissed him. But, it felt so natural. At that moment, I felt that every guy I ever kissed paled in comparison, and I found the right one at last. The kiss was not the problem. It was Nate. I brought up Nate and how I slept with him. Why?

The phone rings. I pick it up. "Jojo?"

Corey's furious, abrasive voice barks over the line. "No, it's Corey, you dumb-ass douchebag. What in the hell did you do?"

"What makes you think I did something?"

"Because Jojo wouldn't have come over to my house, crying over *your* simple-minded ass."

"Look, let's leave it alone, alright? I don't want to get into it with you."

"Lionel, what is wrong with you? We are talking about your best friend. The one you knew since you were knee-high to a grasshopper. It does not take a rocket scientist to find out what is going on here."

"What are you talking about?"

"Don't play dumb with me. You and Jojo. He loves you and I know you love him. I can tell from the way he touches you. The way you touch him. You do things for each other that no one else can. This whole fight was unnecessary, and it wouldn't have happened if you weren't so insensitive."

"How would you know? You weren't there to hear everything that went on. He said some fucked up shit too, you know!"

"Deal with him about that on your own time! I'm talking about the shit YOU said... and fuck the *how*. Let me tell you *what* I know. I know that you have this block about being with him because he is your 'best friend'. You see the chemistry, but you pull the saintly act. Whatever idiot that said 'being with your friend is wrong' needs to have the shit knocked out of him. I believe that if more married people started off being friends, we would have less divorces. No, I think *your* problem is that you still have Nate in your system."

"Again, we only fucked once! Then we decided to be friends. I *told* you that! We're not getting back together, for sex or anything else."

"Methinks thou doth protest too much, but that's beside the point. It's not your fucking Nate that I'm concerned about. If you wanted to fuck a goat, then turn around and say, "Let's be friends", I could care less. I'm more concerned about you and Jojo, and why you threw Nate up in his face. I think the reason you brought him up is because you are too fucking scared to be yourself. You can't even let someone love you who knows you almost as much as you know yourself, supposedly. You and I have had this discussion more times than I care to count. You can't love Jojo the way he needs to be loved, because you can't even love your own goddamned self."

"I really don't need to hear this right now."

"I don't give a flying fuck what you think you need to hear! If I wasn't your friend and I didn't love you, I wouldn't be bringing this to you as real as I am right now. My hat goes off to Jojo, because at least he knows who he is and has become OK with being gay. He may have some self-esteem issues, but his sexuality has not been an issue with him as it has been with you. Lionel, you need to grow up. You have somebody that really loves you, but you're going to push him away. And if that happens, how long do you think he's going to stay there waiting for you to come around? How are you gonna feel when he finds somebody else that will see what you refused to see?"

"Goodbye, Corey." I hang up the phone. Then I do the one thing that cleanses the soul and brightens the eyes but goes to the core of our beings when we know we have made the biggest mistake of our lives. I cry.

*****

I am lying on my couch several hours later. No drinks. No pills. No TV. Just old-fashioned guilt hanging over my head. Two friends I shut out, and because they had the balls to try to teach me a lifelong lesson that I hadn't learned yet. They made me so mad with their needling and probing. What made me even madder is that I know they are right. Thirty-six years old and still acting like a naïve kid. Still worried about what family might say concerning my life. Still trying to fit in a mold that doesn't suit me. The confidence I displayed over the past weeks. What was that? Was I really confident in who I was, or was it just a show for my friends' benefit? Why was it so hard to love me?

Corey's words haunt me as I lie here. Scared to be me and allow someone to love me for who I really am. I'm gay, but still as confused as someone closeted. Do I really know myself as much as I think I do? If I did, I would be more comfortable with who I was, and it wouldn't matter who knew about my life if I was happy with it. I think back to our childhood. Jojo was always different. Always alive. Always free. That's what I loved about him, and still do. But there were times when his comfort in his sexuality made me insecure about my own.

I go outside to catch the night air. I sit on my stoop, listening to the sounds of the Light Rail and the Metro. Suddenly, I feel a horrible sense of desolation. I pushed my best friends away. The same thing I called Corey to the carpet about, I did to both him and Jojo. It crosses my mind to call Peep and tell him what happened. But, I don't. Instead, I sit back on the step and listen to the sounds of Baltimore City. I look up at the sky and study the constellations of Cassiopeia and Andromeda. My mind travels back to the conversation Corey and I had in the car a few months ago. Am I living a life or a lifestyle? I have everything I could possibly want; a beautiful place to live, a nice car, a fat pocket, a decent expense account, and friends who really do care about me, plus a man I've known my whole life who loves me. Maybe I've been living a real life but became so vested in trying to fit in that it became a lifestyle.

I hear a soft footstep, I turn and there is Jojo, standing there beside my stoop. He kicks at the base of the step. I studied the grooves in the cement of the weathered sidewalk.

"Hi."

"Hi."

"I thought you'd be home by now."

"No. Just out taking in the night air."

"Yeah."

Silence.

"Nice night."

"Yeah, not too cold."

"Not too hot either."

"Yeah."

Silence.

"Weatherman says it might rain."

"Good, we need it. Baltimore has been going through a terrible drought."

"Yeah."

I feel him wanting to say something. I want to say it as well. But the words are choking in our throats. Then, some kinetic force pulls our eyes to meet and gaze as we both blurt out.

"I'm sorry!"

Jojo takes on this sheepish look on his face. I see it and a low rumbling begins at the back of my throat as I chuckle. He begins to join in the mirth. In the space of five seconds, we are laughing uncontrollably, holding our sides, then throwing our arms around each other.

When our hilarity ends, I wiped the fresh tears from my eyes. "Come on inside, boy!"

We pass through my door and sit down on my couch. "I just have one question." I ask.

"And that would be?"

"Am I really a Mama's boy with no balls?"

"Again, you are putting words in my mouth. I never said that you didn't have any balls. I just said you needed to grow the ones you got. But you are a mama's boy."

"Well, so are you."

"But, I had no choice. Mama was the only one that raised me, remember?"

"Yeah, yeah, smart ass!"

"But there's nothing wrong with being a Mama's boy. It shows that you value her. But, I gotta tell you. You letting her disapproval have free rein in your life will keep you from really being free enough to be you."

"I know."

"My turn to ask a question."

"Well, what is it?"

"Do you really see me as a faggot?"

"No, I don't."

"You said…"

"I said that you don't seem to care if people label you as one."

"Does that bother you?"

"Sometimes, it does."

"Why?"

"I guess I'm not as comfortable with my sexuality as I know I should be."

"Do you think you will ever be?"

"The truth?"

"Yeah."

"I don't know."

Silence. Then Jojo talks.

"I don't know a lot of things. But I do know that to be comfortable in any romantic relationship, you have to first be comfortable within yourself. Otherwise, that self-hate will continue to be a problem. I'm not saying I got it all together. I still struggle with my physical appearance, but I'm trying to work past what I can't change."

"Me too."

"I am not going to lie. You really hurt me by what you said. I had been called 'faggot' so many times, but I didn't expect the word to come from my best friend's mouth."

"I'm sorry. I really didn't mean to hurt you."

Jojo lets out a huge sigh, then he squeezes my bare thigh as he says, "I guess I should be more patient with you. After all, you came up in a household where being gay was being condemned."

"And I should be more embracing of you and applaud you for having the balls to be yourself."

"I guess we both said some stupid stuff."

"Yeah, and invented stuff we didn't say."

"Lion."

"What?"

"About Nate… Are you really thinking about getting back with him again?"

"No. After we had sex, we talked. We decided that we would be friends. No sex. No petting. Just friends."

"Then why did you bring him up?"

"I guess because I was scared of the moment we shared."

"What moment?"

"You know."

"You mean this?"

He leans towards me…

He closes his eyes…

And he kisses me on the lips.

The kiss lingers, then becomes stronger and more eager. I break the kiss.

Jojo look exasperated. "Lionel, what is wrong with you? Like I said before. Friends can kiss."

"I know, but…"

"Look Lion, we are both adults, so let's just put it on the table. Would it be so wrong for us if ever we were in a relationship?"

"No, it wouldn't. But…"

"But what?"

Silence.

"Lion, you can't deny that we have attraction. I feel it and I know you do too. Isn't it ironic that we have the same birthdays? We've known each other for thirty-six years and in that time, we have slept with one man after another, men that we had to get to know, but didn't measure up. We don't have to do that with each other. We connect so much when we talk. We spent years teaching each other to where we know each other by heart."

"But, I don't want to ruin our friendship." I say, bounding up from the sofa. Jojo gets up and stands in front of me.

"How could we ruin what we spent years building? That is the reason I came back here, because our closeness really matters to me. We worked hard to establish that."

He got me there.

"Lion, I always felt something for you. I have always loved you, more than a friend. I love you like I love my own soul."

Talk, Lionel. Say something! Words are stuck in my mouth. I look at the ground.

"Lionel, look at me. Look me in my eyes and tell me that you are sure that this will ruin our friendship, and I won't bring it up anymore."

I can't. Oh God, I can't.

"What are you afraid of?" Jojo demands, strong purpose in his voice.

"Nothing!"

"You're acting like you are afraid of me."

"I'm not!"

"Yes, you are. You are afraid that I'm going to hurt you."

Silence

"Lion, I would cut out my own heart before I do that."

Oh my God! No one has ever said that to me.

"Don't be afraid of me. I love you and I know you love me. I know you do. I can feel it all over you."

I feel powerless as his hands guide my forehead down to his lips and kisses it...

Then he turns my head to kiss my left cheek...

Then my right cheek...

He draws back, our faces inches apart...

Our breath blows hot on each other's faces, as we inch closer...

Closer...

Closer...until our lips touch and press. Our mouths open as I feel his tongue in mine. *Is this Heaven? If it is, I don't ever want to come down to Earth again.*

After our kiss, we draw apart with our hearts in our eyes. The dreamy haze and the sparkles float around us. I can almost hear a love song that has never been written, yet it has Jojo's name in it. We want to go upstairs to my bedroom, but as we stare into each other's eyes, we both say one word.

"Slowly."

I caress his cheek as he closes his eyes, savoring the moment.

Suddenly I realize the darkness of the night. Jojo shouldn't be walking home alone. "You want me to walk you back home?"

Jojo chuckles, "I would like that, but my car is down the block. Besides, I think you and Corey need to have a conversation."

"Yeah, you're right."

Jojo's hand lifts to trace along the contours of my face. His fingers feel feathery soft. He trails them down my chest where he draws an invisible heart.

"What are you doing?"

"Giving you a memory." He then lifts my hands and kisses them. "I'll call you when I get home. Goodnight, Lionel."

"Goodnight, Joseph."

He gives me one last look of love, then passes through the door. My stomach is churning as I watch him from the threshold as he strides to his car. My head is light. My palms are sweaty. I am feeling an unfamiliar explosion of emotions like guilt, pleasure, passion, pain, wonder... Emotions that wash over me now like a tidal wave. His open and loving personality gave a key to my locked door of feelings. Could it be that, for three plus decades, Joseph Stanley Thompson the III held the golden key to my heart, while I was looking at guys who could barely pick the lock with a copper bobby pin?

I call Corey. He answers on the third ring, "Mr. Davis, what can I do for you?"

"Can we talk?"

"I don't know. Can we, Mister I Don't Wanna Hear It So I'll Hang Up on My Friends?"

"Do you always have to make things so hard?"

"Deal with it. Your hanging up on me and hurting Jojo was hard on the both of us."

"Look, I just called to say I'm sorry."

Silence

"Ok, so say it."

"I said it already."

"Technically, you didn't. You said you *called* to say it," I can almost hear him smile over the phone.

"OK, Smart Ass. I'm sorry."

"An apology coupled with name-calling, Hmm. You really do know how to sweet talk a man." I hear a lighthearted chuckle in his voice. His subtle way of saying, "I forgive you."

CHAPTER THIRTEEN:

"HELP"

"I really don't know what the hell I'm doing here."

"Well, let's just break it down. Why do you think you're here?"

"I guess to make some form of sense in my own fucked up life."

"Why do you say a 'form' of sense?"

"Because I really don't think that we as human beings can make ultimate sense out of our lives. I think that happens only when we die. But since we just live from day to day, all we can do is guess at what we 'think' makes sense."

"Interesting way of looking at it," Dr. Banneker observes. He sits back in his chair with a very composed face and he writes in his legal pad.

I am sitting in the office of Dr. Edwin Banneker. He is a sixtyish, small framed white man with a surprisingly deep and comforting baritone in his voice. He has understanding, greenish hazel eyes that are alight with youthful energy and laughter. His narrow and angular face sports a strong Roman nose, thick and well-shaped lips, and a receding chin with a curly black goatee to match his abundant and full black hair with a vast shot of silver running through it. I take note that his face is unwrinkled and peaceful. He wears a rainbow tie-dye T-shirt with torn jeans and sandals. Very unconventional for a psychiatrist, I know. But these days, even professionals enjoy and embrace clothing to fit their personality, so I can overlook that.

His office is what throws me. Eclectic is the word I would use. The paneled walls are mahogany, as is the medium sized desk. On opposite sides of the desk are two large, bright, colorful vases with willow branches pouring from the inside. The desk is strategically placed between two tall windows with multicolored drapes, providing a peaceful view of Madison Avenue. His degrees and awards are on the wall directly behind the desk. Ok, it is obvious that this shrink loves abundant colors. But, in the corner of the vast room, he has a faded floral armchair placed on a bright yellow rug. Lord, it is ugly as hell. It has big scarlet poppies over a sickly greenish yellow background… and it has *ruffles*! But, when I sat down in the chair, I sank into a reverie of comfort. I felt as though the chair was hugging me, making me feel safe. Above the chair was a bulletin board with fabrics of different colors pinned on them.

I tried to see Dr. Lofton, but he was booked up on appointments. That has me a little bummed out, because Corey told me that he had a very good feeling about him. So, I asked Dr. Lofton if he would make any type of recommendations, and he highly recommended Dr. Banneker. Aside from the chair, I feel a bit skeptical. His office is an acquired taste and so is he, if you go by first impressions. I think to myself, *I hope I'm not making a mistake. Maybe this dude isn't wrapped too tight. This space is a little weird.*

"I don't know how I can make sense of a mother disowning me, or me having a romantic relationship with someone I've known as a friend all my life. Now, everything that is disclosed in this office will be kept confidential. Right?"
"Of course."
"Not too long ago, I found out that my father was bisexual."
"And how does that make you feel?"
"I don't know."
"Well, aren't you gay yourself?"
"You would be correct with that assessment."
"So, with you and your father sharing that commonality, what is the first thing that comes to your mind as it relates to how you feel?"
"Anger."
"Why anger?"
"Because, with him having more experience at this than I did, he might have helped me through it. But then again, he was closeted. So, it does not seem logical to go to him for advice or help if he's not really sure how to navigate it himself."
"Are there any other feelings that come to mind?"

"Well, I feel a little bit of sadness."

"Why sadness?"

"Because between my mother and my father, I always felt that I connected more with him. I felt I could talk with him about anything."

"Did you share your sexuality with your father?"

I look at him like he's crazy.

"Why the reaction?"

"Based on recent events surrounding my mother, I think that coming out to anyone at that time would have been unwise. I didn't know what was going on then. In fact, I'm glad I waited until I was grown and gone before I told her, because she might've thrown me out of the house."

A slight nod from the doctor.

"Do you know what she did one time?"

"No. Do you care to share?"

"She saw my best friend Jojo and me hugging when I was ten. Suddenly, she started screaming at me… She ran down the stairs, grabbed me, and threw me in the house." I pause, catching my breath. When I look up, the doctor looks at me as if to say, "Continue."

"She grabbed an extension cord and told me to strip… I hesitated, knowing that the pain of that extension cord would linger for days, and it would be another week that I would have to wear long shirts and long pants to hide the welts. My hesitation caused her to backhand me across the face. I stripped off my clothes and I began to cry. She screamed at me again. 'Shut up with that goddamned crying! Be a man! I'm not raising my son to be a faggot. Boys do not hug each other, and you are going to be a man if it kills me. Get across that bed.' I must not have moved fast enough for her, because she started hitting me with that extension cord. Some of her blows hit my balls. The pain was terrifying, but all she would say is 'Shut up and stop crying.'" I feel a tear course down my face as I relive that painful memory. "How do you stop crying when someone is beating you? I felt like I was looking down at myself as that extension cord cut across my back and drew blood…all because I hugged my best friend."

Suddenly, I stop talking. Noticing my tears, Dr. Banneker gets up and grabs a box of tissue. He sits it down in front of me and gestures for me to take some. Then he resumes his seat.

"Is that the only time she hit you, or was that time typical of others?"

"Typical, but at least I didn't get it as bad as Andre got it. He had to put up with shit being thrown at him and her using him as a literal punching bag. She was beating on him constantly until he moved out."

"Did your other siblings get hit as bad?"

"No. Well, my sister Rhonda didn't get hit at all. Roland, Brenda, and my twin brother Dean got whippings but not as bad as Andre and I got. I guess because we were the ones who resembled our father too much."

"You said that your twin brother did not get it as bad. With you both resembling your father, why wouldn't he have gotten the same punishments?"

"She always considered him the 'good' twin. I believe he was being abused in other ways, but he would never question or stand up to her. I respected her, but Andre and I were the only ones who would question the right and wrong of how we were treated. We had too much fight in us, just like our Dad. Even so, she was always on his case talking about how he's not a real man, no matter how much he provided for the family."

"Examining how she treated you and your brother, do you think that she was probably treated that way when she was a child?"

"I know my grandmother did the same shit to her. I got a hint of that one day when we were at her house, and Mama said something she didn't like. She backhanded Mama across the face hard and told her between clenched teeth and in a dead hateful voice, 'Bitch, watch your tone. You don't want to try me. It would do you well to remember the respect you owe me, and if you can't do that, you can take those brats and get the fuck out of my house.' There were other hints of varying abuse, but Mama rarely talked about her past. Whenever she did, she would become enraged."

"Let's travel away from that subject for a minute. How are you sleeping?"

"I was sleeping well until I found out this news about my dad. Now, I'm lucky if I get six hours sleep."

"Is there anything else about your dad that bothers you?"

"I don't want to talk about it."

"Why is that?"

"I just don't."

He writes in his pad. "What medication have you been taking for your insomnia?"

"I was taking Doxepin, but I ran out of pills."

"When was the last time you took it?"

"Two months ago."

"With this latest bout of insomnia, how have you been getting to sleep?"

"Vodka."

"That's pretty risky. If I was to write you a new prescription of Doxepin and you continued to drink at bedtime, it could be dangerous. Even fatal."

"I know. I would never drink if I knew I was going to take Doxepin."

"Good. But, considering your use of vodka, I think I should hold off on giving a prescription. In the meantime, I suggest a form of activity before you go to bed. A walk or a jog. Maybe aerobics. It will make it easier for you to go to sleep. Do you have something in your house, like an exercise bike?"

"Yeah. Down in my basement."

"How do you feel about transferring it to your bedroom? This way, right after working out, you would be in the most convenient place to rest."

"Worth a try."

"Good. Well, good first session. I will see you next week. We will reevaluate the Doxepin option in a month, but you must lay off the vodka for a while. Otherwise, I cannot write the prescription."

"Fine." I rise to go, but the bulletin board with the multicolored fabric catches my eye. "I gotta ask, Doc. What's the story with this board and these scraps?"

His face lights up with a mischievous glow and a wide, unreadable smile. "Many people ask me that and I will tell you what I tell them… You will know in time."

I scowl as I think to myself, *I hate surprises and secret shit. I am one foot away from not coming back to this certified nut!* But for some unknown reason, those thoughts stay buried in my brain and trapped behind my lips.

*****

"So, how did your first session go?" Corey asks, as we are setting up the card table in the living room. We're over at his house preparing for the meeting with Peep, Jojo, and Jimmy. We decided to discuss the plans for the cruise over cards. This is good, because I get to pick his brain about some things before the rest of them get here.

"Honestly, I don't know if I can do this."

"Why is that? I mean, correct me if I'm wrong. But, did you not tell me that seeing a psychiatrist was a good idea?" He recaps, as we turn the table on its legs and head into the kitchen for the snacks.

"Yeah, but I had hoped to get Dr. Lofton because you said that you felt really comfortable with him."

"I do, but what's the matter with the one you have?"

"He's a little bit weird for my taste."

"Since when was a psychiatrist not seen as weird? Dr. Lofton dresses in dashikis. Jojo's shrink dresses in tutus. Unique people do unique things, and shrinks are in a class all by themselves. Maybe it's their way of embracing their truths, something they are trying to get us to do."

"I know that, but this one wears tie-dye t-shirts and torn jeans. He has a strange fixation with rainbow colors. His office is like a psychedelic light show without the lights. This guy seems a bit nutty to me. I am willing to bet my bottom dollar that when he goes home after work, his neighbors get contact highs from smelling Mary Jane."

"And if he did, why is that your business? It shouldn't matter what he is doing with his spare time. It is more important to focus on what he can help you with during the time you're paying him for. As far as his style. It takes all kinds. He could be posing as the world's most modern hippie, but I really don't think Dr. Lofton would've referred him if he didn't think he could help," Corey says, as he dumps potato chips in a large bowl.

"Yeah, I suppose."

"Come on. Just give Dr. Banneker a chance. What have you got to lose? My sessions with Dr. Lofton have really been helping. Every now and then, we need a little cray-cray to dance our nae-nae!"

"Are you coming to grips with your feelings about the attack?"

He stops and looks blankly ahead. "Very slowly. I did file the report and the police are looking for the gang members I described. I'm still a bit on edge, but I talked with Garrett about that last night and we both agreed that closure is not going to come overnight."

"And how are you two doing? With everything that's been going on, I haven't talked with him."

"We are getting to know each other. No pressure. But, I can't shake this feeling that I know him from somewhere."

"College, maybe?"

"No, not college. His eyes and face look familiar though." He shrugs, and we take the chips back to the table.

"Maybe he's somebody you met at the Link," I volunteer as we sit down. "He mentioned that you two talked before and you had a pleasant conversation."

"Yeah, we did." He still looks perplexed.

"Did you talk with him about the cruise?"

"I did. Unfortunately, he said he cannot go."

"So, his friend decided to sit it out?"

"No, both his friends are going. They decided at the last minute to do it."

"Why can't he go?"

"For two reasons. One, because he has to work. And two, because he is dealing with some shit involving his crazy ass cousins, his sister, and her husband, Sam."

"I forgot about that drama. Don't tell me. They kicked his ass, right?"

"How did you know?"

"Because he told me that Sam was beating on Rachel."

"Right. Well, they really fucked him up. They messed his face up so bad that even his own mama wouldn't know him. Then, one of them hit him in the side with a crowbar while the other stomped on his back and kicked him in the head."

"Garrett told me that they would go after him."

"Well, he was right. But the worse thing about this is Sam came over to his mother's house, begging for Rachel to come back and, sad to say, she did."

"You have got to be shittin' me!"

"I ain't lying baby. She went back to that bastard and it's a shame before God. Garrett said he is most concerned about his nephew. That atmosphere is too much for a kid to deal with." He breaks off, focusing on a porcelain figurine of a preacher playing the piano.

"Mike Jr.? Yeah, I'm concerned too." I look at Corey's face, and I see tears puddling up around his eyelids.

"Corey?"

"Yeah?"

"You alright?" Corey breaks out of his tear-stained trance. He wipes his tears.

"Oh yeah, baby. I'm alright."

"I don't know if I buy that. It seems like you are dealing with something other than the attack."

"I was just thinking about some things I went through when I was a kid."

"What happened?"

"I can't discuss it right now."

"But Corey…"

"Can we drop this please?"

I raised my hands in surrender. "OK."

After a few minutes of silence, he resumes the conversation, "Have you talked to Nate lately?"

"No, he texts me every now and then to check on me. But we haven't orally talked since our 'encounter'."

"You know, Lion? I know you said it isn't going to be sexual between you and Nate. But, being the realist that I am, I doubt that you can just turn it off that easy."

"Nobody said it was going to be easy, but we both are endeavoring to let go."

"You'd better, because you know Jojo's got eyes for you."

"Aw, Jeez. Is it that obvious?"

"Duh! Peep and I were not just born yesterday. I already told you. We saw it multiple times and it isn't just on his side either. You have been checking him out too. We just figured it was a matter of time before the deal was closed." He then looks at me and does a double take. Then a look of joyful awareness spreads over his face.

"Hell naw!!!"

"What?"

"The deal has already been closed."

"What are you talking about?"

"'What are you talking about?'" He mimics. "Come on, Lion. I can tell it in your face. You both got Cupid's foot up y'all's asses!"

"Corey…"

"Corey, *my* beautiful butterscotch ass! I smell love and marriage in the air, baby. You see, that's why I'm concerned. If you are in love with Jojo…"

"We're taking things slow. We haven't even had sex yet," I interject.

"What does that have to do with anything? Personally, I consider it wise to wait."

I look at him, shocked that these words came from the very one who would clean up being in the middle of a full scaled orgy.

"Yeah, the 'ho' said it! And the 'ho' cautions you that you may need to limit your time and texts with Nate if you have feelings for Jojo."

"Again, Nate is a friend."

"Even so, we are talking about your ex. Whether he is a friend or not is irrelevant. You don't need anything to complicate what could be a lasting relationship. As far as you and Jojo are concerned, I say that it's about time. All I wanna know is when the wedding is."

"Will you please quit jumping the gun?" I retort, half-joking.

The doorbell rings. He gets up to answer it. I pull him back down, "Ow… Bitch!"

"Corey, don't you mention a word about this in the meeting." I whisper between clenched teeth.

"It ain't like they don't already know." he says as he goes to the door. Peep and Jimmy walk in carrying foil trays and a big wooden bowl, followed by Jojo carrying a glass vessel. He gives me a wide smile, which I reciprocate. *Oh God, I love his smile.* In all the years we have known each other, I can't understand why I never noticed it's dazzling quality before.

"HEEEEEEEEY!" Peep drawls. He looks at the chips. "Oh Corey, potato chips?"

"Did you kick in any money for anything else?"

"No, but we did come prepared," Jimmy says.

"What y'all got?" I wonder.

"My twelve-layer lasagna and a big garden salad," Jimmy informs as we trek into the kitchen to put the food on plates.

"And I baked garlic bread from scratch. The butter and garlic will make you hurt yourself!" Peep brags.

"And I brought my ambrosia salad for dessert," Jojo offers.

"Oh, I know it's on now!" Jimmy bellows joyfully. "Sign me up for two bowls, one for now and one for later on!"

"Damn! It's a good thing I made two big punch bowls worth!"

A good thing indeed! Jojo's ambrosia salad is the best anybody in our circle has ever tasted! No doubt you heard Irene talking about it. He goes to this farmer's market on 32nd Street and buys the freshest, sweetest pineapples and mandarin oranges he can get. That's all I know about the recipe. I have been trying seventeen years to get him to tell me how he makes it, but he digs his heels in and won't tell me a damned thing!

"Now why did y'all bring these dishes over here? I already bought the chips," Corey laments as he pulls the ice and beverages from the fridge.

"Well, I just thought that it would be good to have a nice meal over discussing plans for the cruise," Peep informs. "You can either put them back in the bag and in the cabinet. Better yet, just throw them away. You know those chips are full of saturated fat."

"So is the garlic bread... and throw them away, my foot! You know how much these chips cost, fool?"

"Well damn, chile'. When you put it that way, give them to that nice boy, Alex. He is too skinny. Good looking, though. He'd look sexy with some meat on his bones".

"Hey, hey, hey!" Jimmy says, pretending to be jealous. "Watch it now!"

"Oh baby, I'm just stating facts. You know you are my bugga boo!" Peep says, smacking him on the lips.

"Uh, can y'all get a room please? You're melting the ice!"

"Aw, hush Corey. You know you love it. And if that boy Garrett was in here, you would be melting more than the ice!"

*****

That night, we discussed the cruise and our plans in detail. Corey did not mention his discovery, but he and Peep kept making sly remarks and innuendos. Like, when we were going back to the table, Peep suddenly says, "Uh... Lion,

I think you need to sit next to Jojo. After all, you *are* going to be rooming together." To which Corey says, "Among other things." When I asked him what he meant, he just told me, "You really don't want me to spell it out for you, baby". Through the quips and the jokes, we confirmed our intentions of flying to Miami on the day before we set sail. Corey's friend couldn't go, so he ended up asking Alex to go, and he accepted.

As plans for our vacation accelerate, Jojo and I become closer. He comes over to my house and places himself in my arms as we talk about our lives, our childhood, the differences between our mothers. I'm falling in love with the rise and fall of his musical voice. But he shared something with me that shocked the hell out of me. We had a man in common that we both messed with, my cousin Jamaal! I asked him when they first started messing around, and he told me that it was on his junior year. Color me upset! But, I had to reason that neither one of us knew we were both getting sexed by him. It is wonderful knowing Jojo in this way. I am a bit worried about him though. Despite all we have shared with each other, there is still something he's keeping quiet about. I knew about the physical abuse inflicted by Mike, and the bullying he endured in school. But something tells me that there is a great hurt, a past pain that is eating away at him and corroding his chance for a happier life. It scares me, because I am beginning to connect romantically and mentally with him, and it makes me helpless and frustrated because he won't tell me what's going on.

I did curtail my drinking. I rode on the exercise bike and took walks as Dr. Banneker recommended, and the exercise did tire me enough to get to sleep. But I'm having nightmares about my Dad getting killed. One nightmare I had was my Dad bending over and getting fucked by a faceless man. Then magically, they switch places and Dad is fucking him. I see my mother standing in the doorway, holding a sawed-off shotgun, and just as she fires the fatal shot at Dad, at the man, then directly between my eyes, I wake up in a cold sweat and a dry mouth. Now, I am back in Dr. Banneker's office. A month has passed, and I now have a refill of Doxepin. It has been four sessions, and I feel a little more comfortable with him each time I come. I guess it was because of a picture I saw of him and a tall Indian man, smiling and gazing into each other's eyes.

"I think I am a little lost."
"Why is that, Lionel?" Dr. Banneker asks.
"Well, now everybody in my circle knows about me and Jojo."
"What brings the lost feeling?"

I weigh my thoughts a moment before I respond. "You spend years building a friendship that is more potent than most friendships today. Suddenly, you go to a whole new level. Watching the friendship growing into more is scary, exhilarating, and wonderful at the same time. I've never looked at Jojo as someone to spend my life with."

"And now?"

"And now, what?"

"I mean, how do you see him now?"

I look down at the yellowish carpet. A twofold fear attacks me. One is a pleasant fear that I do see a life with him; a romantic life filled with ups, downs, fights, makeups, laughter, and tears... We would go back to the blissful days of childhood when we held each other in joy and in pain. A memory comes back to me. A memory of Jojo coming home bloodied and beaten, drenched in foul-smelling urine, holding on to his ribs. Patches of his beautiful curly hair were torn out and a huge bump had bloomed on the back of his head.

I remember helping him into his house and into his bathroom...

I remember telling him to shower up and I would be right there...

I remember lying him down on his bed...

I remember getting the first aid kit and dressing his wounds...

I remember holding him when it was all over... and us drawing apart... gazing into each other's eyes... then kissing. No tongues. No adult complication. No lustful eyes. Just a mind-blowing kiss that lingered. It was a very angelic, beautiful kiss that could only be shared by the young or the youthful. It was a kiss of discovery between two hearts that found each other, not only in friendship, but also in kindred spirit. It was then that it hit me. The feeling of déjà vu I felt in the car when we went shopping was merely a beautiful reminder of the act of pure innocent love between two teenagers of fifteen.

The other fear came in a stream of paralyzing questions. *What will my family think? Who else would disown me? How will I survive without my family's love?* My eyes travel to the open window and I hear the tinkling melody of windchimes, as the wind blows upon them. I hear a beautiful strain in my heart, unrestricted to meter and harmonies with words that ring sweetly:

> *True Love is as beautiful as a sweet twinkling melody.*
> *True Love is as free as a gentle blowing breeze.*
> *True Love cannot be contained.*
> *True Love cannot be explained.*
> *True Love ignores what the heartless onlooker sees.*

"I see someone I love truly with my heart, my soul, and my whole body, and I know that he loves me the same way."

Dr. Banneker sets his pad in his lap and nods slightly.

*****

"I'm scared."

"Why are you scared?"

"My family…"

"What about your family?"

"They don't approve. They won't approve."

"Is your life based on the approval of your family?"

Ouch! Good question. Minutes tick by. I break the silence by asking this question.

"Is it wrong to want the approval of your family? To desire their love and acceptance just so you can live peacefully?"

"Is it?"

"I'm asking *you*," I snap.

"Why ask me when the answer differs from person to person? I can only tell you that there are certain questions only you can provide the answers to."

Two ouches.

*****

"I wish I didn't care what my family thought. It's because of them that I'm so conflicted with who I am."

"What do you think their thoughts are based on?"

"Easy, the church."

"So, your family is very religious?"

"Yes."

"So, it's not just your family. It's the church as well, yes?"

"I guess."

"What does your family believe as far as your sexual orientation?"

"That it's something we go to hell for. That we needed to pray to God, and pray, and pray until we are delivered."

"And have you prayed that often for your orientation to leave?"

"Yes, sometimes five or six times a day."

"Who told you that you needed to pray it away?"

"My mother and my pastor." *A long silence.*

"Do you remember when I told you about my mother beating me?"

"Yes. It was obviously very painful for you to relive it."

"Later that day, she…" I stop. My breath quickens.

"She what?"

I feel tears coming. "She dragged me to the church to talk with the pastor. She told him that she didn't want a punk for a son, that I hung out with Jojo more than I did with girls, and it made her sick, Then he…"

"What did he do?"

"He and Mama made me kneel at the altar. I can still feel her hand gripping my neck," I whisper hoarsely. "It almost felt like she was about to choke me. The pastor then took a bottle of oil and said, 'Lord, help this fallen sinner, evil from the womb.' And then…" My voice chokes off as I begin to cry uncontrollably. A runny film of mucus travels down my nose as I babble in words barely coherent. "He poured the whole bottle of oil on my head and was screaming in my ear."

Suddenly I hear my voice say the words, "Pray harder!" It gets louder, matching that of my memory, shouting the words over and over, "PRAY HARDER… PRAY HARDER… PRAY HARDER." I crumple to the floor, my abundant tears staining my shirt and falling on the carpet. A thirty-six-year-old man, curled in fetal position, wondering how much harder he can pray.

Chapter Fourteen:

"ASSOCIATION"

"Are you feeling all right, Lion?" Jojo says, as we are at his house, drinking cocktails and listening to "Claire de Lune" by Debussy while watching a brilliant fire in the fireplace. I am holding him in my arms as we talk.

"Yes, I'm fine. Why do you ask?"

"Because for the past two days, you seemed very preoccupied. It's like you have a lot of stuff on your mind, but you don't really know how to get it out."

"I do have a lot of stuff going on. Work really has me jumping. You know that guy I told you about? The one with the crazy machismo commercial ideas."

"Yeah."

"Well, he came back to our firm and told my boss that he wanted me to work on his campaign."

"You're kidding!"

"No sir. He told Mr. Alexander that he wouldn't work with anyone else but me. Mr. Alexander tactfully made mention of the difficulty I had with him on the 'Jump' commercial. After hearing that, he made a promise that he wouldn't be so testy. I guess he's really close to the deadline for the commercial to air and he needs to get something done right away."

"So, are you working with him now?"

"Yes."

"And how has that been going?"

"Fairly well. He kept his promise and we are putting the final changes on the commercial tomorrow. I'm just hoping that nothing will happen between today and tomorrow that would disrupt the flow." He twists his head around to look at me with interest.

"Well, what concept did you finally agree on?"

"Sit up, and I'll tell you," I say excitedly.

I love telling him my ideas. His eyes either light up when he loves them, or his face scrunches up when he doesn't. We draw apart and sit facing each other.

"Well, I came up with the idea of showcasing successful black men, doing what they do in their field. Picture this. Urban music comes on. I have one sharp executive getting ready for work. He sprays the cologne on, gets dressed, and as he walks into the M&T building, he says, 'I reach for the heights in the board room'. I have another in the locker room taking a shower where only his chest is showing. He sprays the cologne, puts on his basketball uniform, and the film cuts to him hitting a slam dunk. When he comes down, he looks at the camera and says, 'I reach for them on the court'. Another is getting ready for a show on stage. He sprays the cologne on him and dresses in his flyest outfit. As he goes out on the stage, he hears cheers and says, 'I reach for them on the stage.' The camera does a three-way split showing all of them doing what they do. A voiceover says, 'Who says that you can't reach for the stars in whatever you do?' It cuts to each man as they split the phrase, 'When I look my best, think my best, and smell my best…' The screen goes black and a deep voice says, 'I can't help but be my best.' Then, there's a shot of them doing a slow-motion high jump in their outfits. Then, we have a freeze frame as the words appear under them, 'Jump: The Sky's the Limit.'"

"That is brilliant!" Jojo's eyes light up brighter than Rockefeller Center on Christmas.

"You really think so? What I was aiming for is something that would not only get rid of the machismo crap, but it would showcase strong intelligent black men in their professions doing what they do."

"Strong black male role models. This will make a positive impact on the kids watching it. I like it," Jojo says as he gives me a quick kiss.

"I do too. It's a hell of a lot better than those other ideas he came up with."

"Yeah, they sucked to the pinnacle of suckivity."

"Where did you come up with that word?"

"I just heard it someplace." He snickers.

"That's not even a word."

"How do you know that?" Jojo playfully swats me on my leg. "You know that people make up words every day, and the Webster's Dictionary gets bigger and bigger. I believe that there are a lot of words that make sense and they haven't even made it into the dictionary yet. This could be one of them."

"How insightful of you," I say as I grab and hold him as before. As I hold him, I smell the citrus on him.

"You made ambrosia salad again, didn't you?"

"What makes you think that?"

"I smell mandarin oranges."

"Well, no I didn't make any. That is just my smell-good."

"Well, it does smell good," I say seductively.

"Thank you," Jojo says softly.

"Are you ever going to give me that recipe?"

"We'll see. We don't know each other *that* well yet!" Jojo coyly banters.

"I got thirty-six years that says we do."

"We're not talking about the friendship years. We're talking about the romantic years that I hope to experience with you."

"Touché!"

"How are your sessions going with Dr. Banneker?"

I stare straight ahead. The silence is deafening. Jojo breaks it.

"So, that is what the preoccupation is all about."

After meditating, I inform, "I'm a bit unnerved. He's causing me to revisit things in my past that I am not comfortable with. He woke up an incident that happened in my childhood."

Jojo turns his body so that he can look at me while talking. "Do you want to tell me? If you don't want to, I understand."

"No, It's ok. We are seeing each other now, so there are things you should know."

"Are you going to hold me to that same principle as far as my dirty little secrets?"

"No."

"Then maybe you'd better not tell me, because things that sensitive should only be shared when the other is ready to share his."

"I don't mind telling you… and I'll wait until you are comfortable enough to tell your story."

"Ok, then. Tell me."

As I relate the story to him, he listens with his eyes wide open at the callousness my mother and the pastor possessed while trying to turn me straight. I saw a worried expression on his face when I shared about the savage beating I received for hugging him. When I tearfully finished my story, he sat up and gestured for me to come to him. His embrace gives me life. Then he speaks. "Now I see why you had the troubled relationship with your mother. It makes sense now."

"What do you mean?"

"It makes sense why you were stalling on me and putting me off. To go through that, it's no wonder you didn't pursue a relationship with me."

I think about this as I shift my position, my back on his hardening, muscled chest. He squeezes me in his beautifully sleek blue-black arms. The word *conditioned* comes to mind. Hmm... I remember hearing that term in my psychology classes while in undergrad. When someone has hammered an idea into your head enough times, you subconsciously cling to that idea without even knowing why. I ponder this as we listen to the mellow sounds of the piano and the logs crackling in the fireplace. "Lionel?"

"Yes?"

"Did you tell Dr. Banneker what you discovered about your mother?"

"No."

"Why not?"

"I just didn't," I snap defensively.

Jojo gets quiet.

"I'm sorry."

"It's ok. I didn't mean to upset you. I just asked because it was really bothering you."

A loud and sharp crack in the log startles me. The sound brings back painful memories of the switch my mother used to beat me with and the hard, stinging slaps delivered from her abrasive hands. But the sound I hear most is the sound of my heart breaking every time she hit me. I touch my left calf and I remember the time she saw me giving a brotherly swat on my wrestling teammate's ass. She beat me with a splintering thick paddle she called Old Faithful. One of the blows landed on my leg and a large sharp splinter lanced through the skin, drawing blood that took forever to clot.

"Do you really think I should tell him about it?"

"If it's bothering you that much, I think you should. Besides, the more you acknowledge what happened, the better your chances of being free from it."

I lifted myself from his embrace and reached into my pocket for my wallet. I pulled out the dog-eared letter my brother found.

"What is that?" Jojo asks.

"The letter written to Mama by Daddy's lover."

"How did you get it?"

"Dean mailed it to me. He wrote that he was sending it because he wants to leave it to me as to what we should do. He also said that maybe Mama does need to face the consequences for what she did."

"What *are* you thinking of doing with it?"

"That's just it! I don't know what to think or how to proceed. But at least this gives me a small amount of closure as to how things happened the way they did."

"I think you should tell Dr. Banneker. Maybe he can help you channel these emotions and indirectly advise you on what to do."

"I'll think about it." I put my wallet, letter and all, in my pocket. Then I look at Jojo, with a mischievous feeling stealing over me, "Now come over here and give me those lips."

"You can't have them. They're attached to me!"

We wrestle playfully from the couch to the floor, then we kiss. Sounds of moans, Debussy, and a crackling fire fills our ears as we share love of the innocent. Love of the romantic. Love without the temporary feelings of infatuation. A night spent without copulation, but still singed with red hot fire generated by the love in our hearts.

*****

"My mind is going in circles, Doc." I pace back and forth, agitated.

"Can you pinpoint the reason?" Dr. Banneker calmly replies.

"It's not just one reason. It's all the stuff that has happened in the recent months."

Dr. Banneker nods, "From everything you've told me, there *is* an element of mind boggle."

"Yeah. It's been overwhelming having to find out about this secret life my Dad had, planning for the cruise, working on the Jump commercial…"

"How is that going?"

I sit down in the chair across from him. "Surprisingly well. We finished the final cut last week and he said, 'That's very good. Very JUMP.' Whatever that means."

"Didn't you tell me your feelings on the cologne?"

"Yeah. It really stunk but someone must have gotten to him before he came back to the firm, because his new and improved concoction smells like cologne should smell. Not my type of smell-good, but it smells decent. Maybe he went back to the chemist and did another workup."

"So, he signed with the company?"

"For this campaign, yes. I know my boss is astronomically happy. That is a multi-million-dollar account and a huge financial bonus for me. After this win, he told me to enjoy my vacation and that I earned it," I add, beaming.

"I'm confused as to his affluence when his cologne left much to be desired by the consumer."

Well, this is new! The doctor is giving shade. Dry shade. But shade, nonetheless. I laugh.

"He's an heir boy. I checked him out. His father is Peter MacLaine of MacLaine Oil. Their net worth is estimated at twenty-four billion."

The doctor nods. "Let's switch gears for a minute. Let's talk about Jojo."

"What about him?"

"Well, are things progressing with him as well as you had hoped?"

"A little too well. It is driving me crazy. If I don't hear from him in a day's stretch, I get a little anxious until I hear his voice again. We are always at each other's houses, just talking about the various situations we faced. And many times, we can finish each other's sentences. He is so insightful and compassionate. More than I ever realized. I also thought he was a bit unlearned about some things, but as we spend time together, I am surprised to find out how uneducated I am... and he is incredibly sexy."

"What makes him sexy?"

"Everything about him. He has a beautiful body and lovely eyes and lips, but I'm turned on the most when he talks. I am attracted to his soul and his mind. Every time he shares his point of view about life, I feel more love for him and more contempt at myself for blocking it out so long. Of course, we have the advantage of knowing each other for as long as we have. We know what makes each other happy or miserable. We haven't had sex yet though, and it is not because I don't want to. When I'm around him, I can feel the sexual tension. Both of us want it, but we are wise enough not to press the issue."

"Are you having sex with anyone else these days?"

"That is a bold question, Doc," I say.

"Why is that?"

"Because it just came out of left field."

"Do you feel comfortable enough to answer the question?"

"No, I'm ok with the question. I just wasn't prepared for it."

The doctor looks at me to continue.

"To be quite honest, I haven't really felt the desire to. The last time I had sex was with Nate. I haven't wanted to sleep with anyone else because I'm too concerned about how Jojo would feel if I did it. The more I spend time with him, the more convinced I am that he is the one for me."

"The way you feel now. Let's explore that. Did you feel this way with Nate?"

"I felt infatuation with him. It slowly grew into love as I got to know him. With Jojo, I feel love, solid love that started when we were kids and grew as we grew. We have love that stood the test of time."

"So, are you saying that you are prepared to be in a monogamous relationship with Jojo?"

"More than that."

"Do you care to explain?"

"Well, it may be sudden, but I am thinking about asking him to be my partner in life, my husband."

"I see, and this is a certainty?"

"Why wouldn't it be?"

"Well, there are two things in the statement you just made that suggest hesitation. One, you said that it might be *sudden*, and two, you said you are *thinking* about asking. Why the hesitation?"

I chew on my bottom lip as I ponder. Then I say, "I didn't know I *had* hesitation. If I did, I guess it's because all of this is still new for me. I'm learning how to be at peace in my own skin, but I'm not all the way there."

"So, you still have insecurities?"

I cannot answer.

"Is your apprehension connected to your family in any way?"

Still no answer. I hear the clock on the mantle ticking out the seconds. Then I proceed.

"I guess I *am* still insecure. But my fear is that I will not get over my insecurities. My father died not fully accepting who he was."

"He was shot to death, correct?"

"Yes."

"Do you know the person who did it?"

Again, I cannot answer.

Five more minutes elapsed. Afterwards, Dr. Banneker speaks, "How have you been sleeping?"

"A little bit better. I still have those dreams ever so often but I'm getting a little bit better."

"So, do you need something other than Doxepin?"

"Let's see how the next two weeks turn out, and then I'll be able to answer that question."

"You mentioned the need to sleep peacefully two sessions ago, but we never explored the details as to what that meant. Is it safe to say that the content of your nightmares is the main cause of your restless sleep?"

"When isn't it?"

"You sound cynical. Are these nightmares affecting your daily emotional balance?"

I sit there for the next two minutes, pondering the question, then I ask the doctor, "Is my time up?"

"No, you still have ten more minutes."

"I have to go, Doc."

After uncomfortable silence, the doctor adjusts his glasses and says, "Very well, I'll see you next Monday."

"Whatever," I say, darting out the door.

*****

"I just don't feel comfortable about talking about it, Doc."

"And why's that?"

"I just don't." Thoughts echo through my head. *If I tell him, there's a chance he may tell the police. I could be responsible for putting my mother in jail for killing my father.* I look at him and see his understanding eyes, but a poker face. *No. There's no way that he could tell anyone. His ethics will not allow him to.* "Do you really want to know what is in my nightmares?"

"Only if you care to share."

I take a deep breath and muster my courage. "I dream about my mother killing my father." I look up for a reaction. The doctor doesn't look surprised or even puzzled. But there is a faint line of interest in his forehead. He motions for me to continue.

I pull the letter out. "I got this letter from my brother, Dean. It was in my mother's box of keepsakes."

"What does the letter contain?"

"An apology."

I tell him about the letter, my father's affair, and my mother's anger that compelled her to kill him.

"May I see the letter?"

Skeptically, I surrender it into his hands. He peruses it quickly, then hands it back to me. He then sits back with an unreadable expression on his face. After a few minutes, he speaks.

"As you hold this letter in your hands, what feeling do you associate with?"

"I feel pity but anger for the one who wrote it. I also feel a sense of justice."

"Justice? I don't understand what you mean."

"I just don't think that a man should have to go to jail for something that he did not do. It might have been brave for him to do that, but I also think it's stupid. My mind is telling me to report this to the police and clear Troy's name."

"Given the intentions of the person who wrote this letter, do you think that is wise?"

"What do you mean?"

"I mean, from the looks of it, he has resigned himself to what he felt he had to do."

"But I don't know if *I* could feel at peace with that. My mother shot and killed my father and his lover is taking the rap."

"And why does that concern you?"

"Why wouldn't it concern me?" I shout. "Because he's my dad!"

"Would your father want you to fight this battle for him?"

I get up and I walk to the window. I look out on the avenue and watch the hustle and bustle of the people walking along the sidewalk. At length, I answer in a small voice, "No."

"If your father were here now, what do you think he would say?"

I turn to look at him. "He would tell me to let it go, for my own good."

The doctor nods.

"But I don't know if I can do that. All I know is that I mixed up with my emotions. I feel anger, I feel hate, I feel like someone needs to pay for my dad's death, and that person is walking around scot free while an innocent man is rotting in prison. I'm all jumbled up."

Doc looks at me for a moment. Then he stands up. "Come with me over to the bulletin board."

We stand in front of the bulletin board. After a period of silence, Dr. Banneker speaks, "I want to do a small exercise with you. Look at this board. What do you see?"

"A worn board with fabric of different colors."

"That is obvious. But what about your mind's eye? What do you identify with when you look at this board?"

I think for a minute.

"Confusion. Chaos. As jumbled up as I feel right now."

"Ok, now I want you to remove the fabric from the board."

It takes time, but I comply.

"Now what do you see?

"A worn board."

"Not very exciting, is it?"

"No."

"Hmmm…"

"Doc, I'm confused as to what this exercise is supposed to prove."

"You will know in time. Let's just continue with the exercise. Now, I want you to pick three fabrics of any color and place it back on the board."

I choose red, blue, and blue-green swatches and I place them on the board.

"Any reason you can think of as to why you chose those colors?"

"No, I just chose them at random."

"You asked me some time ago about this board and I think now is the time to tell you. This board can represent whatever you want it to. I want you to close your eyes and think about what association you make with this board."

I comply. Thirty seconds later, Dr. Banneker says, "Now, what do you see as you envision this board?"

"I guess I see me."

"Keep your eyes closed. The first color you chose is red. What association do you make with that color?"

"Anger, passion, determination."

"OK, the second color you chose is blue. Association?"

"Sadness, calm, truth."

"Ok, third color is blue-green. Association?"

"Serenity, Focus, Youth."

"OK, you may open your eyes."

"What was this about?"

"*You* can best answer that question."

"I can't."

"Try."

"I don't understand."

"Deep down, you do."

I look at the board, then I catch a glimpse of myself in an adjacent mirror.

"I guess with the board representing me, and the colors representing my feelings, I would say that I am angry and sad, but I still have a need to find my truth, so I can focus on finally living in peace and enjoying life."

"Interesting," Dr. Banneker says, nodding his head approvingly.

"I also think the exercise of taking the colors down, and putting only the ones I choose, is telling me that I oversee whatever feelings I choose to feel at any given moment. I can remove whatever chaos that exists and focus on what's most important."

"Hmmm…" The doctor hums reflectively.

I look at the board with the three swatches pinned on it. After thinking it over, I say, "Maybe I need to explore the underlying cause of all this mess. Then I can decide what to do with the letter."

We sit down, "And how will you do that?"

I let out a sigh, "Well, I know Mama won't tell me what happened because she disowned me. My brothers and sisters *can't* tell me because they were not aware of what was going on. Dad sure as hell can't tell me. So... maybe I do need to find out from the only other person who was there and would know."

"And who is that?"

"Troy Matterson, my dad's lover."

CHAPTER FIFTEEN:

"TO FIND THE TRUTH"

"Are you sure you want to do this?" Garrett says. We are at a coffee shop after playing tennis.

"What do you mean?"

"I mean, going down to your hometown. Based off of what you told me already, it might wake up ill feelings with your mother and your siblings."

"I'm not sure if I want to, but it *is* something I have to do. There are some truths that I need to find out, so I can move on."

"What are you going to do after you have found out these truths? I'm not trying to discourage you from going, but I'm more concerned about you and how it would affect things between you and Jojo."

"How do you know about me and Jojo?" I quiz.

"Please, I have eyes. Besides, Corey gave me an earful."

"Why would Corey be telling my business?"

"Why did you tell me *his* when he was attacked?" he said playfully.

"Ouch."

"I'm waiting for the answer."

"Don't be looking at me skinning and grinning. I asked you first."

"And I asked you second. What's the point? Answer my question," he says with childlike amusement lighting his eyes.

"Because I was concerned."

"That's the same reason he did it."

"Touché. But I think knowing the truth behind my mother's disdain may give me enough peace to move on."

"I'm with you on that."

"How is Rachel doing?"

"She is back at Mama's house, leaving Sam for good this time."

Thank God! "That is good news. What caused her to drop him?"

"He backhanded Mike Jr."

"What?!"

"Yeah, the thing I feared the most was beginning to happen, but she said that after seeing that and Junior's face after it happened, she started thinking about how it might escalate."

"Very wise. A man who would hit a woman and a child is a man who is capable of doing much worse."

"Yeah, but the best part about this is he left town."

"He did?"

"Yep. After that ass-kicking Craig and Melba put on him, I guess he started thinking about what worse things they could do to him. So, he booked. Oh, I forgot to tell you. He didn't show up for the court date, so the case was thrown out."

"That's good news. I was concerned about that. What's next for Rachel?"

"She's going to stay with Mama until she is sure he's gone, then she's going back home."

"So, that's her house? Not Sam's?"

"Yes, it's hers. Mike Sr. left it to her before he died. Sam was just living there."

"Someone should go with her to stay, at least for a few months."

"Melba is going with her."

"Melba?"

"Yeah. You know, the family may cringe at her attending the family reunions because of the trouble she and Craig can stir up, but she's on it when it comes to protecting her own. Besides, I think being around Mike Jr. would influence her for the better. She always had a soft spot for him. You saw how bright he is."

"Yeah, He made me think about some of the youth I lost."

"Oh, come on, Lionel. You never lose your youth. You just become so soiled and jaded that you forget that you still have it."

"You're right."

"Like I was saying, maybe Melba will be a little calmer dealing with the fact that she is in the house with a kid."

"Yeah, let's hope so."

"How is the cruise planning going?"

"Pretty good. Next month is the month we sail."

"Are you nervous?"

"A little. The only boat I've been on is a fishing boat. We're talking about a big boat that is going to be on the seas for eight days. I'm a bit like Corey. I'm scared out of my mind!"

"What is there to be scared about? Look, all you have to do is bring motion sickness pills, some breezy clothes and you'll be fine. Just relax and have fun. Besides, you'll have your friends with you."

"How are things with you and Corey?"

A blush heats his face. "I finally asked him out."

"Get out of here!"

"I did, and it was a nice night. Corey is really fun to be with. We went to dinner on the Harbor and walked beside the bay. Then he took me to this place that had go-carts."

"Go-carts?"

"Yes, go-carts. I didn't think I'd like it, but we had a lot of fun"

"That's Corey for you. He makes people want to say yes to life."

"That is a beautiful quality to have. Very attractive too. Only one guy I knew did that for me."

"So, with you and Corey being as close as you are, have you made the decision to come out to your mother?"

Garrett says in a small voice, "Not yet. Corey and I talked about that last night. I want to tell her, but every time I attempt, I chicken out. Corey said that it will come out eventually, but I should take my time."

"I agree. You alone know the right time to tell her. So, is this infatuation or will it push to love?"

"It's too early to tell. I already know that I like and care about him a lot. Talking with him is like reconnecting to a part of me that I thought had died. I feel like this; the more I'm with him, the more I desire to know about him."

"Strange, I feel the same way with Jojo."

"But you both have known each other for years. I would've thought that you would've known plenty about each other by now."

"I guess when you are in love, every interaction brings something new."

"Yeah. Oh shit, when is your flight?"

"Seven twenty-five. What time is it now?"

"Almost four thirty."

I rise and grab my racket. Garrett rises too. "I'd better get home to pack and then catch the flight."

"Do you want me to follow you home in my car? That way, I can drop you off at the airport and you won't have to pay parking fees."

"I appreciate that, Thank you."

"Ok, let's bounce."

*****

I'm on the plane to Birmingham, and it is cold! I had to ask the pleasant flight attendant, Seymour, for two blankets. Jojo wanted to go with me, but I insisted that I needed to do this alone. As I feel the plane climb the sky, I wonder what I am accomplishing by doing this. Would talking with my father's lover bring me any closer to the peace that I'm seeking, or will it send me back into a tailspin? Memories of my father are vivid in my mind. The hugs he used to give me. The man to man talks by the lake where we went fishing when he was not busy on his job. The whipping he gave me when he caught me skipping school. The difference between his whippings and my mother's is that you felt that he hated to punish his children. With my mother, all us kids had to do is look at her the wrong way and she would slap the shit out of us. Dad would explore the offense to find out where it's coming from.

In many ways, I felt like the roles should've been reversed. My dad should've been my mom and my mom should've been my dad because of the temperaments between them. One thing that kept turning in my mind over and over was this: how in the hell did my parents get together? My mother was the abrasive type, but my dad was always very quiet and meditative.

Unexpectedly, one long forgotten scene with my dad bombards in my memory. A fishing trip.

"Lionel?"

"Yeah, Dad?"

He pulled a bottle from his pocket. "I found this on the floor in your bedroom upstairs. Is it yours?"

My KY Jelly! I was shocked. My heart was beating a mile a minute. I should've hid it better!

"You can talk to me, son. Is it yours?"

"Yes."

"Hmmm."

There was another awkward silence. Then Dad asked the most embarrassing question. "What do you know about sex, son?"

"Dad! Come on."

"No, I mean it." Dad said nervously. "This is serious business now. And you are almost fourteen. I tried to talk to you about this at twelve, but you just said, 'Ew!' So, I figured you weren't ready yet but we're gonna have to talk about this stuff sometime. You're growing up faster than I can keep up."

"I know a little bit."

"Where did you get your information?"

"Well, my friends at school. And Jamaal told me a little bit."

"Oh, he did, did he?" I thought I saw a knowing smirk on my dad's face as he chuckled. What was that all about?

"Yeah."

"Son, I'm gonna ask this question, and I want you to be honest with me."

"OK..."

"Are you having sex?"

"Dad!"

"Come on, just be honest with me. I'm going somewhere with this. Are you having sex?"

"Yeah."

"Are you safe when you do it?" He peered over his glasses.

"Of course, Dad. I am always protecting myself." The silence that stretched between my father and I was only interrupted by the birds and the rushing waters. Then my dad spoke, "Well, what do you know about AIDS?"

"I know that it just came out a few years ago."

"Well, the reason I'm bringing this up is because while I don't want you to always have cum on your mind... You do know what cum is, don't you?"

"OK, Dad, this conversation is embarrassing on so many different levels."

"You didn't answer my question."

"No."

"Those boys didn't teach you very well. 'Cum' is what they call sperm."

"Oh, you mean 'nut'?"

"What's 'nut'?"

I laughed, "Dad, if we are going to talk about sex, then you gotta keep up."

Dad chuckled, "No, young man. Don't get it twisted. **You** have to keep up. All **I** gotta learn is the new terminology. Remember, I've already been down the road you're traveling, and it wasn't that long ago."

"It wasn't?" I gave Dad a teasing look.

"So, you got jokes?" Dad boxed me on the arm. Then, he put me in a headlock, playfully giving me a noogie and laughing. How I loved my dad's laugh. It was contagious. Then Dad said. "Seriously, though. I want you to **always** be careful and protect yourself. AIDS is a serious disease and I've had many friends to die from it."

"I know that, Dad."

"And then there is stuff like gonorrhea."

"The clap?"

He gives me an appraising look. "Well, you aren't **that** unsophisticated, I see."

"I read."

"Alright smart ass, but I tell ya. When you are sitting in the doctor's office, it is not a happy feeling. Between the moments of passion and doing the do. Make sure that you wrap it up. We all choose our own type of pain, but there's some types of pain that we choose, and we don't even know we have chosen it until it's too late."

I thought about his words as I looked at him with pride and love bursting from my heart. I admire his tall, lean bronze frame. His good-natured laughing eyes are complimented by his big, flaring nose and large smoke-blackened lips. And I remember thinking, "I'm going to grow up and look just like this man." Everything I wanted to be was tied to him. We sat at the riverbank, just fishing. I hear my father as he whistles his high-pitched tune.

"Dad."

"Yeah, champ?"

"A minute ago, you said something about choosing pain. Why would anybody choose pain? It seems to me that that would be the one thing that they would stay away from."

My dad let out a huge breath before he responded, "Well, son. If you have someone that you really love, as I love your mother, what hurts them will hurt you too. But you will bear the pain, because you chose to love them for better or worse. That is the type of pain we choose gladly. And I wish that for you, because that pain can always move on, and the good times can begin again."

"Sometimes I wonder why you and Mama got together. You two are so different. I don't mean to be disrespectful."

"No, this is one of those times where I want you to say what you feel."

I hesitated to tell him, but he gave me a green light. "Mama is awfully mean to us kids. When she's not whipping us, she's screaming at us. I know she has to discipline us. But sometimes I think she goes too far. The only one she doesn't do that with is Rhonda, her favorite."

"We have no favorites in this family."

"**You** may not, but Mama does. She lets her get away with most of the stuff she beats the rest of us for. And it gets worse when you aren't around, at least for me. Andre is out of the house, so she can't beat on him."

"What did you mean, 'at least for you?'"

I remember looking out onto the lake and hesitating again. "She tripped out about me and Jojo hanging out all the time."

"Oh, your mother and I talked about that. She feels that Jojo is kinda different in that he is what the older generation would call 'funny'. But I talked to her and told her to leave you alone. If he's your friend, he's your friend, and that's all there is to it"

"So, she's upset because she thinks he's a fag?"

"Don't use that word, son."

"But that's what they call them, Dad."

Dad's voice became sharp. "So? That doesn't mean **you** get to call them that. Besides, you never know how your life will turn out as you become older. The same thing you put down might be the same thing you have to deal with."

More than YOU know, I thought to myself.

"Why are you so comfortable talking about things like this?"

"Well Champ, I have friends who are gay, and they ended up being the best friends I've ever had; just like Jojo is your best friend. That should be all that matters to you."

"What do you mean?"

"Well, if you are friends with someone, you like them for who they are. Their quirks are just a small part of what they are."

Silence.

"Dad?"

"Yeah, son."

"Do you have to go away all the time?"

"I gotta feed my family, Champ."

"But we all miss you when you're gone."

"I miss you too. But if I don't go, my family won't eat. And besides, I only go two weeks out of the month."

"Can't you talk to your boss where you don't have to travel so much?"

"I worked hard to get in the position I'm in, so I have to be careful how I approach this."

"I understand," I said, my head held down.

Suddenly, Dad taps me on the knee. I look at him. "Come on, now. Don't look like your dog just died. I'll find ways, Champ. Your old Dad always does." I *smiled because whenever he said, "I'll find ways," I knew he would do just that.*

Looking back, I chuckle. My Dad was right. He always found a way to do what he wanted and get what Mama and us kids needed. I have no idea what song and dance Dad performed, but he was able to cut back a week. Eventually, he got a more stationary position with the company where he could stay in town most of the time. When he had to travel, he limited the time to three days. Things got better after that, especially after Rhonda moved out. As I reflect on that conversation, I realize that what I shared with Dr. Banneker was not altogether true. Dad would've understood. A tear drops down my face. Being armed with that possibility doesn't make it any better. My Dad is not here. I turn my head to the side and try to go to sleep.

*****

At 12:56am, I pull up to the hotel in my rental car. I grab my overnight bag and go inside to check into my room. All I want to do is get some sleep. I could have stayed at the house and saved the money, but I decided that the alone time would be needed. Plus, I don't want any trouble. Mama is at home and I really don't want a scene. In fact, I don't want her or anyone in Yeti to know I'm here. I sit down on the bed and I text Jojo, Corey, and Peep: "I'm here and safe." The phone rings and Jojo's name flashes across the screen.

"Hello."

"Hey baby."

"Hey beautiful. I thought you would be asleep at this hour."

"How can I sleep when I am concerned? I still wish I could've gone with you."

"I know, and I appreciate that, but this is something I have to face alone."

"I understand."

"I will be back Sunday night."

"Ok. Oh, keep Jimmy and Irene in your prayers."

"What happened?"

"She went into another diabetic shock yesterday."

"Another one? She missed meals again, didn't she?"

"Yep."

"You know, this is starting to scare me a bit. How is Jimmy handling it?"

"As best he can, but Peep and Jimmy feel that Irene is losing her will to live, and Peep is starting to internalize it."

"What?"

"Yeah, she keeps saying she's ready to go and that she's tired."

"That's not good."

"And it is scaring Peep and Jimmy to distraction."

"Maybe we should see if we can take Irene with us."

"Are you crazy?"

"Think about it. This way we can all keep an eye on her."

"Well, we can ask them and see. I'll call the travel agent and see if there is a possibility of her going."

"OK."

"Are you ok, baby?"

"Yeah, I'm OK. I just don't know what I'm trying to prove by doing this."

"You are not trying to prove anything. You are trying to move on with your life. The way to do that is to make peace with your past."

"You're right."

Silence

"Jojo?"

"Yes, babe?"

"Thank you.

"For what?"

"Just for being there. Just for being you."

*****

I walk into the dank, drab, scum-coated visiting area of Donaldson prison. How Andre could stand living so many years in a place like this is beyond me. I see a big fat cockroach wending its way across the wall. I shudder and take my seat at the aged, scratched up, dirty window separating the visitor from the prisoner... and I wait.

What am I accomplishing being here? What feelings am I going to experience as I converse with my father's lover? I feel anger, not only at Mother, but at Troy for pulling Dad away from us. I swivel the chair so that my back faces the window. I wonder when did Dad start messing around with guys. Was it always there? Did it happen later? Questions swim around in my head as I speculate. How I wish my Dad was here. We could have shared so much. He could have really helped me through my discovery of my sexuality. Then again, the circumstances would have been pleasantly altered if he were honest with Mother, divorced her, and lived his life in his truth. I would have went to visit him and he could have shown me what to do. I would have gone to live with him. Lord knows, being in that house with Mother was hell and the flames came from someone who claimed to be on her way to Heaven.

A deep voice interrupts my thoughts. "Hello, sir. The guard said someone wanted to see me." I turn, and through the glass, I see a well-built man with sandy complexion. He was wearing a prison uniform, but his eyes sported glasses with wire frames, making him look somewhat bookish, yet appealing. As he looks at me, his mouth drops open. He absentmindedly sits and picks up the receiver, his face depicting a look of shock.

He breaks the gaze, saying, "I'm sorry for staring but you look like someone I knew from way back."

"Kenneth Davis. Right?"

"Yes," He says, puzzled. His eyes widen as awareness fills them. "Are you his son?"

"I am."

Silence stretches like a gulf between plateaus. At length, he remarks, "You look just like your Daddy."

"Yes, well, never mind about that."

"How are you, kid?"

"I've been better. Over the past few months, I have had to come to grips with some very unsettling facts surrounding my Dad's death."

"What do you mean?"

"My mother said that someone shot my Dad."

"Yes, it was me that killed him."

"That's the story, but while you may have been partway responsible, you did not pull the trigger."

Silence.

"Shall I keep going?"

"Look, kid. I killed your Dad and I'm sorry. You have no idea how much I wish I could take it back. I'm trying to put it behind me. I've been trying to erase his image from my memory, but ten years gives me too much time to reflect on him."

"Reflect on him, or reflect on the lie you told?"

"What lie are you talking about?"

I pull out my wallet and retrieve the dog-eared letter. I unfold it and show him. A knowing, despairing look passes through his face.

"Recognize this handwriting?"

Silence.

"Do you?"

He hangs his head.

After the long stillness, I lay the letter down on the table. Then I begin to talk.

"I don't know who I should be angrier with. My father for his affair and his lying, you for pursuing him even though you knew he was married to my mother, or her for killing him. But even through my anger, I still carry a sense of justice. And I think it is asinine for you to spend all these years in this shithole for something you didn't do."

He breathes a long sigh of despair. Then he looks at me.

"Then, you don't know how much your Dad loved you all."

Suddenly he laughed. "You know, he used to tell me all the time about his kids. How you and Dean were graduating with your Business and Mathematics Degree. He was as proud as he could be. I think Andre and Rhonda were the ones he had the most issue with. Andre was always in and out of jail and Rhonda was with her live-in boyfriend. But when they both came home, Kenneth beamed. He said he was happy to have his family back together."

"Did he ever mention Mama?"

"Yes. They were always fighting about something. In fact, I remember one huge argument they had."

"What was it?"

"When you wanted to go to Baltimore to attend Morgan with your friend."

"They fought about that?" He nodded and continued.

"Yeah, your mother was upset because you were making the break from Yeti and she hated that you and your friend were so close. She was afraid that you were picking up what she called "faggot habits".

I started to feel a little more comfortable around him. So, I relaxed as I said. "Faggot habits, no. Gay, yes."

"I know... and your father knew as well."

"What?!"

"Uh, Earth to Lionel! Yes," he said, as he looked at me like I was crazy. When he said that, he looked uncannily like Corey. I must admit. I understand why Daddy loved him so much. His easy wit and open personality were very endearing.

"How?" I say, trying to suppress a smile.

"He came home from work and heard voices. He tiptoed up to your room and saw you and your cousin fucking one day when everybody else was out of the house."

"He saw me?" I ask in disbelief.

"Yep. He saw you."

"What did he say about it? Was he mad?"

"Hell no! He was laughing his ass off! But he never mentioned it because he knew how deep in the closet you were. He felt that you would have been embarrassed if he told you that he knew."

We spend half an hour talking about Dad. The funny anecdotes Troy tells has me splitting at the seams. Who would've thought I would find a good time visiting somebody in prison and with the very one accused of killing my dad? Suddenly the loudspeaker blares, "Visiting hours are over in three minutes."

Silence. Then I speak, "How did you convince the cops that you did it?"

He lets out a long sigh before answering. "I told them that I threatened to kill myself. He went for the gun and tried to take it from me. That's when the gun went off, killing him."

"Involuntary manslaughter."

"You got it. Then I said that I turned the gun on myself with intent to commit suicide."

"How many years did they give you?"

"Fifteen to life."

"I am so sorry."

"Don't be. The time was well spent. I do my time. Managed to keep my nose clean. And I'll be up for parole in a year."

"It's not fair that you had to spend all that time in prison for something you did not do. The one who really killed him should be in here."

"Looka here, kid," he says, looking me dead in my eye. "I destroyed the man's marriage and he's dead because I couldn't leave him alone. I figured it was right for me to take my lumps like a man. Besides, imagine what would've happened if I hadn't. You and your older brothers and sister would've survived, but the two youngest? Who knows how they would have turned out? Even though they were teenagers, they needed their mother. Their dad was already dead. I didn't want to hear of them losing one parent then dealing with the other on her way to prison. How are they, by the way?"

"They're okay. Both are in grad school and are doing well."

"You see what I'm saying? That is good news! I like to think I had a little something to do with that. Besides, it hasn't turned out all bad. I got a legit job lined up after I do my time. As a bonus, I got a man outside these walls that loves me."

"Visiting hours are now over," the voice on the loudspeaker booms.

"Well, I'd better get back."

"Yeah, I guess I'd better go too."

Troy and I get up and start to hang up. Suddenly it hits me. Maybe I can help with his parole.

"Troy?" I hear myself say.

"Yeah?" He says, putting the receiver back to his ear.

"You got a pen and paper?"

"Yes and no. I got my hand." He pulls the pen out.

"Write this number down on it. 443-992-7129. When you get close to your parole, call me. I'm going to do what I can to make sure that you walk free."

Troy looks at me with tears in his eyes and nods, "I'll do that, kid."

Chapter Sixteen:

"Breaking Free"

"I don't see any specialty stores in here," Corey laments.

"Specialty stores?" I query.

"Yeah, for costumes."

"Ok, I'm lost," Garrett says. "Why do you need a costume?"

"Because, they are going to have a Jungle Party on the ship and I want my costume to be fierce!"

"Somebody is glad to be going all of a sudden!" Peep muses.

"Weren't you the one who said, 'I ain't getting on no boat'?" Jojo follows.

"Well, if I'm going on this cruise, I might as well enjoy myself."

The fellas and I are strolling through the mall, with Garrett and Jimmy in tow. It is four weeks before the cruise, and we are in a buying frenzy. The outing is good for me because it takes my mind off of the facts surrounding my father's demise. It is still harrowing to live with the knowledge of my mother doing what she did, but I decided not to turn the letter over to the police. After talking with Troy, listening to Jojo's advice, and going to a few sessions with Dr. Banneker, I realized that it would be better to allow my mother to come forward and confess. If she doesn't, then that will be her lifelong burden to carry. It certainly won't be mine. Also, when Troy was telling me his reasons for taking the rap, I noticed something in his eyes. Something peaceful and accepting. In addition to his wit, I can see why Dad loved him so much. He really is a cut above the rest. He sacrificed his freedom so that Roland and Brenda could grow up having Mother around, regardless of what she did. Who does that? *Hmmm.* Maybe my dad and Troy would've made a wonderful couple. I heard the love in his voice and saw a slow easy and endearing smile whenever Dad's name came up. It is the same look that Jojo gives to me.

We are trying to get the right outfits to wear. We finally sat down two nights ago to look at the itinerary. And what an itinerary it is! Four huge parties, and all of them had different and exciting themes; The Pride Party, The Jungle, the Eighties party, and of course the infamous White Party, only they called it the White Rainbow Party. Weird, right? There is a huge talent and fashion show. Peep, being the self-proclaimed Guru of Fashion in the group, was interested in that. There is a spades tournament, which was right down Jimmy's alley because he is a consummate spades player. Andre, Dean, and Jimmy would really get along, because whenever my brothers and I got together to play cards, Andre and Dean always teamed up... *and they always won!* Every now and then, it crosses my mind that they cheat.

We are going down the list to see what we need to buy for what party. Peep says, "Hmmm... Now we have our outfits for the White Party."

"And we have the Eighties party stuff from the vintage store," Jojo follows.

"So, all we need are outfits for the Pride Party, and costumes for the Jungle," Jimmy observes.

"I really don't think we are going to find anything of substance in this mall as far as costumes for the Jungle. Maybe we should try another mall. What do you think, Garrett?" Corey asks.

"Well, I think in order for you to have jungle costumes, you might go online to get them."

"You see, Lion? I told you we should've went online."

"Well, we are four weeks away from sail date. We have time. But, if we are ordering online, we'd better do it today."

"Right," Jojo says. "But we can still get stuff for the Pride Party."

"That's true," Peep says. "OK, let's split up and be back here in an hour."

"OK." I prepare to leave with Jojo.

"No, no, no. You go on ahead and pick your stuff out."

"Why can't I come with you?"

"Because I don't want you to see what I'm buying. I'll see you in an hour," Jojo says as he races down the hall.

We all disperse. I decide to go to Rodchester's with Peep. He fit me well last time I went. Maybe he'll find something to fit me this time.

Peep turns and sees me. "What are you sticking around me for?"

"Come on, Peep. You know how to style me. I need your help."

"You don't need my help. Lion. You always had good fashion sense. It just went downhill while you were seeing Nate."

"But…"

"Lion, you can come with me but I'm not going to style you this time. You oughta know by now what works and what doesn't."

"Ok, ok! But that doesn't mean that you can't give me your opinion on things I pick out. Right?"

"Lionel Davis, king of the loophole. Alright, but remember, *you* are picking out the clothes, not me."

*****

"What do you think of this one?" I hold up a satin shirt with an eggshell base and a multi-colored paint-drip pattern along the shoulders.

"Oooh!" Peep rushes over to my side. "This is awesome! Would look fabulous on me!"

"No, Peep! I saw it first!"

"Well, who is the designer? I want to be on the lookout for when he designs something else I like."

I look at the tag. "It says 'DeRantio Meredith'"

"That is a unique name. Catchy. But this shirt says Pride, baby!"

"Yeah."

"You see, I told you that you didn't need my help."

"Why thank you, kind sir!"

I search for the pants, I see off-white billowy slacks that might work. I hold them up. "Slacks?"

Peep looks up and grimaces. "Ok, I spoke too soon. Lion, with a shirt like that, you would not wear off-white. But if you did, you wouldn't want to show up at a club or a party looking like you just put a parachute on."

"Well, what about navy?"

"Hmm… Navy slacks might work. It is one of the colors in the shirt. But it needs to be form-fitting."

"I don't want it to be too tight. Somebody might see it and hit on me. Jojo might get jealous."

"Shit, if you are not going to do anything with the guy hitting on you, you have nothing to worry about."

"I guess you're right. But we may need to go to another store because I doubt if they have the type of pants that will fit this shirt."

"Well, we can go to Sexually Yours. If there was ever a store that would have pants fitting the shirt, that store certainly would."

"Cool. Want to go after we finish here?"

"Ok." I continue to look on the racks just in case when I hear this question, "So, when's the wedding?"

What the hell did he just say? Shocked, I look at him as he rummages through the rack. He glances at me.

"What are you looking at me like that for? You know I am practically psychic, and I smell a wedding in the air."

"Peep, we are taking things slow."

"Slow or not, you two are getting ready to walk down the aisle. You have that same googly eyed 'this-is-my-man' look that Jimmy had with me. It may happen sooner, and it may happen later. But rest assured, there is going to be a wedding. All I wanna know is who's planning it."

"Look, I do have feelings for him. I think there's a possibility that we may partner up. But I just don't want to rush into anything. And weren't you the same one that said that you didn't want me to get someone on the rebound?"

"Lion, this is different. When you and Nate got together, I didn't see the same glowing attraction that you and Jojo have. And the only reason I said that is because you were not sure about whether to go back with Nate, or to be with Garrett or Jojo. Nate is yesterday's news. Garrett and Corey have eyes for each other. And it's obvious that you and Jojo both are devoted to each other."

"Yeah, that's true."

"And I remember standing in this very store when I told you all of this, including the fact that both of you have invested thirty-six years into this friendship. And it saves you time trying to get to know him. Did you not hear me say that?"

"Yes, I did."

"So, what is the hold-up?"

"I guess I'm still trying to navigate through some things. I still have concerns as far as how my family will take this."

"Baby please, ditch how the family will take it! When it comes to matters of the heart, they are the last ones to have any say. Besides, you are talking to the master. I already told you what happened when I got hitched. I went against the church, against my family, and against everything that I had been taught. But when I married Jimmy, I married him because I loved him. I didn't marry him because he measured up to what my family wanted."

"You got a point there."

"Lion, it's like this. If you love Jojo, nothing else should matter. Not your mama, Not your brothers, and not your sisters."

Familiar words. "Sounds like something my father would say."

"Smart man. Anyway, last I heard, you are the only one that has to live in the body that you're in. Do you want to go through your life letting everyone else control your every action?"

"No."

Peep gives me an "I rest my case" look and resumes browsing. He looks at his watch. "It's getting late. Me and Jimmy really have to get to Irene's house. I'm starting to worry about her."

"She still not doing too well?"

"No. Her diabetes is getting worse. And she will not listen when the doctor tells her to get on a diet or eat before taking insulin. And…" Peep abruptly cuts off and looks at the Rodchester's Menswear sign.

"What?"

"Something she said a week ago scared the hell out of me and Jimmy."

"What was it?"

"Well, we went over her house to check on her. She just had this worn-out look in her eyes. Her house was a total mess and she looked even worse. Jimmy checked in the medicine cabinet to look at her medication and it was full. Usually she would be due for refill around this time. Jimmy asked her what was going on and she just kept saying, 'I'm tired of taking pills. I'm tired of shooting insulin. I'm tired of fighting to stay alive. I'm ready to go.' Jimmy's trying to be cool, but this is eating him up."

I go over to him and I put my hand on his shoulder. Peep looks at me and says, "You know, maybe it wouldn't have been a bad thing for Irene to tag along with us when we went for that Fella's night out. I've forgotten how depressing a house can be when you are by yourself. I went through that during the summer vacation after my grandma died. I sat in that house and I watched TV, listened to the clock tick, and wallowed in my own guilty feelings. But, Irene had two good husbands to die. She feels like she has no one here that really needs her." He pauses, and a tear rolls down his face. "Lion…? I think she may die soon…"

I turn him around and hug him tightly. I know that this isn't just eating Jimmy up. It's bothering Peep as well. If there was ever a time that he needed his friends, this is the time.

Suddenly, I remember my conversation with Jojo. What better time to bring it up than now? "Listen, have you thought about her going on the cruise with us?" I say as we draw apart.

"No."

"Well maybe if she got out of the house, and into some new scenery, it may cause her to look at things a different way. Maybe this might make her fight a little bit harder to live."

"But it might be too late," Peep says. "The deadline is already gone. And we're not sure if there any rooms left."

"Well, you won't know unless you call."

"But how are we going to get the money?'

"I can pay Irene's share. We would just need to find somebody who will go with her to pay the other half."

"She could call Gladys. She's always saying that they get along."

"But what happens if she can't go?"

"Peep, I'm sure that the travel agent has someone who would be willing to room with Irene. The cruise is not just a cruise for men, you know. There are women up there too, maybe some around Irene's age."

"I'll tell Jimmy, but I doubt if she will go."

"Why?"

"Well, you know how she is, and I don't think she has ever been on a cruise. It would take Jesus and every apostle beside Him to get her on that boat."

"You think so?"

"I know so. Oooh!" He walks past me to grab a pair of navy slacks off the rack. They are nice! Silky to the touch and a perfect complement to the shirt. "I guess we don't have to go to 'Sexually Yours" after all. Go into the dressing room and try these on."

I grab the shirt and the pants and comply. Inside the dressing room as I change, I catch a glimpse of my face in the mirror. I see a few strands of silver on my temples. Holy shit! When did those grow in? What caused them? Was it genetic? It's probably the stress of the campaign and finding out about Dad.

I emerge from the dressing room and Peep stares with his eyes bulging out.

"Hot, Hot, Hot!"

"What do you mean?"

"You look hot to death. Maybe you had better not get that outfit. You might have sharks chasing you on the boat."

"It really looks good?"

"Hell yeah! Now I am reminded of how I got my name. Anybody looking at that would want to peep at that love basket."

"Ha! Oh, here comes Jimmy. Let me get outta this before Jojo sees it."

Back in the dressing room, I overhear Peep and Jimmy talking. Peep is introducing the idea to Jimmy. He is less than thrilled. But he is receptive to the idea.

"It might be something good for her to do."

"I'm sure that it is nice, but my concern is that if you get Irene Hartfield on that boat, there will be no stopping her. It's bad enough making sure she watches what she eats on dry land. When she gets on that cruise, she is going to pig out. And the food is not all that healthy."

"But at least, we will be up there to watch her."

"That's true. But the question is, "Will she go?""

"We won't know unless we ask. Lionel?"

I poked my head over the door. "Wassup?"

"You presented this idea to me. Would you come with us and talk to her about it?"

"Sure."

Just as I am leaving the dressing room, I see Garrett, Corey, and Jojo walking towards us. Corey and Jojo are loaded wih bags and carrying on their usual chatter, while Garrett just walks beside them, listening. From time to time, he is looking at Corey. I noticed a faraway look on his face and a wistful smile. It's like he's daydreaming about days gone by.

"Did you find what you're looking for?" Peep asks.

"Well, we found the stuff for the pride party," Jojo informs.

"But Garrett was right. We're going to have to go online to purchase our jungle costumes," Corey says.

"So, are we done for the day?" I ask.

"I suppose so," Jojo replies.

"OK, then I'm gonna go run with Peep and Jimmy somewhere."

"Alright baby. I'm gonna go on home and put the stuff away. I'll call you later." He gives me a kiss and heads out of the store. It is kind of hard to miss the furtive looks between Corey and Peep, accompanied by sly smiles.

"Well, me and Garrett are going to go to Towson Towne Center. We will catch up with you later."

*****

We turn on Alto Road and pull up to Irene's enormous sky-blue and white two-story house. I take note of the yard. The beautiful flower beds and the immaculately kept lawn both testify to how Irene keeps busy. As we walk up the stairs to her wraparound porch, I can't help but admire how neat and clean it is. There are two white rockers and a small white table between them. They are stationed on the left side of her whitewashed door. Over the porch banister, a hunter green screen is rolled up, ready to be released to keep the sun from baking the person reclining at leisure in the rockers. On the right side of her porch hangs a very inviting porch swing. Whenever I come over to Irene's house, I always feel like I'm at home in Yeti, Alabama.

Jimmy knocks on the door and opens it. "Mama, it's me."

"Jimmy, what are you doing in my neck of the woods?" I hear Irene's clear and beautiful voice coming from the kitchen. She appears through the door and advances towards us with a limp she hoped we wouldn't notice. She hugs all of us, then she stands back to give us a onceover. "I swear, y'all look more good-looking every time I see you."

"I could say the same thing about you, Irene," I say as I look her over. Her vanilla wafer brown skin with reddish undertones glows as it catches the sun shining through the window. Her face showed a bit of crow's feet and smile lines, and I see dark circles under her eyes, but that does not detract from her inner beauty and peace. It radiated from her like a flame warming cold campers. She came out wearing a floral print Blouse, blue jeans, and white sneakers. Her long silver hair is hanging in a braid down her back. She has always been a beautiful woman. Yet, I can't help but notice that when I hugged her, her body felt so frail and bony. She is not even my mother, and I'm starting to worry about her. How she can keep her yard and this house looking so nice, even in her condition, is a mystery to me.

She smiles at all of us with obvious pride in her eyes. "How is Mama's handsome babies doing? Y'all want something to drink?"

"Yeah, you got a Corona?"

"Now Jimmy, you know good and well that nobody touches my Coronas but me. But I got some forties. How about that?"

"Hit me with one."

"Alright baby."

She goes into the kitchen to grab a forty for Jimmy. At length, she calls out to Peep and me. "Uh, did y'all want forties too?"

"No thanks, Mamacita. What else do you have?" Peep says.

"I got some cokes in the fridge."

"Hmmm... Well, I've been drinking a lot of water this week. I guess I can treat myself. How about you, Lion?"

"I'm fine with it."

She comes back into the living room and hands us our drinks. Then, she plops down in her favorite chair. "So, I know y'all are excited about that cruise comin' up"

"Yep. We're really looking forward to it."

"I know you are. Cruises can be a lot of fun."

Jimmy suddenly looks at her. "You've been on a cruise before?"

"Chile, it has been so long since I've been on one. It was long before you were born. But my daddy used to take me all the time. In my younger days, I might've gone eight or nine times on cruises. I had a good time on most of them, but the last two cruises I took were torture. On both occasions, I was sick the whole time. That was when I swore that I would never have my ass on the boat again."

All three of us look at each other with a "what now" expression on our faces. Then Jimmy speaks up, "Well, that kinda puts a dent in what we were going to ask you."

"What do you wanna ask Mama?"

"We wanted to know if you can come with us," I inform.

"Well, the story I just told you also gave you my answer."

"Maybe this time will be different."

"Baby, I am seventy-one years old, and one of the things that you learn by the time you get to my age is that there are some risks you just don't take. Besides, I've gotten sick four times this year because of my Diabetes. The last place I need to be is on a boat."

"Well what are you going to do while we're gone?"

"Oh baby, you know I got Sandra Jean up the street. If there's anything going on or I'm feeling a little lonesome. I could just call her, and she'll come by and see about me." Peep and I exchange sly glances. I think to myself, *One wonders what those two do to cure her 'loneliness'.*

"Well, for what it's worth. You don't look sick at all. You look pretty good."

"Well, that's because I'm naturally beautiful, baby. I get that from my mama's side of the family. My dad's side of the family were a bunch of deadbeats, so I hope I ain't got nothing from them."

For the next hour, we just sit around laughing and talking about life and all the current events. About this crazy government that can't seem to get along. Then, in a total switch, we started talking about LGBTQ issues and gay bashing. It was then that she asked about Corey.

"How is my other baby doing?"

"He's adjusting, given the circumstances. In fact, he's talking to a friend of ours and we think it's getting serious," I report.

"That's a blessing. Hopefully, this will stay serious. Lord, it would do my soul good to watch that boy settle down. Whoever he is talking to is doing him a world of good. I am seeing a little bit of a change in him. Not as wild and more reflective. But, I'm still very concerned about him. I read something about two days ago, and it was talking about why people do the things they do. It said many people are haunted by their past lives, and they use different behaviors as mechanisms to cope. When I was reading it, I thought about Corey. I asked him one time about his people and where he came from, and he just shut down. I'm not sure, but something tells me that there is something else eating at him other than the gay bashing. I think something happened to that boy in his childhood."

"Well, whatever it is. He won't tell us anything," Peep says.

"Yeah. I mean, we get hints about his past. But he won't come all the way out and tell us what's going on. At least he's talking to the therapist and he filed a report on his attack, so that is a step in the right direction," I follow.

"Yeah, it's a good thing he's getting help. Jimmy, do me a favor. Grab my purse from beside the couch."

"This one?" He says as he holds a black bag up.

"Yeah that's the one, baby. Pass it to me." When she gets it, she opens it up and takes out a fifty. "I want you to go down to Calloway's and grab me a carton of Newports."

"Mama, you know good and well you are not supposed to be smoking. You already got diabetes. What else are you trying to get? Lung cancer?"

"Baby, every now and then I need a drag of my cigarette. Next to you, my bridge players, Sandra Jean, and all of y'all, I love a good cigarette. Shit, you oughta be glad it ain't a joint."

"Yeah, but Mama…"

"Don't argue with me, boy. Just go to the store and do what I say. And you make sure you watch Old Man Calloway. Every now and then, he tries to gyp people for their change. Go on now."

"All right Mama, but I still don't think you should be smoking." He gives her a kiss and then goes out the front door.

"Felipe, look out that window. Is he walking or driving."

"Driving."

"Shit, I was hoping that he would walk so I could have a little more time. There is something I want to talk to you two about."

I study her face, which looks very urgent and solemn. "Irene, you alright?"

"Not really… and this is rough to say… You see, the thing is: I went to the doctor and my latest prognosis was not good. He said that my Diabetes has reached its final stages, and… I need to start making plans for what's going to happen when I'm gone."

Peep looks thunderstruck. "Irene… You can't be serious."

"Felipe, I'm getting sicker and sicker every time I go into the hospital. The doctors say there's nothing that they can do, because I wouldn't let them cut off my foot two years ago."

"What are you talking about? You said that they assured you that things were looking up with your Diabetes and that there was no need for amputations."

"That's because I didn't want Jimmy worrying about me. You know how he gets. He would want to be around me all the time. And I love him too much to let him tie himself down and wallow in unnecessary guilt. I have been trying to push him out into the world since he was a teenager, but he's always held on to me and he's still doing it as an adult. I can't guarantee him that I am going to be around for much longer. To be honest, I think my passing will finally force him to live his life. Besides… the pain in my foot is getting a lot worse."

She reaches down and pulls up her pants leg. Her ankle is a stark contrast from her vanilla wafer skin tone. It is almost a dark purple.

Peep suddenly bounces up and paces the floor. Then he stops and looks at her. "Irene, I don't understand. If amputating your foot would've improved your chances for living longer, why wouldn't you have done it?"

"Felipe, I don't want to live my life as a cripple. Did you see that yard out there? That flower bed? This house and how clean it is? The things God enabled me to do for other people? Those are things that I do because I enjoy the fact that I can still do them. And it's even better to have a friend like Sandra Jean come over and sit with me so we can play cards and do some other fun things, to keep me from going stir crazy. Whenever I can do those things, it's like I'm reliving the youth that I lost. But if I got my foot cut off, the only thing I would be is pitied. I don't want people looking at me saying 'Poor Irene'. That ain't no way to live."

"But Irene..."

"Look honey, I've had seventy-one good years on this earth. I've had a lot of fun and God has blessed me during those years. But I'm starting to hear His voice telling me it ain't long. I'm tired of fighting this disease. I'm tired of battling every day to stay alive. Now the medicine they are prescribing is not working. I'm beginning to see the handwriting on the wall. It's saying that it's time to go, and to be honest… I am ready to get out of here."

Peep sits down and puts his elbows on his knees, and his hands to his cheeks. I put my hand on his shoulder to let them know that I understand. I feel moisture behind my eyes.

"Don't do that. Don't y'all start crying. I ain't gonna have that in here because it will depress me and make me cry too. And I've already cried enough tears. I need you to be strong now. The reason I told you is because I want you to know in case something happens to me. And I don't want you to say anything to Jimmy because he ain't gonna handle it right. Sons expect for their mothers to live forever, but it just doesn't work that way. I have tried to tell him, but every time I try to talk to him about this, he keeps saying that I ain't gonna die. He's stubborn and mule-headed just like his daddy." She gazes into the fireplace at the other end of the room and goes silent for a minute. Then she says, "The doctors gave me until November. And unless the Lord says different, I'm trying to make plans before that time. I really need for ya'll to rally around my son. Be there for him. He's going to need all your love and all of his friends when I go."

Concerned, Peep reaches out to her and grabs her hand. "Irene, you know I love Jimmy, and I love you just like I loved my grandma. I'm praying that this does not happen. But if it does, you know that all of us will stand by Jimmy and help him through this."

She pats his hand. "Thank you, baby. I'm praying to at least stick around until after the holidays. Prayerfully God will extend my life just a little while longer, so I can be with my son and Sandra Jean for Thanksgiving and for Christmas."

"You're in my prayers, Irene." Peep goes to her and hugs her. Then, he straightens up comically and asks, "Wait a minute. I hear you talking about Sandra Jean a lot. Is there something going on between the two of you?"

"Listen up, Precious. I'm gonna tell you just like I told Jimmy when he asked me that question."

"What is that?"

"Mind your own business!"

We all laugh. Peep excuses himself and goes to the bathroom.

"Lionel?"

"Ma'am?"

"I'm gonna tell you something your Mama should've told you."

"What is that?"

"You are a good person. You are a good friend. And you are a very good son."

I go to hug her and wiping my eyes, I tell her, "Thank you, Irene. I really needed to hear that." I step back from her. "And I'm going to say something that Jimmy ought to tell you every time he sees you."

"And what is that?"

"That you are just as good a person. That you are a better friend. And you exceed as a mother."

"Humph!" She looks in a nearby mirror and raises her hands to smooth the errant curls on the side of her head.

"Shit, honey. You have never been righter!"

Chapter Seventeen:

"*Cruisin*'"

Cruise day is finally here! We decided on the week before that we were going to come down the morning of the cruise. This way we wouldn't have to worry about paying for extra hotel fare. Our costumes for the Jungle Party came just in time. Two days before! We ordered them online at Corey's house when Peep, Jimmy, and I left Irene's. Garrett was already there. Don't ask me what they were doing!

Since we decided that we wanted our costumes to be a surprise from one another and Garrett was not going, we decided that we would spend twenty minutes with him in front of Jojo's laptop to pick out our costume, while the others found something else to do in the house. We are browsing an online store that he recommended, The Erotic Jungle… and the costumes are phenomenal! He gave me good insight about mine.

"What do you think of this one?" I asked him, looking at a tan leopard costume.

"Hmm. I don't know if I would choose the leopard one."

"Why not?"

"Well, with your bulky frame, a leopard might be a bit slim and slender for you."

"So, you trying to say that I'm fat?" I jokingly poked him.

"No. I'm just saying that you might put that thing on in your room, but later you will have nothing but scraps of cloth after your muscles start ripping the shit."

"Point well taken."

"How about this lion, to go with your name?"

"No, I don't want to be too predictable. That would be the easy option and the rest of the group would expect me to get a lion costume."

"Well, your choices are kinda limited. You can always go as a Brahma bull."

"Nah. That's not a jungle animal. Besides, I'm still feeling feline animals."

"Well, what about this tiger?" He pointed to a picture of a tiger costume. It was a very tight body suit expertly crafted with fur sewn into the suit to make it look like a real tiger. What was even better is the model wearing the suit. He looked about my build and size. The suit showed off his muscle definition although it covered his whole body. There was a headdress masking the top part of his face, orange and black feathers around his neck and shoulders.

"I like it. How much is it?"

"A little over four hundred."

"Damn, man! That's a whole lotta money"

"Well, look at the material, the feathers, and the way the fur is sewn on to the suit. Whoever made this suit spent a lot of time and effort sewing it. That type of effort doesn't come cheap."

"I see what you mean but I don't know if I'm prepared to pay that much."

"Well, look at it this way. You can always use the costume for whenever you and Jojo want to play dress up," Garrett poked my back.

"Geez, does *everybody* know about me and Jojo?"

"Please. You two hang around each other all the time. And there are telltale signs that we see when y'all decide to come up for air. Ye gads, if you two were any stiffer, we would pole dance."

"Shut up, boy."

"Hey, you know I'm telling the truth."

We shared a laugh. "So, you want to purchase it?"

"Yeah. Let me grab my card," I said, reaching in my pocket for my wallet and getting my Mastercard.

"It's a shame that you are not able to come with us," I said as I typed my information in.

"Well, what can you do? I got to work and support myself. Besides, while y'all are cruising, my sister is moving Sam's things out of the house and I'm going over there to help her."

"That's decent. I'm just glad that asshole is gone."

"Me too."

"I know Corey is not happy that you are not coming with him."

"I know."

"You two doing OK?"

"Yes, although we had a little bit of a hiccup."

"What about?"

"Well, I was over here about a week ago and we had a nice little fire going. Corey went to the bathroom and I went to the bookshelf. I picked up an old song book of piano sonatas by Debussy. It had to have been like forty-five years old. I just felt drawn to it. Anyways Corey came downstairs, saw me with that song book, and screamed at me to put it down. He took me by such surprise that I dropped the songbook and one of the pages drifted into the fire. It was a title page. I know because I saw a little bit of it before it burned up. It had the name Bradley and it said, 'to Ihre Nachkomme, From Madame I.'"

"I know. He reacted the same way with me. I looked at that book myself."

"But at least you didn't burn any pages. It wasn't anything with any music in it; it was the title page, and that page must've meant the most to him because it was a gift. Why it said Bradley, I have no idea. But he went crazy. He just started screaming at me. I had to stop him from diving in the fire and burning his hands. He ordered me out of the house and said he needed some time alone."

"That's weird."

"Yeah, but we made up for that. He said it was just a page and that the book was a keepsake, falling apart from years of use. It was given to him by his first piano teacher. I thought that would be a way to talk about our pasts, but he closed up before I could even get my foot in the door. He just wanted to change the subject, so we did."

Corey came in the room. "Are y'all done yet? I got to pick out my outfit."

*****

Fast forward to today. We all learned a valuable lesson. If we are going to travel with Corey anywhere, we need to make sure that we tell him to be ready six hours before. We told him three. Big mistake. When we went over to his house, he was still asleep! We had to use our key to get inside and wake his ass up because his phone was off. It's a good thing that he started back sleeping without deadbolts on the doors, or we wouldn't have gotten inside. He bounded out of bed and begged us to wait ten minutes for him to take a shower and get dressed. He took thirty! Thank God he was already packed, and his luggage was in the trunk of his car. Because of our blunder, we had to rush to catch the Light Rail to the airport. We almost missed our flight.

Now we are in this cruise terminal. We went through the security checkpoint and left the bags at the designated place for the attendants to take up to our cabins. We got our cruise cards and are now sitting in these uncomfortable ass chairs waiting for our zone to be called.

"Corey, the next time we have to travel somewhere, can you just try to be a little bit timelier?" I complain.

"Aw, Lion. Get off my dick. I said I was sorry. I had a long night."

"Something tells me that that long night had to do with Garrett," Jojo teases as he crosses his beautiful legs.

"Yeah, you had to say goodbye in your special way," Jimmy teases as he gives Jojo a hi five.

"OK, let's put this to bed. This might shock the hell out of you, but we have not even had sex yet. We're just trying to get to know each other better. We have been intimate, but we've never even taken our clothes off in front of each other." All of us are staring at him with open mouths. Corey, the slut of the bunch, not having sex. That's like Dom Deluise saying no to a plate of ribs.

"What are you looking at me like that for?"

"This just takes us by surprise. This can't be the same Corey that we know. Not that we're complaining."

"Well, I can't be having sex all the time."

"Speaking of having sex, how long have you gone without having it?"

"Three and a half months."

"Have you at least jacked off?" Peep asks.

"Uh… yeah?! I'm not a hermit! I can jack off every now and then. My balls are not blue."

Just then, the loudspeaker calls our zone. "Zone twelve. Zone twelve. You may make your way to the ship. Zone twelve. Zone twelve. You may make your way to the ship."

"That's us. Let's go y'all." Jimmy says.

We walked towards the ramps and suddenly I collide into someone.

"Oh, I'm sorry. I wasn't looking where I was going."

"It's quite all right." The cheerful voice belonged to a lady of average height and slim dancer's build. She's wearing a pink shirt and white shorts with white sandals. Standing next to her is another woman, similarly dressed but in a yellow shirt. She is a little taller than her and has a sturdy build. "Looks to me like you're very excited to get on this boat," the other woman says good-heartedly.

"Yeah this is our first cruise. Well, at least for some of us," Jojo says.

"Oh, a first timer. Funny, I didn't see you at the party last night?"

"We just got to Miami today," Peep says.

"Well, what are your names?"

"I'm Felipe, and this is my partner, Jimmy."

"I'm Lionel, and this is my friend, Jojo." I look at Jojo and I catch a look of consternation on his face. I think to myself. *If we are boyfriends, why am I so ashamed to say so?*

"Let me clean that up. This is my boyfriend, Jojo."

I looked again, and Jojo has a better look on his face, almost appreciative.

"And my name is Corey. My boyfriend couldn't be here, so I guess I'm cruising solo."

"Well, your boyfriend may not be here. But you have a whole ship full of friends just dying to meet you. We are two of them. My name is Sheila," the first lady says.

"And I'm Jade. I'm *her* partner."

"It's nice to meet you both," I say as we all shake hands with each other.

"Uh, I don't want to break up this little meet and greet, but maybe we need to hurry and get on board, so we can sit *down* and do it," Corey informs.

"Yeah," Jade says. "We had better get going. Come on baby. I got your bag. We need to go straight to the bar. I feel a margarita calling my name."

"Now Jade," Sheila begins. "We need to be very careful not to drink too much. You know how both of us get when we are tipsy." Jade then looks at Sheila and then starts laughing wickedly.

"OK, I don't think we were supposed to see that," Jimmy says.

"Something tells me that y'all ain't babies. So, you know everything there is to know about life over the rainbow. If you don't, welcome to your crash course!" Sheila says.

We walk up the ramp and into the ship. We had to sit on the Lido deck until our rooms were ready. When we get to our rooms, our luggage is already on the sofa. Jojo and I sit on the bed.

"Well…"

"Well, we're finally on the boat." Jojo says, in a serious tone. he unpacks and puts his clothes, including the garment bag holding his costume, into one of the closets.

"Jojo, is something wrong?"

"Nothing."

"Come on, Jojo. Tell me."

Jojo pauses for minute, then he turns around to face me. "I'm just a little bit confused about your hesitation when you were introducing me to Jade and Sheila."

"I caught that look in your eye. That's why I went back and corrected it."

"And I'm glad you did, but I'm starting to wonder as to whether or not you would have corrected it if I hadn't given you that look."

"I don't know."

"It showed me that maybe we're not as ready for this as we think we are."

"What do you mean?"

"I mean if we're going to be together, I don't want you to feel like you have to hesitate when you introduce me."

"Jojo, this is just going to take a little bit of time."

"Time is not something that's on our side. We are thirty-six years old, soon to turn thirty-seven. Around this age, we need to be sure."

"I'm sorry. I didn't mean to upset you by my hesitation."

Jojo goes to me and caresses my face. "I don't think you meant to. I just need for you to understand that I've had these feelings for you ever since we were teenagers, but I don't want to rope you into this if you're not ready."

"Baby, you're not roping me into anything that I volunteer to go into." Jojo then kisses me. "And besides, I've been so used to calling you my friend or my best friend. It's going to take some getting used to, calling you my boyfriend or hus…" I catch myself before the word comes out.

"Or what?"

"Or my lover."

Jojo looks at me. I see a little bit of the same expression he gave through the introductions, but he puts it away with a dazzling smile. "Fair enough."

We kiss again. "So," I say in a cocky way. "We got forty-five minutes before we have to go to our muster station."

"Then let's not waste a second of them," he says as we sink inch by inch onto the king size bed, kissing our troubles away.

*****

We are now on the Lido deck and the cruise has commenced. It took forever for us to get through the muster station drills, but here we are. At last, we can relax! I am looking out on the horizon and it is amazing to see the contrast of dark and light in the sky. The clouds billow over the waters, reminding me of the kind of beauty that only nature can possess. Scenes like this never fail to convince me of the existence of God. I feel a sweet peace steal over me. Now I can see the allure of cruising. Looking at these blue green waters, wondering what is happening beyond the surface and what type of marine life exists. Are there sharks? Whales? Of course, I know there are fish. This is the first time that I have been close to God and really felt the beauty of what He created. People can go to church and talk about God's love and majesty. It is nothing compared to being out here where you feel at one with Him and at peace.

I must admit that after being dragged for years, I go to church very sporadically. When I do go, I go to Corey's church. I have tremendous issues with religion, because I believe it is all about control. However, I do believe that there is a God and that He created a spiritual connection that threads through all humanity. Many people fail to acknowledge that. When I look at the majestic mountains of clouds and the vastness of the sea, it makes me wonder how immeasurably vast and connected the universe is.

A year before he was killed, my father and I went on one of our fishing trips. At some point during the trip, he told me that in the universe, we have innumerable particles of bacteria in the air. He told me to imagine that those particles are windows of opportunity. "This world is only a tiny speck in the universe. That tells me that we all have a place we belong to. We all have a love we can cling to. Most importantly, we all have a purpose to live up to. It just depends on how we find it." I walk along the walkways, breathing in the liberating and cleansing air misted by the sea. I feel an enlarging of my heart and a love I can barely contain. What a beautiful feeling!

I am also pleasantly surprised at how big the ship is, as well as the array of black gay men and women all in one place. This beats The Link any day. And everybody seems very friendly. We met a few more couples like Jade and Sheila. Most of them were very pleasant. There was this older lesbian couple that especially captivated me. We met on the Lido deck. They introduced themselves as Nadine and Clarisse, and they kept us laughing our asses off. Of course, there are always a few rotten apples in the bunch. We met quite a few single guys that were so haughty and stuck up that I wanted to tell them to pull the sticks out of their asses. But I had to remind myself that maybe this is the reason they're single.

I go back to the area by the Lido deck and I spot Corey on the side of the pool, with his bare feet plunged in the water. He's looking a little down.

"Corey?" I call to him as I take off my sandals and sit beside him, sinking my feet into the water.

"Hmmm?"

"What's wrong?"

He takes a deep breath. "I guess I'm just missing Garrett. I had a good time with him last night. I hate that he couldn't come. Plus, I feel kind of out of place on the ship."

"I know."

"And that coward Alex chickened out at the last minute saying he didn't want to get on the boat, so I had to end up paying for a room by myself. I'm not sure why I let y'all talk me into this."

"Because we all needed it. Every now and then we need to get away. Especially from Baltimore."

"Yeah."

"This is what I want you to do, Corey. Don't think about the drawbacks on this cruise. Think about whatever good can come from it."

"Yeah, I'll try. I have met some nice people. But let's face it, I've met some mean ones. I guess no matter where you go, you're going to run into bitter bitches."

"True, but are you going to let those bitter bitches dictate what type of time you're going to have? Where is that Corey that doesn't care about who sees him having a good time? I seem to remember someone telling me, 'There are times when you have to tell your depression that this is where it stops.'"

"Yeah. I did say that."

Suddenly we hear a deep familiar voice. "Sounds like good advice to me."

We turn around and Garrett is standing right in front of us! We both stand up, gaping.

"Oh my God! Garrett?" Corey exclaims, ecstatic. "You came?"

"You didn't think I was going to let you get on this cruise by yourself, did yuh?"

"You sneaky motherfucker," I joke, swatting him on the shoulder. "You told me that you had to work."

"Yeah! And you said you had to help your sister move Sam's stuff out of her house," Corey follows.

"Well I'm full of surprises. Actually, I called the travel agent the day that I told Corey I couldn't go. I did it, so I can see the surprise on his face. I had two weeks of vacation time I never used last year, so I decided to use it. And as far as everything else, I had to come up with some type of alibi that y'all would believe."

Corey bounded around those lounging chairs and threw himself at Garrett, kissing him. "I can't believe you came."

"Well, I couldn't disappoint you. Nobody wants to be on a cruise depressed. After you told me that your friend Alex bailed, I knew I made the right decision."

"Who are you rooming with?"

"With Ricardo."

"I got a room to myself."

"I know. You told me. Worked out for the best I'd say, we won't have to look for places to be alone."

"Well, I'm gonna let y'all enjoy your moment. Garrett, I am glad you came, particularly if it puts a smile on Corey's mean mug. I'm going to find Jojo. We'll see y'all at the White Rainbow Party."

*****

What a time we are having tonight! We're at the White Rainbow Party and it is phenomenal. It started at nine o'clock and it closes at midnight. The lights in the ship's clubroom switch colors every twenty minutes. The first color was red, then it proceeded through the entire color spectrum, turning the sea of white outfits into whatever color being used. It is now black lights and the outfits are glowing an alluring azure blue. The dance floor was even more impressive. It was lighted with white fluorescent bulbs and very durable.

I was standing over at the bar when the fellas come over.

"Come on, Lion. Come on and dance," Corey says.

"Yeah, baby. You are sitting over hear looking all unapproachable," Jojo reproves.

"Nah, I ain't that much of a dancer."

"You oughta quit lying! Remember that huge house party we went to in college? You cleared the floor," Peep reminds.

"I cleared the floor because I ate those burritos before I got to the dance. It had nothing to do with my rhythm."

"Oh, that's right," Peep recalls, laughing. "It was so bad they had to spray the place." The other guys snicker.

"Shut up, Peep!"

"Uh, baby," Jojo drawls. "I don't know if I agree with what you just said. I seem to remember that you had a whole lot of rhythm in high school. You cleared the floor then, and it had nothing to do with any burritos."

"Jojo, it's been a long while since I've been dancing. I might be a bit rusty."

"Well maybe it's time you got back in practice."

"I could not agree more," Garrett says. "Besides, the rest of us are out here. Come on, have a little bit of fun!"

"Why do I smell adult peer pressure?" *And coming from Garrett of all people,* I thought.

"Well, if it is adult peer pressure, it is the kind that you need," Corey says, grabbing my hand. "Come on, Lion. You're getting your ass out on that dance floor if I have to drag you out there."

I look at him then. "Well, somebody is not depressed anymore. I wonder why," I say as I look at Garrett.

"Shut up, get out here, and dance." He pulls me out onto the dance floor, just as this song called "Let Me Have Your Sex" by Insatiable starts. I feel a little self-conscious as I step onto the illuminated dance floor. I mean, if the guys at the Link danced like they were auditioning for Alvin Ailey, these guys danced like they were cast in a Bob Fosse musical, especially the guys from ATL. Besides, looking at all these beautiful bodies on this dance floor makes me a bit nervous. But, as I look deeper at many of the people on the dance floor, there are those who are not dancing or voguing like the others, but they are content with bopping their heads to the beat. I relax my tensing muscles and begin to sway with the music. It is like the pumping house beat is rumbling the dance floor and taking my body over. Before long, I was shaking my ass, twirling my body, and moving with precision to the beat! I couldn't stop myself! My body starts moving with the pulse of the beat. Before I knew it, an hour had passed. Suddenly, Jojo dances in front of me, and I take one look in his eyes and my hunger for him grows with every passing second. I grab him and twirled him around and we start to enter a seductive dance. Jojo is shocking the hell out of me! He talks about my rhythm, but his rhythm is wonderful. Where I went, he went. My left foot back, his right foot forward. My right foot back, his left foot forward. Our torsos are parallel to each other on every movement we make. I guess we both still got some killer moves in our old ages, because the crowd surrounds us to watch as we nearly make out on the dance floor, and they are hooting and goading us to continue! I am not sure what dance we are doing, but with our bodies pressed together in sexual pose and our outfits damp from the sweat, I am eager to have him! We can't continue with the dance. I need him… and from the hunger in his own eyes, I can sense his need for me! As the crowd resumes dancing, we mutually agree to ditch the party. I spot Corey dancing with Garrett and I signal him over.

"What's up y'all?"

"We're going back to our room. Y'all good?"

"Yeah, we'll see you for breakfast in the morning. Y'all have a good time."
We can't leave here fast enough!

*****

As we enter our cabin, I can feel the heat from his body as he walks in front of me. Maybe it was the wine I drunk at the party. Maybe it was those lights in the smoldering heat of that moment. Maybe it was how Jojo glanced back at me with a come-hither look as we enter the cabin. But all I know is after Jojo closes the door behind him, the heat of the moment overtakes both of us. He turns around with a wild, hungry look fraught with sexuality pouring from his beautiful eyes.

I position myself in front of the bed. Without warning, Jojo throws himself on me and I lose my footing. We land on the mattress where he wildly kisses me. I feel his full, hard sex pressing against mine. Our breathing becomes labored with the desire for one another. He rips open my shirt, with the buttons flying all over the place, my Morét Giordana shirt that cost ninety-six dollars. Yet, the cost of the shirt is the least thing on my mind. I respond in kind with his tight, white, sheer muscle shirt that accentuates the definition in his chest, showing only a hint of those love handles he hates so much, (I have always found them sexy). We liberate ourselves of the pants and underwear, and the sight that meets my eyes is delicious! He has a love toy, which I always suspected was large, but the rigidity, the girth, and the length is downright intimidating! I pull back a bit.

"What's wrong?"
"I had no idea you were so big."
"Can you clarify big, please? You mean big body?"
"No, I mean big jimmie."
"You're a fine one to talk. You are just as thick and long as I am."
I respond with a cockiness, "Yes, this is true."

We resume kissing, our hands frantically roaming the hills and valleys of our bodies. The air in the cabin turns humid as sweat drips from our pores, and our bodies become slippery, dampening the comforter, And the air is set on seventy degrees! The blue-black beauty of this man's body excites me. I think of his throbber and how it would be paradise for him to unlock my passions with his "key". I feel his hard, round, baby smooth ass with an abundance of hair in the crevice. His walls would feel like I'm in the canoe traveling down a tributary between two mountains of waterfall. I slip two of my fingers in, and the wetness combined with the sweat makes the sensual valley sleek and inviting.

I sniff the air and all I can smell is sex as well as the sweet, pungent aroma of anal secretion. My lips part is I do something that I've never done before, even with Nate. I let out a long, shuddering, moan of relief accompanied by the magnificent breath of true love and ecstasy. I have lived next to this beautiful man for eighteen years as a teenager and stuck with him for longer as an adult. But I was unaware of how sensual, gorgeous, breathtaking, sexual, intriguing, intelligent, and feisty he is. And he loves me. He loves…*me*! He desires me just as much as I desire him. The sexiest man on this boat to me, and we are in this bed, in this cabin, on this ship for seven days… Together. Suddenly, he pushes back and looks panicked. He tears from my embrace and runs out on the balcony, still naked. Holy shit! What just happened? I rush behind him to find him sitting in one of the chairs. The tears are falling from his eyes and they are barely noticeable among the coat of sweat on his face… And his body. The light of the moon shines on him, making his body glisten. Oh my God, how I love this man!

"What's wrong, Jojo?"

"I'm sorry, Lionel."

"For what?"

"I just think we need to pump the brakes for a minute."

"What? Why?"

"It just hit me that I may be putting too much pressure on you."

"What are you talking about?" I say as I sit in the adjacent chair. I put my hand on his knee, and he flinches. *Uh Oh.*

"I feel like I'm pressuring and crowding you to be in a relationship with me."

I'm puzzled. "I don't understand. What we were just about to do in agreement is what you call pressure? The way we *both* felt on that dance floor while we were dancing is considered pressure?"

"That was just the heat of the moment, Lionel. We both wanted sex with each other and you were unsure before it got to this point."

"Unsure about us?" I feel heat on my face, chasing away the coolness of the night air.

"Right," he says with conviction and measured tightness in his voice. "You hesitated in front of that couple, and when we talked about it this afternoon, you almost said the word 'husband', but you switched it to 'lover'."

I feel my anger rising. "Why are we bringing this up now?"

"Because I don't want another lover. I've had enough lovers. I want commitment. Look Lionel, I'm deeply in love with you, but I don't want you in my romantic life or in my bed if it's just going to be about sex."

"And what makes you think I'm just interested in sex with you? Sure, I wanted it and I know you wanted it too… but that is not all I see in you." I suddenly feel hotly offended. "And I thought that it was not all you saw in me." I jump up from the chair and head back inside.

"Wait, Lionel!"

"Wait for what? You pretty much said that I'm only interested in you for sex. And after all these years of knowing and loving each other, I thought you knew me better. This clearly proves that you don't. You know, I think this is more about whatever it is from your childhood eating away at you that you won't tell me." Jojo looks at me then, stricken.

"Now tell me I'm wrong."

Jojo looks away. "That's not it at all."

"Jojo, that is a lie and you know it. You know how I know? Because you are looking away. You always look me in my eyes when you are telling the truth, and your eyes aren't darting all over the place like they're doing right now. I try to tell you everything that's going on with me, but you're keeping secrets from me just like you kept the secret of Andre and Rhonda beating you up. You felt more comfortable telling Corey that shit than you felt telling me." I stop, struggling to catch my breath… and my emotions. "Well listen up, Jojo. Just like you can't have a relationship with someone who just wants sex, which I don't, I can't have a relationship with someone that I can't trust to tell me the whole truth." I go back into the room and hastily throw on some clothes. Jojo comes in, distressed.

"Lionel, please wait. Where are you going?" He says as I put on my flip-flops and head to the door. I turn around.

"For a walk. This conversation has soured everything for me tonight, and we have to be on this goddamned boat for seven more days. I need some air."

I huff out of the room, slamming the door shut. Going down the hall, I'm furious. But more than that, I am scared that the door slamming shut is symbolic of the outcome of our relationship.

CHAPTER EIGHTEEN:
"DAMAGED GOODS"

I sit at the bar on the Lido deck. Completely miserable. And this gin and tonic is not helping. It's just making me tipsy on top of my misery. The people on the deck are minimal. Only two or three are carrying on lively conversation.

He thinks that I'm just in this for sex… but he is a locked box that no one can open. I wonder if this had anything to do with Mike and his abuse. The whole evening started off so well, all of us enjoying each other's company, and then the two of us finally on the threshold of becoming sexually intimate with one another, after waiting for so long.

Then again, I must ask myself this question. *Am* I in this for sex? I never *really* looked at him in this way, this sexual way, until two years ago. Even when I was with Nate, I saw Jojo's body filling out and becoming more muscular. I think of the looks I stole at his ass and at his crotch. The peeps at his legs. The look I gave him when we went to the Link. OK, I have to take it back. Hmm… Maybe he is right. Maybe I was in this for sex. I looked at him a little like that when we were teenagers.

But then, I think of other things. The kisses we shared since deciding to enter a relationship slowly. The fiery passion we both had for each other, but both of us felt it necessary to wait. The looks of love we shared over ambrosia salad, over playing board games, and sometimes we sneak looks even when we were around the other guys. Most of all, I think of the time we spent over the years. The way I just enjoyed the nearness of him, even as teenagers. People would pick on me just for being around him, but I didn't care. I just wanted to be with him because I loved him. Maybe I loved him more than I knew at that time.

Oh God, what am I going to do? I have to be in the room with him for the next seven days. How am I going to do this? How can I face him? Thoughts come pouring into my head, torturing me. *See?* I think. *I knew it was going to be trouble mixing it up with best friends. I knew nothing good would come of it. I knew this would turn out this way. And yet, I did it anyway.* As if on cue, I feel a strange warmth in my heart that overrides those questions. That warmth assured me that it felt right. It felt good. It was crazy and exhilarating at the same time. I took a chance and it felt good. Oh God, what is this going to do to us when we go back to the Mainland? Are we going to be ill at ease with each other? Who knows? Maybe I need to go to Corey's room and talk to him. He might have some advice. Maybe I could talk to Peep. He's had experience with things like this. Or even Jimmy? But neither one of them had the length of knowledge about their mates that Jojo and I have. Maybe it's not a good idea to talk with Corey about this, but he would probably let me stay in his room for tonight so that I could sleep on it.

A pleasant male voice interrupts my thoughts. "Excuse me."
I start. "Uh, Yes?"
I turned to see a tall dark-skinned young man in his twenties with close-set, but cat like eyes, flaring nostrils, and thin but beautifully shaped lips surrounded by a full mustache and goatee. He has a scar on his chin, which for some reason looks very appealing. Oh, he's attractive. *Snap out of it Lionel, you have someone that loves you.*
Holding a flute of champagne, he asks with concern, "You look a little bit lost. Are you OK."
"Yeah, I just had a little fight with my boyfriend."
He nods his head and sits down opposite from me. He sets his glass down on the table. "I can tell. You look like you lost your best friend."
"I hope I didn't. I've been in a friendship for almost thirty-seven years with him."
"Thirty-seven years? Well, in all that time, I'm sure you have had your share of arguments. How long have you been in a relationship?"
"Almost four months."

"Ah, this is your first fight as a couple, yes?"

"Yes."

"Well, to me, it can't be any different than all the fights you had as friends for thirty-seven years. At least you've known by now what makes the other tick, right?"

"Yes, that's true."

"If you'll pardon an outsider, and I don't know the situation, but it has the ring of cold feet to go deeper into this relationship. But look at it this way. You have such an advantage. With knowing each other for so long. I'm sure during that thirty-seven years, there were all sorts of thoughts about what it would be like if you were in a relationship."

"You know, a few months ago, I would've denied that. It would've been true, but I still would've denied it. But now, I have to say that I have thought about it all throughout that time… and on more than one occasion."

"Well, acknowledging that you've thought about it is half the battle. You know each other very well. You've been close friends with each other. You've just decided to seal the deal, that's all."

"You're right. I don't have any idea why I'm sharing this and hearing such good advice with someone I don't even know."

"Well, I haven't really given advice yet. I'm just observing, but I will tell you this. If you love him and if you know he loves you, then don't let him go."

"Wise words."

"And as to knowing me," he says and sticks out his hand. "Hi, my name is Charlie Moore."

"Pleased to meet you Charlie. I'm Lionel Davis." I firmly shake his hand.

"Lionel." I turn and see Jojo.

I turn slowly back around, suddenly feeling offended again.

"Well, I'm going to go ahead and let you both talk," he says as he gets up. Then he holds his glass up in the air. "Here's to thirty-seven years, and I pray that you two have thirty-seven more." He disappears.

"Lionel, we do need to talk." Jojo sits in the same chair that Charlie abandoned.

"I think we said enough to each other for one night."

"I haven't said enough. I have a lot of things that I need to say. And I want to start off by saying I'm sorry."

I look at him, not sure how to express my feelings. *Yes, I love him. But I'm starting to feel doubts again.*

"Some things did happen in my childhood that I didn't want to bring up. I just don't know what you see in me. I've caught you looking at me wondering about what it would be like if we were together. I caught that look not just when we were adults. I saw it when we were kids. I wanted you for so long. But now that I finally have you, I am scared."

"Scared of what?"

"Scared that I would be giving you damaged goods."

"What do you mean 'damaged goods'?"

Jojo gets up and faces the sea. He goes silent for a few moments. Without turning around, he asks me, "Do you remember when I told you that Mike used to beat on me and Mama."

"Yeah, I remember."

Jojo exhales. Then he says in a voice choked with painful remembrance, "That's not all he did."

"What else?"

His face crumples, as if his next words are going to kill him. I stand up on my feet and go to his side. I place my hand on his shoulder.

"What happened, Jojo?"

Tormented, Jojo claps his hands over his mouth, squints his eyes to keep the tears from falling, and cringes. He is unsuccessful. The tears fly from his eyes.

"When I was nine years old... and that whole year before he left... he... He..." He stops, uncontrollable sobs begin to wrack his body as he stutters.

"Jojo... You can talk to me."

As his body bows in pain, and his face contorts with agony, he gushes out the words, "He raped me."

I don't hesitate. I move behind him to do what his father should've been there to do. I held him and squeezed him, transferring love and protection from my body to his. His tears fall, cleansing my arms as well as baptizing his cheeks. I feel tears from my own eyes baptizing his shoulders from the evils of his childhood. Now I see why we were so close. He was trying to live through the rape and abuse his mother's boyfriend inflicted, as well as the abandonment of his own father. I was trying to live through the constant humiliation, abuse, and disapproval of my own mother. The only bright spots in my life were my father and him. For him, it was his mother and me. I turn him around and hug him.

"You are not damaged goods, baby. You are a person who was abused. It's not your fault. It's Mike's." I squeeze him again, tenderly. "I can see why you say you are damaged goods... and why you feel so low about yourself. When someone is abused, they forget how beautiful they are. But Jojo," I say as I pull back and I lift his chin up. "I promise you. I will love that abuse away... or I will die trying."

The look on Jojo's face is hopeful, full of illumination, still sad but willing to embrace the future and to try to forget the past.

"Come on. Let's go back to the room."

We walk towards the sliding doors and as I look back I see Charlie with a questioning expression on his face. I give him a wave to let them know that things are fine. Charlie gives me back a thumbs-up to let me know that I'm going in the right direction.

We walk back to the cabin. Once we walk in and the door is shut, we shed off our clothes and climb into bed. I lie staring at the ceiling. I love him…but I don't know what to do. I desire him… but I waver at touching him, and the reason is not because he said he was "damaged goods". I don't consider him that way at all. It is because I am afraid of hurting him more than he has already been hurt.

I want to marry him, but I am fearful of what that means. I entered a relationship with Nate, but when the subject came up about marriage, we would both skirt the issue and reason that since we were living together, that was a form of marriage. I feel as though I am on the edge of the highest precipice on Mount Everest, seeing only canyons and valleys below me. I feel wings on my back. I know I can fly, but I am unlearned in its art.

I hear a sob and a whisper of sniffles, I turn my head towards Jojo. He has his back to me, and I see a few small pits in his back, almost like large splinters that were dug out and the skin was left to heal and scar. I touch my calf and recall the splinter from my mother's paddle.

Connection.

I reach for him and pull him close to me. I spoon his body, using mine as a protective shield. I prepare my body to communicate with his. I want him to know that I will protect him. I will nurture him. I will love him… *I Will Love Him.* Comforted in our embrace, Jojo relaxes as we weave a beautiful tapestry of conversation in the curtains of the night.

*****

"I still can't believe he surprised me on this cruise."

"Why is it so hard to believe? I mean, Garrett strikes me as the type that if he could, he would surprise you every day, the same way he did last night."

"He has that impression on you too, huh?"

"Yep," I say as I pile cantaloupe on my plate. "Not only that, but I think he really loves you."

"How can you tell?"

"Because when you were in that attack, all he could talk about was how brave you were. He asked about you so many times. I'm surprised you still have ears attached. In fact, he was the one that sent those 'Secret Admirer' flowers."

"He did?"

"Of course!"

"Wow!"

"Surprised?"

"No, but that's good to know," Corey says while grabbing a bowl and spooning oatmeal into it. As we're waiting for the slow line to proceed, Corey looks like a locked purse with contents bursting to come out.

"Where is Jojo?"

"He's back in our cabin, sleeping."

"Did y'all talk about anything especially hot?" he says as the line starts making progress.

"No, but we did talk about a lot of things like our childhood and different things that happened. Of course, we talked about our positive statuses. I told him how I got mine from a piece of rough trade I met at the Link. He told *me* that he got his from that fool we all couldn't stand."

"Oh, the days of being young and not quite bright. We've all been there. At least ours came where you didn't have to take all those huge horse pills. I thank God for those one-a-day meds. They really do help the situation."

"Yeah, true. Anyway, we talked about how many relationships we had before we decided to come together and what we went through in high school that we didn't tell each other. You know, all the basics."

"Nothing earth shattering?" He quizzes, spooning brown sugar, raisins, and dates into his oatmeal.

"All I will say is that everything we discussed is helping us to learn more about each other and I'm interested in knowing more. It's funny how you live next-door to someone for all these years as a teenager and are still close friends as adults. You think you know everything there is to know about them. Then what they tell you proves that you really didn't have a clue."

There's a little bit of silence. Then Corey says, "I usually don't pry into other folk's business."

"Since when?"

"Since always!"

"Uh, I think I need to step back from you. I don't want the lightning that is sure to hit you to bounce off on me."

"Shut up, Lion. Will you listen to what I got to say, please?"

"OK, OK! Someone is touchy!"

"Are you thinking about popping the question to him?"

A long silence stretches between us. At length, I finally say, "Yes. But what makes you ask that?"

"Well, do you remember when Jimmy was courting Peep?"

"Yeah?"

"I have noticed you staring at Jojo while he talks and it's not a hungry stare or a sexual gaze. I see you narrowing your eyes while you smile at the things he says. Peep did the same thing with Jimmy. It's almost like you're sizing him up to see how he would fit as far as a marriage is concerned."

"You've noticed that?"

"Of course. I told you that I smelt the wedding coming. And I have to say this. It's a good thing that you dealt with your feelings and animosity with Nate before getting into this relationship."

"True." We are silent for a few minutes as we grab the hot food and our juices. Then we sit down by the window.

"So, are you ready to turn thirty-seven?"

"My God. Don't remind me!"

"What are you talking about?"

"Well, when I was picking out my clothes for the cruise and trying them on, I noticed a few gray hairs."

"Oh please. That is inevitable. When you get older, you're going to get gray hairs. It kind of comes with the territory."

"But I didn't want to get them this early."

"You do know that there are people who get them earlier than you do, don't you? Nowadays there are boys in their teens who start graying, and it has very little to do with stress. It has more to do with their genetic make-up."

"I am sure you have a basis for this conclusion."

"And you would be right in your certainty. One of my students is eighteen years old and he has a huge stripe of gray hair on the front of his head. Being curious, I asked him how he became gray in that area. I assumed that he went through a lot of stress, but that wasn't the case. He told me that his father started graying around the age of fifteen, and in the same area. You ought to be glad that your hair waited this long to start turning gray. At least you don't have any bald spots."

"Yeah, that's true. Let's change the subject. All this talk of aging is depressing. Did you and Garrett talk about anything interesting last night?"

"Yes."

"And what might that be?"

"He wants us to get in an official relationship."

"That's great. What did you say?"

"I told him I'd think about it."

"Uh oh. Why?"

"I don't know if I'm ready for a relationship."

"Why the hesitation?" *Boy, does that sound familiar! That is the same thing Dr. Banneker would ask me.*

"Well, you know all the lowlifes that I've dated."

"Yeah. So? Between all four of us, we can run an assembly line on how many lowlifes came across our paths. But I seem to remember that you have met some promising ones along the way."

"What do you mean?"

"Well, remember that good looking doctor that really had eyes for you?"

"Yeah."

"Do you remember why you dropped him?"

"No," he lies.

"I do. You dropped him because he lived and had his private practice in Park Heights."

"I hated going over to his house and office and dreading the thugs looking at my car. With his credentials, he could've lived and worked someplace safe, like Timonium or Towson."

"But Corey, I talked to him about that. I asked him that very same question and he told me that he wanted to go where the need was."

"I guess he was just too good for me."

"OK. I am going to let that one slide right by, even though I don't agree with you. But what about Greg Wilson?"

"What about him?"

"You dropped him because he became busy with family matters. His mother was in the hospital battling cancer. He needed to be with her, but you didn't think about that. You just dropped him because you said that he was not making time for you."

"I did not drop him, I just told him that maybe he needed to call me when he found the time."

"And he did! But, and I'm just telling you what you relayed to me about the conversation, you told him that you needed to be with someone who has time for you and that the relationship, as is, would not work."

"It wouldn't have."

"But where is he now, Corey?"

"He got married to some dude."

"Some dude who knew about his busy schedule and his mother but decided to hang in there."

"What are you getting at, Lion?"

"I'm just saying that throughout the time that I've known you, you have had many promising men to come into your life. But for every good man you had, you would find some type of trivial physical flaw in them that you would tell me about later. You would almost look for a reason to fight and drop him."

"Can I help it if I have standards?"

"Well, of course you can have standards. We all have standards, but there are many who exceed the standards you set, and you still reject them. I'm seeing a pattern here. Now Garrett really likes you. It's obvious, otherwise he would've kept his ass in Baltimore. How do you feel about him? And I don't want to hear "he's too tall", "he's too dark", "he's not athletic enough", or "he's not musical enough". How do you really feel about him?"

Cory gets quiet. His face becomes reflective. I can tell he's thinking about everything I just said. Whenever he's in deep thought, his face scrunches and his brows meet in the middle of his face. Then his face relaxes.

"I really do feel like he could be the one. He understands me. I like our conversations and his steady gaze when we talk, like he is interested in my mind and how I see things." He then sits back, folds his arms, and looks out at the horizon. A sweet, relaxed, and peaceful look settles on his face. "Last night, he took his hand and put it on my heart. And I felt the frequency of his pulse throb with the beat of my heart. And I was shocked that his heart and my pulse were throbbing at the same frequency. I then noticed that we even breathe the same. I have not experienced that since being with Zachary."

Oh my God, the look on his face. What a look of love! It is mixed with happiness and wistfulness. I don't know who this Zachary is, but I can tell he is the first guy that has ever touched my friend in that way. I have never seen this look in the time that I've known him, and it is very endearing and inviting. I take out my phone and snap a picture before he could relinquish the expression.

Corey comes out of his spell. "What did you do that for?"

"Because I want to show you something. And maybe this is the reason the others didn't work. Look at this."

"Oh Lionel, you know I hate to look at pictures of myself."

"I think you would want to look at this one."

I show him. He looks at it, meditating. "The picture is not half bad."

"Notice the look on your face."

He notices but he does not say anything. I take this as my cue to explain my rationale concerning his expression.

"This look that you have... I have not seen it with that doctor, or Greg, or anyone that crossed your doorstep. I see that same look in your eyes that you see in mine when I look at Jojo. I don't know if your expression is saying marriage right now. But I know it's a window to your thinking about a future with Garrett."

Corey then looks at me.

"Some time ago, you told me about the difference between living and a lifestyle. I don't know what has happened to you in your past, but it has forced you to live a jaded life where you are distrustful of everyone that crosses your path, even us sometimes. You have to decide what life you want to live: a jaded life or a life filled with chances just waiting to be snatched up. And I think you ought to snatch up *this* chance at love. If you do that, I believe that you can really live and have that same life you told me about."

Corey stays silent.

"I will say this though. I think you would be happier when you find your peace with whatever happened to you in your life. Otherwise, you'll be going into this relationship with a whole lot of baggage. Garrett may love you to pieces, but he strikes me as the type that will not tolerate baggage from others, nor will he have others projecting it onto him. No self-respecting man would."

Usually he's the one that gives me the advice. It kind of feels good to help *him* for a change.

"Your time is up, dear. My fee, if you please."

He digs in his wallet and pulls out a dollar. "In the words of one Lionel Davis, 'Here, Take your stinking buck!'"

I pluck it from his hands. "Thank you, dear."

I start to eat my now cold food. Then I hear Jojo's voice calling my name. "Hey baby, why didn't you wake me up?" He asks me as he sits down in the chair beside me. He kisses me on the lips.

"Well, you looked like you were really resting well. And I didn't want to disturb you. I was going to bring you breakfast."

"Well, the thought was sweet. You can bring me breakfast tomorrow." Jojo smiles, then looks around. "Where is Peep and Jimmy? Garrett?"

"Ten to one, their asses are still in bed. And with all that partying they did last night, I'm not surprised," Corey says.

"What's on the agenda for today?"

I pull out my cruise guide. "Well, it says here that we have a fun day at sea. But according to the Rainbow Pride schedule, the spades tournament is today. It starts at four. And there is a workshop entitled, 'Alone: By Force or By Choice'. That is at one."

"And that is one I will be skipping," Corey says.

"Corey, I really think you ought to go to this one."

"Why?"

"Let's just say that it will be a continuation from your sessions with Dr. Lofton."

"OK, I'll go to the workshop but one of you will have to go with me."

"Why don't you ask Garrett to go?"

"There's a thought," Jojo agrees.

"I'll think about it. What else is going on?" Jojo and I share a look between each other. Change of subject.

"The fashion show is tonight, followed by the jungle party."

"Oh, I can't wait to show off my costume!"

"Neither can I!"

"And neither can I!"

*****

Jojo and I are now in bed. He has his head on my chest as he sleeps. I hear him snoring. Chuckling to myself, I palm his head and recount the events of the day.

It was wonderful. Corey and Garrett did go to that workshop, run by a psychiatrist, Dr. Elmira Whitaker and her partner, Dr. Brianna Jones-Whitaker. Because we thought that it might have information to help us, Jojo and I decided to go as well. They broke down the components of being alone and explained that there are two words to sum it up: Loneliness and Solitude.

During the workshop, I expressed that I always thought the two concepts were the same. She replied that my view was a common misconception. I was surprised to hear that the two concepts are quite different. Solitude is the joy of being alone. Loneliness is the agony of it. She also went on to say that solitude was a positive need. It clears our head. It gives us a new way of looking at things. In addition, it gives married couples and committed relationships wonderful discoveries to discuss when they are together. This is how they learn about each other. I thought about Peep and Jimmy, my parents, and my relationship with Nate. There were times we enjoyed being together, but we also enjoyed being alone because we were able to think and assess things that could only be dealt with individually. Peep and Jimmy had spaces in their own house to get their solitude. I'm drawing a blank when I think of my parents and their solitude. Mama was always down Dad's back about something, whether it was significant or trivial. And I believe Dad needed his solitude to get away from her. That would explain why he flew out for those two weeks or spend almost hours just sitting in his car and listening to music before he came into the house from work. Maybe that was why he practically ran into Troy's arms. I laugh to myself. I am truly Kenneth Davis' son. When Nate was tripping, I used my work as my solitude. With me out of the house, Nate felt loneliness which explains why he went to Shawn. He was wrong but as I sat in the workshop, I began to understand as well as examine my part in how it all played out.

Both Jimmy and Garrett went into the spades tournament. They are awesome players! They went all the way to the final game, where they had to beat last year's champions: Sheila Sykes and Charlie Moore! Well, Sheila and Charlie won, but Jimmy and Garrett still got trophies for coming in second place.

The Jungle Party. Boy! Tarzan and Jane would have been proud. The expansive party room was decorated in lush ornaments. Green simulated vines hung from the ceiling and ivy leaves dangled from them. The posts were covered with crinkly brown paper and vines were taped and wrapped around them. Someone put a realistic boa constrictor among the vines on each post. The costumes were phenomenal! There were people dressed as lions, leopards, koalas, baboons, and every jungle animal you could think of!

Corey showed up in his outfit. It was the talk of the evening! He came in a sheer, satiny, rich blue bodysuit, a bird mask with a blue plume on the crown, and a fan of flowing feathers on his backside. A peacock!

"Corey, there are no peacocks in the jungle!" Peep points out.

"There is one now!" Corey retorts.

Garrett came in a panther costume. It was made with short, but shiny, black hair sewn into a netted body suit. It made me wonder if a real panther was killed to make the costume. I asked him this and he said that the costume was made much like mine, human hair cut short, dyed, and sewn into the body suit. His head was adorned with panther ears and his face was painted. He even had contacts to make his eyes appear catlike. It was so like him. Quiet, meditative, and stalking his prey: Corey! The latter was in heat for him all night!! It was hard to tell who was hunting who!

Peep played it safe. He came as a sexy ranger on safari. He had a tan outfit that clung to his frame. His shorts came up past his thigh, showing his powerfully defined legs. The top four buttons of his short-sleeved shirt were unbuttoned, displaying a barrel chest of abundant black and silver hair. His biceps strain the sleeves of the shirt as they bulged! I had to tear my eyes off him, especially when Jimmy came in, dressed in a black bear costume. He had the headdress, ears, and muffs with claws of a bear. The open vest, shorts, and furry jack boots had the same Tama fur. But his large chest, his brawny arms, his rock-like lower thighs, and his bulky calves were bare. Since Jimmy was a naturally furry fella, the plentiful black hair on the visible parts of his body made it unnecessary to do a whole costume.

But let me tell you what shocked me! Jojo and I wore the same tiger costumes and we drooled to see each other in them! Garrett, with his sneaky ass, was right. It was sexy! On Jojo, it looked as though it was made for him. The hardness of his body through that fur sewn body suit makes me shudder to see him in it. I pulled Garrett to the side and asked him, "What gives? Why did you have us dressed the same?"

"Because, with you two being the only people in the group who grew up together and the way y'all have been all over each other lately, I just thought it would be interesting to see how y'all would like dressing together."

"OK, I can get with that. But I noticed that mine has a zipper on both the crotch and the asscrack! Why is that?"

"There are some things you must find out for yourself."

*****

And find out we did! Jojo discovered the same "surprises" in his own costume. Of course, we kept zipped up during the party. But as the night flowed past like water, our libido became prominent and the hunger we had for each other last night was nothing compared to the hunger and animal like attraction we had for each other tonight. We run back to our room and, again, the moment we shut the door was the moment we leapt onto the bed jockeying for position. Kissing and groping. It is a good thing that we decided to paint our faces and go for the catlike contacts with glowing golden irises, instead of doing the masks or headdresses. The only thing we had on our heads were the ears. My crotch zipper went down. He lay on his stomach on the bed. I straddled his body and pulled his ass zipper down. And there was that blue-black ass, highlighted by the light of the midnight moon that shone in the cabin. Now we know why the zippers were here! I didn't even see that in the description. Way to go, Garrett! I threw aside his tail. I parted his cheeks and with my tongue, I lick the twitching wonder of his sugar pink sphincter. Oh, the taste of his ass! It was sweet and warm like black coffee. As I allow my tongue to swirl deeper inside his sweet candy cavity, I hear his heavenly moans and I direct my eyes to his muscular, hairy, massive forearms and his dark hands with beige fingernails clawing the white pillows. The muscles on his back begin to contract as he grinds his hips. I taste guttural sweetness as I swirl my tongue with more intensity. Strangé said that the smell of her panties was the essence of sex. That ain't shit! I am tasting the essence of *his* sex. His fluid sex. His juices become like an aphrodisiac for me. The more he moans and writhes, the more I desire him. The crack of his ass becomes slippery with his secretions and my saliva.

"Oh Daddy!"

"Hmmm?"

"Daddy eat me!"

"Mm-Hmm!"

"You like your baby's juices?"

"Mm-Hmm!"

"I've been saving these juices for you."

"Yeah baby."

"I have waited years for this."

"I've thought about it for years."

"Wanted you for so long."

"I want you right now."

"I need you right now."

"Tell me how much you need me."

"Like I need my next breath."

Another exhale escapes my lips. An exhale of relief. An exhale of life. An exhale of love.

"I need you like I need my life!"

"Come on daddy. Give me that dick!"

"You want this dick, baby?"

"Yes daddy!"

"Are you sure, baby?"

"Come on daddy. Don't make me beg. Please baby. Give me that dick."

I can't stand it anymore. I pull my tongue out of his ass and stand up to take off my costume and put my condom on. He practically flies out of his. I guess we don't need these costumes anymore. Now it's just me and him. Onyx and Topaz. Our faces painted orange and black. Our contact laden eyes are golden and shining. I lay on top of him and he embraces me. His deep pink lips part open, inviting my tongue coated with his sex to become one with his tongue. Our juices mix. My shaft is hard and pressing against his puckered rose. It is then that he puts his hands on my ass and pulls me into him. "Come on. Quit stalling. I want your dick."

He then pulls me with a mighty heave and my jimmie goes all the way in. Skin to skin we pressed. Onyx and Topaz. Almost the color of the costumes we discarded. Dark chocolate and caramel, we mix like a Snickers candy bar. We melt together in our sweat. Our bodies slipping and sliding together. For the next hour, the only thing on our minds is each other. We scream words of love. Words of undying devotion. We scream obscenities, but they are loaded with the love we shared for thirty-seven years. Suddenly, he screams with joy and my screams join with his as our sexual glue erupts from us simultaneously.

"Oh baby. You are hot!"

Throughout the night, All I hear are our moans adding sensuous music to the beautiful symphony of love we composed in the shimmering darkness, highlighted by the full bright moon. All I smell is his sweet aroma. All I see is his black beauty. All I feel is the heat of love we have between us. Years of him waiting. Years of me wondering. As we satisfied each other repeatedly, I berate myself. *You dope, how could you have been so blind to wonder so long?*

I am now holding him in my arms... and I'm *still* wondering... only now I am wondering if I can ever let him go.

Chapter Nineteen:

"SHADOWS COME FORTH"

The days passed like a blur. It is now Friday afternoon. Peep, Jimmy, Sheila, Jade, Jojo, and I sit in those spacious domed chairs on the Serenity Deck, watching the beautiful sunset. As I watch it dive into night while painting the sky the colors of vermilion, violet, and blue, I breathe a sigh of sadness that it is all going to end on the day after tomorrow. Jojo and I occupy one chair, and the other two couples occupy the other available two chairs.

"So how long have you been doing Rainbow Pride?" Jimmy asks Sheila.

"Oh, we've been going on this cruise for five years."

"Five years?" Peep asks.

"Yep, five years," Sheila says. "We fell in love with it from the start. Mark and Keith are decent, salt-of-the-earth people and the cruise just did something for us that we needed."

"And what was that?" I ask.

Jade asks Sheila, "Should I answer this, baby?"

"Go right ahead," Sheila says.

"Well, it gave us a place where we could really be ourselves. You see, I work as a lawyer and in my profession, everything is all about depositions, court cases, and sometimes pro bono work for first-time offenders. If that's all you have to look forward to, life can be pretty boring."

"Well," Sheila interjects. "There are some good things to be had from it." She looks into Jade's eyes smiling. Jade responds in kind.

"That's true, baby. Sheila and I met at the law office. She was working as a paralegal."

"That's right. I was assigned to work with her, typing up depositions. Updating legal documents. Doing research. And she needed them quicker than I could prepare them."

"Right," Jade says laughing. "So, I told her on more than one occasion that I needed certain documents… like *yesterday*."

"So, one day," Sheila takes over. "When she asked me about a certain deposition and I gave her my catchphrase, 'No worries. You'll have it', she said, 'I don't want to have it later, I need it now. I will give you twenty-four hours to prepare it.'"

As we listen to the story, Jojo and I are smiling with amusement.

Jade goes on. "So, she tells me, 'You and I both know that you don't need this deposition until next week.' I said that it was beside the point and that I needed them then because I didn't want to wait until the last minute. Other words were exchanged, and she quit on the spot."

"You quit?" Peep asks.

"Yeah, honey," Sheila continues. "I was working long hours. Getting hardly no sleep. And the top it all off, I was extremely cranky that morning. My coffee machine did not work and anybody that knows me knows that I do not go without my coffee. So, I was feeling a bit cranky."

"She stormed out of my office and I had to get another paralegal. I was so mad at her for making me do that because she was hands-down the best paralegal I'd ever worked with… and she turned me *on*! I didn't see her for a year. Then, as fate would have it, I saw her eating calamari in a swanky restaurant. I think it was calamari with marinara sauce."

"No, it wasn't," Sheila reminds her. "It was calamari with ranch dressing."

"It was marinara, baby."

"No love, I remember it was ranch dressing."

"Well it was one of those sauces. Anyway…"

Sheila looks at us while pointing at her and saying, "Did she just punk me?" We chuckle.

"Anyway, when she saw me, she had this mean look on her face. I almost didn't approach her, but I decided to do so with an apology."

"So, she apologized and then we got into another argument on whose fault it really was that I quit. I said it was her fault for being so inflexible with the documents."

"And I said that it was *her* fault for not having the documents when she should've had them."

"At the end of it all, we decided that both of us was at fault and we called a truce. We still argue and disagree. She says its blue. I say it's red."

"Pardon me for asking, but why are y'all still together if y'all fight so much?" Jimmy asks.

"Should I get this one, baby?" Sheila says

Jade raises her hands as if to say, "Be my guest."

"Well, the best way I can answer that is we discovered that what one of us was lacking, the other had. And seventy percent of the arguments we made up anyway, just so we could enjoy our make-up time."

"Before you ask," Jade interjects. "I would just like to say that it never got physical."

"Except that one time," Sheila reminded her.

"OK," I say skeptically. "You do realize you just told me that the fight became physical. It starts my mind wondering if you were throwing blows."

"Oh no baby, nothing like that. She made me mad about something on her birthday. I forget what she made me mad about because it was stupid. But I do know this, I took that cake and dumped it on her head."

"And I took the Vanilla ice cream and I smeared it in her face."

"Anyways, she was huffing and puffing. So was I. Next thing we know, we sprawled over the dining room table kissing, with her chocolate cake on my face and my vanilla ice cream on her. The rest of it, use your imagination."

"Oooh, freaky." Peep fans himself. We all laugh at that shared memory.

"That night also sealed the deal. I knew that this was the woman I wanted to be with for the rest of my life. So, I snatched her and married her. Of course, the people in that small town were so bigoted, especially our families, that we had to move."

"Where y'all livin' now?" I ask.

"We live in San Francisco."

"Have you seen your family since getting married?"

A dark cloud passes over Jade's face as she shakes her head no. Sheila plants a kiss on top of her head.

"It's kind a hard for her to talk about her family, especially her father. See, her father disowned her."

I look at Jojo. "Sounds familiar," I say to him.

"What about your parents?" Jojo asks Sheila.

"They're dealing with this like any typical set of church parents. They are praying for my sinful soul and hoping that I'll find a nice man to marry. They just can't get it through their heads that I'm with the one I want."

"The fact is," Jade cuts in. "When you have a good feeling about something, it pays to be adventurous and go for what you know. And when I married Sheila's crazy ass seven years ago, it was the best thing I could've done."

"You are a fine one to talk about crazy," Sheila says as she smooches her.

Jade looks at her watch. "Well, it's almost dinner. We better get down there and get dressed."

Sheila says as they rise, "We will catch up to y'all later. Enjoy yourselves."

"You too," I say.

As we watch them leave, Jimmy says, "I can't get over those to getting together. They are like two different people."

"Well, I guess it's true what they say. Opposites do attract," Peep informs.

We resume watching the sun almost completely set. What a beautiful sight!

"It is just beautiful here. I can't believe we are going back in two more days," Jimmy says as he holds Peep.

"Yeah. I wish your mother could've come," Jojo says.

"Yeah, she really would've enjoyed it," I agree.

"Yeah, especially after her visit to the doctor and what he told her," the words fly from Peep's lips.

"Told her what?" Jimmy says.

Holy shit! I am dumbfounded. It's gonna hit the fan now!

"Feli, what are you talking about?"

Peep can't speak. Jimmy stands and comes closer to me.

"Lionel, Mama talked to you while I went to Old Man Calloway's. What did she say?"

I'm too flabbergasted to speak. Jimmy turns back to Peep.

"Felipe, don't bullshit me now. I want you to tell me the truth. What did the doctor say?"

"Listen, I don't want to talk about this right now. Can we please go back to the room?"

"No, we can't go back to the room. Obviously, you and Lionel know something about my mother that I don't know, and it is something serious. Now tell me what it is."

Peep exhales and looks downcast. "The doctors told Irene that her diabetes is getting worse and there's nothing more they can do. They gave her three more months to live."

"What the fuck?" Jimmy shouts.

"Baby, calm down."

"You're telling me to calm down and you just told me that my mother could be dead in three months. How long have you two known about this? Has it been two months? Has it been three?"

"Jimmy, Irene told us at the beginning of this month. She didn't want us to tell you because she knew that this would be your reaction."

"But even so, I am your husband! You should've shared that shit with me. This has to do with my mother. This has nothing to do with her eating cake and ice cream and shit like that. This is my mother's life! Are there any *other* secrets I should know about?"

Peep jumps up. "Now wait a minute, Jimmy. It is not like I plotted to keep it from you. Irene asked me to! Like I said, she knew how you would take it. She also told me that every time she would try to tell you about it, you wouldn't listen."

"Jimmy, try not to blame him. When Irene told him, he didn't want to keep that a secret from you."

"The way I see it, you are just as much to blame as he is."

"Now, wait just a minute..."

"You both should've told me!"

Jimmy spins on his heel and heads from the area. "Jimmy, where are you going?"

"I need to think," Jimmy throws back as he leaves.

*****

Tonight's dinner is very dismal. Jojo and Garrett did not join us. Jojo was tired and Garrett had a little bit of food poisoning that kept him in his room. The only conversation to be had is between Charlie, Sheila, and Jade. The exchange between Peep, Jimmy, Corey, and myself is monosyllabic. For the first time during this cruise, Peep and Jimmy aren't sitting together. They are seated at opposite ends of the table. Corey and I sit side by side, but it seems irreverent to have any type of conversation as we are silenced by the pall of hurt between Peep and Jimmy.

Charlie, Sheila, and Jade begin to sense that something is going on, so they finish their food and excuse themselves. Now it is quiet. Jimmy and Peep cannot even look at each other because every time Jimmy tries to look at Peep, he sees him pleading with his eyes for him to understand. Every time Peep looks at Jimmy, he sees him reproaching with his eyes that he should've been told the information that Irene told us. At last, Peep rises to leave. I see Jimmy's eyes as he watches Peep's movement out of the restaurant. When he leaves, the only things we hear are conversations going on at the other tables and the silverware clinking with the plates at our own.

Enough of this bullshit! "So, we are just going to sit here and not say anything?"
Silence.
Then, Corey gets up and says firmly, "Well, I don't have much to say because I have nothing to do with this. This is between you, Peep, and Jimmy. But I will say this to Jimmy. Dude, the only reason they did not tell you is because they were looking out for you."
Jimmy looks down at his plate, a tear escapes his eye.
Corey sees this and nods sympathetically before saying, "I get it... You're scared of losing her. I would imagine that if I had a mother like yours, I wouldn't take the news too well, either. I may not know what it's like to have a mama, but I've lost enough good people to know that none of us are going to be around here forever and it would be crazy to think that there is an exempt status for dying. Jimmy, you've done everything you can for Irene. No one could've loved her more than you, but now that you have this news, do this for me. Once you get back from this cruise, cherish the time that you have with her while you got it. Lionel, I'll catch you later."
Corey then walks off to catch up with Peep. Jimmy looks at me. "I still think y'all should've told me."
"Jimmy, what would you have done if we *had* told you? What *could* you have done? The way you are carrying on right now, you don't even have to wait for her to be buried six feet under; you're doing it right now by smothering her and not letting her go."
"I just don't want my mama to die, Lionel. Is that wrong? I love that woman. She's my mama. There were so many things I wanted to tell her. So many things I wanted to share with her."
"Oh Jimmy, set it to music, why don't ya? She is still living. And like Corey said, why don't you use this time now to share whatever you want to share with her. Make memories with your mother instead of mourning her before she even transitions. She ain't dead yet."
Jimmy says nothing. I then remember in detail the conversation with Irene. It might help him to know what was said.
"Jimmy, do you want to know something else your mother said?"
"What?"

"She said that she is ready to go. She's tired, Jimmy. Tired of this disease ravaging her body. She also asked us to be there for you and we are not going anywhere. We're going to see you through this. And technically, Peep did not make that promise."

"He didn't?"

"No. He just listened to her tell him that she did not want him to say anything about it. And let me tell you, he struggled with this. Put yourself in his position. Imagine it being his grandmother who kept trying to tell him that she was going to pass on, but he wouldn't listen, so she confided in you to have somebody to talk to about it. And she told you not to say anything. Wouldn't you feel some type of conflict between your loyalty to your grandmother-in-law and your husband? Peep loves you both and wants the best for you. He wanted to tell you, but he didn't because he saw this as an opportunity for you to take a few days to enjoy your life without worries about Irene."

I see him breathe a heavy sigh of resignation and his eyebrows go up. "Well, Feli must've been in a tight spot. I'm not sure what I would've done in that position. I guess I better go talk to him." He gets up. I join him saying, "Well, I'm gonna leave this restaurant with you because the food kind of went downhill ever since I've been up here. I'm not trying to get food poisoning like Garrett."

*****

We are retiring on the deck at the back of the ship, enjoying drinks around the table. It is 1:20am and we just left the Pride party. Apparently, Jimmy and Peep talked about everything, because they are both sitting on the chair, with Peep between Jimmy's hairy Herculean legs and wrapped in his arms. We are playing a game called Three Facts. It's a game that my friends and I played in college. It's a fun marriage between Spin the Bottle and Truth or Dare. The only thing is when the bottleneck points at you, you have to share three facts about you, or strip! Well, Corey obviously does not want to share, because he is sitting next to Garrett damn near naked. Of course, I don't see Garrett complaining. Garrett spins the bottle, and the point lands on Jimmy.

"OK Jimmy. Three facts or strip."

"Hmmm. Well, I was not always this big. When I was in high school I was a beanpole with no shape. That's fact one. I've never went to my Junior or Senior prom. That's fact two. I have tried cocaine before. That's fact three."

Peep is shocked. "You never told me that. How long ago was it since you first tried it?"

"I was twenty-one."

"Was that your only time?"

"No. I had a serious addiction from then until age twenty-five."

"What stopped you?"

"Well, one of my buddies that I was snorting with had a bad reaction to the cocaine that we were smoking. He started tripping out and ended up naked and on the ledge. I actually had to talk him back inside. It scared the fuck out of me. But hey, the things you do when you're young and stupid."

"Well I'm glad you didn't have to hit bottom before you got clean," Peep says, snuggling his body against Jimmy.

"You and me both," he says.

"It's my turn." I spin the bottle. It lands on Corey again. He sucks his teeth.

"Why does it have to keep landing on me?"

"It must like you," Garrett teases.

"Yeah. Now you're going to have to tell us three facts eventually. You are already down to your swimming trunks and shades. After two more spins, you're going to end up naked and I am not trying to get put off this boat because of your indecent exposure."

"OK, OK! Let's see, three facts about myself. I used to play for the high school choir while I was in high school, and baby, they paid me like a pro! That's fact number one. I once had a prison pen-pal. And he would write me the dirtiest letters about how he wanted to flip me and fuck the shit out of me. Of course, when he got paroled, that never happened. That's fact number two. And I slept with one of my college professors. That's fact number three."

"You didn't!" I say, shocked.

"I did and let me tell you. It was good. He didn't look like much with clothes on, but when he took them off, talk about the body of a god. He was light golden brown, and his dick was golden brown with a pink head."

I clear my throat, "Um, Corey?" I gesture towards Garrett who is looking less than pleased.

"Oh, come on babe. Don't be looking like that. That was years and years ago. And I needed to up my grade," Corey cajoles, giving him a smooch.

"My turn", Jojo says as he spins the bottle. The point lands on Garrett

"OK Garrett," Corey says. "Three facts that no one knows about and make them good ones."

"OK, I hail from Miami originally. I was adopted when I was twelve years old and rescued from the Yancey's Home for Boys."

Just then, Corey's head swivels around.

"Yancey's Home for Boys? You were in that shit pit of an orphanage?"

"Shit pit isn't even the word to describe that hellhole. And those counselors were even worse. A pedophile and a savage."

There is an awkward silence. Then Corey says with his head down, "Mr. Haines and Mr. Baker."

There is complete tension hovering over the atmosphere.

"Wait a minute. How do you know about those two?"

Corey's eyes are bright with blinding tears. He says, "I was housed there when I was a kid. I had to fight every fucking day that I was in that hellhole. And I know about Mr. Haines because... that sicko molested me."

"Oh my God," I hear my voice breathe out. His voice lacks his usual strident tone. Bitter sobs erupt from the very core of his body. The tears start coming faster from his eyes and his face is filled with fear and anger. I grab him and hug him tightly, and he clings to me for dear life.

"That sick bastard! That cruel son of a bitch stole my childhood away from me! He made me kiss his stinking dick. His ugly, stinking, white dick! Then he made me suck it. The bigger boys would make me blow them until I got the balls to fight them. He knew I would fight him, so he drugged me. And it was when I was too weak to fight... that he raped me."

Garrett's face is drawn. He stands and pulls Corey up with him. He wraps his arms around him and gives Corey a kiss of comfort. The rest of us just sit there, in horror of what we just heard.

"Corey," I say. "Is this what you have been bottling up inside you all this time?"

He turns and nods soberly as he and Garrett resume their seats beside each other, holding hands.

"Why didn't you tell us?"

"Because, I was embarrassed, humiliated. I had to work twice as hard in my studies and drown myself in music, just so I didn't have to think about what happened."

"Again, Corey. That is something we would've understood," Peep laments.

"I know that, but ..."

"Look, don't come down too hard on him," Garrett says protectively. "Rape and molestation are scary issues to talk about."

"Yeah," I agree, looking at Jojo and squeezing his hand. "The important thing is that he is talking about it now."

"I know I should've done it sooner. Pop Kennedy kept trying to get me to talk about it. But I wouldn't. I wanted to block everything out."

"You called him Pop Kennedy?" Garrett asks humorously.

"Yeah."

"Who is Pop Kennedy?" Jimmy asks.

"He was the mental health counselor at Yancey. The only decent one in the bunch," Garrett informs.

"Yeah, he was also my adoptive father. It was from him that I felt how beautiful music could be."

"Wow, he must have adopted several kids. He adopted a very close friend of mine around the same time I got adopted."

Corey turns to stare at him, "When was this?"

"It was in 1994."

"I'm trying to think... I don't remember a guy named Garrett that went to Yancey."

"That was because I switched names after I graduated High School. Garrett is actually my middle name"

"What was your real first name?" Peep asks.

"Zachary. Zachary Middleton".

Corey then looks up at him. Tears of remembrance start piling up in his eyes. "Zach?"

"Yeah," Garrett says with a puzzled look on his face.

For several seconds, Corey just sits there gaping at him. Suddenly, he bolts up, grabs his clothes, and leaves the table.

"Corey," Jojo shouts out.

"I'd better go after him," Garrett volunteers.

"No. Let me. Y'all stay here."

I chase after him, confused about what I just heard and shocked by the revelations I have just received. Corey is speeding briskly up the steps to the Serenity Deck. He is almost running at breakneck speed. I have to break into a jog to catch up with him. I bump into someone. It is Sheila.

"Hey Lionel."

"Hey Sheila."

"Is everything OK? What's wrong?"

"We are fine. Just trying to catch up to my friend."

"Oh yeah, I saw him speed through here. Is there anything I can do?"

"No, thank you for offering. I just need to talk to him. He just ran off after some upsetting news."

"Well, by now, he's probably on the Serenity Deck. Let me know if you need anything. Jade and I will be right here."

I race up the wrought iron stairs, bypassing different men who are talking, hugging, and kissing. I'm starting to worry. I don't know the bottom of Corey's story, but it must be something completely devastating for him. I walk the deck and circle around to the starboard side of the boat, and there, fully clothed and leaning over the railing while looking out into the nothingness of the dark, is Corey.

I hasten up to him. "Corey, what is going on?"

No answer. Just him staring out and letting the tears fall.

"Corey, I'm going to ask this again… and if we are friends, you will tell me what is going on."

He turns around to face me. He is working his mouth, but no sounds are coming out.

"Alright Corey, come over here," I say as I grab his hand and gesture over to a few chairs over by the pool. We sit down. His head, usually held so proud, is downcast.

"Corey, come on. It's me. You can talk to me. It's Lionel. Tell me what's wrong." I hear desperation in my own voice. It must have reached him because Corey is raising his head to look at me again and as I look into his eyes, I see a strong man suddenly becoming feeble.

"Lionel?" I stand to turn and see Garrett and I walk over to him.

"Is he OK?"

"Yeah. Listen, let me just have a few moments alone with him. I think I need to see what's going on. Tell Peep and Jojo that we will meet up later at the Lido deck."

"OK." Garrett slowly turns around and starts walking towards the wrought iron stairs. Abruptly, he turns around and kneels in front of Corey. "Let me just say this, and I'll leave you two alone. Corey, look at me."

Corey raises his head ever so slowly and looks at him. Garrett lifts his hand to wipe his eyes and stroke his face. "I know about what happened with those two evil bastards and I know they hurt you. I don't know what set you off when you heard my real name, but I want you to know and remember that I love you. I won't hurt you like they did." He then kisses Corey softly on the lips and makes his way down the stairs.

I sit back down. Corey lets out a long sigh full of sorrow as if the world is on his shoulders.

"My name is not Corey."

What in the world did I just hear? "Come again?"

"My real name is not Cordell Kennedy. My real name is Simon. Simon Lee Bradley."

You could've knocked me over with a feather. All these years we've known him as Corey. So many questions rush through my mind. Why the name change? Why the deception? Why did he hold all these feelings in for so long and how was he able to do it? Amid the barrage of questions, there's only one that I opt to ask.

"Why the name change?"

"That's all you are going to ask? You're not gonna ask me about what happened in my past?" He asks, almost hopeful.

"No. I'm not gonna ask that. If what you said at the table is any indication as to what went on, you don't have to spell it out."

Corey gets up and walks towards the railing. He resumes leaning on it and looking out into the bleakness of the night and listening to the rushing of the waters. Then he begins to talk.

"It's like this. I was born Simon Lee Bradley. My parents were named John and Carolyn, both drug addicts. My mother didn't want me, so she gave me up... But my life hasn't always been bad... and you know that. You, Peep, and Jojo have been the best friends anyone could ever have. That's what made my life bearable up to this point... Do you want to know how I got so good at music, at playing the keys?"

"If you want to tell me."

"I had two gifted musicians who raised me. One was a sweet German woman. She taught me how to sightread, how to play the piano, and how to appreciate the beauty of music. That's where that book of sonatas by Debussy came from. She gave that to me when I was five years old. The other was the one I was always talking about. The one I called my dad."

"Reverend Kennedy?"

He nods his head. "He was the one that taught me how to feel whatever I played. He instilled in me how passionate and heartfelt music should be. He gave me love... He always made me feel like I belonged someplace. He gave me hope."

He pauses for minute to look up at the star laden sky and the ghostly moon. "I wanted to change my name because I didn't want to be reminded of anything that happened in that godforsaken orphanage. Pop Kennedy named me after his son who was killed."

"What happened at that orphanage?"

He just stands there with new tears in his eyes. "Not only were the two counselors at that orphanage pedophiles and brutes. But they were also racist. Zachary and I were the only black boys in there... Mr. Haines made me blow him almost every night when I was ten. It was then that Zachary taught me how to box and how to fight back. My friend Lawrence started teaching me how to kick in the nuts. He was the only white boy that I had a close friendship with. Him and Zachary, well Garrett, were the bright spot of being in that orphanage.

But when Mr. Haines raped me, and I saw the blood the next morning, I felt like my soul had died... He stole my childhood from me."

"Did you talk to anyone about this? Was there another person there that could've done something about it?"

"There was the orphanage director, Mr. Chrone. I told him what happened a month after Mr. Haines first made me suck him off, and he said that I'd have to prove it and that, without proof, it was my word against Mr. Haines. I knew I was done for when he said that. Afterwards, for a time, I just gave up."

This is heavy. At this moment, I start thinking about my family and how good I had it. I dealt with religious hurt and hypocrites, but I had a father who loved me. My family and I didn't always get along, but I, at least, knew who all of them were. I was abused for anything my mother considered "faggot" habits, but I wasn't being raped or molested.

Corey, on the other hand, was frequently abused in every sense for years before he found Rev. Kennedy. That had to weigh heavily on his mind. Moreover, he had no blood family that he could lay claim to. It was a blessing that the adoptive parents were good to him, but it's nothing like having your own family. He had to make do with what life threw him; abuse and all. I look at my friend, admiring his strength and his courage in keeping it together for so long.

My mind goes back to our graduation. I remember a sea of people there, and among that sea was my father and my mother. I remember Jojo's mother being there. By this time, Peep's grandmother had already passed on, but he had his aunt Myrtle, and she was there. Corey graduated with honors and was a celebrated student pianist at Morgan State University, but he had no one there to cheer him on. By this time, his adopted father had died. I remember looking at his face and seeing the same front that he has put on for years. The same wide smile. The same happy expression. He broke down a couple of times because he missed his adoptive father, but he kept that smile. Little did we know, that smile was hiding so much hurt, so much rage, so much humiliation, and so much sadness. I reach to grab his hand.

"How did you end up in that orphanage in the first place?"

"My first foster parent died from a heart attack and there were no family members that could take me in. The day that I found out she died, I went totally batshit. I screamed. I clawed. I wanted to hurt the world for cheating me out of having a family. It was then that I felt this prick. I faded into blackness... and when I woke up, I was in the orphanage... I felt the exact same way when Pop

Kennedy died. I wanted to scream the anger I felt at God for taking him from me and for taking my chances a way at having a real family. But all I could do at that time is what I did best. I put on my mask and I smiled. You know, there have been times when I thought about killing myself behind that damn mask. Even on this goddamned boat. I thought about ending it. I thought, well my family is gone so what do I have to keep me here?... Oh Lionel... sometimes I just ask myself, 'How many times am I going to have to keep smiling when I'm hurting? How many times am I going to have to laugh just so that I won't cry?'"

I grab him and without resistance he grabs me back and we hold each other. The same way he held me when my dad was killed. I feel his heartbeat and his body quaking. I hear him screaming out his sobs held in for so many years. If I could go back into his past and erase what he went through, I really would. I hear myself say, "It's going to be OK. You don't have to put on a mask for us. We are hurting too. All of us. But, you know something? I believe through divine design that there was a wise reason all of us met, to be each other's support." I release my hold and playfully push him. "And who said that you don't have a family? A lot of times my father used to say this, and I don't profess to be the Best Christian in the world. Sometimes God will take a natural family that doesn't really mean you any good and replace it with a family of friends who want only the best for you. And just look at how you have been blessed already."

Corey looks at me, "Oh yeah? Like how?"

"You had a mother through that German woman. You had a father through Pop Kennedy. JoJo, Peep, Jimmy, and I were sent to you as your brothers and we ain't going nowhere. Also, think about this. Even while you were in that orphanage, you were given two brothers: Lawrence and Zachary. And as fate would have it, one of those brothers is coming back to you to be your special friend for life; and this guy could love you at a level that even the three of us are not capable of. You got a second chance at love with the very one who taught you how to really love another man. So, you haven't lost anything. You gained a whole mountain of people who think the world of you."

We hug each other tightly once more and this time, Corey pushes me away. "Let's not be getting mushy. This ain't one of those corny TGIF shows on Friday nights with that sappy music that plays in the background every time there's a lesson to be learned."

"Corey, if memory serves me correctly, I remember going over to your house and seeing all of those corny TGIF shows in Blu-rays on your shelf."

"I could be collecting them because I want some ideas as far as music is concerned."

"From that same sappy shit music that you were talking about?"

"Hey. It takes all kinds."

"I meant to ask you, how is that symphony coming?"

"Well," Corey grins bashfully. "I finished the last movement, just before we got on the cruise. Two of the movements were composed in the month I went under the radar."

I slap him playfully on the shoulder. "And you sitting up here on this 'woe is me', suicidal tip? All this 'mask' shit? Well, I can't really say anything about that, because all of us have masks that we wear. But you just gave yourself three good reasons why you ought to hang in there. You got brothers who love you, you got a man who worships the ground you walk on, and you got a huge work to finish and to premiere on the world's stage."

"But I still have to clean up the score."

"So? The first draft is finished, and you know how to clean the score. Make it happen."

Just then, Peep, Jimmy, Jojo, and Garrett trudge up the stairs. Peep exclaims, "Corey, if you scare me like that one more time, I'm going to take off these tight ass shoes and beat you with them."

"You couldn't beat shit coming out of a horse's ass." Corey says laughing.

"Are you OK?" Garrett asks, with love in his voice.

Corey looks at him reflectively, A sweet smile curves his lips. "Yes, Garrett. I'm fine. I got something to show you. Someone gave me this. Maybe you know him." He reaches in his pocket, pulls out his wallet, and retrieves a yellowing photo. He gives it to Garrett. Total recall is all over Garrett's face as he gazes at the picture, then closely at Corey. His face begins to shine with love. He lets out a huge laugh and an abundant joy spreads all over his body. "No fucking way! Simon?!"

Corey smiles a genuine smile of happiness. "Yes baby, it's me. Simon Lee Bradley".

Suddenly, Garrett rushes over to him and picks him up and swings him around, bouncing him as they turn. I am laughing and enjoying the scene, while Jojo, Peep, and Jimmy just stands there looking confused.

"Zachary, you nut! Put me down!" Corey says, laughing.

Garrett complies with amazement shining on his face. "I'm sorry, baby. I just cannot believe this. All these years of looking for you and here you are right in front of me."

"You've been searching for me?"

"Yes! No wonder I couldn't find you. I never would've guessed."

"Same thing here! I was wondering what happened to you. This is off the charts!"

"All I want to know is what we call you now. Simon and Zachary, or Corey and Garrett?" I ask.

"Well, you've gotten so used to calling us Corey and Garrett, so y'all might as well stick with that." Corey then looks Garrett in the eye and smiles. "The names Simon and Zachary... are reserved for us to call each other."

"You know it, baby," Garrett smiles as they embrace, and Garrett lifts him up again, spinning him around by the pool and yelling out. "Oh, we got so much to talk about. And I can't wait!" He suddenly releases Corey and Corey lands in the pool!

"Holy shit!" Garrett lets out, shamefacedly. Corey swims up and trudges up the pool steps. "I'm sorry, baby."

"Goddamn, man! You're happy to see me, ain't ya? Well, I 'm happy to see you too. That doesn't mean that I want to get my good clothes all wet!"

Next thing I know, I hear a splash. Garrett jumped in the pool too, swam around, and came out with his clothes dripping. He stood in front of Corey and held him gently.

"Now, we're both wet."

"Oh well, let's give each other a wet kiss," Corey replies. And they commence. I then hear someone clearing their throat.

"Uh, does someone want to clue us in?" Jojo inquires.

"Yeah, spill the tea, *Simon!*" Peep follows.

Corey turns toward us and grins. "Ok, uh, y'all had better sit down. It's a long story."

*****

"Alright, you broke-ass motherfuckers." Miss Laura, A fifty-nine-year-old MC, lets out. "I bet y'all blew all your hard-earned money in the casino... Uh, huh. And some of y'all did some weird shit to get the money...You blew the money just like you blew that trick before yo' asses got on the boat... Hmmmm... And you honey, I know you got money. With all the dick you been getting on this boat, they oughta install a turnstile outside your door."

The audience roars.

"But shit, baby. We are on vacation and we came to have fun. And between shuffleboard and dick, I'll take dick any day of the fucking week! But, addressing the dick-getter, don't have no shame in your game, chile'."

"Believe me, baby, I'm loving it," The audience member yells out, laughing.

"Well, you certainly look like it! Give me some of that glitter. You are shining, baby. Glowing! Yaaaaas! That's what good dick will do for ya!... Uh-huh! You ho' motherfucker!"

I almost piss my pants. This lady is off the chain.

"But seriously, you are enjoying life, honey, and I wouldn't want to live a life I couldn't enjoy. But I tell ya. It's a sad fucking day when a bitch gotta compete with all these juicy muscular asses in here. Tight... wet... almost virginal..." She spots someone in the audience and yells out, "What you looking all sanctimonious fuh! Almost doesn't count... Ha!... For those of y'all who really are virgins, Mama got the answer. A good stiff drink and a hell of an ass eater. Then, tell him to ease it in and make you lean back. Chile', if you get enough dick in you, your ass go'n be spread wider than my cunt on a three-day pass."

Another uproarious laugh from the audience.

"You know, I ain't go'n hate on my Rainbow Pride babies. They know how to pull some men. It seems like the older I get, the more I'm seeing macho men crossing over to the other side. I guess a good stiff dick will bring the bitch out of the Incredible Hulk... Honey, you know how these men are in daylight, walking around like this..."

She then walks around on the stage, swaggering and tugging her crotch.

"And by nightfall, they got their asses and legs up in the air, like this..." She drops to the floor and demonstrates, spasming her body. The people in the audience throw back their heads and laugh.

"I think both me and my twat are going into involuntary retirement. You wanna know the fucked-up thing about that?"

"What?" The audience hollers.

"I ain't even sixty-five yet. I can't collect Social Security. It'll be sweet to lay on my ass and do nothing but collect checks every fucking month. Now give me a big dick to put in it, and I'll be the happiest bitch in ATL."

The audience loses its composure in the hilarity of the moment. Miss Laura's voice becomes very matter-of-fact. "I hear tell that there are two gentlemen on this boat celebrating a birthday. Beautiful thirty-seven, and three friends of theirs wanted to present a gift to them in a song. Are Lionel Davis and Joseph Thompson in the room?"

Oh my Gosh! As we stand, the audience erupts in a round of applause. I look at Jojo and he has this bewildered look on his face.

"Look at Mama's babies! Ain't they beautiful? Yes, indeed! We just want to wish you a happy birthday. And y'all make thirty-seven look damn good. Sit back down and relax as you listen to the sounds of Corey Kennedy, Garrett Peterson, and Felipe Hartfield. Come on, let's give them some love."

The audience applauds as my three friends get on the stage and launch into a beautiful song Corey wrote. The shock of the evening is Peep! His voice is magnificent! I knew he sang in the church choir at Unity and Love, but he's never taken a solo. All these years, I never knew he could sing like that. When Corey blends his voice with Peep's and Garrett plays his saxophone, I feel love for this beautiful, diverse group of people I have called my friends for all these years. I listen to the words of the song:

Love makes me beautiful
Love makes me strong
Love lets me know that I belong
Love gives me courage
To carry on.
Love lets me know I'm not alone

I will be fearless
I will always fight for love
Yes, I will shield you
With the help of God above.
My arms will hold you
Love and console you.
Yes, I will choose pain to stand for love.

During this song, I look at Jojo, and he looks at me smiling his sweet smile. I put my arm around him and listen to the masterful performance of my friends. One line stands out for me:

I will be fearless.

As they finish the song, Jojo, the audience, and I give them a standing ovation.

I will be fearless.

My palms are sweaty as I think of a life with Jojo, the one I have known since being born on the same day, raised for eighteen years living next to each other, eating ramen noodles with him in college and laughing at the TV shows we liked mutually, and crying on each other's shoulders due to failed relationships. But the image that I remember most was the day I held him, dressed his wounds, and told him I loved him at the age of fifteen.

I will be fearless.

I suddenly call out, "Miss Laura, may I have the mike, please?"

"As long as you don't stick it nowhere where the sun won't shine."

Amid the laughs, I take the stage. Garrett goes and sits next to Jimmy, and they both lean forward with anticipation for my announcement.

"I would like to thank my friends for that wonderful song. Knowing Corey, he wrote it. That's how gifted he is. We all have been friends for a long time and I could not think of a better birthday present than the one I just heard."

The audience applauds with approval. I wait for the applause to die down. Then I continue, "There was one line in the song that resonated with me. 'I will be fearless'. Fearless is standing up for who you love and to be able to take on the world to protect him. Fearless is kissing in a room full of people who look down on you. Fearless is being able to leave what you know to travel through uncharted territory. And Jojo… you are the one. You have always been the one and I believe you will always be the one that I want to be fearless with." I pause and look down at my hand and see my class ring. I take it off. I hear the audience gasp and someone saying, "Oh my God, I smell a proposal." An eighty-seven-year-old lady yells out, "Go' head on, honey! Go ahead and get your man!"

I laugh and turn back to Jojo. "I know that this is not a real ring, but I'm hoping that it will do for right now, because, Joseph Stanley Thompson the III, I love you. I'm not afraid to say it anymore. I don't care if my family knows, or my job, or anyone who won't understand. That is their issue, not mine… I would be honored if you'll partner with me in life. Jojo, will you marry me?"

Jojo, with his mouth open, advances and steps onto the stage. Suddenly, he slaps me! It was a light slap, but it was a slap! "Ow, what was that for?"

"For two reasons. One, because you waited so long to ask me. And two, because I want both of us to remember that part of being fearless means to choose pain that you didn't know you signed up for." Then he grabs my shirt, pulls me to him, and kisses me passionately, among hoots and cat-calls from the audience. Releasing me, he says, "This is the other part of being fearless. That it's not always going to be pain, but there is also joy. So, Lionel Shedrick

Davis, my answer is yes without question. I will definitely marry you!" I then sweep him up and kiss him just as passionately! He said YES!

The audience erupts in cheers and hooting. Corey and Peep are standing at the piano yelling, "It's about time!" Jimmy and Garrett slap each other a high five. Throngs of people gather on stage to congratulate us, but all we see is the darkness behind our closed eyes as we hold our kiss and imagine a future of stars and roses, with anticipation of darkness and thorns.

COME ON WORLD. WE ARE READY FOR YOU!

CHAPTER TWENTY:

"LISTEN TO ME"

I'm still reeling from the fact that I proposed to my best friend on a cruise ship. I felt a freedom that I never felt before. The freedom to love without question, without fear. I felt the resilience of my youth every time I looked in Jojo's eyes. I got my life every time I danced with my fiancé and my extended family; Corey, Garrett, Peep, and Jimmy. The crowning glory was when I told my brother Dean that I planned on marrying Jojo. He said, "Well, I'm gonna say what Dad might've said. If he makes you happy, go for it." I laughed with unbridled love to hear those words. I believe they meant more because they came from a person whose bloodline I shared. Then again, Dean was always the most open-minded of us all.

I don't know if it was the water or the wine, but being on that cruise with Jojo, and experiencing the reunion between Corey and Garrett, as they will always be to me, made me realize what I had to do. I had to confront my mother and tell her how I felt about what she did to me, to Andre, and to my father. Soon enough, that opportunity came. No more than two days passed since my return before I got a call from Roland. He said that there were complications with the surgery, and that I needed to come to the hospital in Atlanta. A large part of me wanted to say no, but another part of me told me that it was time to face her. I go to a specialty store to buy a get-well gift for Mama, A beautiful and shimmering crystal snow globe with a mother and child in the snow.

I take the plane to Atlanta. This time, I'm not going alone. I have Jojo, Corey, and Garrett with me. Peep and Jimmy couldn't go, because they had to work and look after Irene. We all walk into the hospital.

"Zach, I think I want to go to the gift shop. Walk with me?"

"Sure, Simon. Are you two going to be ok?" Garrett asks

"Yeah, we'll be ok," I assure him.

We watch as Corey and Garrett walk slowly and blissfully down the hall, hand in hand. An older couple look at them with disgust. But they may as well be on the moon, because all Corey and Garrett see are each other.

Jojo and I get in the elevator.

"I'm nervous."

"Don't worry. I'm here."

I hug him as the elevator opens. We walk down the halls of the hospital to the cancer unit. When we get there, I think about all the evil things Mama said about Jojo. I want to spare him from her craziness. "Jojo."

"Yeah, babe?"

"I think I need to face Mama alone."

"Are you sure?"

"Yes."

"Ok, I'll be downstairs in the gift shop with Corey and Garrett if you need me. Do you have the gift?"

I pull the fragile snow globe from my bag, "Yes."

"Ok then." He turns away.

"Joseph?"

He turns in pleasant surprise. I walk to him and kiss him with a fervor that scared me. I sense people staring but all I can see is my baby. When we pull apart, I say.

"I love you."

"I love you too."

I turn to go in. But I hear Jojo call my name.

"Lionel".

"Yes?"

"Say my name again."

A wide smile hurts my face as I utter, "Joseph."

"My name has never sounded more beautiful." Smiling sweetly, he turns and walks down the hall. I enter the unit and walk up to the desk.

"Excuse me ma'am. But can you point me into the direction of Lynetta Davis's room?"

The desk attendant looks at the roster on her clipboard. "Room 336".

"Thank you."

I locate the room. Standing in front of that door, a momentary seizure of panic overtakes me. What if she is the same? What if she rejects me again? What if we get into another fight? Then I tell myself what Dr. Banneker would say, "Why the What-ifs?"

I slowly open the door. All my brothers and sisters are standing around our mother as she is resting. Roland and Brenda jump up. "Lionel!" They rush to beat a path to my side. I give both a huge hug and squeeze. One that my dad would've been proud of. Dean walks forward and warmly swats me on my arm. "About time you came down. We didn't know if you were going to be able to come." I shake my brother's hand.

"You should have known that I would find a way," I retort, sounding just like my father. A look of remembrance passes Dean's face, lighting his eyes and broadening his smile.

Andre mumbles a half hello and gives me a small but pleasant smile. Rhonda just stands there with a hateful look on her face.

"How was the cruise?" Brenda asks.

"Yeah, did you enjoy?" Roland follows.

"It was awesome. Very peaceful. You get to think about things differently when you are on the water. You know what? We oughta plan a family cruise."

"I ain't getting on no boat," Roland jokes. "There are sharks out there."

"Come on, Roland. It's really fun. They have games, activities, they even have a basketball court."

"What?!"

"Yeah."

"On the boat?" Brenda exclaims.

"Where else would it be in the middle of the sea?"

"Ok, Smarty."

"Did you come in here to talk about your vacation, or to see about your mother?" Rhonda's contemptible voice rings out.

"I actually came to talk to Mama," I say to Dean, ignoring her.

Dean informs, "Sure, but she's kinda groggy. They just wheeled her from surgery."

"How did it go?"

"Very well. They got the cancer out."

"Thank God!"

"Yeah, thank Him indeed."

"Do y'all mind if I have a few minutes?"

"Why? To make more excuses about that disgusting lifestyle you live? I don't think Mama wants to hear that crap," Rhonda snaps.

"Rhonda, do us all a fayva' an' shuddup!" Andre's deep raspy voice explodes. My head turns. Wow, Andre speaks up for me.

"It's the truth, Andre, and you know it."

"An' it wud be de fam'ly ho' to poin' dat out."

"Enough!" Dean shouts. "I'm sick and tired of all this bickering about nothing. Rhonda, he came all the way down here after months of him and Mama not speaking. The least we can do is let them have that time,"

"Uh, Dean and Brenda, let's go to the cafeteria. I am kinda hungry," Roland says.

"You are always hungry," Brenda jokes. "Andre, are you coming?"

"Naw, I already ate. But I'ma wait out in da waitin' room and let Li'nel talk tuh Ma. And Rhonda's waitin' out dere wit' me."

"The hell I am. I'm not leaving here until I'm good and goddamned ready to!"

"Yuh good and goddamned ready right now! Or, I'll beat yuh ass like Mama should've done when we was kids. Get yuh spoiled ass out in de waitin' room!"

"Don't be threatening me!"

Andre actually grabbed her arm and forced her from the room. It's just me and Mama. She opens her eyes and sees me. I see the hatred on her face as she glares at me, then she looks away as if she can't bear the sight of me.

"Hi, Mama."

No answer.

"I brought you a gift. It's a crystal snow globe. You always liked them." I place it on her food tray table.

Silence.

"Mama, we need to talk".

Still no answer.

"OK, you don't have to talk to me. You don't even have to acknowledge that I exist. I don't expect you to... since you said that I'm dead to you. But that also means you can't hear me... and since you can't hear or acknowledge me, I'm going to take this opportunity to say what I need to say."

She purses her lips as she painfully turns her body toward the wall.

"I've been hurt by you for a great many years. You always gave us kids a hard time, but I think you picked on Andre and me the most. It's like we couldn't do anything to please you. You always favored Rhonda more. You believed everything she ever told you, even when it was lies to get me, Andre, and Dean in trouble. I have to see a psychiatrist now to put to bed all of the nonsense that you put in me. All the resentment that you gave me because of my friendship with Jojo. You practically forced us to go to that church and listen to that preacher scream hell and damnation into our brains. I don't advocate not going to church because I believe in God. I know church is the way to learn more about His love. It's sitting through the yelling and screaming that we are sinners of the worst kind that I have a problem with... and I carried that problem for thirty-six years."

A muscle twitches on the left side of her lips.

"I remember every humiliating word you said to me. I remember all the horrible things you did to me. Forcing me to strip while you lashed at me like a mad woman with those switches, extension cords, and that splintering old paddle of yours. I had to wear long shirts and long pants to school even when it was ninety-degree weather. I had people asking me why I was wearing those heavy clothes when it was almost summer. And half of the time, the beatings were for trivial reasons."

The deadness of her silent and contemptible reaction to my words is sucking the air from the room. At this point, I only have one thought: Say my piece and get the hell out of there.

"Not only did you put me through hell. Sunday after Sunday, you let that hypocritical preacher of yours damn me to hell. You praised that man like he *was* God... Would it interest you to know that the same "sanctified" preacher you loved also committed the same 'sins' that he condemned others for?"

She just lies there with angry tears rolling down her face.

"You didn't know that, did you? That preacher that you loved so much made a shameless pass at me... and in his study. He pulled out his long, ugly, black dick and told me to give him some head and had the gall to get pissed when I refused and walked out."

I pause to take my breath. I walk over to the window as I continue, "In case there is a slight chance that you care, I'll put your mind at ease and say that at least he wasn't a pedophile, not with me. This happened when I was twenty-one years old. I came to him for help. I came to him because I thought that if anyone had any answers, the preacher that we followed for years would have them... He took advantage of that opportunity to hit on me. It did not help that I went to church with you that following Sunday and heard him preach about sissies, faggots, and men who wanted to be women. I should've stood up and said something then, but I chickened out. Instead, I went back to school more confused, more depressed, and more grief stricken than before.

"I came to him because I had questions as to why someone would randomly kill my father, a man who was wonderful to me. A father who I wanted to see when I was chosen as "Man of the Year" at my Marketing firm. A father you stole from me when you killed him."

Her lips are parted and trembling. Her eyes are wide and troubled, but she stays silent.

"Yeah, that's right." I pull the letter out of my pocket and stride to the foot of her bed. "I have the proof. How I got it is not important. You let your prejudice and bigotry take rein and you killed my father... You could have divorced him... You could've separated from him. No one would've expected you to stay with Dad when he was unfaithful to you. I admit he was wrong for what he did, but that did not give you the right to steal his life and deprive us of a father we loved. Then you let somebody who *really* loved him take the fall for what *your* maliciousness had caused... The sad thing about all of this is that you are unaware of the consequences your hate and intolerance can cause... Even worse, I don't even think you care." The tears are threatening to fall, but I force myself to keep them back.

"Do you know how we paid for that operation you just had? Andre, Dean, Roland, Brenda, and I paid for it. I had to lend them their share because the surgeon's office requested payment right away, but do you want to know who convinced me that I needed to help my mother? The very one you gossiped about and called a faggot... Jojo." I move to see her face and she turns it away.

"Tell me, Mama. Where was your favorite child, Rhonda, when all of this needed to be paid? Nowhere in sight. She did not contribute one red cent, but she's your *favorite*. You held her in higher esteem than the rest of us and now I see why. You are both one and alike. Both of you are selfish, judgmental, manipulative, and hateful. Both you and Rhonda had lying, murderous tongues that you used to kill the esteem of the rest of your children, but you had to take it a step further and commit the actual deed. You call out the faults of others while you cover the sins you commit."

I crumple the letter in my hand. "I could take this to the police right now, but Troy and Jojo convinced me not to... I don't want to be responsible for any more hardship. This family has already faced enough. I don't want it to mess things up between me and Jojo. And as much as I hate to say this, I don't want the memory of your cruelty to mess up my life, because I don't want to end up like you: hateful, bitter, and holding on to everything that corrupts what you could be... You've been carrying these burdens around for years and I believe it manifested into the cancer you had spreading in your body. But Mama, you have been given another chance to make things right and I'm begging you, for the good of your own soul, to lay that burden down now... because if you don't, it will kill you."

Folding the letter, I go to the side of her bed and place it on the tray table. "This is one of the many steps I'm taking to find my focus and my truth, so I can finally enjoy the life I have left with Jojo, with my friends, and with the part of the family that loves me for who I am... I need peace, Mama. So, I want to let you know that I forgive myself... and I forgive you."

I slowly walk to the door and open it, and I hear a crash to my left. I feel an abundance of blood trickle down my face from a glass shard that flew and cut my cheek. I look back at her... and I see sick satisfaction on her face. The same expression she had when whipping me mercilessly as a child. I look at the floor and I see the shattered round pieces of glass, the simulated snowflakes, and the broken porcelain figure of mother and son. I reach up to catch a pool of blood on my fingers. Walking over to and stopping at the foot of her bed, I wipe the blood on the blanket covering her body. I then look at her horrified face and utter the only five words my heart will allow me to say.

"Goodbye Mother. I love you."

I leave the room and I hear a loud, tormented, insane wail from behind the door. Rhonda jumps up and bolts into the room, looking at me with daggers for eyes. The door slams shut.

I pass by Andre. Suddenly I hear my name. "Li'nel?"

"Yeah?"

"Uh... I'm sorry."

"Sorry for what?"

"Fuh not speakin' up fuh yuh sooner... And fuh what I did to Joe... I was wrong."

I look at him. This muscle-bound thug-life brother of mine... apologizing? I am stunned.

"I neva' hated yuh. I neva' hated Joe. I hated maself fuh believin' all de mean crap Ma said about me and lettin' muh life turn to shit."

"Your life didn't turn to shit. Even though she used you as a punching bag, at least Mama considers you a real man."

"If I was a real may'n, I woulda setta betta example when we was growin' up... I don't even think she know what a real may'n is... Daddy was one, no madduh who 'e loved... He took care a bidness and did what 'e had to do... You are one... Yuh decided to navigate thru' yuh life yo' way... A real may'n ain't got no problems doin' dat."

"Andre..."

"Yeah..."

"Based off what you're telling me, you are a real man, too... You moved out of the house and told Mama that you were no longer her punching bag. You've always been a real man. You just forgot what Daddy taught us about what a real man was."

A nurse comes up, "Sir, do you realize that you're bleeding? It's a small cut, but kind of nasty."

"Yeah."

"Here. Take this gauze. Press it on the cut and wait here. I'll get you a bandage."

There's a long silence as Andre looks down, tracing the floor design with his foot.

The nurse comes back with antiseptic and a bandage and tries to apply it. Andre steps forward and grabs it.

"Nah, I'll handle dat."

The nurse nods and walks off.

"Now I'm warnin' yuh. This gone sting."

"I've been through worse."

As he applies the first aid, I am taken by the love and concern I saw in his eyes. I feel his love for the first time in years. My mind goes back to us playing in the projects. I fell, skinning my knee. He did the same thing for me then. Funny how a gesture can jog your memory.

Doctoring over, he puts his hand on my shoulder. We walk slowly towards the waiting room door. "When yuh git backta Baltimo', tell yuh fiancé dat I wish'm well."

"How do you know about us getting married?"

"Dean tol' me, fool!"

"Oh, he did, did he? Well, I'm not the one you need to be telling that too."

"I know dat."

"Why don't you come to the wedding?"

"Nah man!" Andre laughs. "I'ma leave dat to y'all an' slip'm a call. Besides, I ain't got de clothes fuh dat."

"You don't need them. Come however you want to. You can come in jeans, a pullover, and some Tims… or I can rent you a tux."

"Yuh ain't gotta do dat! I can rent muh own tux. I'm doin' a'ight now wit money… and I'm gettin' it honest".

"Then you can rent your own doggone tux," I playfully punch him. "Just come because I want my big brother there."

"Aight, name de' day an' yuh got me dere."

"We haven't set the date yet. We talked about a long engagement, but we'll let you know."

"Cool. Now, git on outta here. Call me when yuh git backta Baltimo'."

"Will do, bruh."

I start for the door when I hear him call my name again. I turn.

"We bruhs... and I likes yuh."

"You just likes me?" I said, laughing.

"Oh, come on may'n. Don't make me say it. Ye already know wut I'm talkin' 'bout, bruh."

"Say what? I ain't making you say nothing."

"Good, cuz I ain't gone say it." He laughs and I join him.

"You already did.... And I love you too."

I hold out my hand. He grips it in his. Then, he uses his force to pull me in for a tight embrace. WOW! Wasn't expecting that. I feel his tears on my shoulder. Before I know it, tears are coming from my own eyes, but for the first time, they are not tears of pain. They are tears of love for a brother I know loves me no matter what. They are tears of happiness for a brother I thought lost. They are tears of hopefulness for the start of a beautiful friendship between two men, related by blood but different as night and day. And as I hug him, I feel that his tears are coming from the same place.

I draw apart from him. "You know, you could tell him yourself."

"How?"

"Come on down to the gift shop. He came down here with me."

"Aw, shit! I was tryin' to ease into it!"

Just then, I see Jojo, Corey, and Garrett walk through the door to the Cancer unit.

"Hey baby, we just wanted to come up and make sure that you are O..." Jojo breaks off as he sees Andre. Corey has a disgusted look on his face. Garrett looks confused.

"Andre, these are my friends, Corey and Garrett."

Corey mumbles out, "Pleasure..."

"And you already know Jojo."

Andre looks at him and Jojo stares back at him.

"Uh, Joe... I uh... I wanna uh... say dat I was wrong fuh what I di' when we was kids. I was stupid... I was young an' not thinkin' straight... An' I am sorry."

Jojo walks up to him with an unreadable look on his face. "No, you are not sorry."

Andre looks down.

"Idiots, deadbeats, wife-beaters, and even bitchy queens are sorry."

Andre snaps his head up.

"You, sir, are a grown, intelligent man who decided to apologize for what he did as a young, unlearned teenager… And Andre?"

"Yeah?"

"Apology accepted."

Jojo holds out his hand. Andre takes it and gives Jojo a wide, beaming smile.

"Welcome tuh de fam'ly, bruh."

"Well, well, well! It is about time. You finally got some sense. You are to be applauded, sir," Corey yells out in true Corey fashion.

"Sir, keep your voice down. We are in a hospital," The nurse cautions.

"So, chile'? It ain't like we're in a library!" She looks shocked.

Andre lets out a huge laugh! When was the last time I heard him laugh like that? We trip out of the Cancer unit.

"Oops, did I say that?"

"Uh, yes you did, baby," Garrett informs, smiling.

"Well, maybe she needed to hear it. Might wrench the stick out of her ass!"

"Ok, Li'nel. Yuh friend is crazy," Andre laughs out.

"Well, like I always say, 'Ya need a little cray-cray to dance your nae-nae'". Corey goes over to Andre and wraps one arm around Andre's muscular shoulders. "And let me tell you the tee." He goes on, pausing to dig a finger in Garrett's side and making him laugh aloud. "You are just getting a sample of my craziness. And you haven't even met Peep. Let us all walk to the car, while I illuminate thee, brother of my brother from another mother!"

"Peep? Who dat?" Andre asks.

"That's our other friend in Baltimore," Jojo says.

"Why yuh call'im Peep fuh?"

Corey stops walking. "You know what? I don't know. Jojo, do you know?"

"You got me. I called him that because Lionel did."

"Right! Why did you start calling him Peep?"

Aw shit! "I'll let Peep tell you that story."

CHAPTER TWENTY-ONE:

"THE LAST WORD"

It is a cold November day. I rush down Madison Avenue to get to Dr. Banneker's office. What a crazy day! While I was on the cruise, another account was shoved my way. A cat food account. The person inventing the cat food is a tall, brawny, rusty haired white man wearing a red flannel shirt and blue jeans. His name is Martin Stowman. He's one of those eccentric types that keep a lot of cats around them, and he even bought one of the little furballs with him! Now looks can be deceiving. He looks like a homeless person on the street, but this man has beaucoup money. Stocks, bonds, t-bills… the whole nine. He looks like he could be a gorgeous guy, and I'm talking drop dead! Yet, smelling this man made me want to throw his ass in the shower, clean him up, then call Jump cologne and send them a new poster boy. It took everything in me not to hurl in my wastebasket after smelling all that cat shit.

Anyway, my car would not start, today of all days. So, I decided to take the Metro downtown. When it lets me off on the Upton platform, I run all the way down to Madison Avenue like someone half possessed. I race inside the building and into the elevator that goes to the fourth floor. Out of breath and panting, I open the glass door to Dr. Banneker's office and greet the secretary. "Lionel Davis to see Dr. Banneker. I have a three o'clock appointment." She tells me to proceed to his office and that he's expecting me.

I knock on his door and walk inside at his invitation. "Hello Dr. Banneker, I am sorry that I'm late."

"Oh no. You're only late by two minutes. Have a seat."

I plop down onto the familiar chair and I remove my coat and scarf to drape them over its arm.

"So, how did the cruise go?"

"I thoroughly enjoyed it. I'm making plans to attend again next year."

"I take it that there were a lot of interesting things to see and do?"

"A whole lot of things."

After filling Dr. Banneker in on the wonders of the cruise, he asks me, "How do you feel now after taking this vacation?"

"I feel more relaxed. More refreshed. I feel like I'm ready to take on different things. It's always good to spend time with those you care about and to set aside time for that one special person."

"I see. And how is Jojo?"

"He's doing well. Swamped at work. But doing well. We spent a lot of time on the ship together and all of it was quality time. We talked about a lot of things and learned a lot about each other. And do you know what amazes me, doc?"

"What's that, Lionel?"

"How brave and fearless Jojo is. He told me about some things that he went through. I'm not at liberty to discuss all of it, but it is quite a story." I sit back and look reflectively at my nails. "After years of seeing us as two different individuals, it amazes me how our lives are the same."

"I don't think I follow."

"Well, I'm the sports type and he's the artsy type. I'm the type to play it safe. He takes chances. I'm hesitant to displease my family. He holds no hesitation if it is therapeutic for him. The things that made us alike were our struggles. We both had bullies. His were in the school while mine were in the home. Both of us wanted that special someone that we could claim. Of course, he knew for a long time that he wanted me, but I was not sure about my feelings for him. We both want more than sex has to offer. We both loved each other romantically before we were even conscious of it."

"Let's go back to your family. How are they progressing?"

"Rather well. Better than I expected. Of course, my mother and sister reacted predictably to the news of my engagement to Jojo, as well as my need to live my life on my own terms. Oddly enough, I acquired unlikely allies."

"And who might they be?"

"My brothers and younger sister. They have been very supportive. Especially Dean and Andre. Andre has really taken to Corey, who keeps him in stitches and Garrett hangs with him when he's in town."

"Sounds like progress."

"Great progress. He's thinking about moving here."

"Hmmm... that is interesting."

"Very. I'm starting to discover what the motivation behind it is."

"Care to explain?"

"Well, on one of those weekends when he came to visit me, Jimmy, Peep, and he were at Garrett's house playing cards, and Garrett's sister came by. His eyes popped out of his skull, according to Garrett. I believe he is smitten by her and Mike Junior. She felt the connection with him as well. It got to the point where the rest of them couldn't even play spades because Andre was so busy talking to Rachel. So, they decided to let them talk while they played regular cards."

"Interesting. So, there is no awkward energy between you and your accepting siblings as it relates to the differences in your sexualities?"

"Not at all. In fact, something tells me that Dean may be on my team."

"How is that?"

"Well, he has always been very quiet and open minded, and he's never brought a girl home for the holidays. It's always been this old college friend of his, Angelo. My mother was so blind that she didn't see the exchange of looks between the two of them. There is infatuation there. Now... whether they did the do is another question."

"So now you know the reason he is more accepting of you and yours."

"Correct."

"How do you now feel about your sexuality and where you are in it?"

"Well, most days I don't even think about it. I see myself as just another man, gay or not. There are times when I wonder why this had to be my lot and if the Creator hates me because of my being gay. But I remember something that my friend's mother-in-law told me when I was visiting her at the hospital."

"And what did she say?"

"Irene said that God knows about every person in this world. Their idiosyncrasies. The way their minds work. What they hide in their hearts. He even knows about the ones that do the most evil. But he loves all of us the same."

"Interesting concept. I don't think we've talked about her. If we did, can you refresh my memory?"

"She's Peep's mother-in-law." I sit back and fold my arms. I become sad. "She's not doing too well right now. They put her in the hospital two days ago due to her getting sick again but she's hanging on in there like a real trooper. She said that she's praying to be here past Thanksgiving and Christmas, and I'm praying that for her too, because I think it would be hard for Jimmy if she was to leave before that time."

*****

Peep and I are inside the City Café, drinking mochaccinos. It is colder than my evil aunt Mavis outside. Thank God for central heating. I'm looking over at Peep and I'm a little bit concerned. He is looking very depressed. This is not like him at all.

I am talking my head off about my engagement with Jojo, as well as my confrontation with my mother. He just sits there with a vacant preoccupied expression on his face.

"Hello? Earth to Peep!"

Peep comes out of his spell. "Huh?"

"You are a million miles away. What's wrong?"

"Nothing. Well, it is something. I'm sorry. I'm just tired and so is Jimmy. He's been up in that hospital for two weeks. Irene keeps trying to get him to leave but he won't. She almost has to yell at him, and that is not good considering her condition."

"Has she gotten any better?"

Peep shakes his head. Something in his eyes tells me that the news is grave.

"To be honest, Lion, I fear the worst. She said that she was praying about her being here for the holidays. But the way it looks, she might not make it to Thanksgiving."

"But we can't predict what we don't know. All we can do is just pray and see how everything will turn out. She might make it past Christmas. You never know. That *is* what she wanted, right?"

Peep sits back and reflects on what I said. After a couple of seconds, he nods. "You're right. There's no sense in us getting anxious about what we don't know."

"Right. So, let's change the subject, shall we?"

"We shall." He brightens a bit. "How are your sessions with Dr. Banneker?"

"They are going really well. He's helping me see things in a different perspective and to be at peace with what happened with my mother and my dad's lover."

Peep has his mouth open. "Your daddy had a lover?"

"Yeah. His name is Troy."

"Fool! I can't believe you didn't tell me!"

"Well, Jojo's the only one that knows about this."

"Mmhmm… Why am I not surprised?" Peep says, smirking.

"Anyway…" I hesitate. Peep looks at me for moment, then he gestures for me to hurry up and come out with it.

"Well?"

"Well, like I said, Dad and Troy had a long affair. From what I'm understanding, they really loved each other."

"How long had they been in the affair together?"

"For ten years."

"And your dad died when you were in your late twenties or early thirties."

"Actually, my early twenties."

"So, he started the affair with him when you were a teenager."

"Yeah, but that isn't the worst part."

"What is?"

"My mother was the one that killed Dad."

"Oh shit!" Peep breathes out. "How did you find *this* out?"

"My brother Dean found a letter from Troy. He's doing time for it."

"OK I'm lost. If your mother killed your dad, why is Troy in prison?"

"Because he felt like it was his fault for going after my dad when he knew he was married."

"I feel where your mother was coming from. She was in a rage, but I am shocked that she took it to that extreme. Then, she let somebody else swing for her crime. How low can you get?"

"I know."

"Where is the letter?"

"Well, Dean sent it to me and left it up to me what we should do. But I gave it back to my mother."

"You what?"

"I gave it back to her."

"Lionel, what did you do that for? That was evidence that would've exonerated Troy."

"I know, and I fought with myself about that. But I went to see Troy in prison and told him what I was going to do, and he himself told me not to. He said to let it go. He had a lot of peace in his voice when he said that. It was a forgiving peace. Anyways, I thought about it and afterwards I knew that this is what my father would've wanted me to do."

"Chile', you are brave. I would've made her ass swing but if you feel at peace with the situation, then fuck it."

"I'll drink to that." We hold our mochaccinos up for a toast and knock them back.

"Is Dr. Banneker taking on new patients?"

"I don't know."

"I'm asking because I'm thinking that Jimmy might need a professional to talk to after Irene goes."

"I'll ask him and see what he says. And let's let that be the last statement on this subject, because we did say we were changing it."

"OK, OK! So, about what you found out. Does anybody else in your family know?"

"Other than Dean, no."

"Speaking of family, how's Andre."

"He's doing fine. Making good money as a truck driver. He's actually thinking about coming up here."

"To live?"

"Yeah."

"Why would he want to come to this shit pit called Baltimore?"

"Why would he want to stay in that shit pit called Yeti?"

"OK, I see your point. Besides I heard that some people down there are country dumb."

"Wait a minute. You are talking about my hometown." I joke.

"Your point being? Besides I didn't say all people. I did say some."

"I hope you ain't talking about *me*."

"Well..." I throw a playful punch at him.

"Of course not. You're not dumb. Dense as hell sometimes, but not dumb."

"Correction, all of us are dense as hell when it comes to life."

"Touché. So, Corey told me that y'all were thinking about doing a New Year's Day party."

"Yeah, and Corey said that he's not buying the chips this time. In his words, 'Bring your own shit!'"

"That works for me. I hate chips anyway!"

"Great, so on to more important matters. How come you never told me that you could sing like that?"

"Like what?"

"Like you did on that cruise!"

"Please. I sing like that on Sunday mornings at Unity and Love Church. You just rarely come by there. Otherwise, you would've heard me by now!"

*****

"To the new year. 2019!" Corey says, lifting his glass.

"To new lessons that it brings," Jojo follows.

"To new opportunities and new points of views," Peep philosophizes.

"And thanks to God for Irene sticking around past the new year," I conclude.

"Cheers," we all say as we click our Champagne glasses and sit at the round card table.

"Guys, I'm going to go under for a few weeks. I'm just letting y'all know this now so that y'all don't trip if you don't see me."

"Everything all right?"

"Yeah, everything is just fine. I'm just working on some things with my symphony. I'm trying to correct and proofread the movements."

"I remember you telling me about that on the ship."

"Yeah, I'm trying to plan a debut concert of it in August."

"No shitting?" Peep says.

"No shitting!"

"Well damn, Corey. It is about time. You've been working on that thing ever since we were twenty years old."

"Longer than that."

"When did you start it?"

"When I was fourteen. I had just left the orphanage to live with Pop Kennedy."

"Well, you just make sure that we are front row center."

"Of course, you're going to be front row center, right next to Zach and his family."

"Aha, so I take it that you met his family."

"Yes, and they are really sweet people. Wait until you meet Eunetta Peterson! She is a ball of spitfire and smart as a tack. I was at her house for Christmas, and she unexpectedly sat Zach and me down and asked us. "So, what's going on between the two of you?"

"What?"

"You heard me right. And you know how Zach gets when he starts blushing. His jaws get all dark purple like plums. Of course, he tried to play dumb, but Eunetta wasn't having it. She told him, 'You can't fool Mama. I see the way y'all be looking at each other across the table. There is definitely love in the air, and I sho as hell ain't talking about no bluebirds.' When we came clean, Zach asked her how she felt about this and she said that she didn't know that much about it and had no desire to know all the details because of all the shit us gay folks have to go through. But she said, 'If y'all make each other happy, then to hell with what everybody else got to say.'"

"So how are things between you and 'Zaaach'?" Peep asks Corey, teasing.

"Gravy baby. Gravy. In many ways, I feel the same way I did when we were teenagers. Granted, a lot of years have passed, and we have so much that we need to learn about each other. But we are taking our time and I think things are gonna work."

"Do you hear wedding bells," I tease.

"What are you talking about?"

"Well, you heard 'em for me and Jojo!"

"As I said, and I stress now, we are taking our time," Corey annunciates in his smart-ass way.

"Touchy, touchy!" I say

"And since we're talking about wedding bells, when are you and Jojo gonna say some I do's?"

"Well, we have decided to embark on a long engagement just to make sure that this is what we want," Jojo says.

"Is this OK with you, Jojo," Peep says. "I'm only asking because you have been after Lion for a very long time."

"It was actually my idea, Peep. We know each other as friends. Now we want to get to know each other as lovers *and* friends before we stroll down the aisle."

"Wise move," Peep says.

Corey's cell phone rings. "Excuse me, y'all. Hello?" After a few seconds, He leans forward and says, "Yeah, this is Corey Kennedy. Who is this? ... Oh, Darrell ... Yes, I met you on the cruise. What's going on? ... Are you serious?"

We're sitting there just looking at him, not knowing if we should celebrate or console him.

"OK... Well, I would have to talk to my attorney... And we would have to talk terms... OK, next Tuesday at three... At the Belvedere... OK, I'll see you then. Thank you... Goodbye!"

He hangs the phone and brings his fist up to his mouth. A pure and beautiful smile shines from behind his fist."

"Well?" Jojo presses.

"That was a guy I met on the cruise named Darrell Alston. He is a recording artist. He wants to record the song we did up there!"

Peep and Jojo both stand up and start jumping up and down and congratulating Corey. He says with a laugh, "What are y'all carrying on about? It's just one song."

Peep is astounded, "Do you know what that *one song* can do? That is a foot in the door, boy! It can open a lot of options for you!"

"Peep is right," Jojo agrees excitedly. "That song was fire! Everybody who heard it was wondering how they could get a recording."

I stay quiet and seated through all of this, dumbfounded at what just happened.

Corey looks at me, "Lion, your silence is scaring me. What do you think?"

After a few seconds, I stand and tell him, "I'm just amazed. I'm glad you stressed to him that you have to discuss the terms, and if the terms are right, I say go for it!" I clasped his hand and pull him to me to lift him up and give him a huge bear hug!

"Damn, man! Put me down! You and Zach love slinging me around, don't ya?" Corey yells, laughing.

For the next few minutes, the positive energy in the room makes us lightheaded. Along with the new year, a window of opportunity was opened for my friend. An opportunity to share his gift with the world. I beam at Corey with pride at how it took a whole lot of heartbreak and hurt to create just as much beauty and happiness.

Peep's phone rings. He sees that it's Jimmy and he goes to the kitchen to answer it. We are still on our high from the news, but it comes to a screeching halt when Pete comes hurriedly in the living room. His face is contorted with worry.

"Peep, what's wrong?"

"Y'all, I need to get to the hospital," Peep says, his voice cracking. "Jimmy just said that Irene is doing worse and she is asking for me. She may not make it through the day. He needs me down there."

"Well, let us come with you," Corey offers.

"No," Peep says firmly, his tone shocking us. "Stay here. I'll be fine. I just need to get down there."

"Peep, one of us needs to drive you at least, to make sure you get there safely. You're in no position to drive right now," Jojo points out in concern.

Peep suddenly explodes, "I said I will be fine! I can handle this myself! I don't need you at my side for every single bad thing that happens. I will handle this!"

OK, this is a different side of Peep that we have not seen. Usually he's very much in control. Very poised. But this side of him is frantic and full of vexation. Peep notices the look on our faces. "I'm sorry, y'all. Really, I will be fine."

"Listen, like Jojo said, I would feel better if you have somebody driving you, especially when you're this upset," I calmly implore him.

"Listen, I really do not want to yell again. Just let me do this by myself."

"You don't have to yell again. Just give me the keys, because I'm not letting you leave here by yourself. One of us is going with you. The keys!" I hold out my hand. After hesitating, Peep surrenders them. "All right. Now, let's haul ass. We have to get on the beltway." He walks out the door to go to the passenger side of my car.

"Corey and I will take my car and follow you there," Jojo assures.

"No, with something like this. It might be best not to crowd him or Jimmy. I got him. Y'all just pray that we get there safe. I'll call you to let you know what happens."

*****

I speed down the beltway to get to the hospital. We have the misfortune of being stopped by a patrolman. When I tell him what the problem is, it is like talking to a brick wall. He detains us for five minutes while he makes his report. He comes back to the car with a ticket and a shit eating grin. "Have a nice day, boys." I pull out onto the street, muttering the word, "Asshole!"

We pull up to the hospital parking lot, dash into the hospital, and wend our way through halls. I can feel Peep and his pain. I can almost feel Jimmy and his grief, and I haven't even seen him yet. When we walk into the hospital room, Jimmy greets us. His eyes are bloodshot, his hair is disheveled, and his face is grief-stricken, but that is nothing compared to looking at Irene. She looks so thin and emaciated. The color of her rich golden-brown skin with reddish undertones was replaced with a ghostly grayish shade of impending death. Irene can barely talk or move, but she motions for Jimmy to come to her side. She whispers something to him. His tear-stained frown momentarily becomes a smile. What did she whisper to him? I wonder. Of course, I will never ask. That's between him, her, and God. She kisses him goodbye. Then she motions for Peep and me to come closer and she kisses both of us goodbye.

We step back from her bed and watch as she weakly raises one trembling hand. She points to herself and gives an OK sign. Then she points at us and gives the same sign. Jimmy chokes out in understanding, "She'll be OK... We'll be OK."

She then drops her hand and breathes her last. Her face, once alive, is now cold and still. Irene is dead. Jimmy sits at her bedside and slowly bows his body down inch by inch in resigned grief. We hear the rumbling sobs and cross the room to console him as he feels the searing pain going through his body. As I drape my arms around him and Peep, I feel a grief of my own. Then, a smile of remembrance stretches across my face. She got her answered prayer. She was here for the holidays, and God gave her a bonus. She was here to see a new year. The first year of her eternal peace...

CHAPTER TWENTY-TWO:
"THE CONCERT OF LIFE"

Irene Hartfield was funeralized at Unity and Love Community Church. The service was glorious. As I glanced around the packed church, I am in awe of the amount of LGBTQ ladies and gentlemen that came out to pay their respects. She was obviously well respected and greatly missed. The large choir, conducted from the organ by Corey, sang to the rafters. The pastor of Unity and Love, Reverend John Washington, gave an astounding eulogy. He spoke of her in such awesome conviction and admiration. We sat there amazed as organization after organization came up and conveyed the heartfelt sentiments on what Irene Hartfield did for them; running the soup kitchen, chairing the annual Thanksgiving Dinner for the homeless, president of the Baltimore chapter of the Association of Equal Treatment for Women, moderator of the LGBTQ Center of Hope, and the list went on. I had no idea Irene did so much. She was a busy bee. Jimmy just sat there acknowledging those who came to the lectern and consoled him as they gave remarks, an unmoving rock of bravery and strength. It was when the morticians wheeled Irene's pearly blue casket by him that he broke. It took considerable effort for him to hold himself together, but the tears flowed from his eyes to his lapel and the sobs shook his body violently. They put Irene's casket in a white hearse with a rainbow stripe. Then, they led a police-escorted processional down North Avenue to the cemetery on Moravia Road. There, they laid Irene to rest.

Shortly after the funeral, Corey went into complete seclusion for an entire month to correct and refine his symphony. The only time he came out was either for work or for times when Garrett would drag him out of the house, reminding him that for anything to render good results, he needed balance. I am glad Garrett reminded him of this. We were afraid that he was going to come out with the same busted look he had after the attack. But that fear proved to be groundless because when Corey finally emerged from his cocoon, with the symphony completed, his appearance took all of us completely by surprise.

His skin gleamed with youthfulness and purpose. His eyes sparkled with a light that only the creatively gifted can possess. His smile was wider and more self-assured. His demeanor was more poised and at peace. In fact, Corey was glowing! My first thought was that it was the feeling of accomplishment, but the more I thought about it, the more I was compelled to come to a different conclusion. Corey had some inspiration to pour that happiness into his whole being, and much of that inspiration came from Garrett, or as he would call him, "My Zach".

He then went to work planning the concert. He called in some favors from The Harbor Boys' Choir and the Maryland Chamber Orchestra. He also wrote proposals to different music organizations in the city to assist him with funding. He had more than enough money in the bank, but he was determined to only pull from it when all other avenues were exhausted. I asked him why and he said that he wanted to sharpen his negotiation skills. It was rough hearing the word, "No," "We can't help you," or "We don't fund unknown composers", but Corey kept it moving. He called and called until the CEOs of the organizations got tired of him calling and gave him funding just to get him out of their hair. On a sunny June day, Corey called me with excitement brimming in his voice to tell me that he was *finally* conducting and performing his own symphony!

Pete, Jimmy, Jojo, Garrett, and I are now sitting front row center waiting for the concert to start, and we are dressed to kill! There are four empty seats next to Garrett. I suppose that they are for his sister, nephew, and mother who are running late. Hmm... who is the fourth seat for? I take a minute to look around the auditorium and I see a packed house! I see many of Corey's students on one side of us and his academic colleagues on the other. Behind us are members of different organizations. Even the mezzanine and the nosebleeds are filled! I had no idea that Corey was so well known. A thought goes through my head. *It's amazing how we have tunnel vision as it relates to those we love. We only see Corey as a friend, a piano teacher, and a first-rate musician. Apparently, to all these people, he is much more.* Now I see that different people can see different facets of one person. I think of how often we take those we love for granted, like wallpaper on the walls. I look at Jojo sitting next to me. I grab his hand and kiss it tenderly. Jojo looks at me with the same tenderness and love in his eyes. Without warning, I hear a condescending, self-righteous voice behind me exclaim, "Now this is a shame before God. Disgusting! Flaunting their sinfulness in public!"

Peep heard this. *Oh boy,* I think to myself. *She is about to get it now!* "Now, you wait just a damn minute, you support hose-wearing, ugly purse-toting, bigoted old cow..."

OK, I need to defuse the situation. "Peep, sit down. I got this." He sits. *I need to put this dumb broad in her place without causing a scene and ruining Corey's big night.*

"Excuse me, ma'am. Did I hear you say that me kissing his hand was disgusting?"

"You didn't hear me stutter!"

"I bet it makes you sick, doesn't it?"

"All gays make me sick."

"Well, let's see if we can make you sicker. Joseph, come here. I want to show you something." I cup his head and give him a sweet and loving kiss on his lips.

Well, that lady was pissed! She bolts up from her seat and says, "I'm getting the hell out of here. This place is crawling with sin!"

"And it will leave with you once you take your ignorant ass out of here!" Peep retorts.

She pushes her way down the row in a huff, mumbling and cursing, "I'm getting the manager. She'll have you kicked out of here."

"Go ahead and get her. We have witnesses to prove that you started this whole thing with your name calling and bigoted bullshit," Garrett speaks up.

"That's right," an elderly lady says. "These here boys weren't doing anything to you, missy. And I will be a glorified witness to that."

Well, she has nothing else to say, so she picks up and hauls ass out of here.

"Well, somebody is coming out of their shell," Peep says, looking at me, then Garrett. He then turns around and addresses those in earshot, "Now, does anyone else have anything to say? No? Good!" He sits back down.

JoJo looks at me, squeezing my hand with an abundance of love. "Thanks, Lionel."

"Anytime, baby."

"Feli, I can't take you anywhere without you reading folk," Jimmy jokes.

"Baby, she needed reading. She'd better be glad I didn't say anything about that ugly ass mumu she calls a dress. All of them flowers were giving me allergies just looking at 'em."

Just then, I see Rachel and Michael Junior come through the door. Walking with them is a petite and lovely older lady with laughing eyes, a wide smile, and a welcoming expression. Her skin is the color of a brown paper bag. Her silver hair is done in a French roll. She is wearing a sparkling black dress with a plunging neckline, and a simple string of pearls. Small gleaming pearls glint on her earlobes. Garrett stands up to greet his mother, who gives him a kiss on his cheek. "Hey, my baby. I'm sorry we are late. The traffic was crazy."

Peep takes one look at her and jumps up. He addresses those nearby. "Take a lesson, folks. Now, this is how you dress for a concert."

She laughs. "Oh, don't you be carryin' on about me."

"Why not, honey? It's the truth. And this young lady and her son are killing it too."

Indeed, they were. Rachel looks flawless. She must have spent the whole day preparing especially for the occasion. She had her long lustrous brown hair in an upsweep, with beautiful curls dangling from the crown and a tamed bang that framed her face like a half moon with a chin. She comes dressed in a luxurious royal blue formal gown with a small train that drags behind her. She has a beautiful white sash draped from behind her back and over the crooks of her arm. She's wearing a simple silver necklace and small dangling earrings. Homegirl had it going on!

Mike Jr. is standing next to her with his curls tamed back in a ponytail. He is dressed in a nice Royal blue jacket with a white shirt, black pants, a blue bowtie, and black shiny shoes. He beams a wide smile at me.

"Everybody, I would like for you to meet my mother, Eunetta Peterson. And you already know my sister and nephew: Rachel and Mike Junior". Rachel shakes hands with everyone, then comes over and hugs me.

"Lionel, it is good to see you again."

Mike Jr. waves. "Hi, Mr. Lionel!"

"Hi, Junior!"

"Hello y'all," Miss Peterson says. "Y'all are Corey's friends, aren't you?"

"For the past seventeen years."

"It's real nice to meet you all, and it will be nice to see Corey again. He is all my Blueberry can talk about. This wonderful boyfriend of his who can play the stank out of a piano."

"Ma!"

"Well it's the truth, ain't it? It would be nice to hear Corey for myself. These are our seats?"

"Yes ma'am."

I feel a tap behind me. And as I turn, I encounter my oldest brother, Andre. I gotta say, he cleans up very well! His tuxedo fits him like a second skin and his black shoes are polished to a blinding shine. His hair is braided in neat cornrows. His satiny milk chocolate skin shone along with the sparkling light in his large expressive eyes. And his smile dazzles as he looks at Rachel and Junior. He looks just like a younger version of my dad.

"Brudderman! Whaddup!" I greet him as I slap him five.

"Jes' chillin'. Hangin' out wit' muh favorite motha', lady, and lil' may'n. Can't wait tuh see muh crazy bruh do 'is thang! Fellas, how are yuh feelin'?"

"Doing great, Andre." Peep stands up and greets warmly with a handshake Andre taught him. "Thanks. And I gotta say, you are killin' folks in that tux, muh bruh!"

"Well, wha' can I say. Now yuh know where Li'nel gits it!"

"Yeah. From Daddy!"

We all laugh.

The curtain goes up as we all sit down. The stage is filled with musicians and their instruments. Just then, Corey strolls from the left wing. He looks magnificent in his beautiful white tux with tails. His shining curly hair tumbles about his head with the sides tapered. He flashes a thousand-kilowatt smile, full of child-like joy. He bows gracefully before the audience and waits for the applause to subside. Then he turns towards the orchestra and raises his hand and baton. The musicians position their instruments to play. Then as he brings his baton downward, they commence with the concert.

The first movement is phenomenal! As I listen to the instruments, I am astounded with the grace and beauty the symphony contains. The first movement was called "Happy Place". It had a small jazz flavor. The piano was a perfect complement to the flutes chirping over the strings, the French horns, the bassoons, and the oboes. I got the impression of children playing a game of hide and seek.

Two more movements called "Pain" and "Heartache" float in the air. It is like the aroma of an Oriental Musky cologne filling my nostrils with its sweet spicy scent. As the movement of "Pain" is being played and the boys' choir sings the hurtful song, I feel the blows from my mother's splintering paddle. I sense the hurt from remembering my sister Rhonda's humiliating words spoken to my brothers, my father, my sister, and me. I glance down the aisle at Andre, and his eyes are wet with tears. He sees me looking and he straightens in the seat, wiping his eyes to appear unaffected. He did this when we were kids. I laugh with affection. That is so like Andre... Very emotional... but always trying to keep his usual stoic demeanor.

My heart rends on the movement "Heartbreak". It reminds me of my break up with Nate and my mother's rejection. My tears are puddling around my eyelids. I wipe them before they fall. I guess it's gonna take some time, at least for the latter. Jojo looks at me and asks if I am alright, and I nod my head to let him know that I am.

The applause after those movements is thunderous! I even hear one of the students say while applauding, "Mr. Kennedy is my piano teacher!" Another student, a girl, says, "Boy, bye! Mr. Kennedy is *our* piano teacher. You ain't the only one studying with him."

Corey takes a bow and steps off the platform. He takes his place behind the piano and signals for the musicians to rest their instruments. Corey begins his next movement, "Anger". It starts with feathery, foreboding strokes in minor key. I feel his swelling intensity and anger as he played with vigor and hurt in his heart. Each note is perfectly played. I look at my friend, playing his heart out on this piece. It is as if he's venting about everyone who has ever hurt him. The bullies at the orphanage. The perverted pedophile, Mr. Haines. The gang members that beat him up just for being who he was. This is his vengeance. Every frustration in his life, he is releasing during this performance. He dramatically ends the movement and the entire auditorium of people stands on its feet and claps, lauding his musical genius.

He reclaims his place on the platform and cues the orchestra. The next movement is called "Agony". As the movement passes, it occurs to me suddenly. This symphony is his life told through music! I can't help but admire the strength and tenacity it took for Corey to compose this masterpiece. I never felt closer to Corey than I do at this moment, listening to him tell of his tumultuous life story through beautiful melodies and flawless harmonies. But as I listen more carefully, I conclude that it is not just his life that he based the symphony on. This magnum opus depicts all our lives. Our happiness… our pain… our heartache… our anger… our agony… and finally our love.

We are now at the last movement of the night. He takes the microphone off the stand. He waits for the applause to cease, then he begins to speak. "As we prepare to wrap up this evening, I would like to give thanks to God for the gift of music. It is through music that I can express my loves, my hates, my anger, and my happiness. I would like to thank you all for coming. I would also like to thank the Harbor Boys' Choir and the Maryland Chamber Orchestra. Will the leaders of these organizations please stand and be acknowledged?" A middle-aged black man and a wizened white woman stands as the audience applauds.

"I also wish to give thanks for four of the best friends anyone could ever have. Three of them have walked the hallowed halls of Morgan State University with me for four years, and one married a beautiful spirited man and brought him into the fold. It is an honor to share this once-in-a-lifetime moment with them. I was also blessed last year to be reunited with a very dear companion of my youth. He is and has always been my love and joy. Will Lionel Davis, Joseph Thompson, Felipe and James Hartfield, and Garrett Peterson, as well as Andre Davis and the Peterson family, please stand?"

As we stand and hear the applause, I feel a deep abiding love between us all. Corey, Jojo, Peep, and I have tears in our eyes: Connected by hurts, pains, joys, depression, and bouts of laughter. As I look at them, as well as Andre, Garrett, and Jimmy, I think to myself, *these are my brothers.* I look at Rachel and Eunetta. *These are my friends.* I look at Mike Junior. *He is my hope.*

"The final movement is called 'Love', and I will need your help. This is my hardest movement in that I will be remembering those who I loved and lost. I would like to dedicate this movement to the memory of three special human beings who taught me love. Miss Ingrid Schumacher who introduced the love of music and hard work. Reverend Harold S. Kennedy, my father, who taught me about love between kindred spirits and God's goodness therein. And finally, Miss Irene Hartfield, who taught me to cherish those you have in your life while you got them."

Corey's voice is cracking so much, I don't know if he's going to be able to get through this movement without crying. He looks at me, suddenly shaking. I suddenly remember the sign that Irene gave before she died. I pointed to him and gave him the OK sign, letting him know that he would be OK. This gives him the courage that he needed. He reciprocates the gesture.

"At this time, I want to call my best friend, Felipe Hartfield, and national recording artist, Darrell Alston, to the stage. They will be singing my latest composition recorded by Mr. Alston, 'Love Makes Me Beautiful.'"

As the strains of the violins begin the overture of this movement, I am struck by the lush beauty of how the music melts together. I hear the wonderful voices of Peep and Darrell singing my friends composition, with the boys' choir supporting their vocal prowess, and I think about what that song really means. I begin to reminisce…And the tears continue to fall…

Tear number one… My time with my dad… ***"Dad, if we are going to talk about sex, then you gotta keep up."***
"No, young man. Don't get it twisted. You have to keep up. All I gotta learn is the new terminology. Remember, I've already been down the road you're traveling, and it wasn't that long ago."
"It wasn't?"
"So, you got jokes?

Tear number two… My fall in the gym… ***"I was just in such a rush to leave the house. I thought I would get something after the workout."***
"Lion, what the fuck is wrong with you? You, of all people, should know that it is risky to be running on fumes."

Tear number three… Peep styling me at Rodchester's… ***"This is for you."***
"I don't know."
"Don't tell me you want to go back to the good will and pick those old fogey clothes up to wear again. Boy, put this mess on."

Tear number four… Jojo's advice on the stoop… ***"I think you ought to help your mother."***
"What, why?
"Lion, you have to treat folks right, even when they treat you wrong."

Tear number five… My conversation with Andre… ***"We bruhs… and I likes yuh."***
"You just likes me?"

"Oh, come on may'n. Don't make me say it. Ye already know wut I'm talkin' 'bout, bruh."

"Say what? I ain't making you say nothing."

"Good, cuz I ain't gone say it."

"You already did…. And I love you too."

Tear number six… Corey in the hospital…*"Yes, they hate us. We can't change that. But we can't let them make us hate ourselves. Do you hate yourself?"*

"No!"

"Well, alright then!"

I look over at Jojo and see the magic on his face as he gazes back at me, giving me his sweet smile and mouthing the words, "I love you." I smile and mouth back, "I love you too."

EPILOGUE

Sitting in my raggedy Queen Anne chair, I would generally be writing out ideas to take to my drafting table. But in the year after my mother's rejection, the chair has served a dual purpose: to inspire me in my marketing work and to organize the thoughts of my life as I see it.

On the day of that ill-fated Mother's Day call, I went out for walk on the harbor, feeling very lonely. Yes, my mother is a mean, self-righteous hypocrite, but she is still my mother. I remember thinking. *It is a bad feeling when your own mother tells you that you are dead to her.* I was so distraught that I went to the liquor store to buy a whole lot of different potent liquors. I read somewhere that if you drink liquor to excess, you would die from alcohol poisoning. I thought, *What better way to kill myself than to indulge in my own vice?* I grabbed all my favorite hard liquors from bourbon to vodka and place them in the cart. I took them up to the front to pay for them and the Hispanic cashier asked me if I was getting ready for a party. I mumbled, "Yeah. Something like that."

As he calculated my total, I remembered something from my LGBTQ support group. The moderator gave positive ways to handle depression, and she specifically stressed that these were merely ways to cope, not ways to cure. "There is no cure for depression," she said. "But we stand a better chance of managing it through therapy, friends, and medication if necessary." One of the ways she mentioned involved writing my feelings out to release the hurt that plagued me from day to day.

Writing… I had forgotten about that. I used to write little stories all the time when I was a child of twelve. I shared them with two receptive people: my father and Jojo. My father would just listen with a smile on his lips and then ask me questions about the story and the characters. When I shared them with Jojo, he simply looked astounded and would encourage me to keep writing. Sometimes, he would ask me to tell him a story and I would oblige him out of my happiness that someone wanted to hear what I had to say.

Anyway, when the cashier gave me my total, good common sense stopped me from paying it. I just couldn't see myself drinking to death. I told him to just give me the vodka. He gave me a disgruntled expression, probably because he had to restock those eleven bottles of liquor. But he calculated my new total without a word. After paying him, I went to the drugstore two blocks down and bought a five subject notebook and a bag of pens. I wrote my first entry the night I went to the Link. It contained the feelings about the callous rejection letter scrawled by my mother's hand.

I was pleasantly surprised at how therapeutic writing my feelings proved to be. From that time on, the notebook became like my closest companion, one that I took with me wherever I went. In it, I wrote my feelings and my points of view about life occurrences. I wonder if my friends and partner-to-be ever took up journal writing. After Corey's concert, I asked them to write what they were doing before we met up that night at the Link. Corey, in his usual way, shrilled, "You know good and well I can't think that far back. Pappy is getting old." But he obliged.

I also asked them to write things about them that I don't know. They must've made me promise a hundred times that I wouldn't go blabbing the sentiments. I asked them, "Why are you worried? It's not like anybody else is going to read it." After I swore that I wouldn't, they wrote and gave me their stories one by one. I think it was good to do that, because their entries made my journal even more special.

I look over to the couch and I gaze again at the man I adore as he reads. I smile as I think about the escapades I wrote about, involving him. He kept asking me, "What do you write in that notebook?"
I play dumb. "What notebook?"
"The light blue one. The one you carry with you all the time."

I generally would reply, "I write about my life."

"Are you ever going to let me read it?"

"Are you going to give me the recipe to that ambrosia salad?"

That got him every time, because I was sure that he was going to take that recipe to his grave. But tonight, he surprised me by calling my bluff. He said, "OK, let's go to the store."

He took me to the farmers market and showed me how to pick the ripest, sweetest fruits they had. We then went home, and he taught me his recipe, step-by-step. Well, a deal is a deal. While I am at my drafting table working and eating the delicious ambrosia salad he taught me to make, he is reading my notebook. He thinks I'm working on a campaign, but I've already finished work at the office. I am now writing my last entry to my journal on a few sheets of paper to be added later. After I add this, I'm going to lock the notebook away in a time capsule to be opened long after we all are gone. I'm going to that same drugstore tomorrow to buy another five subject tablet and some more pens.

My friends? Oh, they are doing fine. Corey and Garrett (or Simon and Zachary) are still together, getting more involved with each other with every passing day. Just like Corey heard wedding bells for me and Jojo, I hear them clanging for him and Garrett. Something tells me that Garrett is going to pop the question soon. Don't ask me why, but I just got this feeling. Oh! Remember that song Corey wrote for me and Jojo? Well, after Darrell Alston recorded it, it somehow went overseas and hit number one in Japan. While he's touring over there and singing it, and Japanese radio stations are playing it nonstop, Corey is just sitting back and enjoying the benefits of his royalty checks!

Peep and Jimmy are slowly coping with Irene's passing. Some days are better than others, but Jimmy is now seeing a psychiatrist. I immediately recommended the great Dr. Edwin Banneker. I figured that since he helped me, maybe he could help Jimmy. He goes almost every other Monday and Peep goes to his therapist on Wednesdays. I am noticing that both are slowly letting go of the guilty feelings and letting the love and memories of their departed soothe them and assure them that they are just fine.

Andre did eventually move to Baltimore. What he didn't tell me was that while he was in prison, he enrolled in a student re-entry program and got his High School Diploma. He is still driving trucks, but he's also taking online classes and is studying to become a registered nurse. He and Rachel are in an on-and-off relationship, but we know they really love each other and Mike Jr. *really* likes him a lot. He and Jimmy have become very good friends. When he is not studying or trucking, he is zooming over to their house and kidnapping Jimmy to play basketball or catch a football game whenever the Ravens are playing. Peep says that this is good. It takes Jimmy's mind off of Irene.

Andre, Jojo, and I had a LGBTQ discussion while playing Tonk one day. Jojo wondered out loud why so many people in this world were gay. Andre said something very profound, "Welp, 'magine a worl' wit' nuthin' but browns, blacks, whites, an' grays. Kinda borin', don't cha think?"

"Yes, it would be."

"So, dat ansuhs yuh question. God needed culah when he made dis worl'. Hence, we got da rainbow tribe!"

When he said that, I thought, *This teaches me not to judge a book by its' cover.* Underneath all that muscle and hard-core persona is a very intelligent man that has studied the ways of the world and learned, in his own way, that it takes all kinds of people to make the world work, LGBTQ included.

Dean and I went down to Donaldson Prison three months back to attend Troy Matterson's parole hearing, and I am happy to report that he was granted the parole. He is now living in Birmingham with his steady. I learned this through a letter of gratitude he wrote to me. He included a picture of his intended and the man looks uncannily like my father, Kenneth Davis. I sent him back a congratulatory letter, wishing him the best. He then wrote me saying that his boyfriend is pushing him to go on a cruise, the same one that the fellas and I, along with Dean and Andre, have decided to take again... Rainbow Pride. Hmmm... Now, isn't that a coincidence?

As for me, I'm learning to live, not just exist in a lifestyle. I am remembering my friend Corey's words,

"Lifestyle is different from life. Lifestyles are easy to fake. But you can't fake life. You have to live it."

I'm finding my way... Unlocking my happiness... Discovering my Cray-Cray to dance my Nae-Nae! I am living.

I AM ALIVE!

I am accepting my life and all the things that make me who I am. I am finding the flame of beauty that radiates from my very core, lit by all my family and friends who love me enough to accept me for who I am. And I... Lionel Shedrick Davis... will add my light to the flame by loving and accepting myself.

Yes, love really does make me beautiful, and if we let love in, it will do the same for us all.

THE END
... OF THIS PART OF THE JOURNEY.

DISCUSSION QUESTIONS

There are no right or wrong answers, as everyone sees things differently than others. These questions serve merely to encourage discussion.

1. What could be some reasons why parents disown their children due to their being gay?

2. How would you describe the personalities of Lionel, Jojo, Peep, and Corey? How are they alike? How do they differ?

3. The subject of Peep's sexuality was never brought up by his grandparents. What do you think their reaction would have been if they were informed? Based on your answer, what differences would it have brought about in his adult life?

4. What could Lionel's father have done to halt the abuse that his children suffered at the hands of their mother?

5. What symbolism do you find in Lionel wiping the blood from his cheek onto his mother's blankets?

6. Other than the physical completion of his symphony and the feeling of accomplishment therein, what intangible qualities do you believe Corey attained?

7. This question is for groups that encourage open discussion on adolescent sexual abuse. Based from Jojo's experience depicted on page 21, what are some feelings that can haunt the child when he/she grows into an adult? What do you think he meant when he considered himself "damaged goods."?

8. How do you feel about the racism that Corey experienced in the orphanage?

9. In reading Peep's interaction with the pastor on page 34, what are your feelings about how the church treats its LGBTQ members? What steps can be taken to lessen the spiritual abuse suffered?

10. Throughout the book, there are examples of sexual promiscuity. For those that engage frequently in the pleasures found in anonymous sex, is it learned behavior through negative conditioning or are there people who

just love the anonymity as well as the sex? Please share why. Again, there is no wrong answer.

11. Corey displays passionate refusal to talk with Dr. Lofton. Why does he refuse the help? Is there is a fear of getting professional help as it relates to us as a people? Where do you believe this fear comes from?

12. Do you believe that there is a stigma attached to those who factor professional help into their journey to peace?

13. We as human beings have been taught to fear HIV and AIDS. What are some of the stereotypes surrounding the fear? What are the myths?

14. This question is one to either answer openly or to meditate on. Is there any occurrence in this book that you can relate to?

15. This topic is outside of what was depicted in the book. Is there a racial difference in terms of how we deal with our sexuality and how heterosexual parents of different races handle children who come out?

16. This question is for any group of women reading this book. You have seen Same Gender Loving concepts expressed from a male's point of view, both in literature and in reality. What are some of the challenges that plague Same Gender Loving women?

17. Life or Lifestyle. Is there a difference to you? What might it be?

Follow Eros Da Artiste on Facebook
https://www.facebook.com/erosdaartiste

or on Twitter
https://twitter.com/artiste_da

Thank you for reading
I CHOOSE PAIN!

www.ingramcontent.com/pod-product-compliance
Lightning Source LLC
Chambersburg PA
CBHW030343020726
47493CB00003B/661